WHIRLWIND

Also by DAVID KLASS

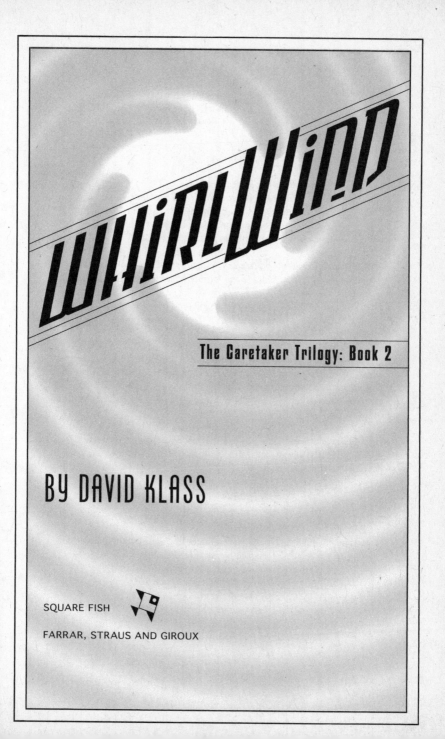

WHIRLWIND

The Caretaker Trilogy: Book 2

BY DAVID KLASS

SQUARE FISH

FARRAR, STRAUS AND GIROUX

SQUARE
FISH

An Imprint of Macmillan

WHIRLWIND. Copyright © 2008 by David Klass.
All rights reserved. Printed in December 2010 in the United States of America
by R. R. Donnelley & Sons Company, Harrisonburg, Virginia.
For information, address
Square Fish, 175 Fifth Avenue, New York, NY 10010.

Square Fish and the Square Fish logo are trademarks of Macmillan
and are used by Farrar, Straus and Giroux under license from Macmillan.

Library of Congress Cataloging-in-Publication Data
Klass, David.
    Whirlwind / David Klass.
        p. cm. — (Caretaker trilogy ; bk. 2)
    Summary: Jack finds himself embroiled in another dangerous adventure
when, after a six-month absence, he returns to the Hudson River town where
he grew up to find his girlfriend P.J. only to discover that she is missing and
everyone believes him to be responsible for her disappearance and the death
of his family.
    ISBN: 978-0-312-38429-6
    [1. Space and time—Fiction.   2. Interpersonal relations—Fiction.
3. Adventure and adventurers—Fiction.   4. Ecology—Fiction.   5. Science
fiction.] I. Title.

PZ7.K67813Whi 2008
[Fic]—dc22

                                                                    2007014160

Originally published in the United States by Farrar, Straus and Giroux
Designed by Barbara Grzeslo
Square Fish logo designed by Filomena Tuosto
First Square Fish Edition: March 2009
10 9 8 7 6 5 4 3
www.squarefishbooks.com

LEXILE 770L

For Madeleine

WHIRLWIND

1

April Fool's Day in Hadley-by-Hudson. Spring chill cutting sharp as a blade. Dusk descending. Musty smell of nearby river clotting my throat. Had enough sentence fragments? My English teacher said they were a weakness of mine. But that was nearly six months ago, when I was a senior at Hadley High School, leading a normal life. My biggest concerns then were chicks, flicks, and fast cars, roughly in that order.

Nothing normal about me now.

Parents gone. Friends lost. Old life vanished. Sense of security evaporated. Belief in the sanity of day-to-day existence drowned in the deep Atlantic.

But I still like sentence fragments. They generate pace. You want pace? Stick around.

Main street of Hadley. Six in the evening. People I know, or at least used to know, climbing in and out of cars. Buying groceries in the co-op. Picking up dry cleaning. Heading home to eat dinner with their families.

They pass me. Rub shoulders. None of them give me a second look. Don't you remember me? Jack Danielson? Straw-colored hair, piercing blue eyes, and above-average brain power, except when I do something really stupid. Once gained three hundred and forty yards in a school football game.

No, they don't remember.

Can't blame them. So much has changed.

Swore I'd never come back here. Too many memories. There's the Rec Center where I played hoops. The liquor store where we used to get Dan's older brother to buy us six-packs. The ice cream shop where P.J. and I would split double-chocolate cones with sprinkles.

P.J. Her house is three blocks from here. Do I dare? Yes, that's why I'm here. I tried my best to run away from this moment. Tried to pretend I could make a new life. Realize there's no explanation I can give that will satisfy her. She'll be furious at me for disappearing. Maybe we can never repair it. Never regain what we had.

Trust gone. Foundation of relationship caved in.

Doesn't matter. Have to try. Because I still love her. That's why I came back. Pure selfishness. Clinging to last possession. My love for P.J. is all I've got left.

Pass Mrs. Hayes. My third-grade teacher. Her eyes flick over me. And then away.

Not completely her fault she didn't recognize me. I've taken a few precautions. Wearing a cap, tilted low. Dark scarf, wound high. Grown a scraggly mustache, my first. Hair hasn't been cut in three months. It falls to my shoulders in straw-colored mop.

But I can't hide my eyes. Supposedly the windows to the soul. That's what Mrs. Hayes didn't recognize as she walked by me holding a sack with toilet paper and cat food peeking out the top.

New windows? Or is it a whole new soul? Did what happened to me change me to the point where I'm no longer myself? Or is this still me, walking away from the center of town, heading slowly up Elm Street?

No doubt my Firestorm adventure and the long journey home transformed me. I've been so lonely. Spent so many sleepless nights staring up at the stars, trying to figure things out. Why was I chosen? If there's a God, why did he or she let things get so messed up? Is our Earth really so fragile? If this is the Turning Point, can we save it? Do our lives have meaning, or is it all for nothing?

Many questions. No answers. But when you agonize long

enough, it doesn't matter if you come up with answers. The questions and the pain change you.

I know I'm very different from the guy who drove P.J. home from the Hudson River make-out spot six months ago, his mind on sex and football. But is he still recognizably part of me? Is there any Jack Danielson left in me?

Only one way to find out. Last remaining touchstone. The ultimate litmus test. P.J.

Here's a sad but true definition of home: it's where you go to find out if you're still you, or if you've become somebody else.

Less than two blocks from P.J.'s house. I slow down. Scared out of my mind. This was a bad idea. Should have tried to make a go of it in England, where I landed after my Firestorm adventure. Or joined the crew of the tramp steamer that brought me back across the Atlantic to America. Could have stayed in Maine, in the small port city where it never stopped snowing. Might have hung longer in Boston, where I got a job stacking crates. Guy in the warehouse needed a roommate.

But I had to come home. A soft voice kept calling to me. Whispering across the months and the miles. "I'm still waiting for you. Come home, Bozo."

P.J.'s nickname for me. Not very respectful.

Less than one block from her house. I can see the outline of her roof against the evening sky. The walls. My God, she's inside there! She's been there for the last six months without me. Doing her homework. Eating cereal for breakfast. Talking to her friends. Dreaming her dreams.

Half a block. Her window. No light on. Maybe she's studying at the library. I should go check there first.

No, don't leave. If I chicken out now, I'll never come back. Better to be a man and tell her what happened.

Sure, just tell her the truth.

Hi, honey. Sorry. I didn't mean to disappear. But members of something called the Dark Army came one night and killed both my parents. It turns out they weren't my parents after all. They were just sheltering me.

I'm from a thousand years in the future, when things are pretty bleak. I was sent back to find something called Firestorm and save the oceans, thereby improving living conditions centuries hence. A telepathic dog and a beautiful shape-changing woman helped me. I did what they asked. I found Firestorm and I destroyed a giant trawler fleet. But then the dog and the woman blinked out, leaving me alone. And now I'm back. Sorry I didn't write or call. And how have you been the last six months, P.J.? Did you have a good Christmas? And how's the French Club?

I stop in my tracks. What the heck am I doing here? I can't tell her the truth. And I won't tell her a lie. So I can't tell her anything. I know in my heart I can't come back here. Don't belong anymore. Been away too long. Caused too much grief. Passed the point of no return.

I turn slowly, and take a half step away. Then a hand grips my arm. "Jack? Is that you?"

2

A thin man. Balding. Strong hands. A printer by profession. Always been nice to me. His eyes unnaturally bright as they stare at me. Glad to see me? Can't be that. I must have caused his daughter great pain. But he's almost smiling. Gripping my arm tightly.

"Mr. Peters? I . . . can't come in. How are you? How's P.J.? I'm sorry. I should go."

I babble excuses and awkward questions as he leads me up the walk toward the front door.

"No, don't go," he says with quiet forcefulness. "You must come in. Don't worry about anything. It's important that you come in. Please, Jack."

Five seconds later the door swings closed behind us. I'm in P.J.'s house. "Ruth," he calls. I'm dimly aware that he pauses to lock the door. "Look who I found out front! He didn't even want to come in."

P.J.'s mom hurries in and stops short at the sight of me. A look of momentary shock on her face. Deep worry. Flashing pain. Something very wrong here. She's trying to hide it. Get out, Jack. You hurt her daughter and this sweet woman is stunned that you've shown up.

"Of course you had to come in." Mrs. Peters nods. "It's bitter out there. Let me get you something hot to drink."

Mr. Peters excuses himself for a second.

I find myself seated in the kitchen. Familiar old wooden table. P.J. used to make me hot chocolate here when I walked her home from the library on winter evenings. Sometimes she would bring me delicious cookies that her mother had baked. I would sit in this very chair and she would sit next to me, in the rickety chair in front of the refrigerator. If her parents weren't around we would hold hands and smooch. I once smooched her so hard her chair tipped over and her hot chocolate scalded both of us.

"Would you like some cookies?" Mrs. Peters asks me now. Not "Where have you been for the last six months?" Or "Why did you break my daughter's heart?" Or "Please leave before she sees you, and never, ever come back."

Extremely weird. But what can I do? I take a cookie. "Thanks." Pop it in my mouth. Delicious.

Mr. Peters comes back into the kitchen. He's taken off his jacket. Seems very hyped up. Almost feverish. "Good," he says, "you served him a cookie."

"And I'm making him some tea," his wife adds.

"Good. Tea. Good thinking. Yes. Tea."

I'm looking from one to the other. Are they out of their minds? What's going on here?

"I owe you two some sort of explanation," I say. "You must think awfully of me. I want you to know how much I care about you. And P.J." My voice breaks.

"You don't have to explain anything," Mr. Peters says quickly, glancing out the window. "Where's the tea, Ruth?"

"Right here. Piping hot."

"Great! Milk, Jack? Sugar?"

I stand up. Starting to get freaked out. "Who cares about tea? Why aren't you curious about where I've been?"

Mr. Peters is trying so hard to smile that it looks like his face may crack apart. "Sit, Jack. There's no need to rush off." He tries to push me back into my seat.

I resist the pressure. Somewhere down the block I hear sirens. Could there be a fire nearby?

Mr. Peters pushes harder. "You really must sit."

I pivot away so that he stumbles and almost falls.

Mrs. Peters screams. I look at her. She's holding a cleaver. "Damn you, park your butt in that chair or I'll cut your nose off," she threatens. All warmth and hospitality gone. "Where's my P.J.? What have you done with her?"

The news registers—P.J.'s missing! I take a step back just in case she's serious about hacking off my nose.

Sense a blow coming from behind. Dodge sideways. Mr. Peters with a baseball bat. It smashes across the wooden table. Salt and pepper shakers splinter. Napkins take wing like a flock of doves. "Where's my little girl?" he demands. "Tell me or I'll beat it out of you."

Sirens getting louder. Not a fire. When he disappeared, Mr. Peters called the police. They were pretending to be nice to keep me there. Setting a trap.

I run for the back door. Mr. P. swings again. Connects. Not a home run. Maybe a double. Sharp pain in my right shoulder. But it doesn't knock me off my feet.

I make it to the door. Also locked. Mr. Peters is coming after me with the bat. I get the latch open. Half run and half fall down the steps.

Spotlights converge on me. I can feel the heat on my face. Didn't know Hadley had this many police. Cops crouching behind their cars, guns in hand. Ten, fifteen, twenty of them. All ready to fire and turn me into Swiss cheese. "This is Chief Parker," a deep voice announces through a megaphone. "We have you covered. There is no escape. Lie down on your stomach. *Get down right now.*"

I could run for it. But somebody might get hurt. And what would be the point of running? I need to find out what happened to P.J. So I get down.

Dry smell of winter grass in my nose and throat.

Policemen run toward me. Kneel on my back. Search me. Cuff my hands behind me. Hoist me back up to my feet.

Mr. Peters standing there. Red-faced with rage. "What did you do to my little girl? Tell me!"

"Nothing, sir. When did she—"

He swings, and all I can do is roll away from the punch. Feels like it loosens the teeth on one side of my mouth.

Pretty good right hook for a middle-aged printer.

I buckle but don't go down. "Nothing, Mr. Peters," I repeat, looking straight into his enraged black eyes. "How long has she been gone?"

His wife stands next to him, sobbing.

A big man approaches through the evening shadows. Shoulders like a water buffalo's. Neat uniform, as if to make up for destructive acne. Chief Parker. I played football with his son, Chris. Tough kid. Tough dad.

"Hello, Jack," he says softly. "Long time no see."

"Hello, sir."

But he's turned away from me to look at Mr. and Mrs. Peters. "Don't worry," he tells them. "I'll get some answers out of him. We have our ways."

3

Police holding cell. Jack all alone. No other prisoners tonight. No drunks. No vagrants.

Stone wall. Bars on three sides. A locked square cage. My hands are still cuffed behind my back. Painful. Not much circulation going on there. My mind roiled by what's just taken place. P.J.'s missing, maybe even dead! Her parents blame me. Probably the whole town does. And the worst of it is maybe they're right.

A few lines of poetry come to me in the silence of the jail cell night. Always loved poetry. Read a good poem once, remember it forever. This is from "To Althea, from Prison" by Richard Lovelace:

> *Stone walls do not a prison make,*
> *Nor iron bars a cage;*
> *Minds innocent and quiet take*
> *That for an hermitage;*
> *If I have freedom in my love*
> *And in my soul am free,*
> *Angels alone, that soar above,*
> *Enjoy such liberty.*

But unfortunately I don't have a quiet and innocent mind. I have a troubled one, tortured and in tumult. The reason I fled from Hadley six months ago without trying to contact P.J. and my other friends was to avoid endangering them. I sensed that if I reached out for help to those who cared for me, I would be dragging them into whatever dark hole was opening around me.

So I ran, to Manhattan and then to North Carolina, and finally to the open ocean, and my only consolation was that my friends, my teammates, and especially my girlfriend were slumbering on in Hadley, safe and oblivious.

And now P.J.'s missing. Maybe it's a coincidence. Maybe she ran away to try to start a career as an artist in a big city. Or perhaps she was kidnapped and the ransom demand has been long in arriving.

Dream on. It's not a coincidence. There's only one way her disappearance makes sense. Her parents are right. This must be linked to me. But who took her? And why?

Footsteps approach. The door to the cell block opens and shuts. Big shadow. Loud footsteps. Chief Parker.

He unlocks my cell. Steps inside. "Hello, Jack."

"Hello, sir. What happened to P.J.?"

"We'll get to that," he promises as he locks us in together. "How do you feel?"

"I'm okay. My wrists hurt."

"That's too bad. How does it feel to be a celebrity?"

I look back at him. "Huh?"

"You're already on the evening news. The FBI is sending a team from Manhattan. They should be here in about an hour. And reporters are heading our way, too."

"The FBI?"

"They'll take it right out of my hands. Small-town police chief. Multiple-murder suspect. Missing teen queen. Lotta bigwigs are gonna see an opportunity. Push me right out of the way. So you know what's gonna happen first?"

I shake my head very slowly.

"You're going to tell me everything. Come, sit down."

4

Chief Parker pushes me back to the cot. He sits on the one chair. "Let's have a chat. You want to go first?"

"You said I was a multiple-murder suspect?"

"The autopsy on your mom was not conclusive, but the medical examiner was pretty sure it wasn't the burning house that killed her. A burning house doesn't chop a woman nearly in half."

I fall off the cot to my knees. Throw up.

He just sits there and watches. Then he reaches out. Grabs my hair. Hauls me up and deposits me on the cot again.

"And your father. I always liked your dad, Jack. We used to sit next to each other at football games. He was very proud of you. A nice dad like that doesn't deserve to be torched inside his car and pushed off a hundred-foot cliff into the Hudson River. Took us a while to find him. They died. You disappeared. No other suspect. No motive. A real mystery. And here you are. Like to clear it up for us?"

My voice comes out a tinny whisper. "I'm so sorry. They deserved better. I don't know what else to say."

"Then let's talk about P.J.," Chief Parker suggests.

"Is she dead, too?" I gasp.

He leans forward. "Are you confessing?"

"No, I don't know anything."

"What were you doing outside her house tonight?"

"Coming to see her. I thought she might be home."

Chief Parker studies my face. "Her father says you were hiding in the shadows."

"I hadn't seen her in months. I was trying to decide whether it was a good idea to come back. What happened to her? Is she dead? Hurt? Missing? Please tell me."

"So you don't have any answers?" the chief asks.

"No. None."

"What about your parents? Any answers there?"

"None that you would believe, sir."

"Try me. You were a good kid once."

"Still am. But there's nothing I can tell you."

He stands. I'm still sitting. Never realized how big he really is. Towers over me. He's winding something around his right hand. Looks like a dark towel.

"Twenty-three years I've been a cop and you can count the number of times I got rough with a prisoner on the fingers of one hand." As if to demonstrate his point, he holds up his right hand and folds down fingers one by one. "But sometimes you have to do things you find repugnant."

His right hand is now a fist, big as a cantaloupe, the knuckles cushioned by a dark wrapping. "Don't make me hit you," he says. "Talk. What happened to your dad?"

"I don't know, sir. I wasn't around to see—"

His fist slams into my stomach. I gasp and sink to my knees. He hauls me up by my hair.

"Your ma was a nice lady. Who cut her up and torched your house?"

"The Dark Army."

"What?"

"Mutants, cyborgs, and chimeras from the future."

He squints at me, red-faced with rage. Another punch. Right in the testicles. I fall over on my back and writhe on the floor. Tears of pain faucet down my cheeks.

Even with my hands cuffed, I could fight back. Eko taught me enough martial arts moves so that I could probably turn the tables on the chief. Kick him unconscious. Take his keys. Free myself. Make a break for it. But what would be the point? I deserve this beating. I'll take it like a man. And when the FBI come, they can put me in thumbscrews. I'll take that, too.

What is it about you pathetic humans, that you not only march meekly to the slaughter, but find ways to justify the executioner as the ax is falling?

Familiar canine telepathic voice. Shocks me even as I writhe on the floor in agony. Gisco! I'm glad that he's alive, but I'm in enough of a mess as it is. Trapped and betrayed by the parents of my sweetheart. Beaten by the father of my football teammate. Not to mention punched in the testicles, and soul in torment.

Please go away, I tell Gisco telepathically. You only bring trouble, and I've got enough of that as it is.

How can you say such a thing, old bean? There's a special bond of love and trust between a boy and his dog.

The last time I saw you, you promised you would never, ever leave me, no matter what. And then you instantly blinked out and vanished into thin air.

Hardly my fault. But we can sort all that out later. The salient fact is that we've got to escape right now.

Dog using fancy SAT word. Where is he, anyway? How did he get inside this police station?

Chief Parker hauls me up by my shirtfront, choking me. "Are you gonna start talking or do you need more?"

I look back at him. Shake my head slightly from side to side. More. His fist slams into my rib cage. Knocks me across the cell into the stone wall. I bounce off hard and bang my head on cell's toilet. Almost black out.

Fight back! Get his keys. I'll help you escape.

Why would I want to do that? Give me one good reason.

I'll give you two. First, he told you the FBI's coming. They're about to pull into the parking lot.

That's a good reason?

It's not really the FBI, lamebrain. It's the Dark Army. If they take you into custody, it'll be the slow neural flay.

What's the other reason?

Sorry to have to be the one to tell you this, but the Dark Army already took your friend P.J. She's at their mercy. If we don't find her, there's no telling what they'll do to her. Time is of the essence. You're the only one who can save her.

Chief Parker reaches down and grabs a shock of my long hair. "You really need to visit a barber," he says. "Or maybe I could just pull it out for you."

"I don't think so," I tell him.

"What?"

"I've had about enough of this." I pull loose from his grip.

"Oh, is that right?" He steps forward.

I spread my feet to the width of my shoulders, settling into a fighting stance. "Yes, sir," I tell him softly. "More than enough."

5

I turn sideways to present less of a target. Circle slowly, feet never leaving the ground. Somewhere between ballet step and boxer's shuffle. Forward and to the side.

"C'mere, you lying punk," Chief Parker growls, and reaches out for me.

I let him grab me and then twist my body and use his weight and forward momentum to throw him. He's a big man and he goes down hard. Gets up surprisingly quickly. "So you learned a few tricks? I'll fix you, you bastard."

He throws a right hook that could tear my head off. But it doesn't connect. I run away from it to rear of cell, jump and kick off stone wall, and somersault back behind him. He spins around, mouth wide open. Never saw anything like that before. "What the hell?" he gasps.

I don't want to torture him so I end it quickly. Leap up off the left leg. Straight snapping kick with the right. Ball of foot catches him on point of chin. Snaps his head back. He collapses like a sack of potatoes.

I grab his key ring. Snap the cuffs open. Hesitate. Unclasp his gun belt. Hope I don't need it. Never wore a gun in a holster on my hip.

First time for everything. Surprisingly heavy.

I unlock the cell door and head out. Through the empty cell block. There are overhead cameras. Chief Parker must have turned the surveillance system off when he came to persuade me to talk.

Unlock the metal door at the end of the cell block. Hurry silently through a dim hallway. Pass an empty side room. Glance in. Changing room! Uniforms hanging on pegs.

Two minutes later I'm dressed like a Hadley cop. Blue pants and shirt. Black shoes. Long hair tucked inside a police cap.

Jack, we're running out of time. I can feel them coming.

Uh-oh. Me too. Prickles of cold all over my skin.

I head out into main station area. Pick up a file and hold the papers in front of my face. Pretend to be reading them intently. Police cap tilted down over eyes.

Half a dozen people there. Dispatcher answering phones. Two young cops at coffee machine discussing the Knicks' dismal season. Female cop and dog control officer trying to wrestle a rhino into big cage. "He doesn't have any tags and there's no sign of a collar," the female cop is saying. "He seems well taken care of, but I don't know what his owner was thinking, letting him out like that."

"Maybe the owner was thinking he eats too much," the dog control officer suggests. "A dog like this can eat you out of house and home."

No, not a rhino. Gisco! He infiltrated the police station by getting himself picked up by some kind of suburban pest sweep. Now they're trying to lock him away. Then, no doubt, off to the pound.

"I like small dogs," the lady cop offers. "Chihuahuas. Toy poodles. Nothing bigger than a retriever."

"Anything would seem small next to this four-legged tub of lard. Look at his legs! Like tree stumps! And his tail! Like a dust mop!"

"At least he's well behaved. Come on, Jumbo. Into the cage."

Call me Jumbo again and I'll bite your ears off.

Chill, Gisco. She's right. You have put on a few pounds since I last saw you.

Big dog swivels his head in all directions, looking for me. *That's muscle tone. No need to insult me. Where are you?*

No insult intended. But for a dog that vanished into thin air, you're now looking rather substantial. I'm the guy in the uniform that doesn't fit.

Oh, yeah. I should have recognized you by your smell.

You're no rose garden yourself.

The aroma of a healthy dog is one of the world's finest smells. It has a complex bouquet, like a fine wine.

Or a shallow latrine.

How dare you?

Just telling the truth and . . . Gisco, let's get out of here! The Dark Army!

Sure enough, two tall men in blue jackets and khakis hurry through the front door. Both wearing sunglasses.

Gisco backs into the cage.

I step into a corner and pretend to read my file. Watch them out of the corner of my eye as they flash I.D.'s and demand, "Where's Chief Parker?"

"In with the prisoner," the dispatcher tells them. "Scott or Glenn, wanna take these gentlemen to the cell?"

The two young cops are excited to have FBI agents in the station. Lead them away down the hall.

I look up from the file in time to see Gisco plow forward, busting the wire cage door like it was spaghetti. The dog control officer tries to grab him. She's a big woman, but he shakes her off like a flea. The lady cop pulls out a stun gun. "Back in the cage, Jumbo, or I'll deep-fry you." He doesn't waste time dodging, just runs into her and right through her. She fires the stun gun as she's falling and shoots the dog control officer.

There's shouting. Screaming.

Dispatcher runs to try to help.

Alarms sound. Lights flash.

"FBI agents" and two policemen hear the commotion. Their footsteps pound back down hallway.

I slam door to block them. Barricade it with desk.

Gisco and I dash out the door of the station. Cold night air.

Should we run for it?

No chance. They'll be after us in seconds. We need some wheels!

As if on cue, a police car zips up. Young policeman inside. My God, I know him. Zach Mills. Used to play football with him, when I was a freshman and he was a senior. He sees my uniform. I stand in the shadows and hope he can't see my face. "What's going on?" he asks.

"Prisoner trying to escape! They need help inside."

Zach always had quick reactions. He's out of the car in a flash, running for the station. Unfortunately, he's taken the car keys with him.

Know-it-all dog seizes control. *It's not difficult to hot-wire one of these primitive vehicles. Hop in. Reach under the dash. Find a black wire and a red wire. Rip them out from the steering column and wind them together . . .*

A few seconds later, we're ready to go. I always wanted to drive a police car. Peel out. Turn on the lights. Flashers. And the siren. This is cool!

You're going the wrong way.

This is my hometown, snout face. Don't tell me where to go.

They'll put out an all-points bulletin. Get cars from neighboring towns. Block all key roads.

You're exaggerating. That stuff takes time.

Turn on your radio.

I switch it on.

Excited voice of dispatcher. ". . . Suspects are fleeing in a Hadley police car, license plate B25897. They are considered armed and extremely dangerous. Suspects last seen at Hadley Station, heading south on McDermott. New York State Police issuing all-points bulletin. Chopper 47 now airborne . . ."

I turn off radio. Okay, you made your point. How do we get away?

Sirens blare behind us. In front of us. Spotlights sweep the streets. There must already be a dozen cars out looking for us. They're closing in!

One chance. The river. And step on it.

6

Back roads to Hudson. Breakneck speed. Screeching around curves. Streaking down straightaways.

Police car handles well. Lights and flasher illuminate winding tarmac sloping to dark river.

Crest a hill. See lights up ahead. Roadblock.

Watch out, Jack.

I see it. That's why I turned off onto this road.

This is a road?

More like a dirt trail. Down to a private swimming beach. Only local kids know about it. I used to come down here with P.J.

Sorry about P.J.

How do you know the Dark Army took her? Have they hurt her? Do you know where she is? Why would they go after her? She's just a normal American girl.

All excellent questions. But there are two good reasons why we might want to discuss them later. First, there's a police helicopter heading our way.

Sure enough, I see the chopper. Flying in circles, its spotlight bathing trees and rooftops in a streaming golden halo. Okay, what's the second reason?

Dog sounds nervous. *We're about to go off a cliff.*

Up ahead, the trail we're following disappears into blackness. That's not a cliff, I explain to Gisco. Just a very steep descent to the river.

Dog is not calmed by my explanation. In fact, he sounds terrified. *You're sure you've gone this way before?*

Dozens of times. Hold on, my furry friend.

Dogs can't hold on. We don't have fingers!

Whose fault is that?

Down we go. Police car bumping, thumping, spinning, crashing over rocks and mud. Always walked down this trail, picking my way. Never drove down it before. Come to think of it, it is a lot like a cliff.

Gisco is hunkered down so low on seat, it appears that he's trying to crawl inside the upholstery. *Why did I trust you? You're going to kill us!*

Car careens over a rough patch. Gisco attempts to scrabble still lower in his seat. He reminds me of a soldier during an artillery attack, trying to dig a subbasement to his foxhole. I can't even see his head. It's buried under his massive shaking forelegs.

We're almost down the hill, Gisco, I reassure him. There's no need to be so scared.

Me? Scared? Hah! Fear is something I conquered in my puppyhood. He peeks up from between trembling paws.

Just then, we hit a monster bump. The front hood bucks skyward, the car teeters for a second on its rear wheels, and then we start flipping madly, end over end.

I hear a loud yelp of canine fear and pain.

Sparks shoot. Glass shatters. Metal grinds rock.

I am hurled sideways into Gisco. He is spun upside down and wedged against a side wall. We're all tangled up with each other. My right arm is bent around his hind legs. I spit out what tastes like a noxious whisk broom. It's Gisco's tail, which ended up in my mouth.

Yuck. You okay, Gisco?

No. Call a team of surgeons. I am seriously injured. Bones cracked. Organs ruptured. Can't move a muscle.

This might be a good time to heal quickly and get out.

Why is that?

The helicopter must have spotted our crash. Here it comes! The Dark Army won't be far behind! Gisco?

Somehow the big dog has pried the door open and he's already sprinting toward the river. I spot his dark shape galloping across the tree line, with the girth of a hippo and the gait of a racehorse. For a dog with cracked bones and ruptured organs, Gisco's covering ground fast.

I squeeze out the door and follow, just as the police helicopter bursts over treetops. The bright search beam sweeps down on the car wreck, and frames it in a silver circle whose perimeter jiggles as the copter hovers.

I sprint after the dog across rough terrain in darkness. Dodging trees. Leaping rocks. A few hundred yards ahead, moonlight burnishes the dark band of Hudson.

Swish, *swish* of night breeze in tall grass. Musky smell of river mud. Angry whine of mosquitoes. No, wait, there are no mosquitoes when it's this cold!

That's the whine of motorcycles speeding our way!

The Hadley police don't have motorcycles. And even if they did, they couldn't possibly have responded to the car wreck so quickly.

The same Dark Army motorcycle assassins who killed my father! They monitored the police band and learned about the car crash as the helicopter reported it.

Now they're coming for me!

7

Hudson River a hundred yards away. But it's not a level football field. We're talking about trees and rocks, bushes and bracken, on a steep, dark, sludge-strewn slope.

Luckily, during my days on the Outer Banks, Eko taught me how to run in low visibility. I remember the countless marsh channels we raced through side by side, with only the stars to light our way. At first I could barely trot three steps without getting clobbered by an overhanging branch or tripped up by a hole in the muddy bottom. Eko taught me to sense my surroundings, to feel rather than to see.

I'm using that training now. Vaulting over thorn bushes that reach like witches' hands, grasping at me with talon-like fingernails. I skirt weed patches that try to toss green lassos around my ankles. Rocks and boulders do their shadowy best to block me, but I zigzag around them.

I catch up with Gisco and pass him. Come on, let it all hang out. This is the final sprint.

Large dogs are not known for sprints. Trotting with dignity is more my style. But we'll make it. Don't worry.

I'm worried. Motorcycles zooming after us. They sound like angry hornets closing in, with stingers bared.

We reach the mud cliff above the rippling water. Start picking our way down. Hard to get footing.

Big dog tiring badly. Huffing and puffing. *Sorry. Can't make it. You go on without me. Boat anchored offshore. Actually not a boat. No time to explain. Good luck, old bean.*

Come on, fur ball, you can't give up now. Roll yourself down this hill if necessary.

Gisco stops, gasping air. *Can't do it. It's over.*

I stop next to him. Steep mud cliff. Rotund dog. Motorcycles racing up behind us. Only one thing to do.

"You'll thank me for this later." I grab his shaggy coat and throw him forward with all my strength.

Gisco tumbles wildly down the mud cliff, building speed. He's somersaulting snout over tail, faster and faster, unable to stop. Flattens ferns. Bulldozes bushes. Decapitates a willow tree. Cuts a wide swath as he hurtles down over pebbles and through river mud.

Terrified dog yowl all the way down: YAAAAAAAAAAAAA!

I follow in the wake of the one-dog avalanche. Make it to the bottom. Water lapping against bank. Gisco? Where are you?

I'll get you back for that. Don't think I won't. I'm part bloodhound. You can't hide from me.

You're the one who's hiding. Where are you?

Dead. I'm dead and this must be dog heaven. But what would a miserable human like you be doing in dog heaven?

I spot thrashing dog paws. He's upside down with his head and snout wedged deep in what looks like the entry hole to a rodent's nest, dug into the mud bank.

I grab hold of his hind legs and tug.

Ouch! What are you doing?

Trying to pull you out.

Gently, fool. A canine's anatomy is like a finely calibrated Swiss watch.

Beams of light sweep over us. Drone of motorcycles above us. The Dark Army! Atop the mud cliff.

Some of them slide down after us while others raise weapons.

I yank dog's hind legs again, with all my strength. Either I'll rip Gisco out of hole or I'll dismember him.

There's a loud sound of reverse suction, as if a giant bottle of champagne has just been uncorked. Gisco pops loose from the hole and his backward momentum carries him toward the river. I'm still gripping his legs. We splash together into the Hudson, as the Dark Army's laser beams melt the mud bank we were just standing on.

River dark and cold. Strong current catches us. Where are you, Gisco?

Out here. They're coming. Hurry.

Ponderous pooch may not be built for distance running, but he sure can swim. Buoyant as a manatee. Can dive like a walrus. His head pops out of the river, and he looks like a grizzly bear happily hunting salmon in an Alaskan river. *Come on, slowpoke!*

Motorcycles reach river. I glance back and see hideous forms massing on the bank. Rabid red eyes search the surface. Flared nostrils sniff for our scent. Sharp teeth glint in the moonlight. Genetically manipulated mutants and hellishly engineered cyborgs from a future gone mad.

Some of them shine spotlights over the dark waves and eddies. Others plunge into the water and swim blindly into the darkness after us. Still others are busy launching what looks like a racing boat.

I'm fifty feet from shore. Fighting the current with every stroke. The cold saps my strength.

Just a little farther. Gisco is waiting for me, treading water around a dilapidated yellow dinghy.

That's your boat?

Yes, help me in. Dogs can't climb.

What good will getting on board do us? They're coming in a speedboat. How are we going to escape them by trying to row away in that pathetic wreck?

You ask too many questions. It's always been one of your problems. Now shut up and help me in.

I heave dog into boat. Not an easy thing to do. He weighs a ton, and his wet coat doesn't exactly help.

I grab the side of the boat and clamber up and over. Tumble to floor of dinghy. Shivering. Exhausted. But none of that will matter. Because I can see the speedboat setting off from shore. Powerful engine launches them forward like a rocket. Searchlight flickers over river. Shadowy shapes are hunched near the front, weapons at the ready.

Gisco, we should dive back into the river. Swim for shore. It's our only chance.

It's no chance. We'll never make it.

But they've seen us. They're coming! They're much faster than we are!

So what? Let them come. Damn the torpedoes. Full speed ahead. Dog stands at prow of boat and raises one paw, striking a heroic pose, like Nelson at Trafalgar. Right foreleg waves in the air, as if wielding an invisible sword.

No, Gisco's not fencing with shadows. He's operating what looks like a miniature control panel! Using his paws and when necessary his nose.

There's a strange sound, like a long zipper opening.

A transparent bubble encircles the top of our dinghy. Don't ask me where it came from. It appears overhead and clicks tightly shut.

I can see through it, to the stars above. This glass dome is nifty, but I very much doubt that it's going to save us from a laser attack.

And that's exactly what's coming. Because they've spotted us! The speedboat's spotlight pinions us. We're bathed in brilliant white-silver.

The sleek racing craft roars in our direction.

Gisco! You've trapped us in our own pathetic wreck of a boat. Now we can't even swim for it. There's no possible way out of this.

Oh yes there is. One very good way.

Lasers sizzle the water to steam all around us. We'll be vaporized any second. Fried like fish and chips. Or, rather, like dog and boy and chips.

Would you mind sharing it with me? What's our one good way out of this mess?

Down.

8

Gisco, what do you mean "down"? They're going to laser us into subatomic particles at any second. If you have a plan, this would be a good time to . . .

Hold on.

Hold on to what?

A red button flashes on the small control panel. Gisco punches it decisively with his snout. *Voilà!*

And nothing happens.

Button keeps flashing.

Dog punches it again, with less certainty. *Showtime!*

No show. Nothing at all happens.

Gisco? We only have a few seconds . . . !

Strange. It must be low on power. Either that or it doesn't like dogs. Third time's the charm. He hits it a final time. Tries to sound confident, but he's not fooling anyone. *Let 'er rip!*

Nothing rips. Nothing even frays. There's a slight reddish glow, but that's it. My hopes sink with every second. Dog has trapped us in floating frying pan with a glass lid, and we're about to be put on laser burner.

Wait a minute, hold on a second, it's not my hopes that are sinking, it's our dinghy!

Now the water is up to the oarlocks, now it's above the sides of the boat but it's not splashing in, it's washing against the transparent bubble as we slowly descend.

Our pursuers in the speedboat figure out what's happening. Fire a desperate fusillade at us.

Orange-yellow laser beams fork down through the water like the tentacles of a giant jellyfish. They stab all around us. But they don't score a direct hit.

And then it's too late.

Because the water lapping at the top of the bubble comes together to form a liquid ceiling above our heads, and the stars disappear.

We're under the dark surface of the Hudson River. Sinking into an inky abyss.

Gisco, what the hell are you up to?

Weren't you complaining a few seconds ago about my pathetic little wreck of a boat? It just saved your life.

Okay. I admit it's a doozy of a dinghy. But what exactly is

it and where did you get it? Did you bring it from the future?

No, I bought it at Kmart.

Spare me the canine sarcasm.

Spare me the human third degree. Enough questions. We got away. That's the good news.

What's the bad news?

They saw how we gave them the slip. They'll start sweeping the river bottom for us, with every surveillance technique at their disposal. And . . .

And?

We're low on power.

Great. Can't we recharge?

I don't know. I'm not an engineer.

How far can we go with what we have?

Hopefully, far enough to get away.

And then we'll have to surface?

Unless we develop gills.

And they'll be waiting for us, right? I escaped downriver last time. They won't let that happen again. This time they'll be sitting around every bend of the river between here and Manhattan. They'll spot us when we come up for air. Fish us out, gut us, and fillet us. Is that what you're worried about?

You put it well, if a bit too vividly.

What do you plan on doing about it?

We'll confound them. Instead of going downriver to Manhattan, we'll do the unexpected. Sail upriver!

That's your plan? We're going to try to escape by heading in-land? That may just be the stupidest thing I ever heard. There's no outlet to the ocean, there are no population centers to hide in, we'll be easy to track . . .

Hold on, Jack.

Why?

We're about to hit bottom. Don't worry, it'll probably be a nice and gentle landing on soft river mud.

Jarring, scraping impact. Dinghy comes to a grinding stop.

We are motionless in darkness. Mired in what I assume is murky river bottom.

I'm worried, dog. I'm very worried. "Extremely" would not be too strong a word. We're stuck at the bottom of a river. Do you know how to make this thing move?

Of course. That is, I believe so. Or perhaps I should phrase it another way: I can eliminate several methods of steering and propulsion which definitely will not work, but sadly they include all the alternatives that I thought would work, leaving us with . . .

Not a clue.

Indeed. But there's no reason to panic. Hard times require clear minds, as my uncle used to say, before he was torn to pieces by a pack of mutant wolves after fleeing in blind panic right into a trap they had set—

Enough, Gisco. More than enough. Before we find a way to extricate ourselves from this nautical nightmare, I want you to tell me exactly what's going on. What happened when you vanished into thin air above the Atlantic? Is Eko still alive, too? Why is the Dark Army chasing us again? And, most important, how did P.J. get involved in this mess?

Sure, the dog responds. *Good questions. Superb, in fact. Unfortunately I can't answer any of them right now.*

Don't be evasive, Gisco. I'll skin you for a quilt.

It's not that I don't want to answer your questions. The problem is that I'm not feeling well.

You seemed fine when you sprinted out of that wrecked police car. And you just swam like an otter.

A burst of dog adrenaline. But I believe that when you crashed that police car I sustained an injury. Or perhaps it was a lucky shot from one of their guns. Yes, I believe I was hit. Now I seem to be fading out, like a candle in the wind. You're going to have to take over, Jack. I know you can do it. You are our beacon of hope.

Take over what? Why do you need a beacon of hope? We saved the oceans, right? Gisco, I can't work this thing.

Find a way. We're running out of power. I always liked the song "We all live in a yellow submarine," but I have no desire to die in one. Now I need to sleep.

Dog, don't do this to me.

Gisco's telepathic voice weakens. *If I never wake, into the hands of the Great Dog God I commend my soul.*

Gisco? You useless coward. Stop praying to the Great Dog God, get back up, and help me!

I grab him. Yuck. He's covered in muck.

No, wait. That's not slime. It's warm and smells salty. It's blood! Gisco really is seriously injured!

I stroke his head very gently. He's out cold.

It's dark and very quiet. I can hear his shallow canine respiration. Poor fellow.

I'm all alone. At the bottom of a river. With a dying dog. In a futuristic submarine that's rapidly losing power. What could possibly be worse?

As if in answer, I hear something. A faint, cheerful musical whisper. Buzz, buzz.

Maybe it's an insect that will keep me company as I try to figure a way out of this. A friendly firefly. A lighthearted ladybug. Buzz, buzz, buzz.

No, wait, not buzz, buzz, buzz.

Drip, drip, drip.

Water! Dripping from the bubble ceiling.

We've got a leak!

9

grew up near the Hudson. Went swimming in it. Fished in it. Used to make out with P.J. in a car parked high above a scenic river lookout. But I never wanted to die in it, or rather under it. Never had a desire to personally contribute to the sediment on the river bottom.

Dark sub. Unconscious canine. Tons of water above us, slowly leaking into craft. All in all, not such a great situation.

I step over prone Gisco to miniature control panel. Always been good with new technologies. Pick up new computer skills the way babies catch the sniffles in winter. Expose me to something once and I've got the hang of it forever.

But this isn't like any computer I've ever seen before. And whoever put this dinghy together didn't bother to stick an operating manual in the glove compartment.

In the light of the flashing red button I see a few weird symbols on the panel that might as well be Egyptian hieroglyphics. A couple of funky-looking dials. Nothing remotely like a screen. How can I take over the steering of this submarine if I can't read the controls or see an outward projection of the thinking processes taking place inside?

Short answer: I can't.

Drip, drip, drip. Leak getting worse fast.

Not much time. Better try to think out of the box. But I'm in a box, under a river, stuck in mud.

I sit. Force myself to calm down. Breathe regularly. Okay. Stop thinking like a Mac user from the twenty-first century. I need to discard every assumption I have about computers. Because if, this thing is from a thousand years hence, the odds are that nothing I know is going to help.

I've read books and articles speculating about what the future of artificial intelligence will be. The big disagreements seem to be about whether computers will ever become conscious. But whether they achieve consciousness or not, everyone seems to agree that in the far future the relationship between humans and machines will be less and less human-directed, and more and more of a collaboration.

So maybe I should stop trying to take over the steering of this sub. Because maybe the sub doesn't need me to grasp a steering wheel, or pull a rudder.

That's an old way of thinking.

This sub is probably fully capable of freeing itself from the river bottom and steering us to safety. What it probably needs is guidance and direction, not operation.

But how do I direct it? What is the mechanism of establishing collaboration? I've never seen it done.

Wait a minute. Maybe that's not true.

I remember Eko at our beach house on the Outer Banks. Every time we came home, she would check a device in the living room that measured the threat level to our security. It was a blue cube. She wouldn't say anything to it, or turn any dials. It would bathe her in a bluish glow. And when the glow faded, she would have her answer.

I spread my hands on either side of the control panel. Come on. Turn on. Bathe me in some kind of glow.

Nothing happens.

I address it telepathically. Hello? How are you today, Sub? Can you read me? Is any of this registering?

No response, audible or telepathic. Nada.

Drip, drip, splash, splash. The water is starting to stream in, in a widening rivulet.

I'm frustrated, furious, and very scared, staring at the control panel with its blinking red button.

That's the button Gisco kept pushing to get us going. It's what brought us down here, to the river bottom. I assumed it must be the "down" button.

But it's unique. The only blinking button on the panel. *There's no "up" button.*

So what if it has nothing at all to do with steering the sub? What if it's actually the way in?

When Gisco was trying to get us to move, he kept hitting it. He punched it three times with his snout before it finally responded and gave off a reddish glow.

The cube that Eko used to consult in the beach house on the Outer Banks gave off a similar, bluish glow. First she would gently stroke it, as if conjuring it to life, and then spread her hands to either side and commune with it.

Maybe these things don't need to have a key turned in their ignitions, or a switch flicked on. Perhaps what they need is brief physical contact with the person they're about to collaborate with. Maybe in order to get on the correct wavelength, they must establish the right chemical or electromagnetic bond. Gisco said in frustration that this sub didn't like dogs. Maybe he was right. Perhaps touching the panel gives the sub a chance to scan a user's body chemicals down to his DNA and establish the necessary link. Possibly it's not programmed for dogs.

I get to my feet. The trickle of water splashing onto the floor of the dinghy has increased to an ominous little waterfall. Any second the tons of water above us may crack apart the bubble ceiling, and the river will force its way into this sub like Niagara Falls prying open a tin can.

I touch the red button. Hi. Jack Danielson here. I'd like to establish a collaboration. We have a little leak problem to fix. Then we need to get off the river bottom and head north. Do you read me? Can you answer?

Nothing.

No, not nothing. A faint reddish glow emanates from the panel. But no words come back at me. No operating instructions are projected with holographs.

A faint reddish glow is cheerful enough, but how is it going to get me out of this mess?

Wait a minute. Something has changed. I can still hear Gisco's shallow breaths, but beyond that, the tiny sub is now completely silent.

No more splash, splash, splash. The leak has stopped.

Did you do that, Yellow Submarine? What next?

No answer. Just a flickering nimbus in the darkness.

I stop trying to talk to it telepathically. It clearly doesn't have that ability. But, at the same time, it glowed after I touched it, and it stopped the leak when I asked it to, so it must be aware of me.

I put my hands into the center of the reddish flame. Try to open my mind to whatever's reaching out to me.

A very strange thing happens.

✴

10

I am Jack Danielson, standing before the control panel of a souped-up dinghy at the bottom of the Hudson River.

But I am also the dinghy. I am aware of the water all around, pressing down on me. I feel the darkness and the cold. I am weak from my ebbing power supply.

This is not the kind of back-and-forth telepathic contact I have with Gisco. It's less about communication and more about a deep symbiotic sharing of knowledge and abilities for practical purposes.

The Yellow Submarine is not alive. It has no ability to feel joy or sadness, no soul. I can't tease it the way I tease Gisco and expect it to crack jokes back at me.

At the same time, it's also not just a machine. It has a narrow but definite sense of self-awareness that seems close to human consciousness. It doesn't fear death as a great unknown, but if the water pressure crushed it, it understands that it would not be able to function or serve anymore. It knows it would become a useless piece of river-bottom debris. That prospect disturbs it in a way that feels oddly similar to my own greatest fears.

No, it desperately wants to function and to serve. So it allows me to merge with it. Welcomes me.

I complained that the people who built it didn't include an operating manual, but now I see that's not true. This dinghy is its own operating manual. It has a comprehensive knowledge of its own abilities, which it's eager to share with me, now that we're pals.

Jack Danielson cannot see in darkness, so lights blink on, not because I flipped a switch but because the craft understood that there was a need for more illumination. We understood that need together. Just as we need to get moving, and so the sub rocks once or twice and then we power forward, out of the muck, and begin a journey northward.

Now we're moving in the right direction. Sharing a sense of purpose and accomplishment. Solving problems together. Sub and boy. Boy in sub. Boy running sub. Sub showing boy what to do each step of the way.

Want to go faster? Shall we turn? Need it to be a bit warmer inside? No problemo. Done.

Who's in charge? Who's more dependent? Who's smarter? Where does the power lie in this complex mingling of mind and machine? I can't say.

But I do know the answers are not simple. Things have changed a lot from the day a caveman picked up a piece of flint and chipped it to make a tool. Now the tool invites the man inside for a shared experience in problem solving.

We're fifty feet beneath the surface of the Hudson. Moving northward at ten knots. Lights kept low to avoid surface detection.

I slowly disengage. Not painful, but it makes me lonely for a second. Like stepping away from a part of myself. But I'm no longer needed. We made our decisions together, and now the sub will carry them out.

I pull off the blue police shirt that I took from the Hadley station. Drape it over Gisco like a blanket.

It's all that I can do for him now. The blood has dried on his fur. I stroke his ears and he stirs faintly.

Heal, hound, I encourage him telepathically. A big old war dog like you has made it through many battles. Come through one more. And because Gisco is out of it and can't hear me, I add in a soft, pleading whisper, "I need you, old friend. I don't want to lose you again."

The dinghy must sense my deep concern for him. A faint reddish glow envelops Gisco from snout to paws. Perhaps the boat has the power to keep him alive, or even to somehow heal him.

It certainly couldn't do any harm.

I sit with my back against the wall. Listen to Gisco's labored breaths. Feel scared for him. But also curious.

Why did Gisco come back to Hadley for me? How did he know I'd be in the police station?

Is this his submarine, or did someone leave it in the river for him? If it's his, why didn't he know how to work it better? If someone left it for him, who are they and where did they go?

Haven't had this feeling of complete mental meltdown for a while. Drowning in a sea of my own fears and ignorance. I know nothing about myself. Don't have a clue what I'm supposed to do.

Can't figure out who's after me and those I love. Chief Parker's grim descriptions come back to me, conjuring up awful images.

The woman who raised me, and who I still think of as my mom, sliced in half and left to die in a burning house.

My "dad" torched inside his car and pushed off a hundred-foot cliff into this very river.

Now the Dark Army is chasing me again. Why? What do they want from me? Only Gisco can answer these questions.

If he dies I'll have no one.

Except P.J. But maybe not even her.

My love. My touchstone. The reason I came back to Hadley. Now she's gone. Vanished. No, not vanished. Vanished would be better. P.J. was targeted.

For no reason I can think of. She wasn't part of this. Just a sweet American girl who fell for the wrong guy. She was taken because of me. It's my fault.

At least I settled the question of whether I can ever go home again. Hadley is gone for me. The people I grew up with, my childhood friends, my parents. All out of bounds forever more.

Strange to give up on the concept of home.

I shut my eyes and try not to feel so awfully lonely.

But sleep will not come for someone as miserable as I am. I could sit here and count Dark Army ghouls jumping over fences from now to doomsday, and I wouldn't sleep.

Then I feel the cloud. Soft as a child's security blanket. It settles around me. Not a fluffy white cloud. It's reddish and flame-like. The dinghy.

It's trying to heal Gisco, and it's also taking care of me. It senses that I need to sleep. It's looking out for me. Worrying about me. So it reaches out gently. Invites me back, to merge with it again. Not because it needs me to help steer or to solve a navigational problem.

It just wants to alleviate my loneliness and misery.

I accept the offer. Sink into the flame till I'm no longer a boy sitting with my back against the wall of a boat, but rather I'm the boat moving through a dark river.

I feel the cold density of the water as we nose our way through the depths. The hostile embrace of the pressure from tons of water above us. Like tentacles wrapped around us. A constant octopus squeeze. But we'll be all right. We were built to withstand far worse than this.

Nice to be a machine without worry.

Circuits humming. Power supply low but everything still functioning perfectly.

I sink into the strangest sleep of my life.

11

This can't be a dream. Dreams come to you in your safe, warm bed, woven from the delicate gauze of sleep.

This is vivid, visceral, brutal.

I feel myself being ripped out of my own body. Borne aloft at furious speed. What part of me is being taken? My mind? My spirit? I can't resist. Pulled as if captive on a magic leash. Spun as if caught up by a whirlwind.

And then plunked down suddenly, in a strange new place, like Dorothy crash-landing in Oz.

My God, I've been transported. Moving down a river in twilight. No, not the Hudson. This makes the Hudson seem like a pathetic, trickling stream.

The size of this river! The thrumming aliveness of it! Green all around me. A greener green than exists in New York State. This is the emerald of children's fairy tales, of the giant leaves that shade Jack's beanstalk.

I drift off into that magical green canopy. A giant snake slithers through the water. Its spade-shaped head trowels the surface. Its body unspools and recoils.

An endless variety of birdcalls trill from high above. Chirruping solos and warbled duets. Soaring avian arias and pessimistic passerine blues ballads.

Something with me, above me, around me, keeping tabs on me as I move through the green jungle. A keenly intelligent gaze. Human eyes! Spooky. Ghoul-like. Egyptian mummy eyes, encased in a sand-dry face.

The face is ancient, but the eyes are alive. Childlike. Mischievous. The wisdom in that face! The humanity! It's the face of someone who exists outside of time and place. An Einstein. A Gandhi. Then I hear something, above the chittering of the birds and the chattering of the monkeys . . .

Music! Flutes and drums. Rattles and tambourines.

Human voices. Chanting in a language I have never heard. A lullaby? No, more threatening. A war ballad?

That wise old face now closer. He's right next to me, traveling down the same river. We're in some sort of canoe. "Who are you?" I ask. "What are we doing here?"

The old lips open. One word. "Destiny."

"Destiny what?" I press. "Whose? Yours? Mine?"

But he's not looking at me anymore. He's looking out at the river and the trees.

Banks on both sides, pressing in on us. Trees linking branches to form a green canopy overhead. We're not on the amazingly wide river anymore.

We've turned off, lost our way. We're on a fast-moving stream, being squeezed tightly between cliff walls.

There's a ferocious roaring up ahead. Lion? Jaguar?

No, it's a river growl—the throaty roar of a watery torrent smashing down a steep, rock-ribbed mountainside.

"Destiny," I hear whispered one last time.

We hang on the lip of the abyss, and I glimpse what lies before us, if we should make it through the rapids.

A wondrous diamond-shaped valley is surrounded by cliff walls. Four rivers spill into that sheltered valley in a succession of cataracts, hissing down into the same boiling cauldron.

A lush island floats serenely in the center of this wild whirlpool, a jungle Eden. I glimpse towering trees and pink flowers as big as umbrellas. Giant men are on the island, too—I see their shadowy faces. Frowning. Primordial. "Don't come here!" they warn. "Stay away!"

We plunge over the lip of the abyss. Our canoe can't take this battering. We spin and smash and frothing water blinds me, and I scream as we lose all control. I hold on desperately as we whirl down into certain death.

I'm in transit again, not my body but my essence—my mind, my consciousness, my spirit.

An endless dark passage. Someone is with me. That old mummy. His arms are upraised. He's reaching out to me. Pleading for help. Summoning me to fight with him.

Yes, it's a call to arms. A summons to duty from a great distance.

Fly to me, he's saying without words. Come quickly, Jack. Time is running out.

Where? I ask. Who are you, old man? How do you know my name? Who is time running out for? I need a little bit to work with on my end. Who's chasing me? Is P.J. there?

No answer. But something has drastically changed. I'm not in a canoe anymore. No longer in a steaming jungle. It's cool now.

Cold, even. Dreams shouldn't feel chilly.

Music gone. Birdcalls muted.

Silence.

Also, I'm not moving upriver anymore. Or downriver.

Cold. Quiet. Stuck fast.

Dream over. I open my eyes. The dinghy has surfaced and its bubble ceiling has retracted. I'm now in a shabby yellow boat, scraping against a dark and pebbly bank, near some power lines.

What are we doing here, where the Dark Army may spot us at any moment? Why did the dinghy steer us to this Hudson River beach?

It's a smart machine—smarter than I am in many ways. There must be a logical reason.

I glance up at the power cables. They're bowing slightly toward the boat, as if being pulled by an invisible force. The reddish button on the dinghy's control panel is pulsing wildly, and it occurs to me that the boat may be renewing its power supply after the previous night's adventures.

I realize to my horror that the dinghy is now completely silent.

I don't hear Gisco's labored breathing. Did my furry friend pass away during the night? I wheel around and spot the big dog lying silent and still.

*

12

For a long moment I fear the worst. Then I see Gisco's massive chest heave in and out, and he gives a little snore. I realize the big dog is sleeping normally.

I reach over and gently shake him. Gisco, can you hear me? Are you still in pain? Can you open your eyes?

Gisco yawns and his eyes pop open. *Boy, do I feel a hundred times better. Must be the spring air. The only thing I need to complete my recovery is a hearty country breakfast. Eggs. Scrambled, I think. A slab of honey ham. And perhaps some hot biscuits slathered with gravy.* He sits up and looks around. *Where are we, by the way?*

Somewhere upstate. The dinghy pulled over while I was sleeping. I think it may have run out of power, and it's recharging from those cables. Maybe you should worry less about breakfast options, and more about the Dark Army finding us. They could be closing in while you fantasize about ham and eggs.

Try not to worry so much. It's bad for the digestion. The Dark Army will never figure out my brilliant ploy of heading upriver. So let's go find the local doughnut shop and see if they make a honey-glazed—

Gisco never gets to finish the thought because at that moment there's a distant thud followed a few seconds later by an earth-shattering BOOM.

Something strikes the ground near us, with enough impact to knock me off my feet. "What was that?" I ask, getting to my knees.

Gisco peers around, suddenly very worried. *The Dark Army.*

I thought we outfoxed them by heading upriver.

I may have been overly optimistic.

Meaning what?

I believe we've sailed right into an ambush.

I look around. The morning mist is burning off the hills that slope to the riverbank.

There! On a hill a mile away, I spot the glint of dawn light on laser guns and black motorcycles. As I watch, the bikes roar into motion and speed toward us.

And there—on a road, much closer! What looks like a combination of a sports car and a tank. It's built for speed, but it has a long gun on a roof turret that is pointing in our direction! The muzzle is smoking—it must have fired whatever missile just missed us.

And there! Far out in the river! An armada of speedboats, sailing right at our yellow dinghy!

The dinghy also seems to sense the ambush. The power lines swing back to normal, as if released from an invisible grip. We pull away from the bank.

Jack, get down! Incoming fire!

I turn my head just as the mini-tank belches out a red-tipped missile that streaks toward us.

Gisco and I dive face-first to the bottom of the boat at the same second.

The missile flies right over where we were just standing. Its speed makes the air hum.

As soon as it passes us it begins to slow, as if realizing that it missed, and veers into an acute turn.

This is clearly a beacon-of-hope-seeking missile—it comes whistling back at us to take another shot.

Something warm on my wrist. I glance down—the wristwatch that my father gave me is turning bright blue. A sapphire beam streaks out of it and touches the nose of the missile. It turns the projectile very slightly toward a massive oak tree that stands on the shore.

Huge explosion. Oak tree incinerated. Mud and grass and pieces of wood rain down.

I wait for the monsoon of wood, sod, and shrapnel to subside. Look up. A pillar of white smoke rises into the air where the tree stood. Brush fires lick all around.

I glance back up the hillside. The Dark Army killers slalom through the forest on their sleek motorcycles. They fire laser blasts that ignite the trees between us and make the rocks glow like hot coals.

The turret of the mini-tank swivels as it corrects its aim—the next missile will surely finish us.

Our dinghy is moving into deeper water, picking up speed. But we'll never get away in time.

A beam of light snakes into the water near our bow, and steam shoots skyward with a deafening HISS.

The motorcycle riders have dismounted and now crouch on the shore, firing lasers at us!

Dense black smoke billows out from the dinghy's motor and enfolds us in an inky cloud that screens us till we're safely out of laser range.

But there's nowhere to go on a river, and no place to hide.

The mini-tank rumbles to the bank and quickly converts to a combination gunship and amphibious transport vehicle. A few Dark Army motorcycles roll onto it, and then it sails out into the river after us at a surprisingly fast clip. Its big gun swivels in our direction.

Meanwhile, the speedboats close in for the kill.

13

As the speedboats get close, they let loose a colorful futuristic fusillade. Blue plasma nets, red paralysis darts, and white-hot laser beams streak across the water toward us.

The dinghy tries its one trick. The transparent bubble rises, and we start to submerge.

This worked before and I have high hopes that it will work again. But as we sink, the mini-tank belches something toward us that is not a torpedo. It's a nasty ball of black energy that re-forms and reshapes as it crawls toward us like a giant spider.

Water covers the top of our bubble. We're down, but we're not safe yet. Because the pulsing energy blob has reached us! It hovers, inches above the surface.

And then it dives down after us! I press the blinking red button on the controls. Jam my palm against it. Need to warn the boat that the monster is still chasing us.

Now that I know how to merge with the dinghy, I can do it much faster. It's aware of our pursuer. We're aware. Working together. We take evasive action as the jellyfish of energy points tentacles at us that break off and zap down like dark thunderbolts.

I'm Jack Danielson standing in the dinghy. But I'm also the dinghy, darting back and forth.

Unfortunately, dodging isn't enough. One of the energy blasts strikes us a glancing blow. We need to fight back or we'll be shredded. Can we? Do we have any firepower?

Oh yes we do! I can feel the coldness of the river on the hull. I tingle at the energy blasts all around us. And I sense a small shutter opening in our hull. Fire in our belly. I help direct it, spew it out.

The jellyfish of dark energy dives right into our weapon's path. It flails its tentacles, turns from black to glowing red to radiant orange, and disintegrates.

For a moment I share a powerful feeling with the dinghy. Joy? Can a machine feel joy? Achievement? Victory? Definitely a kind of comradeship.

Then I feel the wound. The blast that hit us punctured our bubble. Water is pouring in. Too big a hole to fix. We have to go back up.

When we surface I see that our brief underwater duel has carried us beyond the ring of speedboats that encircled us. They spot us, turn quickly, and take up the pursuit.

Down! Gisco orders. The dinghy swerves as a nasty bit of artillery whistles past our bow.

Jack, get down flat! Present less of a target! The pigeon-hearted pooch leads by example, pressing himself to the bottom and flattening his massive belly till he looks like a throw rug covering a bowling ball.

I don't get down. I'm still merged with the boat, still bathed in the reddish glow.

I am Jack Danielson crouching before the control panel of a souped-up dinghy that is taking evasive action as it's chased across the Hudson River. "Do something," I am saying to the dinghy. Or not saying, but rather thinking and feeling.

But I am also the dinghy. I feel the frenetic hopelessness of the chase, the strain of my motor, the quick read of incoming missiles and lasers.

One primary need—to escape. One grim certainty—escape is impossible. The speedboats are drawing closer. We'll never reach the far bank in time.

A laser weapon slices the stern and I—we—feel it come searing in. The dinghy wants desperately to save us, but it can't. It's not fast enough. It's outgunned. I feel its bitter frustration—our mutual frustration.

Then I feel something I don't understand. It grows out of that frustration, blossoms incongruously from the grimness of our predicament.

Joy. Elation. Certainty of purpose tinged with nagging regret.

The bond between boy and boat is fractured.

The dinghy swerves wildly and I'm knocked off my feet. I press myself to the bottom next to Gisco, mystified. How can the boat be so jubilant at a time like this?

Another laser strike! I don't need to be mind-melded with the dinghy to feel this one hit. They've got our range now. We'll be fish food in seconds.

Jack, we've got to get off now!

Off the boat? How is that going to help?

No time to explain. Abandon ship!

Gisco has climbed up from his ruglike recline and is now perched at the rail, ready for a dive into the drink.

There's no way out, I tell him. We might as well go down with our dinghy.

The dog locks his jaws around my shirt and tries to drag me over the side. I fight back. I'd rather be blown up on board a friendly craft than flash-fried in the river.

Gisco is strong, but not strong enough to drag me over the rail. He's got me half over but I'm resisting.

Then the dinghy bucks like a bronco. It dips and twists, and dog and boy both go flying.

✳

14

We splash down hard into the cold river. I hit face-first. Sink and come up sputtering.

The bank is a hundred yards away.

Come on, we've got to swim for it. Gisco sets out for shore in an Olympic-quality dog paddle.

What's the point? I ask. We'll never outrun those speedboats.

Instead of swimming, I tread water and just watch hopelessly as the black speedboats come on, their laser weapons turning the water around us into a sauna.

The mini-tank that is now an amphibious carrier of Dark Army motorcycles is also closing in fast. Even if we did make it to the far bank, those motorcycles would chase us down in seconds. There's no possible escape.

The yellow dinghy does not stay close to us. It turns in a quick circle and heads directly back, toward the speedboats and the amphibious mini-tank.

Lasers punch holes in the kamikaze dinghy's sides. A missile just misses it, and nearly capsizes it. But it steams right for them at full speed.

Is it my imagination, or is it starting to glow?

Maybe it's on fire. The lasers could have ignited it.

But the reddish glow doesn't seem to be a natural flame. It's flickering. A cherry nimbus spreads out from the damaged boat and licks the waves in its own wake.

The reddish glow touches me in the water and I feel something strange. Not a telepathic message from a machine. The boat can't think, the way I can.

Yet for one last second I become part of it. I share its strange mixture of joy and regret, its implacable sense of mission and the sad knowledge that it will never be able to serve again. And even a trace of something akin to a friendship ending, or at least a comradeship cut short.

The bond is broken. I gulp down river water and cough it back up. The dinghy is now far from us—already nearly halfway back to the pursuing boats. The glow that emanates from it changes color, from cheery cherry to savage scarlet smoldering with yellow-black.

And it's pulsing! What the heck is happening?

It's going hypercritical! Dive, Jack!

What's going hypercritical? The dinghy? Where are you? I look for Gisco, but he's vanished.

Something grabs my left ankle and yanks me under the surface. I thrash wildly and struggle to get away. Open my eyes underwater. See that it's Gisco who's dragging me down, my left leg in his jaws.

Then the sky falls in. The explosion is deafening even though I'm under the water.

The clouds catch fire. Flames rake the surface of the river. I feel the sizzling heat. The shriek of water whistling into steam is all around me, as if I'm trapped in a giant teakettle.

I stay down as long as I can. And then I pop back up.

Silence. Wide, empty river. Smoke clearing to reveal that the dinghy is gone. And the speedboats and the mini-tank are gone, too. There's a board here, a bit of charred motorcycle there, but nothing has survived that blast.

The yellow boat gave its mechanical life for us. It knew that it was destroying itself and would never serve again. But it was the only way to take out our Dark Army pursuers. That was the joy the dinghy felt. One last great act of service.

Come on, the dog demands.

Don't you understand? It sacrificed itself for us. The dinghy's final heroic act hits me hard. I flash to my mother, hugging me goodbye for the last time, and my father, shooting off his foot to get me to leave him, and then turning to make a last stand while I fled.

I get it. Now it is for us, the living, to honor its sacrifice by making sure it didn't die in vain. Let's go!

It couldn't die, because it was never really alive, I muse, my mind still reeling.

Good, then if it couldn't die we don't need to mourn it, so let's just va- moose.

Are you really so self-centered that when noble comrades are blowing themselves up for your sake, all you can think about is saving your own stinking skin?

Yes, Gisco admits, *that's exactly the effect that danger in my imme- diate vicinity has on me. And right now I'm thinking of saving my skin by swimming as fast as possible to the bank and getting the hell away from here before more Dark Army fiends come looking for us.*

I have no doubt they'll come, I tell him, but what's the point? We run and hide, good people die, and we run again. My mother, my father, the dinghy. What is the point, dog? Enough!

This is a really unfortunate moment for you to become Hamlet and play the "To be or not to be" game, Gisco says. *Sure, life sucks some- times. But you have to keep going till the great boot squashes you. P.J. is still alive, but she's in mortal danger. I know exactly where she is and who took her, and I even know why. If you don't save her, she'll perish for sure. That's what you have to live for. Do you take it or leave it, that is the question.*

I can't leave it, but I'm not ready to take it yet. I fire off questions: Who took her? Why? Where is she?

She was kidnapped by the leader of the Dark Army, the baddest man of the far future, the dog informs me. *Now let's swim for it. Every second is critical.*

Why did he take her? I demand.

For reasons of personal vengeance, Gisco says. *He has a score he wants to settle with you.*

Where did he take her? Where is she right now?

South, Gisco responds, and starts dog-paddling for shore.

South, where? I follow up. New Jersey? North Carolina again? Are you going to try to trick me to the Outer Banks a second time? How do I know that you didn't kidnap her yourself? No, I take that back. I don't think even you would stoop that low. But I know how tricky you are, and that you've got your own agenda. Tell me one thing: if this evil warlord from the far future kidnapped P.J. to even the score with me, how can you be so sure she's still alive? Give me some concrete proof!

Proof, shmoof. Gisco is twenty yards away, dog-paddling for all he's worth. *The Dark Army will send reconnaissance. It's swim-or-die time.*

I hesitate a second more and strike out after him.

15

Now I know why they call it the crawl. I'm fighting the cold current as I inch my way toward the rocky bank. I must have lost my police cap when I dived off the boat. I reach down and unclasp the gun belt and let it drop.

Gisco is in front of me, setting new swimming speed records for convalescent canines.

We don't communicate. We're both too busy trying not to drown. But his words echo in my mind as I stroke on, trying to ignore the ache in my arms and shoulders.

P.J.'s still alive! But she's in the hands of some fiendish five-star general from the future! And he's taken her to get back at me! Which means it *was* my fault that she was targeted. And she's south, whatever that means.

I'm freezing and utterly exhausted when my toes scrape the river bottom. Soon I'm hip-deep, then knee-deep, and finally I'm completely out of the cold Hudson.

Where to now? I ask Gisco. South to find P.J.? Who is this evil commander who took her? Does he have a name?

No time now for explanations. Let's just get away.

Where?

Anywhere. The dog shakes out his fur, and water flies.

How?

However.

That's your plan? Mindless, headlong flight?

You got it, the huffing, puffing dog acknowledges, as we leave the rocks and fight our way through scrub brush. *The Dark Army knows where we just were. I guarantee you they'll come roaring upriver and find us in minutes. The more we run, the more visible we make our-selves.*

Then why don't we just crawl into a hole and hide?

Because the more we hunker down and stay put, the less chance we have of ever getting away.

So we're screwed? I ask.

Yes, that's a superb way of putting it, Gisco admits. *I don't see any way out of this. But we have to try. Never give up, as my dear grand-father used to say, before he hoisted the white flag and tried to surrender to a pack of gigantic mutant rats who devoured him alive.*

Enough, dog. Here's a road. Maybe we can flag down a car.

Unlikely. It's an unpaved path. Even country bumpkins avoid driving down gravel trails in the early morning.

A car swims into view. No, scratch that. It's a blue pickup truck.

You were saying? I ask Gisco, sticking out my thumb.

You're wasting your time. Even if some rural rube happens to be out for a morning drive, what are the odds he'll stop for a sopping wet teenager who needs a haircut, and a shaggy dog who hasn't had a decent breakfast in days?

The pickup rumbles past us, stops, and backs up.

A family in the front seat. Mother, father, little girl with braces.

"Morning," the father calls. "A little early for a swim, isn't it?"

"Good morning," I shout back cheerfully. "I was walking by the bank and fell in."

"Are you headed to the fair?" he asks.

"Yes, sir, that's where we're headed," I answer.

What are you saying? Gisco demands. *We don't have time to waste at a fair! The Dark Army is converging on us and you want to eat can-died apples and take pony rides?*

What we need, I point out, is to get away from the river as fast as possible. Capeesh?

Capeesh. I just hope this truck has decent shock absorbers and leather seats.

"If you don't mind riding in the back, climb on in," the man says.

The back? What are we, livestock?

"Thanks," I tell the man, "that'll be fine."

"What's your dog's name?" the girl with braces asks. She looks like she's about nine. Pigtails. Freckles.

"I call him Gisco. It's a funny name, isn't it?"

"Yeah, and he's sure funny-looking."

You're not going to win any ribbons at the fair yourself, metal mouth.

"He is a little weird-looking," I agree with a friendly nod. "But I'm fond of him anyway. Looks aren't everything."

"I know what you mean," the girl says. "We have a butt-ugly cat named Socks, but I still like her."

"Sally," the mother says, "that's not nice language."

"I just said 'butt-ugly,' " the girl repeats. "There's nothing wrong with 'butt-ugly.' "

"Say it again and I'll swat you so hard you won't sit down for a week."

Lovely family, Gisco remarks. *Sweet little girl. Charming mother.*

In you go, Mr. Butt-ugly. I give Gisco a boost into the back of the pickup and climb in after him. The truck rumbles away down the winding gravel road at a fast clip, bumping wildly at every turn of the wheel.

16

They're coming. I sense it.

Gisco feels it, too. I can tell by the way he lies flat in the bed of the pickup, groaning each time we hit a bump. This truck does not have new shock absorbers. It doesn't seem to have any kind of shock absorbers at all. We're taking a pulverizing beating.

The gravel path twists like a corkscrew next to the Hudson. Blue water flashes at every bend.

I watch the skies above the river and soon spot jet-black helicopters swooping low. Gisco!

They'll locate the wreckage from the explosion first, the dog predicts glumly. *Then they'll summon help and sweep both banks, and start searching for us inland.*

Sure enough, the helicopters slow in tandem and begin to circle, right above the spot where the dinghy committed nautical hara-kari. In minutes three gray hovercraft glide like wraiths up the Hudson, zeroing in on the patch of rotor-wash-stirred water beneath the copters.

They'll be after us in minutes, Gisco warns.

It was a big explosion, I point out. Maybe they'll assume we were blown to bits and give up the chase.

You don't know who you're up against, the dog sniffs.

Because you won't tell me. If he was the leader of the Dark Army, why has he come back in time? What score does he have to settle with me?

You'll find out soon enough.

He can't be worse than Dargon, I speculate, remembering the chimeric nightmare of my Firestorm quest.

This guy makes Dargon look like a teddy bear.

Do you have any good news?

We're about to turn away from the river on a paved road, which may make this primitive vehicle tolerable.

Sure enough, the pickup reaches a turnoff, slows, and veers onto a two-lane road that heads west. We drive smoothly for a few miles, through forest and farmland.

Suddenly I hear music, and bright colors flash through the web of tree branches. Tents with banners! Carnival rides! A spinning red-and-blue Ferris wheel twirls like a giant pinwheel in the morning breeze.

The pickup turns into an enormous parking lot that is filling up fast. This fair is clearly the big local attraction. We chug into an empty space and pull to a stop, and Gisco and I hop out.

"Thanks," I say to the father.

"Don't mention it," he responds. "Come on, Sally. Want to try that Ferris wheel?"

"Ferris wheels make me puke," the little girl says. "Goodbye, doggy. Sorry I said you were butt-ugly."

Apology not accepted. Scram, brat.

Off they go, through the gate.

We linger outside. What now, shaggy shanks?

That ride in the truck didn't buy us much time. They're close on our heels. I can feel them.

Me too. In fact it feels like they're already here.

That black van at the far end of the parking lot!

I spot it, a half mile away. It's got a satellite dish rotating on its roof. Have they spotted us yet?

I'm not sure, the dog admits, *but I do know that inside that van is every cutting-edge search technology the Dark Army has. Heat sensors. DNA scanners. We're sitting ducks out here in the parking lot.*

What do you recommend?

No choice, Gisco says. *We've got to huddle with the hoi polloi.*

Dog using fancy SAT word. You want to go into the fair?

Correct. It's time to take refuge among the great unwashed, the haughty hound declares, trotting quickly toward the ticket window. *I hope you've got money for cotton candy.*

17

It's early in the morning, but the fair is already mobbed.

Parents with heads revolving like bobble dolls try to keep track of sugared-up turbo tykes as throngs of older kids run rampant, breaking every rule posted on signs. They're playing tag and screaming at each other from rides and kung fu kicking and competing to see who can eat the most junk food.

We plunge into the mayhem.

How about the Tilt-a-Whirl, Gisco?

I'm not a fan of tilting. Dogs appreciate stability.

Then I guess the Death Coaster is out of the question?

Perhaps a corn dog, savored slowly in the shade of that giant apple.

I glance over at the two-story wooden apple bearing the legend EMPIRE STATE—PROUD APPLE CAPITAL OF THE WORLD, and spot a gaunt seven-foot-tall man wading through the crowd toward us. He's dressed in an old-fashioned and ill-fitting black suit, and has a protruding Adam's apple. A boy darts in front of him, and the tall guy shoves the kid fifteen feet out of his way and marches on without breaking stride.

I've seen his type before. An identical zombielike man spotted me in the Hadley Diner six months ago, the night all my troubles began. This one may be dressed like Abe Lincoln but he's a cyborg—part-man, part-machine, and all deadly. Gisco! He's spotted us!

And he's got an axon blaster!

That must be the device in his right hand. It looks like an oversize TV remote. He points it at us and a barely visible orange beam shoots out.

Gisco plows into me, knocking me over just in time. The beam ZAPS a fat woman throwing beanbags at a pyramid of bowling pins. She freezes in mid-throw.

"What's the matter, Mabel?" her husband asks with a laugh. Her throwing arm slowly swings down and she drops the bean-bag on the ground. "That's a balk. Runners, advance." Then he stops laughing as she goes limp and slack-jawed, and her whole body turns to cellular Silly Putty. "Mabel? *Oh my God! Someone call a doctor!*"

The cyborg re-aims. Gisco and I stay low, scuttling around rides as we try to keep him from getting a clear shot. But he's stalking us skillfully, and we're running out of cover. I hear a bell ringing. "Gisco! The Death Coaster is setting off!"

I'd rather have my axons blasted, the dog declares.

"Suit yourself," I tell him, and sprint toward the nearby tracks. The roller-coaster cars rumble by, starting to gather speed for a long climb. I vault the rail and jump into an empty seat.

"Hey," a boy behind me yells, "you can't do that."

"I'll pay when it's over," I tell him.

A second later Gisco hurtles over the rail and crash-lands next to me on top of the safety bar. *You're right, this is the only way out. But how does this safety bar open?*

It's already locked down. Just hold on tight.

Dogs don't have fingers!

That evolutionary failing may cost you dearly.

Gisco takes this personally. *As Darwin would no doubt explain to you, dogs occupied a vital niche in the survival of the fittest and paws were a significant advancement . . .* He ends his learned discourse as we stop climbing skyward and sit for a second looking down at an impossibly steep descent. *Jack, I can't hold on! I'm going to die!*

What were you just saying about paws?

The terrified dog jumps into my lap. *You hold on to me!*

Impossible, old fellow. I need both hands to grip the bar.

What am I supposed to do?

Darwin would probably suggest you adapt.

Gisco looks around wildly, but there's no one else to help him and nothing to be done. As our car begins accelerating downward, he locks his massive jaws around the safety bar.

We plummet earthward. All around me, kids bellow in joyous fear. I hold on for all I'm worth, and glance at the dog.

He now seems to be flying above our car, inverted, like a furry guardian angel. He's literally clinging to the safety bar, and to life itself, by the skin of his canines. Enjoying the Death Coaster, Gisco?

I'll get you back for this. Fingers can be gnawed off in ten bites.

Hold tight, Gisco. Here come the death spirals.

The speed we have built up from our plunge keeps the cars pinned with centrifugal force as we are spun upside down and whipped through five loops.

Blood rushes to my head. My fingers probably leave marks in the steel bar. I've never liked roller coasters.

What's the point, anyway? By now the Dark Army has got the entire fairground surrounded.

We are on the slow part of the Death Coaster, when passengers are given a few seconds to recover. We're rolling along a straightaway, fifteen feet above the ground. Kids wave to us. I scan the nearby exits and don't spot any Dark Army operatives. But I have no doubt that Gisco's right. They're down there.

What I do see is a noisy kaleidoscope of food stands, a Fun House, a booth with a prize pig, a balloonist offering rides, a chance to take photos with a mock-up of Niagara Falls, and about a thousand screaming kids.

This fair is total chaos, I point out to Gisco. There must be a way to squeeze out unobserved. Maybe we could steal a car or hide in the back of a truck.

They can anticipate our need to flee and they've got super-advanced search technologies, the dog explains. *If even a single hair from either of us passes out an exit, they'll know. They're checking every van, every car, everything with a combustion engine for our DNA.*

His words give me the inkling of an idea. Something I once saw in a fair, near Hadley. Gisco, that's it!

What's what?

Maybe we can beat their super-advanced technologies with something primitive. But we have to get off this Death Coaster.

There's no way off this ride. We're starting to climb again if you hadn't noticed.

Look! There's a trampoline tent coming up below.

You're kidding, right? It's filled with kids.

They just emptied it out and they haven't taken in a new batch yet. We've got to try. I contort my body and manage to squirm out from under the safety bar. I stand up in the car.

Jack, we're too high up. We don't have a prayer.

It's dive or die time, dog.

I calculate speed and distance as best I can, and throw myself over the side of the car headfirst. The boy behind me shouts, "Hey, mister, you *really* can't do that."

A second later I hear: "And neither can you, dog. I'm going to report you both."

18

Free-falling. We waited too long to jump. We're going to miss the trampoline and land on a merry-go-round.

I remember Eko's flying lessons on the Outer Banks. How she

made me run through a natural wind tunnel with my arms out-stretched. I felt foolish. "You can learn to do this," she chided me. "Use your whole body. Your legs. Your trunk. Your spirit."

I try to wipe my mind clean. Hard thing to do when you're about to go splat on rearing horses and cheerily painted sleighs. Not to mention the merry-go-round's steel base. Can't worry about that. No fear, no calculation, no thinking at all allowed.

I'm a beam of light swimming through a river of air. Feel its currents and eddies. Ride the wind.

Dog plunging through the air right next to me, making a valiant effort to spread his bulk flat, like a giant flying squirrel who has eaten a few too many doughnuts.

But Gisco's doing it! He's riding the air currents. And I'm also moving slightly sideways. The bad news is that we'll never get ourselves far enough over in the few heartbeats we have left.

The carnival rushing up at us. Garish colors, squeaky voices, blaring music. My life flashing. P.J., sorry I couldn't save you. I would have gone to the ends of the earth. God forgive me for get-ting you into this. Eko, wherever you are, farewell. I should have listened to your flying lessons a bit more closely.

The face of death appears, mouth opening wide to swallow me. It's an aristocratically handsome face, austere, and familiar. It reminds me of Dargon, the villain of my Firestorm quest. But this is an older face. Stronger. Wiser. Crueler. Cold, merciless eyes watching me. Waiting to escort me to hell.

Crash, I come down on the merry-go-round. Bash my head open on a sleigh. A steel pole impales me. It's agonizing. I feel my-self die and . . .

Swoosh, no, it's a giant pillow. At the very last second I moved myself the final few feet and landed on the tentlike roof of the kids' jumping booth! Gisco and I fall on the plastic top and bring it crashing down. The trampoline below is like a massive marshmal-low. We hit it together, and it bounces us right back up into the air.

Down we come again. The whole kiddy trampoline contraption is cracking apart from the force of our fall. Wooden base splintering. Support poles giving way.

Kids waiting on line are loving it. They shriek with laughter. "Look, it's Dumbo! No, he's not an elephant. It's a fat flying dog!"

Their mothers are less pleased. Screaming and yanking them away. Calling the police on cell phones. The FBI. The Terror Hotline.

A fire alarm goes off. A sprinkler switches on. Foam is sprayed by an automatic extinguisher system. The kids hoot and bellow. Toss foam around like snowballs. Christmas in April. It's pure pandemonium.

Gisco, come.

I'm right with you. What's your brilliant plan?

We're off the busted trampoline, darting between rides. I saw this part of the fair from the air, so I have some idea where we're going. Around the Sidewinder. To the left of the Tilt-a-Whirl.

I spot its shadow first, looming, ominous, globular, pregnant. There, dog! That's our only way out.

The Tilt-a-Whirl? Are you nuts?

No, not down there. Look up!

Gisco raises his head and sees the orange-and-black balloon. *A hot-air balloon? You're kidding, right?*

We're out of options. Let's go.

A white-haired man stands on a tall wooden platform in an old aviator getup, ignoring the confusion below as he shouts a pitch he's probably barked out a thousand times: "Tethered rides, ten dollars a person. No reason to be afraid, we're not going to Oz. Come one, come all, there's nothing like riding in Houlihan's hot-air balloon!"

This is our escape?

The Dark Army will never anticipate it. You said yourself they're looking for us in cars, trucks, and anything with a combustion engine. I would guess that there aren't many hot-air balloons floating around a thousand years from now.

True, but they've got helicopters that fly as fast as your jet planes. Once we're up in that thing, when they figure it out, we'll be target practice.

At least we'll be up, up, and away. Do you have a better idea?

No, but that doesn't make your idea good. The dog and I race up the steps of the platform.

"Hi," I tell the man, "we're ready for our trip."

He's wearing what looks like a World War I flying ace's uniform. Helmet. Goggle glasses. Flying jacket. Leather gloves and boots. "I don't take animals up," he says. "It's against the law."

I open my wallet. Hold out a hundred dollars in soggy twenties. A week's worth of stacking crates in Boston. "Are you sure? He's a very well behaved dog."

The old balloonist glances at Gisco appraisingly, then looks at the money, and licks his lips. "Well, I suppose I could make an exception. Are you sure Fido there won't panic and jump out of the gondola?"

My dear fellow, once we're airborne, a force-five hurricane couldn't dislodge me.

"Positive, but we need to go up right now."

The flying ace hesitates a second more and then takes the cash. "I don't know what your hurry is," he says, "but climb in."

19

We climb into the wicker basket. "How high does this go?" I ask. "Hot air rises, so theoretically it can keep going up and up, right?"

The old aviator bends to the controls, switching on a small propane heater. "We're anchored," he points out. "The tether rope is fifty feet. You'll get a good view when we're all the way up."

We start to rise gently. *This certainly beats the Death Coaster. Feather-soft and uplifting in the truest sense of the word. Ask the gentleman if a meal is included with the flight.*

I hesitate, but I'm also ravenous. "Do you by any chance sell food up here?"

He looks at me like I'm mad. "What?"

"Like theme snacks?"

"This is a balloon ride, not a buffet."

I smell pastrami. He's holding back.

Chill, dog. "So, how far can one of these fly?" I ask the grumpy balloonist.

"What's with all your questions?" the old guy demands. "How high, how far, who cares? We're tethered, get it? Anchored like a boat to a dock. We ain't goin' anywhere."

"I get it," I assure him, glancing at the tether rope, which is clamped to the side of the gondola. We're about thirty feet up now, and rising quickly. "It's just that I've seen on TV how billionaires in balloons circle the earth and set new speed records and stuff."

"Those are helium balloons. This is just hot air. They're built for distance. This is an inflated piece of nylon and a basket. You're talking about a completely different animal. This is as high as we're going today."

There's a bump as the tether rope pulls taut and we stop climbing. "There's the Hobbleville Little League field," the old fellow says in a bored tour guide voice. "That's the Gaines family apple orchard. Over yonder's the Maplewood garbage dump." He stifles a yawn with the back of his hand. "And there, you can see the Hudson River over the hills. Nice, huh? Ready to go down now?"

Jack!

I see them! Helicopters, racing toward the fair. Perhaps the cyborg dressed like Lincoln summoned them. They're still far off, tiny mechanized bugs crawling over the hills. But they're moving fast!

"Not quite done yet, sir. One last question. Are you insured?"

Old Houlihan wrinkles his nose. "You mean if one of my passengers gets hurt?"

"No, sir, I actually mean against theft."

He chuckles. "Who's gonna steal an old balloon?"

"I'm afraid that we are," I tell him. "Gisco, keep him over on that side of the gondola. I'm going to cast off."

"Not so fast. I knew you two were trouble," the old guy says, reaching into his pocket and pulling out a pistol. "Now put your hands in the air."

20

I slowly raise my hands. The balloonist swings the gun toward Gisco, who sits down on his rump and raises his front paws. It would be comical if we weren't in such dire jeopardy. "This here is a licensed handgun," old Houlihan grunts, his gun hand shaking. "I was attacked by a crazy owl once, and I keep it handy to scare away birds. I wouldn't want to use it on a young fella or a dog, but don't you even think about moving a muscle till we land and I turn you over to the police."

He bends and his eyes flick to the controls of his propane heater.

I steal a quick glance at the copters. They're much closer. Gisco, we've got to do something.

What do you suggest?

One of us creates a diversion, and the other grabs his gun. Since I'm better at grabbing guns, I think you should be the one to make the first move. Go for it.

This old guy's twitchy. The first one of us who moves is likely to get a bullet between the eyes.

I think you were right about that pastrami. He must have a sandwich packed for lunch. I'll give you first dibs on it.

Gisco considers hungrily. The balloonist has lowered the flame on the heater. We're descending quickly. Down to about twenty-five feet. It's now or never.

Gisco stands and growls.

"Back off, Fido," the old balloonist says, "or they'll be stuffing you for the window display of the Tipperville Taxidermists."

Gisco glares back at him. Lets loose an even more threatening growl.

The old guy raises the pistol. "Or maybe I'll have your head mounted above my pool table." His right hand shakes as his trigger finger starts to tighten.

He takes his eyes off me for a second as he aims. I make a dive for his gun hand.

The pistol goes off with a CRACK. The shot misses Gisco. I have enough presence of mind to jerk the old guy's wrist so that the bullet also misses the balloon.

Houlihan doesn't put up a fight. In a second, I've taken his gun away, and he's lying on his back.

"Please don't hurt me," he pleads. "I have grandkids. Well, I don't exactly have them yet, but I will if that good-for-nothing son of mine ever settles down. Please, I have a loving wife. Well, she would be loving if she wasn't bitching at me night and day."

"Calm down, we're not going to hurt you," I assure the scared geezer as I bend to the propane stove.

"Your dog's about to rip out my jugular."

"He might back off if you tell him where your sandwich is."

"In the backpack there. My wife made it. He can have it. It's got sweet gherkins. I hate those damn pickles. She knows that, but she puts them in anyway."

I crank the flame back up. We start rising again, and I unclamp the tether rope. "How much propane do you have?" I ask him.

"Just what you see there, and one spare tank on the ground. Where do you plan on going?"

Where are we headed? I ask Gisco.

The Amazon, he replies matter-of-factly.

What?

You heard me. Keep watch on him. I'm going after that sandwich.

What do you mean, the Amazon? And how can you think about food at a time like this? Don't you have any self-control at all?

I happen to like sweet gherkins. Even with pastrami.

The big dog begins rooting around in a corner of the gondola like a truffle pig in search of the mother lode.

"We're going to the Amazon," I inform the balloonist.

He looks back at me and then, terrified as he is, bursts into laughter. "What have you guys been smoking?"

"You don't think we'll make it to the Amazon?"

"You couldn't make it to Albany in this thing. It has a range of fifty miles, max. And the winds blow west-east, not north-south. Why don't you nuts give me back my balloon and go your way, and I won't call the police."

Found it! Gisco begins ripping his way through a brown paper bag.

Didn't you hear what this guy said? How are we going to make it to the Amazon?

First things first. Sustenance.

My own stomach rumbles. I realize that I can't even remember my last meal. Okay, sustenance. Give me half.

I've already eaten half. Half is now half of half.

I thought we were partners. Share and share alike.

Be grateful for small favors. I think I smell a bag of potato chips. What are we going to do with the Red Baron? We can't take him with us.

I pop the quarter sandwich in my mouth and chew it slowly, savoring the rye bread and pastrami, not to mention the sweet pickles. We're traveling at about thirty feet, blown by a strong breeze. We've moved away from the fair, out over a forest.

There's a small lake coming up below—actually little more than a pond.

"We've got business in the Amazon," I tell Houlihan. "So we're gonna take a shot at it, winds or no winds."

"You're loony."

"Do you wanna come with, or you do wanna get off?"

"I don't travel with loonies."

"Can you swim?" I ask.

"Like a fish." Then, suspiciously: "Why?"

"Stand up," I suggest. "The dog's not going to hurt you. He's too busy eating."

"You got that right. Look at him gobble it down. He even ate some of the waxed paper."

My compliments to the chef.

Houlihan gets shakily to his feet, looks down, and sees the small lake. "You're kidding, right?"

"It's your choice. But I have to warn you. If you stay on board, we're about to make like the space shuttle."

He squints back at me, then at Gisco, and finally peers down at the pond. "Guess I'd rather risk drowning than be part of a flying nuthouse." He climbs up on the side of the gondola, hesitates, and then mutters an unhappy "Good riddance to you," and leaps.

The old balloonist's legs churn and his arms circle as he falls with a scream. He splashes down feet first, and disappears under the blue water.

Did he make it? Gisco asks uninterestedly.

Yeah, he just popped up. He's swimming for shore. What a grump.

At least he furnished us with a last meal, Gisco says.

Come on, things aren't so bad, I point out. We're flying in a hot-air balloon on a beautiful day over lovely countryside.

As four helicopters with automatic weapons get ready to chase us down, he adds. *Can you spell H-I-N-D-E-N-B-U-R-G? At least take us up and maybe we can lose ourselves in the clouds.*

I glance down at the stove. Love to, I tell him, but we're running out of propane.

21

Dark Army copters roar away from fairgrounds toward us. I can see their mounted guns.

We're in a hot-air balloon without much heat. Not enough propane to rise. No place to go if we descend. We could dive out of the gondola into the pond like old Houlihan, but the copters would circle over us and pick us off like herrings in a barrel.

And then I feel something on my wrist. Gisco, my father's watch is getting warm!

I already know what time it is. The moment of my painful departure from life, and all that is sweet and vibrant. The crickets fiddling in the fields, the robins chirruping in their nests, a pot roast swimming in gravy, all gone. Goodbye, gleaming halls of morn. Farewell . . .

Gisco, it's not just warm. It's hot. Scorching!

I rip the watch off my wrist. It's so hot now that it's burning my skin. Why now? And then I get it.

I place Dad's watch atop the now-flameless propane stove, directly under the balloon cavity.

The blue watch face shimmers and glows. A sapphire luminescence kindles into flame. Air is heated, it rises into the nylon globe, and we start ascending.

I can see the silhouettes of the Dark Army pilots as they climb cloudward after us. But we're going up faster and faster. Already the first misty tendrils of cloud shroud us. Not just cottony white clouds, either.

Massive, ominous, threatening black clouds.

The sunny day has darkened. Did my dad's watch do this, too, or did we drift into a spring storm? Thunder rumbles and it sounds like we're in the middle of a bowling alley with balls striking pins all around us. Lightning flashes by and strikes the closest Dark Army helicopter.

There's an explosion audible even above the thunderclaps. The helicopter bursts into a scarlet fireball that spins sideways across the sky and takes out another copter.

Whatever you're doing, it's great stuff.

That's not me, I tell Gisco. Or maybe it is, in some way. Because it can't be just coincidence that this storm blew up. It can't be just happenstance that lightning bolts are forking down toward the remaining two helicopters, which turn and flee.

Is that a person I see, aloft in the clouds near us? No, that's impossible. It must be just a curious twist of cumulus mist. But its lineaments are so definite, so humanlike. Arms, legs, a torso, and even a head! Flying near us, without effort. Tracking in and out of cloud.

I remember the man from my dreamlike vision on the yellow dinghy—a face that exists outside of time and place. An Einstein. A Gandhi. Not quite a god, but no longer a man. The small figure opens his arms to us.

I open my arms back at him.

Who is it, Jack? Is there another helicopter? Who are you waving to?

"Destiny," the mysterious figure seems to say to me. "Come."

I can't come, I tell him. The winds only blow west-east. If you want us to come, you'd better find a way to help get us there.

"Come," he repeats, and begins melting into the stormy mist. As he disappears, he moves his arms around twice in slow circles, stirring the air like a witch's cauldron.

I feel it instantly, on my back and neck. The winds shift. Blow stronger. Pull us as if they have a will of their own.

Hey, check this out. Gisco was rooting around in the corner of the gondola where old Houlihan stored his possessions. No doubt the dog was looking for the bag of chips. Instead, he's found a compass. It shows that we're going due south. *Beacon of Hope, we're headed to the Amazon!*

22

Moment of truth. At least that's what I'm hoping I'll hear. I'm aloft with Gisco, spinning and soaring through dark clouds. But this isn't like the twister that whisked Dorothy willy-nilly to Oz. These whistling winds are pushing our balloon one way—south. This is a very special storm with a purpose, an agenda. Who stirred up this targeted tempest, and for what reason? It's time to find out. Okay, dog. Let's have the truth, the whole truth, and nothing but the truth, so help you Great Dog God. What the heck is going on?

I can certainly appreciate your curiosity, Gisco replies, sitting back on his haunches.

Then let's have some answers. Why did some warlord from a thousand years in the future kidnap my girlfriend? I thought when we used Firestorm to save the oceans, we created conditions that would end the threat of the Dark Army. Who sent you back to help me? And why are we being FedExed to the Amazon by special delivery balloon?

Excellent, thoughtful, probing questions, Jack. I would love to try to answer them for you, but the truth is you don't have the necessary sophistication in the physical sciences even to begin to understand what has transpired.

Perhaps not. But I do have enough sophistication to know that if I kick your doggone butt out of this gondola, gravity will yank your hairy mass back to earth with enough acceleration to smash you like furry scrambled eggs.

There's really no need to threaten an old friend. I'm completely on your side.

I take a step toward him, furious. What side is that? I demand angrily. The war in the future is over and the Dark Army is vanquished, right?

Not exactly, Gisco replies. *Things are a bit more complicated than that. I really don't know where to begin.*

Why don't you start by explaining what happened after our Firestorm quest. You promised me you would never leave and then you betrayed me by disappearing without even saying goodbye.

I was called back. It's not something I can control. It's like being yanked by a rope around your neck. I think they called Eko back, too. She didn't betray you either, by the way. In fact, I think she was starting to fall in love with you.

Gisco's revelation rocks me. I remember holding Eko tightly as we flew away from Dargon's island. She was dying. I felt her slipping away, and then she literally slipped through my fingers and vanished into thin air.

So she may still be alive? I ask the dog. You're saying Eko may have been transported away from me by people who could save her life?

It's possible. I haven't seen her since. But she may not have been any more in control of her disappearance than I was of mine.

I have trouble believing we're all at the mercy of future puppeteers who can pull our strings and make us appear and disappear.

Yes, it is very disconcerting. One minute you're pondering an island vacation with dear friends, after the successful completion of a mission. The next instant, poof, you're gone. Or rather, yank, you're being jerked away to a very different place and time.

His vivid description makes me recall my own out-of-body experience on the dinghy when I dreamed that I was being transported over a great distance to a mighty river. I had the painful sensation of being ripped out of my skin and dragged along by an irresistible leash. Okay, I tell Gisco, I believe you. Who called you back?

The people who sent me.

My mother? My father? The Caretakers?

What was left of them. Gisco looks sad. *You see, Jack, things had gotten very, very bad.*

How is that possible? We did exactly what we were supposed to do. We found Firestorm and used it to destroy the trawlers and preserve the oceans. That's why I was sent back to the Turning Point as a baby. You came back to help me. Together we turned the future in a better direction, right? Did we save the future or not, dog? It's a simple yes or no.

It's a "not quite," and there's nothing simple about it, Gisco responds. *You see, Jack, by sending you back in time to the Turning Point to change things, we inadvertently opened a very dangerous door, a sort of cosmic Pandora's box.*

23

Gisco's words give me the chills. Come to think of it, it's freezing up here. And the air is soupy thin. I feel dizzy, and I wrap my arms around my shivering body.

I flash back to Dargon in the volcanic cave, warning me that if I used Firestorm to save the oceans I wouldn't be healing the future but rather destroying it. There would be a ripple effect, he claimed, that over the course of a thousand years might alter everything, including my ancestors. So was Dargon right? I ask Gisco. You can't repair a problem by sending someone back in time to change the past? Did I muck up the whole future when I used Firestorm? Did I kill my own parents?

Calm down, Gisco urges. *Dargon was wrong. He was playing on your unsophisticated understanding of time-space. We knew what we were doing. I can't explain this to you, Jack. You don't have the background to understand it. If you tried, it would just confuse and discombobulate you, to the point where you could no longer function.*

I don't have to do much functioning in this balloon, I point out. I'll risk discombobulation. Fire away.

The dog still hesitates. *The human mind is a frail thing. It can't handle what it can't wrap itself around.*

I sense that Gisco truly believes this. Just try, I urge him. What happens when someone travels back through time and changes something?

The hesitating hound looks over at me, and takes pity. *I'm a fool,* Gisco mutters. *But okay, I'll try. You see, Jack, the best scientific minds of your era got this wrong. They wrestled with the same questions as you. Einstein battled with them, too. His Theory of Relativity first opened the door to the theoretical possibilities of time travel. And he didn't like those possibilities one bit.*

I think of Einstein—the wise old face with the playful, child-like eyes. That mental picture brings another image to mind—the old mummy's face I saw in my strange dream on the dinghy, and more recently when he seemed to be flying through the storm clouds near us. I blink it away, and refocus on the Father of Relativity. I've read a lot about Einstein, I tell the dog. I know he thought the cosmos should be logical and beautiful.

Correct, Gisco agrees. *And time travel is fraught with paradoxes. Einstein hated those. For example, there's the Grandfather Paradox: If you travel back in time and kill your own grandfather before he meets your grandmother, then you would never have been born. But, at the same time, you were the one who killed him.*

I try to digest this, and find myself holding tight to the side of the gondola. It's a mess, I agree. Is there an answer?

The top scientists of your era agreed on one explanation. It was first suggested by the work of a grad student named Hugh Everett, in the late nineteen-fifties. As it was developed it got a fancy name—the Many-Worlds Interpretation of Quantum Mechanics. Our universe, the physicists theorized, was just one of an infinite number of universes continually branching out every second like new limbs from a tree, to form a multiverse. So if someone went back in time and killed his grandfather, no paradox would occur because that person would be creating a whole new universe.

Is the gondola whirling more quickly, or are Gisco's explanations making my head spin? I try to concentrate. So if that's right, I ask, my parents couldn't change their polluted, unhappy world by sending me back in time? If I did change something to try to fix their problem, I would just be creating a new branch of the multiverse tree. But their own world would remain as bad and polluted as it was.

Correct, Gisco agrees.

I mull it over. That seems pretty nutty, I finally tell the dog. To think that there are an infinite number of universes, with new ones being generated all the time.

If you polled the leading cosmologists of your era, the vast majority of them were convinced it was so, Gisco says. *It was a fascinating theory. Complex and completely unprovable. Of course, it turned out to be as misguided as the notion five hundred years earlier that the world was flat and explorers who sailed too far would fall off the edge.*

So if it was wrong, what was right?

A Russian mathematician thirty years after Everett pointed in a direction that turned out to be much closer to the truth. His name was Igor Novikov, and he said that Einstein and all the other theorists who worried about time-travel paradoxes had gotten it completely wrong. According to Novikov, you couldn't travel back in time and kill your grandfather before he met your grandmother precisely because that would create a paradox.

I don't get it, dog, I confess. Suppose I traveled back in time and met my grandfather and wanted to kill him. What would stop me?

Suppose you wanted to walk on the ceiling? What would stop you?

Gravity.

And according to Novikov, an invisible cosmic force would prevent you from killing your grandfather.

What force?

Novikov explained it this way. In the absence of time travel, the unfolding present is influenced only by the past. So if you were trying to figure out what to do at three in the afternoon, and you had made a dentist's appointment for then, when three o'clock came you would go to the dentist. Got it?

So far.

But with the presence of time travel, the unfolding present is influenced by both the past and the future. The time traveler is not just making a one-way trip—he's making a loop. So he can't change something that will alter the future part of his loop. Gisco looks at me sympathetically. *All you need to know is that Novikov got that part right. You couldn't go back in time and do something that would wipe out your own ancestors or parents or yourself, because you have already lived in that future.*

I'm so dizzy I have to sit down on the floor of the gondola. So you're saying there's no multiverse?

None.

Time is like a river, flowing in one direction? And if a person makes a journey upriver to change something, he can't wipe out everything downriver because that place exists since he came from it?

Broadly correct. The dog nods. *And it is therefore possible to journey back in time and change the future in predictable ways, just as you could go upriver and change a watercourse knowing that it would have certain foreseeable effects downriver. Your father knew what he was doing when he sent you back. We could predict that using Firestorm to save the oceans would change the future world in the way we needed.*

But you were wrong? My father was mistaken?

No, we were right. He was astonishingly correct in his calculations.

But the world didn't get better? You said it got worse.

Much worse, Gisco agrees sadly. *Horribly, nightmarishly worse.*

✹

24

Gisco's convoluted explanations have brought us to a final conundrum. If my dad was right, and I changed what needed to be changed, why didn't things get better? I ask.

They did start to improve.

What do you mean "start"? If we fixed the problem in the present, why wasn't it long gone in the far future?

Gisco hesitates. *You look like you've already gone twelve rounds. Are you sure you have the stomach for more?*

I look up at him from the floor of the gondola. I am dizzy and light-headed, but I try to shake it off. Ring the bell for round thirteen, I say. I need to know why, if we fixed the problem, the world got worse.

When a significant change is made in the past, it takes a while for the fabric of time and space to reshape itself in the future, the dog explains. *Go back to your river analogy one more time. Let's say the water in the stretch of river where we drink and fish is polluted. So someone is sent far upstream to remove the source of that pollution. Even if they're successful, the water where we live doesn't immediately become clean. It's a gradual process. The river cleanses itself day by day and hour by hour. Got it?*

Sure, I say. But once you remove the source of the pollution, the river gets cleaner and cleaner.

Right. And when you used Firestorm to save the oceans, a thousand years in the future things did start to get better. The oceans became cleaner. Extinct species began to reappear. Whales, wiped out for eight hundred years, started singing in the depths. Dolphins leaped from the surf after half a millennium of stillness. Coral reefs began to bloom like vast undersea gardens, and serve again as the crucial breeding grounds for millions of species. As the oceans healed, conditions on land got much better. The Dark Army began to lose its grip. The People of Dann were proven right, and were on their way to being triumphant—the caretakers of a new Eden.

Great, I say. That's what I imagined after you and Eko disappeared. That's the justification I clung to when I sailed back to America on a tramp steamer. Night after night I sat on the deck alone, and I told myself that even if I had lost everything I valued in my own life, at least I had done some good. So what went wrong? What Pandora's box did we open up?

The dark storm clouds we're flying through blot out the sun. Gisco's eyes gleam for a second as lightning flashes near us.

The Dark Army became desperate, he explains. *Its leader realized that if the Turning Point could be used to tilt the future one way, it could also be used to turn it back in the other direction. He borrowed a page from the playbook of the People of Dann, and he came back to the Turning Point to attack the earth at the crucial moment and turn the future back to darkness.*

We must have entered a new level of stratosphere. The air suddenly seems even thinner. Or it could be the cumulative effect of Gisco's explanations. I can barely see straight. So this commander in chief of the Dark Army came back himself?

Yes. You look like you've heard enough for one day, Jack. It's cold up here. And the way the wind is spinning us is not conducive to clear thinking. Perhaps we should curl up together and take a snooze.

I shiver and struggle to my knees. I'm not going to take this lying down, I tell the dog. So the Grand Poobah of the whole Dark Army is here, in our world? That's why we're heading south? To find him?

I wouldn't call him that to his face, if you ever meet him. Jack, don't try to stand up.

I pull myself to my feet and gasp in several quick breaths. What damage is he doing down there?

Everything he can. He's deforesting the Amazon. Wiping out huge tracts of irreplaceable virgin rain forest, the destruction of which is having a terrible effect on the future earth and strengthening the hand of the Dark Army.

I stagger and almost fall out of the gondola.

The dog catches my leg in his jaw and pulls me back in. He guides me gently down again to the wicker gondola floor. Gisco lies next to me, protectively, like a living, breathing quilt. *Go to sleep, Jack,* the dog advises. *Enough for one day. You'll need your strength.*

To save P.J.? I ask, starting to fade out. How can you be sure she's alive, and that he took her? And why would he do that? If he's accomplishing his objective and turning the future back to darkness, why mess with my old girlfriend?

Because he had another reason for coming back, Gisco says. *An extremely personal one. You killed his only son. He wants revenge.*

25

Soaring through icy air. I can feel Gisco's heart beating. Didn't I read in a Jack London novel that gold miners caught in blizzards in the frozen north slept next to their sled dogs for warmth? Now I understand it. Huddling on the floor of the balloon's gondola with a living blanket that reeks of unwashed dog fur. The gale intensifies, sweeping us southward at increasing speed.

Night comes on, or maybe it's just the storm itself, reaching out tentacles like a giant octopus and squeezing out the sun. The only light source is the blue flame that flickers from my dad's watch. It heats the air beneath the balloon, keeping us up so high I feel disoriented and groggy. I'm confused by Gisco's explanations and still reeling from P.J.'s disappearance and the dinghy's suicide, weak from hunger and cut loose from all moorings.

Time crawls by as we whirl through a seemingly endless vortex of dark storm clouds. Days and even weeks may be passing on the earth far below, but we're somehow above and beyond that. We're off the clock and outside the calendar, in the spin cycle of a meteorological monstrosity. Sunless days blur into moonless nights as we hurtle toward a fateful confrontation in the remote Amazon.

Maybe it's the altitude, maybe all I've gone through since my ill-fated attempt at a homecoming in Hadley, but I sink into a paralyzing listlessness, a deep torpor.

My stomach rumbles—I can't even remember my last full meal, yet I have no desire to eat. My mouth and throat are dry, but even though we sometimes fly through wet mist I make no effort to drink.

I vaguely feel Gisco trying to force potato chips into my mouth. I'm aware of him reaching out to me telepathically: *Jack, are you okay? Give some sign if you hear this. Move your fingers or your toes. Jack?*

I don't move. I still have questions for the dog, and I know he has more answers, but I keep silent.

Deep sleep, like slipping into a yawning cavern. Hallucinatory dreams. I see time as a blue river, flowing right by our gondola. There I am as a boy, playing football along its banks, in Hadley Park.

Time twists and suddenly I'm with P.J. at our make-out spot on the night before all my calamities began.

The dark band of river in front of us. A full moon hanging in the sky like a swollen sex gland.

P.J.'s warm, sweet lips on my own. Our hands on each other's bodies. Our need for each other. Our closeness.

"Not tonight," she says.

"When?" I ask.

"Soon," she promises. "Just be patient." Her face and words fade, and it's like a door closing.

The door opens and P.J. looks out and screams. She's in her home in Hadley, staring outside at something truly terrifying on her front steps.

Whatever it is, it yanks her outside. Her feet rise off the front porch, and she starts to fly away.

I call out to her. Reach with my hands. Grab for anything—an ankle, a foot even.

I miss her, but suddenly I'm airborne, too. Ripped skyward, yanked away, to use Gisco's phrase.

That same out-of-body sensation I felt on the dinghy. I'm pulled out of my own skin. Can't fight it. The pain is unbearable.

Dragged along on a magical leash.

And then set down, plunk, in a teeming jungle clearing.

A building nearby. Concrete. Terrified voices from inside. Pleading for food and water.

It's a prison. Squalid. Rank. Suffocatingly hot. People suffering. Men. Women. Kids. Crowded into cells. Their faces pressed to the bars. Their eyes desperate.

I'm beyond them now, moving down a hallway past empty cells. Shackles dangling. Thick, rusting chains on stone floors, like coiled snakes. Who's imprisoned here? Ghosts?

A light up ahead. Glinting off bars. A solitary cell. One voice, familiar, shrieking in terror. It's P.J.! Calling my name.

She senses I'm near. Begs me to help.

I see her now. Clothes hanging in rags. Her arms chained above her head. Standing helplessly. Facing the door to her cell.

Fingers unlock it from outside. No, not fingers. Something strange going on. The jailer is not human. A shadow shuffles inside. It's as big as a piano!

It crawls toward her. Eight legs. Hairs on those legs. Bristles that twitch. Eight subhuman eyes watch P.J.—a pair in the middle and three on either side. As it crawls forward it makes a hissing sound, by rubbing its jaws together. Its fangs gleam in the bare-bulb light.

A tarantula! It's less than three feet from her now.

P.J. twists away from it in horror. *"Jack!"* she screams. *"Save me!"*

My proximity to her is heartrending. I can see her clearly. I can almost touch her.

It's P.J. and not P.J.—she looks exactly the way I remember her, and at the same time she's changed.

Half a year older. She's obviously been through pure hell. Hair, which was always carefully cut and styled, now long and uncombed. Sparkling hazel eyes now red and swollen. Face and body thin and haggard, as if she's been suffering for weeks.

But the vibrancy I loved is still there—the spirit and courage and resolve to live still burn in P.J.'s eyes, even as they widen with fear.

"Jack, please do something!"

I'm so close to her I can feel her breath, but there's absolutely nothing I can do. I'm just a presence, a shadow, a consciousness without substance.

I have no voice to answer her desperate pleas, no arms to protect her with, no legs to kick away the loathsome creature that slowly circles her.

All I can do is watch.

And I know this is all my fault. P.J.'s connection to me has taken her out of a world of love and safety, to this realm of pain and peril. In a few seconds it will cost her her very life. And I can't save her—I'm present but utterly powerless, culpable but deprived of any chance to redeem myself.

The first bristles of the goliath tarantula touch P.J.'s bare skin. She cringes. Her terror-stricken eyes are now on a level with the spider's own. She glimpses its hunger. Understands that it will devour her.

Its head swings forward. Her breast is punctured by the loathsome fangs.

A cry of pain and fear rips from P.J.'s throat. It's unlike anything I have ever heard . . .

That cry . . . I desperately try to answer.

But I'm airborne. Yanked back and away at tremendous speed.

Hurtling through smoke and fire.

Fighting all the time to stay with her. Shouting her name into the swirling miasma. *"P.J., I won't let you die! P.JJJJJJJJJ . . ."*

Hellfire crackles around me. Yes, I'm in hell. The Devil's booming voice: *"Welcome, Jack."*

No, it's thunder. And the hellfire is lightning.

Jack! Don't do it, Jack.

I'm standing up on the edge of the gondola, trying to jump out, shrieking P.J.'s name over and over.

Gisco is fighting desperately to keep me from leaping to my death. He has a hold of my right pants leg with his teeth.

Jack, I can't hold you any longer.

The fabric frays and rips.

Nothing more restraining me.

The face of death beckons. A handsome old face. Gleaming, sharp teeth. Cold and merciless eyes.

Time to end the pain.

But the frigid air blasting my face has revived me enough to remember who I am and where I am headed. P.J. is in the Amazon and I have to find a way to save her. As inviting as death seems, I force myself back from the precipice, and fall, shivering, into the basket of the gondola.

26

Jack? Are you okay? I've been so worried . . .

How long was I out for?

Days, I think, Gisco responds. *It's hard to keep track of time up here.*

I see what he means. We're still sailing through dark clouds. It could be morning or night. Where are we?

I have no idea. According to this compass, we've been heading almost due south.

I peer over the side. For a moment I think I see the outlines of enormous soldiers marching in columns beneath the swirling black mist. Then they're gone.

Did you see something?

I blink. No. Not now. But I did while I was asleep! It wasn't really a dream—it was more like a vision. Gisco, we've got to do something!

What did you see, Jack?

P.J.'s in terrible danger. She was in a jungle prison. And this . . . awful creature was menacing her.

Sounds like you had a nightmare, complete with its own hobgoblin. Our imaginations really know how to scare us. I once ate a bad piece of cheese before bed, and dreamed a six-headed cat was chasing me around an exercise wheel . . .

No, Gisco, this was too vivid to be a dream. P.J. could see me and I could almost touch her. It wasn't some figment of my imagination or some product of indigestion that was threatening her. It was detailed and real—a spider. A tarantula! But giant-size. What's wrong?

Gisco suddenly looks very upset.

A tarantula? You're positive?

Hairy, with eight legs and eight eyes. Doesn't that sound to you like a tarantula? What is it, dog? A little arachnophobia?

You remember how Dargon was a chimera, a human with the genetic attributes of several different animals?

For a moment I recall Dargon clearly, as I saw him during our last battle on the lip of a volcano. The eyes of a raptor, the aquiline nose, the strength of a bull. A melting pot of nasty animal genes. Yeah, I assure Gisco, I'm not likely to forget that guy anytime soon.

His father also had his DNA monkeyed with. Or maybe I should say snaked and spidered with.

He's gonna catch me in his web like Spiderman? I try to make a joke of it, but Gisco is creeping me out. There's something

spooky and alien about reptiles and spiders, especially the poisonous variety.

Tarantulas don't spin webs, Gisco informs me. *They run down
their prey. But now I believe your vision, Jack. So he is here!* I can feel
Gisco tremble telepathically.

I have quite the reverse reaction. If this is the guy who took
P.J., I want to settle things with him soon face-to-face, eight legs
or not. What's his name? I ask the dog.

*He doesn't have a name. He doesn't have an age, or a place of birth
that anyone knows. He's mysterious for the worst reason. Everyone who
comes up against him dies horribly. They say he likes to do the killing with
his own hands, or even with his teeth.*

I remember the fangs of the spider in my vision. So let me
guess, dog, you're about to tell me I'm the only one who can stop
this spidery sociopath, just like I was the only person who could
find Firestorm?

Nope, you can't stop him, Gisco answers. *No one can stop him. He's
far too powerful.*

I look back at the dog. He's so scared and miserable I think
he's actually telling the truth.

Then why did you bring me back? I demand. Why did you go
to such trouble to find me, and break me out of jail, and get me
on this balloon to the Amazon? Clearly you want me to do something. But at the same time you say we don't have a prayer of
stopping this guy.

*Correct. There's a contradiction there, and you've just put your finger
right on it,* Gisco declares. *I'd love to clear it up for you, but we have a
little problem here.*

Don't try to distract me, dog. I know your tricks.

Gisco is peering over the side of the gondola. He looks about
as worried as an old dog can.

I follow his gaze downward. There, through the swirling
miasma, the gargantuan soldiers are visible again, marching in

endless columns. No, not soldiers, mountain peaks. Rocky, snow-capped, and formidable.

What are they? I ask him, trying to visualize a topographical map of the hemisphere with the different large mountain ranges. The Appalachians? The Sierra Madre?

I believe they're the Andes.

The Andes? I repeat, awed. My God. I've always wanted to see the Andes!

Yes, well, you're going to get your wish. Our balloon seems to have sprung a leak and we're losing altitude fast, Gisco observes, *so I think we're about to crash into them.*

27

We come down fast, spinning out of the stormy sky so that I half expect to land on the Wicked Witch of the West. Or make that South. Because, on closer inspection, these are definitely the Andes. Nothing in our hemisphere could be so awesomely grand.

Jagged, glacier-capped peaks spear skyward to impale us. Twice we almost slam into rocky cliff faces. At this speed the impact would surely kill us. Gisco, we have to try to find a way to steer this thing.

There is no way. It's a primitive contraption not meant for surmounting mountain ranges. The dog lies down on the floor and covers his eyes with his paws.

Then what can we do? Gisco, get back up.

Prostrate yourself. Pray to whatever gods you believe in to spare your wretched life.

How about if we transfer our weight in the direction we want the balloon to move? Or maybe we could lean outside the gondola and alter the airflow? Gisco?

O Great Dog God, you paragon of perfection from your withers to your dewclaws, it is your humble servant Gisco, beseeching you from this precipitously descending dirigible.

If there is a Great Dog God, Gisco, he's written you off long ago as a faithless opportunist who only dials him up in moments of grave danger. So come help me try to steer us into that valley. It's our only real chance . . .

O Four-footed Master, ignore this two-ankled fool. As I whirl through the mountain valley of death, I scrape my stomach before your divine dogness. Be thou my German shepherd, I shall not want, and deliver me from evil, and I swear I won't eat any cake for a year! I'll get up every morning at dawn for a fast jog—

Gisco, stop this. We have only seconds. I need you to help me try to steer this thing! Why should some all-powerful canine give a damn whether you wake up early and exercise, or if you give up cake?

The dog is too frightened to respond. He's lying on his stomach, his whole body quivering in terror, while his thick paintbrush of a tail flails weakly back and forth as if he's waving a flag of surrender to the craggy mountains.

Beneath us, a deep rift of a valley has opened between two colossal peaks. We swoop down into it, and suddenly a boulder as big as a house looms dead ahead!

I close my eyes and prepare for death, but somehow we hop over the giant rock. I blink and glimpse a sheet of dazzling white unfolding in front of us.

Then a jarring bump knocks me off my feet as the gondola touches down on the lip of a glacier.

We career wildly over snow and ice as Gisco and I are tossed around the gondola. I try to brace myself, but it's like clinging to a sled when you're heading down the Matterhorn. Miraculously, we immediately start to slow. Our toboggan has an unexpectedly good set of brakes.

I glance back and understand—the balloon is acting like a giant parachute! We slide off the glacier, skid through mud and ice, and come to a stop near a little mountain stream.

Gisco, we made it! We're alive! You can stop whimpering in fear.

Fear? Those were chuckles, the dog says, standing back up and trying to regain his dignity. *Once more I laughed in the face of death and lived to tell the tale.*

Aren't you going to thank the Great Dog God for your salvation?

There's no time for religious mumbo jumbo now. We've got to see what the damage is to our balloon. It's our only way out of here.

I grab my father's watch, and in seconds we're standing by the deflated balloon, examining a small, jagged rip in the nylon.

At least it's not such a big tear, I say.

Where are we going to find something to patch it with in this mountain wasteland? And, more important, what are we going to eat?

We'll forage for food.

I'm a dog, not a bear. Berries and wild grass are not my style.

Maybe you can find something more to your liking on one of your early morning jogs, I suggest.

Gisco ignores me, and peers down the hill. *There!* he exclaims. *That's the answer to all our problems.*

I see nothing but barren rocky slopes.

Follow the river, the dog advises. *Water always leads to civilization, and civilization leads to a hot lunch.*

Following the stream downhill with my eyes, I spot a mountain hut carefully concealed between two boulders. It must be completely invisible from below. Near it are terraced fields of green crops.

Gisco, that hut was built with privacy in mind.

Nonsense, the dog responds, trotting downhill. *You know nothing*

*about the camaraderie and hospitality of the mountains. No doubt there's
some stalwart campesino inside whose sturdy wife will be only too happy to
fix us a hearty goat stew.*

28

Perilous clamber down pebbly mountainside. The slightest mis-
step will trigger a landslide. Gisco has an easier time of it. Four
feet are better than two on a slope like this, and the potbellied
pooch has the center of gravity of an earthworm. I walk hunched
over, arms out.

Come on, Jack.

This is as fast as I can go. Gisco, I really think we should be
careful.

I can smell food. Chicken. Nicely spiced.

I myself can't smell it, but Gisco is infallible in certain areas.
I'm willing to believe he could sniff out some well-peppered poultry at a distance of half a mile.

I'm sweating despite the cold. I can see the hut more clearly
now. It's made of wood, with branches and leaves strewn across
its roof for added concealment.

We cross what looks like a giant pumpkin patch. Neat rows
of plants. No pumpkins though.

I can smell the chicken now. Gisco's right—it's a tantalizing
aroma. I climb down much faster.

Something glows ahead in a rocky ravine. A fire. The mountain men are having a backyard barbecue!

Two chickens cook on wooden spits! Talk about hitting the
jackpot! Smells pretty good, doesn't it, Gisco?

My dear boy, the word "good" doesn't begin to describe that aroma. I wish I could bottle that smell and use it for cologne. I wish I could crawl into the cavity of that roast chicken and eat it from the inside out. I wish . . .

Gisco, before your appetite gets us both killed, allow me to point out that the longest knife I've ever seen in my life is lying on a rock near those two chickens.

That's not a knife, it's a machete—more of a tool than a weapon. It's used, no doubt, for clearing brush and slicing the heads off plump chickens before they're plucked and spitted. But it's not necessary for unspitting them.

Gisco dashes across a final small cucumber garden, or whatever those green plants are, and grabs one of the spits in his teeth. I can't quite work out how he unspits it, but in a fraction of a second the golden brown bird is no longer being cooked but rather devoured.

I myself haven't had a good meal in weeks. The sight of Gisco gorging himself and the sound of his tongue slurping chicken fat off his lips is more than I can bear.

I grab the second spit, slide the chicken off onto a fat rock, and rip off a drumstick. It's piping hot, but I couldn't care less— I'm famished.

That's the spirit, Jack. Binge with gusto! That's my motto, anyway, the masticating mongrel announces as he practically inhales a chicken wing and snaps the bones in his jaws, so that they sound like small fireworks popping one after the other.

No, wait. Those are footsteps, racing toward us! We both whirl around.

A girl is standing there. I can't tell her age. Eleven? Twelve? Her long black hair is tied in a braid.

I smile at her, and then see my mistake. It's not a girl but a thin slip of a boy. His large dark brown eyes are childlike and bright with life, but they shine out of a face that is haggard with suffering beyond his years. He looks shocked to see us. When he

opens his mouth he's too frightened to talk, so only a few surprised sounds come out. He waves his arms at us wildly.

I guess I can understand his shock. When you're roasting two
chickens high up in the Andes, you don't expect an American
teenager and a corpulent canine from the future to fall out of the
sky and help themselves.

Tell him we're friends, not foes, Gisco suggests. *Thank him for the
superb chicken. Politely inquire if there's any dessert. I believe we're in
custard country, and a nice flan would be just the thing.*

I took French in high school, I inform Gisco. I don't know a
word of Spanish.

Must I do everything? the hound asks huffily, spitting out a
small bone. *Try to get the accent right: Buenos días, señor de las mon-
tañas. Gracias por el delicioso festín de pollo.*

I begin to repeat the words out loud. "*Buenos días . . .*"

The boy waves at us even more frantically. Gisco, I'm certain
he's trying to tell us something.

The linguistically dexterous dog ignores me. *Try this: ¿Tiene
usted algún otro alimento? ¿Un queso tradicional de la región, quizás?*

Gisco, he's trying to warn us of something.

*Don't be silly. He's delighted to have company. Didn't I tell you about
the camaraderie of the mountains? In the Andes, we are all mountain
brothers and sisters—*

Gisco breaks off as two burly men with ragged mustaches
emerge from around a rock outcropping. Both are carrying Uzi
submachine guns, which they point at our heads. One of them
grunts something in guttural Spanish.

What did our mountain brother just say? I ask Gisco.

The big dog doesn't look particularly happy. *He asked his buddy
which one of us they should shoot first, the golden-haired gringo who needs
a bath or the dog-faced pig.*

29

The mustachioed mountain men with Uzis bark a few questions at us. Gisco translates. I try to respond with polite and creative answers. But we can't even begin to explain how we parachuted into their neighborhood.

They lose interest quickly. Bind and gag us, and toss us into the hut. One of them mutters a threat that Gisco doesn't quite get, but it sounds to him like they plan on returning early the next morning to finish us off for target practice before breakfast.

Foul-smelling hut. Tight ropes. Hours drag by.

We've been dumped in a corner, like garbage to be disposed of when the time comes. Knots bite into my wrists and ankles. Gisco has been hogtied.

Ouch. My cramps are starting to cramp up.

It's not the most comfortable position, I agree. What was that again about the camaraderie of the mountains?

This does seem a rather stiff punishment for stealing a couple of rotisserie chickens, even if they were well spiced.

This has nothing to do with poultry, snaggletooth.

What then?

Did you notice that this hut doesn't have any beds?

I'm upside down and facing into a corner. All I can see right now is your dirty feet. Maybe they sleep in hammocks. Maybe they snooze on the floor. I don't see that it makes a heck of a lot of difference. Tomorrow morning they're going to come back and machine-gun us as they eat their huevos rancheros.

There are no beds, no chairs, no table, no clothes. Nada.

I've got Gisco's attention now. *Okay, there's nada. The significance being?*

This isn't a home. It's not a dwelling place.

Then what is it?

A lab, I think.

What?

Don't you smell those chemicals?

No, they muzzled me with some stinking rag. I can't smell anything. If I twist my head, maybe you can tug the cloth off a bit.

Yeah, I've got it. I'm tugging. It's stuck. I'm going to give it a hard yank.

OW! That's my ear!

Sorry.

Okay, that's the muzzle rag. Good. Can you move it a little more? Ah, fresh air! Or should I say foul air.

Can you tell what those chemicals are? Come on, any dog who can pinpoint a chicken at a half mile should be able to spitball a few chemicals in a home laboratory.

The dog sniffs. *Hydrochloric acid.*

What's that used for?

I'm not sure. Gisco sniffs again. *And something fruity. Lime, I think.*

Hydrochloric acid and citrus? Weird. What else?

Alcohol.

Are they mixing margaritas?

Gisco doesn't find this amusing. *Jack, we're in mucho trouble.*

Why? What is it now?

Remember those green plants in neat rows?

You mean the pumpkin patch? Or I thought it might have been a cucumber garden.

Coca plants, Gisco corrects me. *They're using this mountain hut to process a crude form of cocaine.*

A shiver of cold fear travels rapidly down my spine like a

mountain centipede seeking a new hiding place. Are you sure, Gisco? It's hard to believe we randomly crashed our balloon above a nest of drug smugglers.

Growers. Distillers. Smugglers. Killers. Whatever. It explains why they're so suspicious of strangers.

Yes, I agree. No wonder they're planning on shooting us. Okay then, we have to escape and find a way to patch our balloon before they return. Any bright ideas?

No, but some more bad news. Our situation is deteriorating by the second.

Gisco, we're marooned—or maybe I should say un-ballooned—high up in the Andes, imprisoned by drug smugglers, who are planning to return in the morning and Uzi us into condor feed. What could be worse?

I hear footsteps. They must be coming back a little early.

30

The door of the hut is yanked open. I prepare myself to be dragged in front of a two-man firing squad.

But something's wrong. These aren't the thudding footsteps of swarthy drug smugglers. These are the soft, padding, scared footsteps of one relatively small person.

Gentle hands on my back. Tugging me over. The good news is it's the boy with the braid! The bad news is he's holding the machete in his shaking right hand. Is he going to slit our throats? No, he begins sawing at the ropes.

Gisco, it's that kid! He's setting me free.

Remind him not to forget about a boy's best friend.

He looks terrified. I think he's risking his life to help us.

We'll find a very nice way to thank him. Hurry up and get free so you can set me free.

Seconds later the ropes are in a bunch on the floor and Gisco and I are both taking awkward, reeling steps, waiting for the blood flow to return to our legs.

"Thank you," I say to our rescuer. *"Muchas gracias."*

The boy looks back at me, and for a moment his worried face softens just a bit. He opens his mouth, but again no recognizable words come out.

Maybe he's mute, Gisco.

No. He can make sounds. I'm sorry to have to tell you this, Jack, but I think somebody cut his tongue out.

Gisco's observation makes me feel disgust and a surge of fury. This boy is barely out of childhood. He should be playing tag and hide-and-seek. Why would anyone do such a cruel thing to a young kid? I ask the dog.

It's a precaution. They're probably keeping him here as a slave, and they wanted to make sure he stays quiet.

I've seen news stories about child slaves taken from their families, confined and abused, and forced to work their whole lives for scraps of food and the clothes on their backs. Such exposés always seemed distant and remote to me—outrages in countries so far away that I never imagined I would meet such a kid face-to-face.

Now I'm looking back into this boy's dark brown eyes. They're big and frightened, like the eyes of a rabbit that has been chased down and cornered.

I can only imagine the amount of courage it's taking for him to help us, knowing he may be brutally punished for it later.

Gisco's right—we have to find a way to thank him. He looks so lost, so completely alone on this mountaintop.

On impulse I take off the necklace that Eko gave me on the Outer Banks. There's a locket with a tiny image of my mother,

Mira, who lives in the far future. It's my only picture of her, but I sense that this brave, solitary boy needs a mother even more than I do.

I unstring the locket and show him the portrait of the beautiful woman with kind features and lustrous hair. Then I tie it onto the leather thong around his neck.

The boy looks back at me for a long moment, and then motions us to the door and thrusts his arms downhill.

He's showing us the way out, and telling us we should take off, Gisco. And he's probably right.

No, he's probably wrong. Gisco has gone over to the side of the hut that's used for a laboratory. There are vials and chemicals, and bundles wrapped up in orange tarps. *If we try to escape down the mountain either we'll be caught or we'll starve to death. Neither is particularly appealing. This is our only way out.*

A drug lab is our way out?

Check out these tarps. They're using them to make sure their cocaine stays dry and waterproofed.

They look like old raincoats.

Nylon. We can use them to patch the balloon. Gisco begins sniffing various vials and jars of chemicals. *I can improvise a powerful adhesive. It won't hold forever, but it will get us out of these mountains. Let's go to work.*

Gisco has the chemical know-how. I have the hands, critical for pouring and mixing. The young lad with the braid stands in the far corner of the hut and watches as we cook up a steaming witch's brew. Occasionally he snaps open the locket and looks at the image of my mother.

The sun is starting to sink as we finish.

Are you sure this will work, Gisco? It smells awful.

I wasn't exactly baking an apple pie. Let's go.

We hike back up the mountain to where we crash-landed near the glacier. The descent was easy, but the steep climb makes us sweat, even though a freezing wind whistles through the high mountain crags. I'm huffing and puffing by the time we near our deflated balloon.

The boy follows us. He seems intrigued by what we're doing, but also frightened. I see that he's brought the machete along. He has the constitution of a mountain goat—he's not breathing hard as he trails us up the steep slope.

I've heard that mountain sunsets come on fast. It seems to get colder and darker by the second. My hands shake as Gisco directs me to spread his odious adhesive on the torn balloon envelope.

The paste works like quick-drying epoxy. As soon as it's on, I press one of the orange tarps over the rent in the nylon. The pungent mixture hardens like concrete, and now our balloon has a bright orange Band-Aid.

Voilà, Gisco exults. *Not bad, huh?*

Do you think it will hold?

Only one way to find out.

How are we going to reinflate the balloon? I ask. Old Houlihan probably had some special fan or air hose to fill it up.

Necessity is the mother of invention, Gisco declares impressively. *As Archimedes' dog once said, give me a bone long enough, and I will move the world!*

Wasn't that a lever? And I never heard that Archimedes had a dog.

Bone, lever, whatever . . . Gisco's ears prick up and he glances down the mountainside.

What is it?

The banditos have returned! I can hear them at the hut, searching for us. Let's get this thing up, up, and away!

✺

31

Gisco grabs one side of the mouth of the balloon in his jaws, and I grab the other side with my hands. We try to stretch it open, but it's bulky and awkward, and Gisco can only hold his end two feet off the ground.

What's your plan, Gisco?

I was hoping the wind would gust up this mountain crevice into the balloon and reinflate it.

But the wind isn't gusting into the balloon, I point out. It's blowing all around the balloon and blasting me in the face, which might explain why my nose and mouth feel frostbitten, not to mention that it's also getting darker and there are bandits with submachine guns looking for us . . .

Kvetch, kvetch, kvetch. Why can't you look on the bright side? We patched the balloon, didn't we?

A deflated hot-air balloon is of no use at all—

An earsplitting RAT-TAT-TAT of submachine gun fire rattles the nearby rocks. Gisco, they've spotted us!

The dog opens his mouth and spits out his end of the balloon with a resigned shrug. *That's it, then,* he says. *There's no way out of this.*

Maybe we can escape down the other face of the summit. Come on, Gisco. What about looking on the bright side?

There is no bright side. The other face of the summit is a sheer cliff. We've got a deflated balloon and no weaponry to fight back. We're done for, Jack. Lower Gisco into the mountain grave and roll the boulder over his remains. The dog peers around at the windswept crags. *Strange, I always pictured my final resting place as a grassy glen, with willows weeping down while bluebirds sing. Not this godforsaken precipice, which is fit for the fossilized carcass of a mammoth, perhaps, but hardly an appropriate tomb for a dog of culture and accomplishment . . .*

Gisco, snap out of it. You're not dead yet, but they are closing in on us. We have to do something.

Then, suddenly and incongruously, I hear a woman's soft voice, singing.

I turn my head and see that the boy has walked close to us. The locket on his neck has opened, and the eyes of the tiny image of my mother appear to be glowing.

The voice issues from the locket and swirls around us. The song has no words, but it's soothing, as if meant to comfort children—a lullaby from a thousand years away.

I drop the balloon and stand there, numb. Somehow I know that I'm hearing my mother's voice for the first time. It's a sweet and melodic voice, but its true beauty comes from a deep reservoir of personal anguish.

Up till this moment, I felt fury toward this woman in the far future who sent me away when I was a baby. Night after night on the tramp steamer I pulled out the locket and studied her image by moonlight. A dozen times I was tempted to hurl it over the side. How could she have abandoned me to be raised by strangers? What coldness and cruelty would make a mother do such a terrible thing?

Now, hearing the sadness in her song, I consider for the first time the possibility that she might have had her reasons. As I stand motionless on the cold mountaintop, I suddenly understand that events which seem cruel and heartless when looked at one way may appear selfless and even heroic when viewed from a different vantage point.

Regret infuses my mother's voice, pulsing in her pitch and deepening her tone. I wonder what dire events forced her to give me up. Was I her only child? Has she thought of me every day and every night since then, wondering if I was alive somewhere, being taken care of, being loved and fed and comforted, even if by a stranger's hands?

The boy with the braid is also standing motionless, listening to the song, perhaps remembering his own mother. Then, as if sensing something, he walks over and picks up the side of the balloon's mouth that Gisco dropped. He reaches high over his head, stretching it wide open.

Rat-tat-tat, the bursts of submachine-gun fire riddle the glacier above us, sending a snowstorm of ice flakes down on us. The bandits are hustling up the mountainside, stopping every so often to fire volleys.

We're sheltered by the rocks, but they'll soon be close enough to blow us to bits.

The cold wind is no longer blasting me. I feel it slacken and ease off, as it shifts. It seems to refocus itself in a new direction, gusting suddenly and with such power that its blast drowns out the last sad notes of my mother's lullaby.

The young lad of the mountains now stands directly in its way. The whistling wind unbraids his long black hair, which flies wildly behind him as he holds the balloon's mouth over his head with both hands.

The great nylon cavity fills up in a few seconds.

My plan worked perfectly, Gisco observes, recovering from his melancholy ruminations on his final resting place with lightning speed. *All we've gotta do is heat the air, get this thing off the ground, and the two of us can resume our southerly peregrinations.*

The three of us, I correct him.

What?

The boy's coming with us.

※

32

The gondola is lying on its side, facing toward the balloon's open mouth.

My watch starts to grow warm on my wrist. I take it off, and toss it into the big wicker basket. Sure enough, it glows blue, and starts to flame. Within seconds the heat is so intense that Gisco and I have to step back. I worry that the gondola may burst into flame, but most of the heat is directed upward.

Gisco glances at the boy. *Travel light, travel fast, as the old saying goes. We can't take on extra baggage.*

Take your pick. He's coming or I'm staying.

Don't be melodramatic. He may not want to be "saved" by us. Those drug bandits may be the only family he has.

You're the one who said they enslaved him and cut his tongue out.

The point is that charitable as your impulses may be, we have a responsibility to a greater cause—

No, the point is that he risked his life to save us.

As we debate his fate, the boy in question stares at the blue flame like he's witnessing a miracle—the burning bush or the parting of the Red Sea. "It's okay," I reassure him. "Don't be scared. This is our way out."

But the balloon is not rising. Gisco, are you sure this will work?

The scientific principle is simple enough, the dog responds. *Hot air rises through cold air. So when the air in the balloon reaches a high enough temperature vis-à-vis the air outside it, the balloon will be pulled skyward, and we'll be on our way.*

But what if it doesn't reach that temperature before we're machine-gunned?

That's a whole separate calculation, Gisco admits, *with variables beyond my control. But look! It's starting to rise!*

Indeed it is. Now the balloon is an inch off the ground, now three inches. The gondola is pulled upright, and Gisco and I leap in. "Come," I say to the boy.

He backs away a step.

Jack, he clearly doesn't want to join us. And allow me to point out that our chances of lifting off and escaping before the submachine guns target us will be significantly reduced by the weight of an additional passenger.

It's a risk we'll have to take. I'm not going to have another P.J. or yellow dinghy on my conscience. I reach out my hands to the boy, palms open. He can't mistake my meaning—get in and join us.

He still hesitates, fearful of the blue flame.

Our gondola is now a foot off the ground and rising more quickly. In an instant we'll be whisked away from him, the way the Wizard was separated from Dorothy when he made his sudden aerial departure from Oz.

I reach out and grab the boy's thin right wrist, and try to pull him in. He resists with surprising strength, and for a long second we're looking each other in the eye. I don't know what he sees in my face, but he suddenly stops trying to get away and steps toward our basket.

Rat-a-tat, bullets chip away at the rock he's standing on.

The lad gives a desperate leap and reaches up to me. I grab both his arms, and haul him in.

He clambers over the side, flops down onto the floor of the basket, crosses himself, and shuts his eyes tight.

Even though we're rising, the banditos don't have a clear shot at us yet. Our angle of ascent allows us to hug the mountainside, and their fusillades are deflected by boulders and overhangs. But in a second we'll be free and clear, and that will be the end for us.

Gisco, we'll be out in the open, silhouetted by the rising moon. They can't possibly miss us. We'll be the biggest, easiest target in the history of submachine guns.

What choice do we have? Our only way out is up.

The balloon is now level with the highest rocks of this Andean pinnacle. The golden orb of moon glows above us. In different circumstances it would be beautiful, but now it looks deadly. In seconds it will backlight us, and the bandits will blast us into human nacho chips.

Then a tiny corner of the moon grows dark, as if it really is cheese and a rat has nibbled off a crumb. Soon it's a third gone. Then half has vanished. A dark cloud trailing across the sky is slowly covering the lunar surface like a well-placed veil! The cloud will blow off in seconds, but that may be all the time we need.

The winds catch us and lift the balloon away from the rocky crag. We spin wildly, gaining speed, heading right for a neighboring snowcapped peak.

Jack, we're going to smash into it!

There's a jolt and a grinding sound, but it's only the bottom of our gondola kicking ice off the crest.

Then we're on the other side of it, out of danger from submachine guns and rising quickly into the starry vista of the clear and cold Andean sky.

33

The night grows stormy. Claps of thunder boom all around us, like angry Inca gods roaring at three interlopers in their preposterous balloon. Needle-sharp flashes of lightning stitch together a blanket of black clouds that soon covers the mountains.

The boy with the braid responds to this climatic chaos by curling into a fetal position. Is he praying for his life, the way Gisco does when he's desperate? Or is this his way of dealing with the unknown—to hide in himself, the way a turtle pulls its head inside its shell?

Gisco and I stand quietly in the gondola, recovering from our Andean escapade.

My mother's lullaby still echoes faintly in my ears. As I recall her sad voice, I'm also aware that the watch from my father is now powering our hot-air balloon. It feels strange that these two parents from the far future who I've never met, and who abandoned me, have somehow come together to take care of me.

Lightning strobes Gisco's shaggy face, and rolling thunder makes his sensitive ears twitch back and forth.

We spin and dip, and the boy with the braid whimpers.

What are you planning to do with him? Gisco asks.

I don't know, I admit. But wherever we're headed, it has to be better than leaving him where he was.

Not necessarily, the dog conjectures gloomily. *First, we may not make it through this storm. And second, if your spider dream was a premonition of who's waiting for us, the poor kid might have been better off on the mountaintop.*

You don't really believe that.

It was foolish and reckless to bring him, Jack. Now we're responsible for him, and it's going to slow us down and endanger our mission. I understand why you did it. But the moral equation here is all a matter of proportion.

How can saving a kid's life not be moral?

It's just one life. The entire future is threatened by what the Dark Lord is doing in the Amazon. You haven't seen it. I have. A world stripped of its lungs today is a world wheezing its way to a terrible death a thousand years from now. Millions of people are suffering horribly and depending on us. Your duty is to the many, Jack, and not to the few, and especially not to the one.

No, I tell Gisco. Saving the life of one person is just as important as saving the entire world. In fact, if you don't save one person, you can't save the entire world.

How can that be?

I don't know, but it is.

For a while we're both silent, watching as the cloud cover begins to change color, from black to inky purple. We're traveling at great speed now. It also feels like we're descending—I hope our nylon Band-Aid isn't leaking.

Okay, Gisco, I say, you've seen this awful future and I haven't. Explain the contradiction. How am I supposed to save the day? According to you, I can't fight this Dark Lord who's doing so much damage to the Amazon now, and to the future a thousand years from now. You made me come on this trip, but at the same time you say I don't have a prayer of stopping him.

No one has a chance against him. Except for one man.

And who is that?

Gisco's descriptions of people from the future are sometimes tinged with emotions. When he talks about my parents, I can sense his love and respect. When he alludes to the leader of the Dark Army, I pick up on his fear. Now the veneration in his telepathic tone approaches awe: *The only person who has a chance to stop him is the greatest wizard-scientist who ever lived, the Mysterious Kidah. He came back in time for that express purpose.*

Great, I say, then let these two titans of the future battle it out—the Wizard against the Dark Lord. Why do you need me?

Because Kidah disappeared, Gisco admits sadly. *He may be dead or in hiding. No one can find him. And sand is slipping through the hourglass, Jack. Now and a thousand years from now, time is running out.*

Suppose he doesn't want to be found? It sounds to me like your great wizard doesn't want to tangle with the spidery Dark Lord either. Maybe he made himself disappear.

Kidah's courage is indisputable.

Okay. Then where is he? Where was he last seen?

Gisco looks back at me and then raises a paw dramatically and thrusts it down at the purple cloud cover beneath our balloon. *We think he's there.*

I look down. The clouds are no longer purple. Shafts of morning sunlight now make them glow a remarkable shade of green.

Then I realize that I'm not looking down at cloud cover but rather tree cover! Except that it can't possibly be tree cover because forests have boundaries and limits, they thin out and give way to grasslands, but the expanse of rippling green below me seems to go on forever.

The green is laced and flecked with silver that glints in the noonday sun. There are glowing veins and flashing arteries, and millions of tiny, twisting capillaries. Water! The almost impenetrable forest canopy conceals a second, hidden world of rivers, lakes, and swamps.

"The Amazon?" I whisper.

Yes. We're pretty sure he's somewhere down there in Pará or Amazonas state. And if he is, you and I have to find him and get him back on his feet.

Sure, I mutter, staring down at the forbidding tree canopy.

We'll track the greatest and also apparently the most cowardly mind of the future down in the biggest, wildest, and most dangerous swamp in the world. Talk about trying to find a wizard in a haystack. Count me out.

Kidah's no coward. And don't worry about the Amazon, Gisco assures me. *Predatory reptiles and giant insects and fish with teeth are only dangerous when they can sink their teeth into you. That's why we came airmail. You're totally safe up here with me.*

No sooner has Gisco given me this reassurance than I hear the concussive thuds of antiaircraft fire. Luckily, we seem to be out of range.

Unluckily, whoever they are, they seem to have a variety of weapons, and they're not shy about using them.

A heat-seeking missile streaks up through the treetops and rips a nasty gash in our hot-air balloon.

Gisco, we're hit! We're going down!

I know, and there's nothing to be done!

Into the uncharted Amazon.

Uncharted because no one could survive long enough to map it.

Do something!

Don't panic. Remain steadfast as the evening star.

You're the one crying and shivering.

Can't help it, old fellow. Have you ever heard the unfortunate expression "dog-eat-dog"? Well, in the place we're headed, everything eats dog. There are army ants that eat dog. Giant catfish that can swallow a dog whole. Spiders and snakes and even plant species that feed on dog!

Try to calm down, Gisco. Steadfast as the evening star, remember? Anyway, the impact will probably smash us to smithereens before the animals can devour us.

Thanks for the kind thought. You're a true friend.

We're almost in free fall. Once again I reach for my father's watch, and put it on.

The boy stands up and looks around wildly. When he realizes what's happening, he makes a frightened sound and grabs Gisco.

The dog tries to shake him off, but he can't break the kid's iron grip. *Get this mountain boy off me.*

If we make it through the trees we'll splash down in the water. He must sense how buoyant you are.

I'm a dog, not a lifeboat. Here come the trees!

Maybe they'll cushion our fall.

More likely rip us apart!

34

It's like being in five different car accidents at one intersection. We're hit this way and spun that way, tumbled forward and jerked back.

There are loud crashing sounds and flashes of light and dark as branches splinter beneath us and curtains of leaves whip against the sides of our gondola. Outraged birds squawk. Monkeys howl.

Down, down, down we plunge.

Water flashes below. River, swamp, or lake? Can't tell. I prepare for a bellyflop into a piranha pool.

But then we stop suddenly. Gently. And hang in the air, swaying slightly like a decorative mobile.

I peer over the side. The top branches of the forest canopy slowed us, and the understory snagged us. Our gondola now dangles thirty feet above the swampy forest floor. Looking down, I can see tree trunks rising and vines descending, and lots and lots of water.

But there is an island nearby.

Someone else has found it first. Three enormous jet-black caimans lie motionless on the water's edge. They look like mini-dinosaurs working on their suntans.

Gisco, we survived the fall!

Is that good news or bad news?

Come on. I admit there are a few caimans below and God knows what other critters, but at least we're going to have some time to figure out our next move.

Yes, maybe you're right. A forest is just a forest, after all. As long as we remain calm and logical, we'll be just fine. What's that?

What?

That sound.

What sound?

That buzzing. Gisco glances uneasily at the tangle of vines and branches all around us.

I myself do not hear a buzzing, possibly because of the trilling birdcalls and outraged monkey chatter and a thousand other strange barks, whistles, and shrieks that I can't even begin to separate and identify. They ebb and flow around us, beneath us, and above us, an ever-present yet constantly changing cacophony.

A two-inch black bird hovers near Gisco. The dog backs up quickly. *Swat it. Club it. Kill it!*

Calm down. It's just an Amazon hummingbird.

It's not a small bird. It's a giant wasp!

No way. Wasps don't grow that big.

They do here, the entomologically expert dog tells me, visibly trembling. *There are more than seven hundred species of wasps in the Amazon. Their stings are supposed to be the most painful imaginable.*

I've been stung by a bee. It's not so bad.

Wasps in the Amazon hunt tarantulas! When they attack in a swarm of thousands, nothing can stand before them!

Well, the good news is the one that saw us flew away.

Then why is the buzzing getting louder?

I hear it, too. The boy with the braid lifts a large leaf and points to what looks like a five-foot-long inverted ice cream cone, made of thin whitish bark.

That's the mother of all wasp nests! Gisco announces with a telepathic shriek, backing away to the far corner of the gondola. The boy has also retreated as far as possible from the droning, vibrating hive. Each of us is trying to get behind the other, but somehow Gisco always seems to be the one with his back to the gondola's far wall.

Maybe they won't hurt us, I suggest hopefully. I remember reading that many wasps are vegetarians.

When their nest is threatened, they'll kill anything. The one that saw us must have been a scout. He's letting the swarm know we're in the neighborhood. We'll be stung to death in seconds.

I glance at the swampy river below and spot the three caimans lying motionless on the island. Something tells me they won't remain quite so still if we splash down into the water near them. Okay, Gisco, what can we do?

That boy brought a machete. Hack their nest off the tree! It's our only chance.

I tiptoe forward and see that the giant nest is attached to a branch that's three inches in diameter. Slicing it off would be like trying to hack through the barrel of a baseball bat. There's no way, Gisco.

It's the only way! If I had fingers I'd do it. But I don't. You're the one who is anatomically best suited to this battle. All for one and one for all— get to it!

The shrill whine from the nest rises in volume. A few wasps fly out of a hole at the bottom. I see their bright red stingers, razor sharp and nearly an inch long. There's no doubt that they know we're here. I take a deep breath and then step forward. Okay, Gisco, I'll try it your way.

That's the spirit. There's really nothing to be afraid of, the dog assures me, practically burrowing into the gondola's wicker wall to get as far as possible from the enormous insects, who have taken up what sounds like an Indian war cry inside their nest. I have the strong sense that any second the swarm is going to attack in full force.

I feel a surge of adrenaline. Gisco's right—hacking off the branch is our only chance. The boy seems to understand and hands over his machete.

I take it in my hands and creep closer.

Gisco, if I don't cut through the branch in one swipe, they'll swarm over us in a heartbeat.

You can do it, Jack. You're a natural machete swinger if I've ever seen one. I have the utmost confidence in you. I note that even while he's encouraging me, the crafty dog has one foot over the edge of the gondola, preparing for a hasty evacuation if necessary.

I grip the machete with both hands, raise it, take a final step forward, and bring the blade down with full force on the branch. There's a loud CRACK as sharp steel bites into wet wood. The loud buzz rises to a furious crescendo, but by the time the wasps know what hit them their nest is in free fall, heading for the distant swamp.

Gisco steps forward, all smiles. *Well done, Jack. After all, there's no reason to be afraid of a few overgrown backyard pests. Put it there. Shake my paw.*

But before I can accept the dog's hearty congratulations, a tiger springs into our gondola from a nearby branch and looks at us with anticipatory relish, as if someone just rang a rain forest dinner gong.

The boy with the braid takes one terrified look at the tiger and jumps onto my back, wrapping his arms and legs around me. I decide that it's time to remind my canine companion of his pedigree.

Gisco, good news. We're no longer menaced by insects. Now we just have to deal with a tiger.

Spots, not stripes. It's a jaguar.

In any case, it's a member of the cat family, and we all know that dogs love to fight cats. So go to it.

Gisco narrows his eyes and studies the jaguar. *You're right,* he agrees, *the dog was never born who feared a cat, even an overgrown feral feline like this one. I thought they were nocturnal hunters. This one must have insomnia. Or maybe it was stung by an angry wasp as the nest fell.*

Or it could be too hungry to sleep. Don't let that stop you. Take it on, Gisco. Teach it a proper respect for dogs. But watch your jugular.

Jaguars don't go for the jugular, Gisco informs me, squaring his shoulders like a heavyweight boxer trying to intimidate an opponent. *They crush victims' heads in their jaws with one bite. Hence the Indian name "jaguar"—"kill in one bound." But this won't come to a fight. All cats are cowards. Watch what happens when I show this tabby who's the king of the rain forest.*

Gisco steps forward, bares his teeth, and lets loose an impressive growl. It is a truly fearsome sound, which my sophisticated and cultured travel companion has somehow managed to dredge up from a secret reservoir of primitive canine behavior.

The jaguar responds by padding forward a step, opening its toothy mouth, and screeching out the scariest howl I've ever heard in my life. It's a fierce and primordial shriek, halfway between a roar and a bark.

Gisco whirls around and dives off the gondola into the water far below.

The jaguar shifts its hungry gaze to me. Its yellow eyes glint as it takes another step forward.

The boy on my back clutches at me wildly. His arms reach around my head and cover my eyes.

I stumble back, away from the jaguar, trying to pry the kid's arms off my eyes so that I can see what's about to crush my skull in one bite. I trip over the wall of the gondola, flail wildly for balance, and then fall over the side with the boy still clinging to me. Down we drop, toward the swamp below.

35

The water is lukewarm and smells slightly stinky, like a giant bowl of egg drop soup. I knife into it headfirst with the added weight of the boy driving me down. He's clinging to me with such desperation that I'm pretty sure he can't swim a stroke.

I stop my dive, manage to flip underwater, and then my feet encounter something muddy and I kick off the bottom.

The boy isn't cooperating. As I claw my way toward daylight, I also have to fight a no-holds-barred wrestling match. He's much stronger than he looks, and he's clearly hysterical—his nails gouge my arms, and his right arm, which is wrapped around my throat, tightens like a noose.

I remember Gisco's warning—he'll be a responsibility and an added danger for us now, at every turn.

I unpeel the boy's right arm from around my neck. As I break the surface I yank him in front of me. Gisco?

Over here. That fat cat had a nasty attitude, so I decided to take the plunge.

I thought you were going to show it who's the king of the rain forest.

Why bother? This isn't so bad. Nice water temperature, don't you think? Sort of like a mineral bath . . .

Where are we headed? This kid is freaked out and I can't tow him around all day.

That island looks like our best bet, the dog suggests, indicating a mud-and-grass hump that rises from the swamp.

Gisco, there were three huge caimans on that beach less than a minute ago.

Well, they're not there now.

Right. Where do you think they've gone?

The dog suddenly looks wary. *Good point.* He scans the water. *Maybe they swam away.*

I appreciate his optimism, but I'm pretty sure he's wrong. They're closing in on us. That's not just a paranoid guess—I can feel it!

When Eko trained me on the Outer Banks, she tried to teach me how to reach out telepathically to wild animals. I couldn't master the skill, but I did learn to sense the presence of top predators. When I ran into great white sharks, I could hear them— they gave off an electrical hum of pure evil.

Now I'm picking up something with a similarly nasty signal, but on a different frequency. It's not emitting a high-pitched buzz, but rather a low drone, like a thirsty ghost circling toward freshly spilled blood.

Gisco, I can hear them coming for us!

I don't see anything.

The drone comes again, closer. It exudes an unearthly patience as it closes in on us. I sense that countless eons of hunting have given the caimans this stalking maturity—they've been catching lunch this way since dinosaurs roamed the earth.

Gisco, we're being pursued by Mesozoic predators! Maybe you can't see them, but I can sense them, and they're getting ready for a lip-smacking dog-and-boy McSandwich!

There they are, Jack! Gisco treads water and stares, panicked but riveted.

I follow the direction of his fearful gaze. Three faint lines are being traced on the smooth surface of the water by large objects swimming just underneath it.

Don't move. Maybe they haven't spotted us.

As if on cue, six reddish yellow eyes slowly rise out of the swampy water and survey us.

The boy sees the caimans and thrashes wildly. It takes all of my strength to hold him.

Meanwhile, Gisco is also freaking out. *My dear mother did not raise her favorite son to be ingested by a cold-blooded scaly-skinned overgrown handbag. We've got to get out of here!*

The dog starts swimming away at high speed.

I can't possibly keep up with him, but I see that there's no need. The frenzied hound is paddling in a big circle, scanning the swampy miasma with wild glances, desperate to escape but baffled which way to head.

Find us some dry land, Gisco. Our only chance is to make a run for it.

They're faster than we are.

No way. Their legs are like tree stumps.

In a short sprint, a gator's stumpy legs allow it to accelerate and run down a peccary, a person, a horse, or even a highly evolved and extremely motivated dog.

Then we'll have to climb to safety, I suggest.

The terrified dog scans the trees overhead. The rain forest is a contest for sunlight, and a low branch is not much use. The nearest limbs of the understory are at least twenty feet above us. A monkey swings by on a vine and mocks us with a *hee-haa.*

It's hopeless. Jack, we have only one option left.

What's that?

Give them the boy. While they're eating him, we can find some way to escape.

Gisco, how can you suggest such a thing? He's one of us now. All for one and one for all. Plus, he's helpless. What about the famed loyalty of dogs?

Gisco is watching the caimans swim closer. *I can't be loyal to others if I'm being eaten and digested. A dead Gisco is a worthless Gisco.*

So it follows that my first duty as a public-spirited and selfless dog is to save my own skin at all costs. Feed him to the gators and let's swim for it!

Never. Let's try to make a stand against them. We're a pretty formidable tag team.

We're also out of our element, not to mention our weight class. Do you happen to know how caimans kill?

No, I admit, watching the reddish yellow eyes get bigger and bigger. They're no longer distant marbles. Now they look like glowing softballs.

They take a bite. Get a secure grip with their iron jaws. Then they drag their catch down to the bottom to drown it. Down in the mud and silt, they feed on the decaying corpse at their leisure. A feast like the three of us could last for weeks.

I admit it doesn't sound fun.

Give them the kid, Jack. It's the only moral thing to do. You tried to save him. You've been heroic. Now to hell with him. Our duty is to future generations.

For a moment I'm tempted to let go of the boy. Maybe Gisco's right. Maybe there does come a time when logic dictates sheer self-preservation.

The boy has stopped struggling. He's also watching the caimans come on.

I can feel his scared heart fluttering in his chest.

No, I tell the dog. You swim for it—you're a faster swimmer than I am anyway. If I have to end up as caiman snacks, I'd rather not die a coward and traitor.

Suit yourself. Gisco takes a few quick dog paddles away and then stops and circles back. *Damn you for shaming me into this. But then again, I can't outswim them either. So we'll stand and fight, or rather drown and be eaten.*

At least we can draw some blood in return! I point out with as much bravado as I can muster.

Cold blood, Gisco responds miserably.

The boy seems to have sensed our decision, and he doesn't

agree with it. He's pointing in the opposite direction, urging us to swim for it.

I wish I could explain to him that there's no place to go.

He thrusts again with his arm.

I shake my head. "Sorry I brought you here. Running away is not an option. We're going to stand and fight."

He implores me with those big brown eyes. Jabs the air with his finger.

I look back at him for a second. Recall that this is a kid who's been surviving by his wits for years. I follow the direction of his pointing arm.

Nothing. Silver-green water. A few lily pads.

The caimans are thirty feet away now. They never change speed or expression. They just come on, slow and steady, as they have for millions of years.

The boy grabs my hair and uses it to turn my head. I peer over the lily pads and see a dark shape.

Gisco, the kid has spotted something!

Where?

There! A tree. Or at least a log. It's submerged. Covered with moss. Do you see it?

The dog doesn't respond because he's already swimming for the floating log at top speed, using a hysteria-driven four-pawed dog paddle that turns him into a furry Jet Ski.

I follow as fast as I can in his wake, pulling the boy along like an overburdened tugboat on overdrive.

36

Gisco reaches the floating log and scrambles out of the water. I follow along ten feet behind him, expecting at any second to feel a caiman's jaws snap closed like a bear trap on my ankles. Fear turns my kicking legs into propellers and gives my one-handed lifeguard stroke turbospeed. I make it to the log ahead of the ravenous reptiles and give the boy a shove out of the water.

He grabs what remains of a branch and hauls himself up. I follow him, slipping and sliding onto the sludgy, slippery, mossy mound of decaying wood.

The caimans come on implacably through the water like the three fates. If they know that we've clambered out, they don't seem at all fazed.

And why should they be? It's their swamp and we have nowhere to go, no place to hide. Still, it feels good to be out of the murky water, standing in sunlight. Air is my element, and at least now I won't be eaten by something that I can't see.

Gisco, maybe we can kick them away.

Or wedge branches into their jaws, the dog suggests.

Maybe we can even find branches with points, which we can use as spears!

We search the floating log. There are no spearlike branches. Nothing that resembles a weapon of any kind. This was once a mighty tree but the massive trunk has been worn smooth by the water, and the branches and smaller limbs have been softened and stripped away.

The caimans are now less than twenty feet away. Six reddish yellow eyes glint hungrily.

The boy is trembling. I pick him up and hold him protectively in my arms. But of course I can't protect him, and we both know it.

Goodbye, Gisco. You were right, I should have left this poor fellow on the mountainside.

Farewell, Jack. You did the best you could. We were none of us dealt lucky hands. When we die, your Amazon is condemned to stumps and sawdust, and my future will gasp its last rattling breaths. Kidah's out there somewhere in the forest, but we'll never find him.

The lead caiman opens its jaws, and I see a dark, tooth-edged tunnel leading into oblivion. I pray to God that the pain ends quickly.

And then drum music starts up! A deafening snare drum cadence. *Ka-cha, ka-cha, ka-ka-cha!* Wood chips fly, water sprays, and in half a second the top predators of the Amazon learn that there's a higher rung on the ladder.

One of the caimans turns to face the hail of bullets and snarls wildly. I watch as its scaly hide is shredded by dozens of bullets. Its two companions quickly dive down and sink out of sight.

The drum cadence stops.

There is total, eerie silence beneath the emerald canopy. This is a biosphere that understands bloodletting. Even the birds and the tiniest insects seem to be impressed by what has just taken place.

Jack, we've got company.

Two long, sleek outboard canoes motor toward us from either side of the log. Five soldiers in uniform stand motionless in each canoe, and it would be hard to imagine a tougher-looking group of rescuers. The men are short and muscular. I can't see their faces clearly because they're all wearing dark sunglasses and low-slung gray hats. Several of them carry submachine guns.

Still, the enemy of your enemy is your friend, and these roughnecks just saved us from being eaten. I wave at the man in the front of the lead canoe, who is cradling an Uzi in his arms like it's his favorite child.

"Sir, I don't know if you understand English, but thank you for saving us. *Muchas gracias.*"

He takes off his dark glasses and looks back at me as his canoe pulls up alongside our log. His face is not exactly warm and friendly, but he smiles at me and I smile back. *"Não é nada,"* he grunts, turning his submachine gun in his hands so he's holding it by the barrel. Then he swings it like a baseball bat at my head.

I wasn't expecting the attack. I start to duck away, but I'm still holding the boy in my arms and he slows me.

It takes me just a fraction of a second to push the boy down and start to roll away from the blow. But the delay makes all the difference.

The metal butt of the submachine gun catches me on the side of my head with a loud CRACK.

As I black out, I feel myself slipping off the log, and the silvery swamp water closes over me like a shroud.

37

I awake to the tolling of church bells. Are they striking the changing hour or has someone died?

It takes me a few seconds to realize the persistent ringing is inside my head, an excruciating metallic ache that reverberates from ear to ear each time I breathe.

My eyes are sealed shut with my caked blood. I'm lying down, being carried swiftly along.

I force one eye open. I'm on my side in a canoe, sailing quickly down a narrow and winding river. Tree branches reach across it to block out the sky overhead.

My wrists are handcuffed behind me. I twist my body around and glimpse Gisco and the boy lying near me, similarly bound. A soldier with a gun stands over us.

Bam, bam. The jackhammer switches on again. Gisco?

Welcome back, Jack. You haven't moved in three hours. I was afraid he shattered your skull.

He sure swung for the fences. Who are these goons?

They seem to be soldiers of the Brazilian Army, stationed in a remote regiment in the Amazon. They were the ones who shot down our balloon. Then they located us in the swamp, under orders from their commander. Now they're taking us to their base.

Why go to so much trouble?

Maybe they didn't appreciate us ballooning over their stretch of rain forest.

I feel woozy again. Who's their commander?

They call him Colonel Aranha. Are you okay?

Bam, bam, bam. It feels like my head is going to come off my shoulders. What does this colonel have against us?

Who knows? But "aranha" is Portuguese for "spider."

I can feel myself slipping down, sinking away. Did I fall out of the canoe? I reach for something to cling to.

Don't go away again, Jack. Gisco tries to hold on to me telepathically. *Stay conscious. If you go to sleep, you may never wake up.*

But darkness has me. I slip down to the bottom of the river and find a quiet spot, deep in the river mud.

No tarantulas down here. No jackhammers allowed.

I stay down a long time. Feel the sun moving above me. Distant voices. The pull of the current.

No, not a current. Currents are smooth. We're bouncing and grinding along.

And we're not in a canoe anymore. This is louder and faster than a canoe. A car? No, bigger. A jeep?

Whatever it is, its engine isn't exactly muffled. But except for that mechanical roar, all around me it is quiet.

Dead silent. The constant buzz and chirrup of the birds and insects of the rain forest has disappeared.

I crack my eyes open. Mistake. Blinding sunlight floods in. We're in the open. No shade of any kind.

What happened to the trees? I peer out through one half-closed eye. We're in a desolate place. A wasteland.

Charred stumps. Rocks. An occasional empty streambed. All covered by a funereal shroud of cinders.

Gisco, where are we?

Back from the dead, are you? That must have been one hard crack on the noggin. How are you feeling?

These bumps don't make it any easier. What is this place? What happened to the rain forest?

Colonel Aranha is no friend of the trees.

How's the boy?

I don't know. He can't speak and he's not telepathic. He is feisty, though. He tried to bite the arm of the guy who clubbed you, and got knocked down pretty hard for it.

How come you didn't try to bite the guy's arm?

Could it be because he was carrying a submachine gun? Gisco asks rhetorically. *Yes, I believe that was the reason.* Then, excited and frightened: *Jack, look!*

What?

Over there! The gates of hell. And they're opening!

✳

38

Jungle fortress meets desert prison. The scorched wasteland is broken by an enormous fence, topped by rings of razor wire. Guard towers are visible at intervals, with armed sentries standing stock-still.

Only one way in. A massive gate. The buckle on this formidable mesh belt. I try to puzzle out why an army regiment in this remote part of the Amazon might need such a fortress. To keep enemies out? For intimidation? To protect valuables? Or because things are happening inside that are so horrible they are best kept secret?

Our transport vehicle rolls up and the gate slides open. We roll in and the enormous gate closes behind us. I force both eyes open as we rumble down a road toward a compound of low buildings. They look like army barracks—and were clearly designed for functionality rather than comfort or elegance.

They also look strangely familiar.

I recall my vision of P.J. in chains, menaced by a giant spider.

Gisco, I've been here before, in my dream about P.J.

It must be the colonel's base. I hope they have a cafeteria.

It's a prison, Gisco. The people I saw inside it were starving to death. Those were the lucky ones.

You really know how to put the damper on the end of a trip.

Our transport vehicle rolls to a stop. Guards are waiting for us. They wear khaki army uniforms and carry guns and clubs. They drag us out and shove us forward.

I hear awful sounds carried on the breeze. Men begging. Women pleading. The cries of desolate children.

Gisco cocks his ears and looks sad.

The boy also hears them. Recognition registers on his young face. He knows pain and helplessness.

We pass from sunlight to gloom as the prison's heavy door clangs shut. We're pushed and shoved down a series of narrow and dank low-ceilinged corridors.

The cries of misery are constant now. A mother calls her child's name again and again. A man begs for water. The heat is sweltering. This prison was built almost without windows—the afternoon sun turns it into a kiln.

I try to remember the twists and turns of this maze. If we ever manage to escape from our captors, I'll have to find my way back out.

But it's no use. One hallway leads to another, and my head is still throbbing.

An enormous rat runs into the corridor ahead of us and bares its teeth. One of the guards raises a pistol.

Terrific. A sweltering, vermin-infested dungeon. Can you imagine what the mosquitoes are like at night?

We'll find some way out of here, Gisco. If there's an entrance there has to be an exit.

I hope so. But there's an old dog saying: don't bury your bone in too deep a hole or the hole will eat the bone.

Faces pressed tight to the bars of the cells. Women. Kids. Malnourished. Hopeless. I slow down, scanning their faces, searching for P.J.

A guard shoves me so hard I stumble. I whirl around and he's got his club raised. Go ahead, his eyes urge. Give me the slightest chance to club you or shoot you. I've done it many times before, without guilt or remorse.

I turn away and lower my head submissively, and feel his club jab hard into my back.

We turn down another corridor and stop. My handcuffs are removed. Keys turn in a lock. We have reached our new home.

They push me in, and I go sprawling. The boy is shoved in after me, and we end up in a tangled heap. Then the cell door is slammed shut and locked. It takes me a minute to realize that Gisco is not inside with us.

I hear him growl and I whirl toward the bars.

Two of the guards have drawn their guns and are pointing them at Gisco's head. A third guard approaches the dog with a rope coiled into what looks like a noose.

Gisco, don't give them an excuse to shoot you.

Gisco snarls at the guards again. *Once they put that thing around my neck, they can do what they want to me.*

There's no choice, I tell him. They probably just want to take you to the doggy wing of the prison.

Or feed me to the army ants.

I see the guards aim guns at his head. Gisco, if they shoot, they'll kill you for sure. I'll find a way out of here and we'll be together again soon.

Do you promise? I don't like the idea of being alone and at the colonel's mercy.

I promise.

Gisco stops growling and allows the noose to be draped around his neck. As soon as it's on, the guard yanks it tight and Gisco starts choking and gasping for air.

Keep the faith, Jack. I'll be back. They don't know who they're messing with . . .

Two guards grab the free end of the rope and they drag Gisco away like a trussed pig to the slaughterhouse.

The boy and I watch helplessly and then turn back to our cell. It's big for two people. But we're not alone.

39

At least twenty other men and boys are in the same dank, gloomy space. When the guards unlocked the door with guns drawn, the inhabitants of the cell must have backed up to the far wall. Perhaps that's the protocol here. I get the feeling if you violate one of Colonel Aranha's rules, you don't get a second chance.

Now that the guards have departed, our cell mates emerge from the shadows and circle us. They don't look pleased at having two new mouths to share their food with. The oldest must be eighty; the youngest appears to be eight or nine. Most are gaunt, some are frighteningly emaciated, and many of them look desperate to the point of madness.

A tall man with rotting teeth makes a grab for the watch on my wrist. I instinctively swat his arm away.

The contact produces an immediate reaction. Weapons come out. Not guns or knives, but primitive prison weapons—sharpened sticks and stones chipped into hand axes and iron shards that have been chiseled into shanks. Questions and taunts are barked at us, whispered at us, and shouted at us, in a variety of languages I don't understand.

I put one arm protectively around the boy and prepare to fight for my life.

A sturdy, bearded man with what must once have been a barrel chest issues a sharp command. The hostile crowd instantly stops threatening us. Hands holding weapons freeze in midair. Lips barking taunts fall silent.

The bearded man steps in front of us. His hair has gone white and his barrel chest has staved in, but he still looks powerful. His strong face and intelligent eyes mark him as a natural leader. He asks us a question in Spanish, and then repeats it in what I think is Portuguese.

"Sorry," I say. "I don't speak those languages."

His face reflects surprise. "Americans!" he says.

"I'm American. This boy is not. He was kidnapped by drug smugglers in the Andes, who cut his tongue out. My friend—that dog they just dragged away—and I helped him to escape, but then Colonel Aranha's soldiers shot down our hot-air balloon and captured us. They brought us here."

As I listen to my own explanation, I'm sure no one will believe it. From the drug smugglers in the Andes to the balloon, it sounds preposterous.

But the bearded man slowly nods. He looks the boy over as he translates my words into several different languages for the benefit of our other cell mates.

"So you are an enemy of Colonel Aranha?" he finally asks, in surprisingly good English.

"Yes. I think he plans to kill me."

"He plans to kill all of us," the bearded man says. "This prison is a slow death. How did a young American come to be the enemy of a Brazilian Army colonel?"

"It's complicated," I answer. "A family feud."

"Family feuds are always complicated. But if you and your family are enemies of the colonel, you are welcome here." He speaks a few words to his cell mates, and the results are immediate. The hostility vanishes from their faces. More important, their makeshift weapons disappear into pockets, mouths, armpits, and cracks in the floor.

A few of the younger kids in the cell step forward and wave hello to the boy from the Andes. I find my hand being shaken by a dozen unshaven walking skeletons.

"Welcome," the bearded man says, gripping my hand firmly. "I am Ernesto. You are one of us now."

"Thanks. I'm Jack Danielson. But who are you? And where am I?"

"This," he says with an ironic laugh, running his eyes over the walls of the fetid concrete cage, "is what I like to call the future of the free and wild Amazon. I am the governor general. And you have just become one of our citizen-soldiers, which means, I'm afraid, that you will share our miserable fate."

40

Ernesto introduces me to my cell mates, and one tale of woe is sadder than the next. There are four types of people one encounters in the Amazon, he explains, but only three were represented in this prison till I arrived.

First there are the native Indians who hunted and fished in the rain forest for centuries. There are several of them in our cell, from different tribes. He identifies one sad-looking fellow as a full-blooded Korubo chief. Their lands are supposed to be protected by the government, Ernesto says, but they contain valuable hardwoods.

A year ago, loggers penetrated deep into the exclusion zone, and the chief and his warriors defended their preserve with war clubs. Two Indians were shot and a logger was clubbed to death. Now the chief is here, wasting away, while Colonel Aranha uses his influence to help loggers raid the timber on the Korubo lands.

I can't tell if the chief understands what Ernesto is telling me. He looks back into my eyes for a few seconds, his own face sad and resigned, as if he has accepted that it is his fate to die in this concrete cage and just wishes it would happen sooner rather than later. Then he turns away, and peers out the cell's one tiny window.

Ernesto moves on to the second group, the Caboclos. They are of mixed Indian and European heritage, he says, and have retained some of their native survival skills. Many of them love the land and try to protect it.

Ernesto himself is a Caboclo. "I was raised in the forest, in Pará State, till I was twelve. Then I was shipped off to Rio de Janeiro for schooling. I studied law," he tells me, "but what I really loved was taking pictures. I worked as a photographer for papers all over South America. And then I came home to use my skills to expose what was going on in the forests I roamed as a boy."

He founded a group that tried to use modern technology to document environmental abuses. "Sometimes we took the pictures ourselves, and sometimes we gave the cameras to Indians and taught them how to use them."

Ernesto's face radiates pride. "We got photos of wildcat diamond miners teaming up with local police to plunder the lands of the Cinta Larga. We had videos of roads being bulldozed for miles just to get to protected mahogany trees. We posted images on our Web site of the devastation that gold miners are causing in our rivers. Every year they dump tons of mercury into the Amazon basin."

"It sounds like you probably made some powerful enemies along the way," I guess quietly.

"Yes," he agrees, "but I also had many friends. I would never have believed that I could just disappear. But one day as I was driving on a remote stretch of highway my car was stopped by gunmen in army uniforms, and I was blindfolded and brought here. I don't think my family and friends even know that I am still alive."

"Can't they find out?" I ask.

He smiles at my naïveté. "If they ask too many questions, they may be the next to vanish."

Lunch is served—I'm told it's the only meal of the day. It's a watery soup with a few pieces of potato thrown in. As I sip my half cup I understand why the men in the cell look so emaciated. This is a starvation diet.

I'm tempted to give in to despair. But then I spot the boy we rescued from the Andes. He's in a corner of the cell, kicking a stone around with other kids. In this dungeon he's found friends! They've claimed a tiny part of this cramped cell as their own, and are joyfully playing a crude but competitive game of soccer!

Ernesto finishes off his soup and takes up his sad tale. "The third group in this cell are the settlers—newcomers who have no traditional ties to the land. Most were driven here from the cities by poverty and promises of cheap land to farm."

He points to a few men who are taller than the Indians, but now look just as weak and miserable. "But those promises turned out to be hollow—the rain forest exists in a delicate balance with nature, and when the trees are burned and the wrong crops are planted, the soil quickly becomes useless. The settlers fell into debt, they couldn't feed their families, so they rebelled and ended up in prison with the very Indians whose land they stole."

"And what about the fourth group?" I ask.

Ernesto laughs. "You are the fourth group," he says. "We sometimes see Asians, Europeans, and Americans touring the mills, processing plants, and ranches, but never in our prisons. So it's an unexpected honor to have you here."

"You may have another American here," I tell him. "A girl, with brown hair, about my age. Her name is P.J." I describe her to him in detail. Ernesto shares my description with the other men in the cell. Two or three say they think a young woman who fits P.J.'s description was spotted being transported at night through the corridors, always under heavy guard.

When I hear this, I can't contain my excitement. So she is here, possibly even in this very wing of the prison! There must be a way for me to locate her and break her out. "Has anyone ever escaped from this place?" I ask Ernesto.

"Several have tried, and they have died in highly unpleasant ways," he tells me. "Colonel Aranha is a meticulous man. He couldn't do what he is doing if he weren't."

"And what exactly is he doing?" I ask. "It sounds like many different people are involved in destroying the rain forest. Europeans, Asians, and Americans. But also Brazilians. Even Caboclos and Indians."

"Absolutely," Ernesto agrees. "And there have always been corrupt government officials who bent the rules in exchange for bribes, but never on the scale of what this colonel is doing. He's using his powerful connections to help loggers, miners, and foreign companies gain access and break laws. In the last few years, with his influence rising, the destruction of the Amazon has proceeded at an ever-increasing pace. And we who tried to stop it are rotting here, with nothing to do but watch it vanish out our one window."

I look around at my cell mates—Indians, Caboclos, settlers, all wasting away. Skeletal bodies. Toothless gums. Hopeless eyes. "Why doesn't he just kill you?"

Ernesto shrugs. "Maybe it is his sense of humor. He makes us work, destroying what we love the most."

"And what is that?" I ask, almost afraid to hear the answer.

Ernesto opens his mouth to answer, and then closes it quickly as thudding footsteps approach. Guards open the door and I follow the lead of my cell mates and hurry to the back wall of the cell.

The guards enter with guns drawn and point quickly to ten men. Ernesto is chosen, and one of the Indians. I am the last one they single out.

I follow the others to the front of the cell with my arms

raised, and then hold out my wrists to be handcuffed. As the cuffs are locked on, Ernesto whispers to me, "You are about to find out about the colonel's sense of humor for yourself."

41

It's a small, shabby plane that looks like it dates from the Cold War. I just hope its engine is better than its paint job. As we are prodded toward it at gunpoint, I see that it's equipped with floats for a water landing.

It does not, however, have any seats, at least in the cabin. They've all been ripped out, so we squeeze down onto the iron floor. A few seconds after we are all piled in, the old Cessna takes off with a hacking roar and banks sharply. Then it zooms away, flying just a few hundred feet above the treetops.

Peering down through the cabin's windows, I can see the colonel's fenced compound, built near a wide river. Virgin rain forest starts on the far side of that river and stretches away as far as my eyes can see.

We are flying so low that we seem in danger of dipping into the rippling sea of forest green. Every now and then streaks of color flame up at us as flocks of brightly plumed birds take wing together and burst from the trees toward the clouds.

I think of Gisco—what would he have made of my cell mates and their sad stories? And what would he think of this mysterious flight in an airborne junk heap?

Coward though he is, I've gotten used to facing danger with the big dog. It feels lonely to be going it alone. I hope I was right, and the guards were just taking him to another wing of the prison. Something tells me there is a more sinister explanation for why he was dragged away.

Minutes stretch to hours but the scenery below remains unbroken. The rain forest reaches from horizon to horizon, an untouched and seemingly untouchable world. It looks so vast and unsullied that it's hard to believe the shadow of mankind could fall on it.

Ernesto is sitting near me on the iron floor, peering down at the green vista. "You made it sound endangered," I whisper to him. "We could never cut all this down."

He glances at the nearest guard, who is dozing off. "An area the size of France has already vanished, chopped down or burned," he whispers back. "In thirty years it will all be gone. Every animal. Every tree. And the people . . ."

His eyes settle for a moment on an old Indian man who was brought along on this mysterious expedition. The little man is sitting with his legs and arms folded, his body slumping in on itself, as if the weight of the world is very slowly crushing him.

But his glittering black eyes are alive, and as we fly over the rain forest in this airplane that must be so strange for him, I can see him watching the world he knows so well, drinking it in, as his gaze flits from treetop to treetop, from a flock of parrots to a winding silver river.

"Five centuries ago, when the Europeans first came knocking, more than ten million Indians lived in the rain forest," Ernesto tells me. "Today there are fewer than two hundred thousand. Each time a tribe disappears, we lose all the knowledge they have accumulated about the plants and the animals." He pauses as our plane turns sharply and begins to descend. "So the problem is not that the shadow of man is falling over the rain forest," he whispers. "Men have lived there for centuries." The dozing guard, sensing our descent, starts to shift and blink. Ernesto finishes quickly: "The problem is that the wrong men are coming now, for the wrong reasons. Soon it will be gone."

Our plane is now almost at tree level. I look down and see a gleaming river, and two large trucks waiting by its muddy bank.

It seems like we will fly right into the tree canopy, but at the last minute it parts and the Cessna—with its engine hiccuping wildly—touches down on the river. It skids to a stop near the trucks.

Ten minutes later I find myself in the back of an old flatbed truck, rumbling along on a logging trail. This is not the swampy rain forest that Gisco and I found when we were shot down in our balloon. This is nearly impenetrable dry-floored jungle, exploding in all directions with an improbable amount of life, like a child's kaleidoscope constantly turning to new and incredible patterns.

Towering trees piggyback over each other in a centuries-old wrestling match, straining toward the precious sunlight that is almost completely blocked out from our low vantage point. From the canopy, high above, vines dangle down hundreds of feet till their tendrils brush flowers with brilliant petals.

"It's unbelievable," I whisper to Ernesto as we cling to handholds. The truck bounces along over rocks and crashes through low branches that have grown across the path. "The variety of life here . . . and the intensity of it . . . is just . . ." I stop, at a loss for words. "Shocking."

He nods and rewards me with a little smile. "Would you believe that this planet is four and a half billion years old and there are more different species right here in the Amazon than have ever existed anywhere else, at any time, in that whole time span? Or that there are more species of fish in one Amazon lake than in the Atlantic?"

"I believe it," I whisper. "I see it all around me."

"No you don't," he corrects me. He pauses and seems to be listening and smelling and almost drinking the forest in as we crash through it on our big truck. "Most of it you can't see." His tone changes and his words become almost poetic. "The sloths high above us that live their whole lives in the trees, hanging upside down, so that the organs of their bodies are in different places than the organs of other mammals."

I look up. It's hard to imagine that in that canopy so high above us mammals are hanging upside down. Suddenly the air is split by outrageously loud shrieks.

Ernesto smiles. "You won't see howler monkeys either, but you can hear them. They're the loudest land animals. Their screams can be heard three miles away—the only living things that can make a louder sound are blue whales."

The monkey screams fade into the chirping, twittering mélange of jungle sounds. "And you won't see the bats or the snakes or the birds—you might catch glimpses of them, but you could live here your whole life and not see most of them. But they're all around us. Millions of them. Entire and unique species of them." His face tightens as our truck grinds to a stop. "But they won't be for much longer."

"Why?" I ask. "Why have they brought us here?"

Ernesto looks like he's about to answer, and then he just shrugs. I don't think he can bring himself to tell me. I guess I'll learn for myself soon enough.

The guards who took us from the prison appear with their guns held at the ready. My fellow captives and I are taken off the two trucks, released from our handcuffs, and handed large red metal cans. I can barely carry mine—it must weigh a hundred pounds.

"What's in the can?" I whisper to Ernesto.

He looks too miserable to answer. But then, taking pity on me, he gives me one last piece of advice. "After it starts, run behind the trucks to the plane. That's your only chance."

42

The guards direct us to start walking and pouring.

I tip the red metal can and immediately have my answer. Gasoline. The thick and noxious stench of refined crude seems out of place here—it conjures up fleeting images of gas pumps and car engines, and contrasts oddly with the green jungle all around us, and the intense natural aromas of the trees and flowers.

The guards direct us to empty our cans in designated areas, almost as if we're following some sort of pattern or master plan. When my can is finally empty, I'm handed another one, and then a third. My arms ache with the work, and the smell makes me queasy. But I'm even sicker with a dreadful premonition of what is about to happen.

I douse the trunks of great old trees and the outer layers of impenetrable thickets and I swish gasoline on verdant flower beds and tangles of vines. Finally, the gasoline is all gone.

We hurry back to the trucks, which have been turned around in our absence so that they now face down the path we rode up on, toward the river and the plane.

The guards climb quickly into the trucks. They still hold their guns at the ready, aimed out the windows at us to keep us away.

One guard remains outside just long enough to light a cigar. He takes two puffs, and then touches the glowing ash to a bottle-like container with a long fuse.

He draws back his arm and steps forward, hurling the bottle high and far, like a centerfielder making a long throw to home plate. He doesn't wait for the projectile to land, but rather dives into the nearest truck. Immediately, both flatbeds head back out of the forest along the logging trail.

Ernesto and the other prisoners don't hesitate either. They take off after the trucks at as close to a sprint as they can manage. Most are weak from confinement and malnutrition, and some can only manage a stumbling shuffle. Still, they flee with wild desperation, dodging overhanging branches and even pushing each other off the path when necessary. It's a mad, pathetic scramble.

I lag behind for a second, fascinated by this odd race. And then I suddenly understand why they're running for their lives. The homemade bomb that the guard threw lands and ignites. And the rain forest seems to explode around me.

It's not a single circumscribed boom, it's more of a dull roar— I recall the jaguar's cry that scared Gisco out of the gondola. But that was a natural sound, with a beginning and an end. This roar is unnatural and endless.

I find myself running. Sprinting. Fleeing in a wild panic. Now I realize that when they directed us to pour the gasoline, they were laying down a pattern and creating their own way out. The bumpy logging road to the river is the only bridge through the flames—the sole possible escape from this inferno. The trucks are already almost out of danger, rumbling along a half mile ahead of us, nearly to the river and the plane.

For the rest of us, it will be a much closer call. I've always been a swift runner. Fastest in my school, in my town, in my whole county. I got a late start in this race, but now I'm making up for it, flying along at full sprint with my arms pumping and my legs churning.

The heat is all around me. It's like racing through the center of an oven. The rain forest is not green anymore—black smoke is billowing in all directions and has obscured everything. Red flames shoot out of that black cloud and singe my skin and sear my eyes and throat.

Earsplitting explosions go off all around me. Even though I'm terrified of being roasted alive, my mind remains clear and my senses keen. Perhaps this is my body's way of anticipating new dangers. I realize the explosions are giant old trees popping apart from the heat. And then the forest leviathans start to fall.

Till now, the jungle canopy has been its own mysterious world, hundreds of feet up, glimmering in shadow. I crashed through it in the balloon, and I've glided over it from above, so I know it's up there. I also understand it's connected to the forest floor by the massive tree trunks that stretch skyward and the vines that dangle down. But the treetop realm seemed to exist in its own separate and magical space, with its own birds, animals, and insects.

Suddenly the canopy is rent as a giant tree comes crashing down. The ground literally trembles. As the old Methuselah of the forest falls, its leaves and branches crackle yellow and red in the ground flames. A family of parrots fly out of a nest and ignite in midair. Some are flash-fried. Others manage to fly on for a few seconds while burning, and then suddenly veer off and down at odd angles, screeching pitifully till they slam beak-first into the rocky ground.

Crash, a second giant tree falls, and then a third. The green jungle sky is literally collapsing down on us. Suddenly the race for survival includes all sorts of strange denizens of the high branches, most of them ill equipped for flight on land. I see them dying all around me in horrific, fleeting images as I run for my own life.

A family of monkeys leap off a branch of a fallen tree and try to stay ahead of the flames. They look terribly human as they scamper along. The youngest monkey hitches a ride on his mother's back, but she can't carry him at this pace. He shakes off and tries to scramble forward on his own, but the fire overtakes him.

He opens his mouth and gives a scream that is lost in the hiss and pop of wood splitting and sap steaming. And then he is incinerated in an instant as his family members run on ahead.

I see what I think must be a sloth. It's brown and nearly two feet long, and I bet it's graceful enough moving through the tree canopy upside down. Here on land, it's a three-toed slowpoke—it doesn't have a chance in this frantic footrace. As a wave of flame breaks over it and its fur catches fire, the sloth rolls on its side and screams.

I see the river up ahead. The trees around me are crashing and popping and hissing in a deafening cacophony. I overtake the old Indian man who I saw gazing out of the Cessna. He can't run anymore. As I pass him, he sits down on the road, facing away from the fire. He opens his mouth . . . Perhaps singing a prayer or calling to a God. I glance back and see the flames consume him.

Ten of us were chosen from the prison. Seven make it back to the river. We splash and run and swim to the plane. The Cessna's engine is already on. They weren't planning to wait for us.

Seconds later we're airborne, flying over the burning forest. From the air the cloud of smoke looks like a hungry monster as the fire chews its way through pristine jungle with sudden, savage bites. I watch it for a few more seconds and then turn away.

Ernesto is sitting near me, also watching, his face black with cinders and soot. He meets my eyes and says softly, "Colonel Aranha knows exactly what he's doing. To break a man's spirit, force him to kill what he loves most."

✳

43

Gisco was right about the mosquitoes. They come out before sundown, and drone around us all night long.

I hear their hungry whine, slap at them when they bite, and try to forget everything I ever learned in school about malaria and other tropical diseases. We have other unwelcome night visitors, too. Tiny black flies seem to seep right through the prison walls in soupy clouds, landing on our faces and nipping at us. Centipedes slither their way up drains. Spiders like hairy helicopters spin down from the ceiling and tiny reddish brown worms tunnel in sideways through cracks in the walls.

I lie awake night after night, wondering what will be the next loathsome variety of exotic jungle vermin to take a bite from the Jack Danielson buffet. As the long hours drag by, I can't stop myself from reliving the burning rain forest in a vivid waking nightmare.

I smell the stench of the gasoline. Hear the roar of the explosion. Feel the blast-furnace heat. And then trees are popping and crashing around me, and on the walls of the cell I see the desperate face of the young monkey as he slips off his mother's back, and of the Indian man praying on the logging road as the flames consume him.

I ask Ernesto why they burned the forest. "In four months, it will be seeded with rice or soy," he explains. "The grains will go to feed cattle who will end up as hamburger meat in Western fast-food restaurant chains. So, acre by acre, our beautiful rain forest becomes millions of double cheeseburgers."

Even without the torture of waking nightmares and ravenous

mosquitoes, it would be impossible to get a good sleep in Colonel Aranha's prison. There are twenty-three of us wedged into a cell that could comfortably hold ten men. During the day, when we're standing, and a few of the men are taken out for various chores, it's tolerable. At night the situation becomes unbearable.

We have no mattresses, so we sleep on the hard stone floor, each of us seeking a little space and privacy. When one man turns over, it sets off a chain reaction as bodies flip like dominoes and arms and legs flail in the dark. When one of our sick cell mates vomits or has diarrhea, the cell reeks.

The boy from the Andes adapts to this wretchedness with surprising ease. Given his brutal childhood in the mountains, I guess this is not a total surprise. At night he sleeps near me, perhaps seeking comfort or protection, but during the day he seems happy and fearless.

He even gets a name. His new friends, who play soccer with him in a corner of the cell during the day, christen him "Mudinho," which seems to be an affectionate way of saying "little mute" in Portuguese. He appears to like having a name—each time someone calls it out he flashes a quick smile.

I ask everyone again about P.J., but there is no new information. Some claim to have seen a girl matching her description, escorted quickly and under heavy guard. Others, who are taken out daily to clean the prison, say they occasionally manage to exchange gossip with prisoners in different cell blocks. They have heard rumors of a beautiful girl kept all alone in a special cell, whose desperate cries and sobbing prayers are in English.

I'm haunted by these stories, and by the suspicion that they've heard other, even grimmer, rumors about her that they're keeping from me. I feel that she's very close. Sometimes, in the middle of the night, I'm certain I can hear P.J.'s voice crying faintly for help. It always merges into the drone of a mosquito that one or another of my cell mates slaps with a curse.

The sad truth is I've come all the way to the Amazon to find her, and we may now be only a few hundred yards from each other, but P.J. doesn't have a clue I'm here.

After the terrible adventure of setting fire to the forest, I am kept in the cell day after day. There is no exercise yard and I am never selected for chores. The tedium is, in its way, worse than any torture. Sleepless nights follow dreary days in a numbing chain that quickly drains all my strength and hope. And then, after five days of waiting, something truly shocking happens.

In the late morning of our sixth day of captivity, guards' footsteps approach. We all back away to the far wall and wait.

Our cell's door is unlocked. And Gisco is pushed inside.

But it's not Gisco anymore.

44

The big dog is not leashed or chained, but he doesn't growl at the retreating guards. Nor does he look around the cell with the keen intelligence and paranoid curiosity about his surroundings that Gisco always displayed. Instead he plods into the cell, finds an empty corner, and lies down on his great belly.

I hurry over to him. "Gisco, what happened?"

He looks at me blankly, with friendly but glassy dog eyes.

I address him telepathically. Old friend, are you playing possum? Are they watching us? Did they plant some kind of a bug? Did you meet the colonel? Any news about P.J.?

No response. The line has gone dead. Gisco opens his mouth and lets out a yawn. His jowls shake and a sliver of drool spills out and trails down to the cell floor. Now I know something is very wrong. Gisco always had impeccable manners.

I pick up the great head and look directly into those enormous dog eyes. Gisco, I know you've been through something. I won't press you for details. But do you at least recognize me? Give me a sign, old fellow.

Gisco looks back at me and drools again.

To my horror, I realize that he's become a dog. A normal dog. All the humor and intellect is gone. I reach out and pat his shaggy head. His great paintbrush of a tail wags slowly, and he licks my hand. Then he lowers his snout to the ground and goes to sleep.

I try to break through to Gisco several more times, without success. He doesn't seem to know me, or even to recognize my smell. There are no outward signs that he's been harmed—no burn marks or fresh wounds on his body. But his brain has been scrambled. Finally I leave him alone. The truth is I can't bear to see him this way.

Mudinho takes care of him. Brings him his soup and sits by him while he laps it up. Cleans up after him. Strokes his ears and back. Gisco returns the affection, sleeping next to the boy that night, and sitting near him in the cell the next morning, watching him play soccer, displaying that special bond that has existed between boys and dogs for thousands of years.

I can't help remembering that Gisco wanted to leave him in the Andes, and then feed him to the caimans. I guess it's not surprising that a boy who had his tongue cut out should forge a special bond with a dog who has been cruelly stripped of his remarkable communicative powers.

I don't have long to ponder my comrade's condition. The day after Gisco is brought to our cell in such sad shape, the guards return. This time they come for me.

I am not led out with nine other cell mates to burn another forest. They take me alone.

They march me beneath a hole in the ceiling and yank on a chain. The slightly brownish water that cascades down is lukewarm but I don't complain. It's the first shower I've had in a long time. They give me a bar of soap, and watch me all the time I clean myself, perhaps to make sure I don't have a weapon hidden.

After I towel off, they toss me clean shorts and sandals. Clearly I'm about to be presented to someone of enough consequence that they don't want to offend him by ushering me in filthy and stinky.

I have a pretty good idea who I'm about to meet, and it scares me. On the other hand, I've sat in the dank cell long enough. If it is Colonel Aranha, I have a few very pointed questions I want to ask him about P.J. and Gisco.

And then we're on the move again. A fast march through endless corridors. The guards prod me along, their guns always at the ready. The colonel didn't squander much money on decor. The walls are unpainted, the lights dim, the thick iron bars on doors and windows are rusted.

Faces watch me from between those bars as we hurry past. Women. Children. They don't cry out—they seem silenced by a complete and crushing sense of hopelessness.

We climb steep stairs to a new level. Cells in better condition. Most of them are empty, doors yawning open, awaiting their next occupant. They're small and windowless—isolation cells. Every now and then we pass a locked door, and hear screams or moans from inside. The few prisoners on this sequestered ward seem to have been driven insane by the colonel's special brand of hospitality.

The guards all look human—there's no sign of Dark Army cyborgs or chimeras. I guess Colonel Aranha has gone to such trouble setting up his impersonation of a Brazilian Army officer that he doesn't want any ghouls from the future to risk exposing his charade.

We come to the end of the corridor. One door, all by itself. Something familiar about it.

I've seen it before. In a dream.

The door slowly swings open. I glance inside.

There's P.J.! Standing in the center of the room. Arms shack-led above her head. Head lolling to one side, almost on her shoul-der. She's facing toward me, but she doesn't react at all. Then I see that she's blindfolded.

"P.J.!" I shout.

Her head moves quickly. Jerks up. Her mouth opens wide to scream, but her words come out softly, more of a prayer than a plea. It's as if she's afraid of believing that she's heard what she's heard, and that I'm really here. "Jack? Jack Danielson?"

I take a few running steps toward her before three burly guards grab me. Together they must weigh more than six hundred pounds, but they can't hold me back. I drag them forward like a tackling sled. "P.J., it's me. I've come for you!"

And now she believes. I know it because her voice is no longer a prayer. It's a full-throttle wail of desperation. *"Jjjaaaaacccckkkk!"*

I'm just outside the door, dragging what feels like the Brazil-ian national rugby team. They're holding my feet, pinning my knees, clinging with their full weight to my arms and shoulders, but they still can't stop me. For a moment I'm sure I'm going to drag them all right into that cell. Then something soft and foul-smelling is clamped over my face. A towel. Soaked in a noxious chemical.

The acrid smell crawls into my nose and mouth. My knees go weak. I surge forward one final time and then I fall, and as the blackness covers me, I hear P.J.'s voice bellowing out a very rea-sonable request: "Save me!"

45

Snow—a thick blizzard of it, billowing in the wind. Someone is watching me keenly from beneath the white drifts. Two glinting black eyes study me with tremendous concentration and intelligence. I feel dizzy and can't think clearly, but I sense deep down that something is terribly wrong. Then I recall the isolation cell and P.J.'s desperate scream, and I try to struggle to my feet. Strong hands grip me tightly and a soft, musical voice commands: "Don't move."

It's a voice used to being obeyed, and I find myself sitting back down and trying to focus my blurry vision and clouded thoughts. It's not a blizzard, but rather a man with flowing white hair. He's wearing glasses with thick black frames and surgical gloves and tending to me like a skilled doctor. I smell disinfectant. There's an orange flame as he lights something and holds it under my nose. "Breathe through your nose and exhale out your mouth."

I inhale and the bitter stench makes me cough from the pit of my stomach. Almost instantly my vision sharpens, and the fog clouding my thoughts dissipates. I look back with curiosity and undisguised hatred at the old man who just revived me.

"Old" is a misleading adjective for him. It suggests weakness and degeneration, but the army officer standing before me shows no traces of decay or infirmity. He looks enough like his son for me to recognize him. But Dargon was handsome and leonine—he had a dashing movie-star quality, and he dressed the part. This man has no need to show off. With his white hair, in his black-frame eyeglasses, with shelves of books all around him, he looks like a librarian on steroids.

And then there are his eyes. Not quite human eyes. Some basic soft, warm-blooded mammalian quality is missing. They're the empty eyes of a predator without the slightest glimmer of a soul. Cold. Merciless. Spidery.

"I am Colonel Aranha," the musical voice says. "But then, I see you've already figured that out. You recover quickly, my young friend. You remind me quite a bit of your father. You have his strength, and his determination. I hope for your sake you have more wisdom."

This would probably be a good time for me to try to exercise self-control, but I hear myself growl back, "And you remind me of your son. You have his cruelty and his arrogance. I remember that arrogance especially well—it was flashing in his eyes the last time I saw him, just before I threw him into a volcano."

At the mention of his son's death, the colonel tenses. I have the feeling he may lash out at me, but instead he gives me a tight-lipped smile. "Brave words from a young mouth. But we have much to talk about and little time. Where shall we start?"

"What did you do to Gisco?" I demand.

"It's not a name I'm familiar with."

"My dog."

"Ah, yes. A most interesting specimen of canine. After many questions were asked and few were answered, and I started to lose my patience, he had the audacity to open up his mind and take me on. Imagine a chess match, played violently and on many levels simultaneously. How courageous of him to challenge me, knowing who I was."

"What did you do to him?"

"I returned him to his true form, his essence. He was a dog who had learned too many tricks. So I made sure he won't jump through those fancy hoops again. Now he eats. He barks. He lifts a leg and urinates. It's enough."

"It's not enough. He was my friend, and he's worth ten of you."

"Your loyalty to him speaks well for you," the colonel says. "But then it was loyalty that brought you here. If I'm not mistaken, you came to save a damsel in distress."

I look back into those glittering, soulless eyes. "You know exactly why I'm here. You arranged it so that door would swing open and I would see P.J. It's probably a negotiating trick—you want me to know that she's at your mercy. Well, get this—if you hurt her, I'll kill you."

"Don't ever threaten me," he responds quickly. "I have already hurt her, and I will again if I so please . . ."

I jump at him and throw the best kick of my life. Eko, who taught me martial arts on the Outer Banks, would be proud of this kick. It comes at lightning speed, snapped out straight from a horizontal position, the ball of my foot rocketing toward his chin.

He reacts with a level of speed beyond what humans are capable of. Catches my ankle in midair. Holds it there, in a viselike grip, so that I'm doing a standing split.

His head flashes forward, to my sandaled foot, held immobile. I see the glint of white teeth, or are they a spider's fangs? Then I feel a hot flash of pain that makes me cry out. As I twist and turn to try to end the agony I hear bones crunching.

Then he releases me and I fall to the floor and stare uncomprehendingly at my right foot. It's not just bloody, it looks different. Slowly I realize that he's just gnawed off my little toe.

46

I roll around on the floor in agony, blood flowing. It feels like my whole leg is on fire. The pain almost makes me pass out.

Colonel Aranha watches me writhe. A spot of my blood gleams on his right cheek, and he wipes it off with a white handkerchief. "We'll have to try again," he says finally. "It's imperative that we talk. Let me give you something for the pain."

He walks to what looks like a fisherman's tackle box, and returns with a bottle of bright green liquid. When he bends toward me I pull back and clench my fists. "Don't be a fool," he says. "If I wanted to harm you further, you must know now that you couldn't stop me."

I let him squirt some of the green liquid on me. The blood immediately clots and the painful throbbing lessens. In seconds my whole foot goes completely numb. "Better?" he asks.

I nod.

"Shall we try again? Perhaps we jumped into things too quickly the first time around. Let's go a little slower. If I'm not mistaken, this is your first visit to the Amazon. Impressive, isn't it?"

I can't believe a man who just bit off one of my toes wants to exchange polite banter. I look up at him and demand through gritted teeth, "If you find it so damn impressive, why are you destroying it?"

"I'm not destroying anything," he assures me. "I'm just the facilitator. Would you like to see how it works?"

I don't bother to answer. He's like Dargon—so used to being obeyed that his whims have the force of royal edicts.

Suddenly, cottony green holographic images flash across the floor from wall to wall, like a 3-D shag carpet. It's a miniature of the rain forest, complete with rivers and mountains. "Mato Grosso and Pará states," he tells me. "Virgin rain forest. All I'm doing is opening it up by encouraging the building of a few thousand roads."

"Roads to where?" I ask.

"Mahogany trees," he answers. "If loggers spot a valuable tree, they'll cut a road for miles so that it can be dragged out.

Once those roads are cut, the forest can be developed. Other loggers will pour in to harvest the less valuable hardwoods. The more that's cut, the more becomes available. The animals will be hunted for bush meat. The land will be cleared for farming. So the whole trick is getting loggers to cut that first road."

"How much money do you bribe them with?"

"I don't have to offer them anything but information," he explains. "Their greed does the rest. Mahogany is the 'green gold' of the Amazon. A single tree can be worth thousands of dollars. But even the tallest trees can be hidden beneath the jungle canopy. So I designed the technology to pinpoint them by their chemical fingerprints. Would you like to see every mahogany tree in the Amazon?"

Suddenly red dots start flecking the green carpet, and each time one appears there's a PING sound. It becomes a rising crescendo of PINGs as hundreds and then thousands of the red dots appear, alone and grouped in clusters. "This is what I give the loggers," the colonel says. "They build the roads. And the roads open up the forest."

"Loggers chasing mahogany didn't have anything to do with the trees your guards made us burn down," I tell him.

The colonel grins. Ernesto was right—he does have a sense of humor, albeit a sick one. "I thought you might find that little outing interesting. It's incumbent on a warden to make sure his prisoners get enough recreation," he says. "You must have run quite fast to survive."

I remember sprinting through the black clouds of smoke, fleeing for my life. "It was beautiful, pristine forest, filled with life. Why did you make us burn it?"

"There are a few misguided heroes in our government who can't be bribed or threatened," he explains. "They've set vast tracts of land aside for the Indians, and sometimes even I can't get at them. Torching the trees ends the argument. Once the forest is gone, the Indians retreat. And I can bring in foreign investors to plant soy. A few cans of gasoline is all it takes to develop the most sheltered parts of the forest."

"You're not interested in developing anything," I almost growl at him. "You just want to ruin it all."

"How easy it must be for a brash young American to make that accusation," he answers. "Tell me, what corner of the United States, from Alaska to the Everglades, was sacred when America was transforming itself into the richest industrial nation in the world?"

I think back to what I know of American environmental history over the last two centuries and I can't find a good answer. From the near extinction of the buffalo to acid rain, from the bad farming techniques that led to the Dust Bowl to the *Exxon Valdez* spill, I know our own record of preserving natural beauty is not a distinguished one.

He reads my face and smiles. "Did China or Russia show any restraint in developing their own resources? Does Chernobyl ring a bell? Or the damage being done to Siberia and the Russian Arctic by the oil industry? Do you know the harm the Three Gorges Dam is inflicting on Chinese wildlife? Why should the Amazon be any different? It's not a treasure that the whole world owns—it's the possession of a striving nation. And we have the right and the duty to develop it to feed our children and take our place among the powerful nations of the world."

I can't argue history with him: he has deeper knowledge and a far more sweeping vantage point. So I make it personal. "Cut the crap. You're no Brazilian patriot, interested in feeding the poor. You're the leader of the Dark Army. I struck a blow against you when I used Firestorm to save the oceans. So you're trying to poison the future by ruining the lungs of the planet."

His face darkens threateningly, like the sky before a tropical storm. "Okay, to use your charming phrase, let's cut the crap. I can imagine what Dannite lies you've been fed. So you're pure and wholesome children of God, while we're Dark Army abominations who don't even deserve the spark of life? I find your father's definitions narrow and very self-serving, and I have news for you both."

He steps toward me and flexes his muscles, and his shirt shreds and pops off him. His eyes are glowing now—his superhuman intelligence coupled with his subhuman vitality makes him seem at once near-divine and at the same time bestial and despicably loathsome. "You have no idea the misery you caused among my faithful when you used Firestorm," he hisses. "Seven hundred years of bitter warfare reversed by one ignorant boy. My loyal followers—tens of millions of life-forms with just as much right to the planet as anyone else—suddenly in full retreat, pushed to the brink. You healed the earth, but in so doing you doomed all those who were designed or bred to flourish in its decay. We will not yield the future."

He picks me off the ground and slams me against a wall again and again, so hard that it feels like my spine will crack. I try to fight back, but I'm helpless in his grasp. "You foolishly turned the future to light, and now I am switching it back to darkness. All will be as it was. Your father and his Caretaker whelps will melt away in the unfiltered radiation of the sun, they will choke in the sludge of dark oceans, blow away in the howling winds, and be battered down by ice storms. My minions will live on and multiply. That is the fate I decree for the earth. And only one man can possibly stop me. Where is he?"

His hand slides to my throat. He's pinning me to the wall in a choke hold that will kill me in seconds. I gasp and gag as his fiery orange eyes bore in on me.

He eases up, so that a tiny puff of air threads its way into my lungs. "Where is that cowardly shaman?" he demands again. "I know that's why you are here. Tell me where he is or you will die the most agonizing death imaginable. And for no reason at all, because I'll find him eventually on my own. Tell me and you're free to go. Where is that accursed trickster? Where is Kidah?"

I look back into his cold, merciless eyes and whisper, "I can't possibly tell you . . . because I don't know. But you're wrong, I'm not here for Kidah. I came for P.J."

For a moment, I'm certain he will strangle me. As I start to black out, he lets me sink to the floor and lie there gasping.

I don't see him make a signal, but three of his uniformed henchmen hurry in. He motions for them to take me away, and they hoist me to my feet.

He looks at me for a second, eye to eye. "You're a brave boy," he whispers. "Your father is a courageous man, too. But everyone has a limit. Once you see the death I have in store for you, you'll tell me everything."

47

My numb right foot won't support weight and the three guards don't seem inclined to carry me, so they just drag me roughly along corridors and down steep flights of steps.

As we move through the gloom, my guards grow nervous. They're tough-looking men with scars, who have plainly dished out and received their share of punishment, but with every step we take they become increasingly agitated. Frightened. "Terrified" would not be too strong a word.

My imagination runs wild picturing what is waiting at the end of this labyrinth. Is it some high-tech torture from the future, or will it be something more primitive?

I recall Dargon and his great white sharks. As we traverse a gloomy corridor I try to imagine what fearsome Amazon denizens his deranged dad may keep as house pets.

A circular black door becomes visible—it looks like the entry hatch to a submarine. At the sight of it my three guards slow till they're almost walking backward. They begin arguing in whispers, till the burliest of them stops and utters a gruff command. The two smaller guards lead me unhappily onward.

I smell something salty. Decaying leaves? Brackish water? It leaves a slight tangy taste on my tongue.

The guard holding my right arm begins trembling. He does his best to hide it, but he soon turns pale and starts breathing in gasps. I glance at the guard on my other side. He's clutching a small crucifix.

We reach the round door. Neither of them wants to touch its metal handle. I hear something stirring inside. Is it singing? No, it's some kind of oscillating whisper.

The guard on my left reaches out with the tips of two hesitant fingers and pulls the door open, and we enter.

It's a large and well-lighted chamber, about the size of an ice rink. But it's not ice that glimmers under the bright lights. It's water—shallow water, in a deeply recessed pit. The colonel has his own wading pool.

Spigots are mounted on opposite sides, and twin streams of water arc out of them and splash down ten feet to the surface of the pool in a continuous liquid whisper.

I look down into the pit expecting to see caimans or clouds of toothy piranhas, but it's just clear water, empty as a bowl of broth.

A narrow footbridge spans the pool. On the far side of that bridge I see the colonel. He's now wearing plastic bags over his boots and a shower cap on his head.

A dark figure stands behind him. I can't make out the man's features—he's wearing a black mask.

My two guards are holding their breath. Neither of them can take their terrified eyes from the glistening pool.

The colonel utters a dismissive command, and the two guards bolt back out the door and slam it shut behind them.

"Welcome," the colonel says. "We can continue our conversation here without any disturbance. I guarantee you no one who knows of the existence of this room is likely to intrude, at least willingly."

"I saw your guards nearly piss their pants," I tell him. "What the hell is down there? The creature from the black lagoon?"

"Not a bad guess," the colonel says with a chuckle. "I really can't blame my guards. They grew up near the forest and the horror stories of childhood never fade."

I peer down into the pool. The surface eddies as if something invisible is swimming beneath. "Horror stories about what?" I ask. "Ghost fish?"

"A horror that is not supernatural but is far beyond your imagination," he assures me. "But we were discussing my plans for the Amazon. You were wrong about the rain forest being the lungs of the planet. That was a phrase popularized twenty years ago, but even the scientists of your time have already discredited it. Lots of oxygen is produced here, but so is plenty of carbon dioxide."

"Probably from all the fires you help start," I suggest, straining to get a look at the dark figure behind the colonel. I'm pretty sure he's wearing a black cowl. Is he a torturer or executioner? Perhaps he's some kind of sadistic fish or animal trainer whose expertise involves unleashing whatever monstrosity swims in the pool below.

"The Amazon plays a far more complex role than just being the lungs of the planet," the colonel explains. "It's more like a giant air conditioner, with a benign effect on global climate. It's also a major repository of fresh water, which will become the most vital resource in the years ahead. And like the coral reefs that my son was so fond of, the Amazon is one of the earth's irreplaceable breeding grounds. Its diversity is without parallel."

"So what happens when you destroy it?" I ask. "You switch off the air conditioner and dry up the fresh water?"

The colonel shrugs. "The mathematics of forecasting environmental destruction over a millennium are beyond you. It will be easier for you to think of it this way: strange as it may sound, the planet has a consciousness."

I think back to the moment I held Firestorm in my hand, and felt the anger of the earth seething out from the mysterious gem. "I sort of know what you mean. But what does that have to do with the Amazon?"

"Your father and Kidah are trying to awaken and enlist that consciousness in their cause—to create a partnership in order to defeat me. I won't let that happen. Sure, the damage I'm inflicting on the Amazon will have detrimental effects a thousand years from now, but it's also a blow aimed squarely at the meddling consciousness of nature itself. I'm making it back off, so that we humans can fashion our own destiny. None of which will affect your world in the slightest. In your lifetime, the climate changes won't kill you. The dearth of fresh water won't hurt the richest countries. Nor will you miss the variety of frogs and snakes and beetles in this wilderness. So even if I win, you personally have nothing to lose. Which brings us to the question at hand. What shall I do with you?" He lets the question hang in the tangy air.

"I'm sure you've already decided."

"Not completely," he admits. "To work things out, we need to come closer, metaphorically and literally. So, young Jack, why don't you take a few steps onto that footbridge?"

"Not till you tell me what's in the water."

"I thought you might hesitate. Perhaps this will change your mind," he says, and pulls the black hood off the man standing behind him.

48

It's not a torturer. Nor an executioner.

As the dark cowl comes off the immobile figure, long auburn hair cascades down. A pretty face looks back at me expressionlessly. Pale lips part but cannot speak. Two frightened hazel eyes plead for help. It's P.J.—he's hypnotized her or drugged her so that she can't move, but I can tell she knows I'm there.

"P.J.!" I cry out. *"Are you okay?"*

"She's fine," the colonel assures me. "She struggled a bit, which made bringing her safely into this room rather difficult, so I restrained her for her own protection."

For a second I lose control and nearly try to jump across the pool at him. "Let her go, you spidery bastard, or I'll rip your heart out, if you even have a heart."

He looks back at me, and places one hand behind P.J. "As a matter of fact, I do have a heart," he informs me, "and it beats in pretty much the same rhythm as yours. The blood that flows through my veins is every bit as warm and red as your own. And there was a woman a thousand years from now whom I loved as much as you love this bright-eyed gamine, but she was taken away from me forever by your father and his so-called noble warriors."

The colonel's voice remains soft, but his tone sharpens to a knifepoint. "And I had a son with that woman, whom I loved despite his many faults. The impetuousness of youth, unease at the weight of the crown, all these I understood and forgave. My son was also taken from me—he died a cruel death, falling from a great height into a molten furnace. I believe you know the details. So yes, I had a heart, as capable of love as your own, but you and your father have already ripped it out by its roots and I'm tempted right now to return the favor."

He grabs P.J. by the back of the neck and pushes her forward a step. "Walk onto the bridge, Jack, or I throw your ladylove into the pool."

"*Don't you dare hurt her!*" I shout, and my desperate plea bounces in crazy echoes off the stone walls.

"It's very simple—you walk or she swims." He shoves her again. Her toes are now just inches from the pit. There's no time to argue, no time to think. I step out onto the bridge. It's narrow, but as long as I'm careful there's really no danger of falling.

"I knew you wouldn't disappoint me," the colonel says. "Contrary to what geneticists claim, I'm convinced bravery is an inherited trait. Your father remained defiant even when he was at my mercy, as you are now. Keep walking."

I move my arms out wide from my body, and rivet my eyes to the narrow beam. It's not wood—it's hard and shiny, like a plastic. I take a few more cautious steps. My right foot is numb and it's difficult to balance. I'm a third of the way across now. I try to ignore the water beneath the beam, but I can't stop myself from stealing glances. It swirls and gleams.

"You're wondering what's down there," the colonel says, and it's not a question. He knows exactly what I'm thinking. "What did you expect when you walked in?"

"Piranhas," I say. "Or caimans. It doesn't matter."

"It may matter a great deal to you," the colonel corrects me. "People have so many misconceptions about painful deaths. What they fear most is what they should fear least. Trust me, I have experience in these areas."

"I'm sure you do," I admit through gritted teeth.

"A school of piranhas would tear you apart in seconds. The agony would be mercifully brief. Caimans drown their prey, which is a pleasant death in relative terms. What I have here is of a different order entirely. You see, a truly painful death depends on two factors—slowness and method. And then, of course, there is the intangible of mental suffering, and particularly of fear, that can add immensely to physical pain. Take another step, please."

Is it my imagination or is the smooth beam beneath me narrowing? Either that or my feet are growing larger. I take a small step, now moving much more slowly and carefully. The colonel's voice pierces my concentration.

"Experts on vampire bats like to claim that they are the only animals that feed exclusively on blood," he says. "They're almost right. In the entire world, there is only one other such creature. Westerners dubbed it the vampire fish. But the natives here call it the candirú."

The water beneath me swirls as if someone is twirling a straw through it. Suddenly the lights in the room start to dim. The bridge under my feet continues narrowing. When I started walking across, it was more than a foot wide. Now it can't be more than six inches. I feel myself start to tremble, and fight against the panic.

"Where is Kidah?" the colonel demands. "Tell me all that you know and I promise I will spare you. Deny me, and you will learn why the candirú is the most dreaded creature in this vast feeding ground known as the Amazon."

I look back at him, and at P.J. standing beside him, and I try to keep the terror from my voice. "If I knew, I would tell you. I have no reason to protect him. I came here to save P.J. All I know is that Kidah's supposed to be here, somewhere, hiding. I'm sorry."

"Yes, you will be," the colonel promises. "Just as the loggers can't cut down mahogany trees until I reveal their exact locations, I can't destroy Kidah unless you tell me where he's hiding. I know he's here. That's hardly new information. But where, Jack? Perhaps if I tell you a bit more about my spiny friends it may loosen your tongue. Their scientific name is *Vandellia cirrhosa*. But 'candirú' has a much more dramatic ring, don't you agree? They're about an inch long. Translucent. Their fins and spines are white, so they can't be seen in the water. But they're down there. Thousands of them. I breed them."

He pushes P.J. forward, until her toes touch the edge of the pit. "We've reached the point of no return—the sheer precipice of the moment of truth. Walk to me, Jack. Or I shove her in."

49

The light in the room is almost gone. The bridge has narrowed to less than five inches. It shimmers beneath me like an ebony ribbon tapering into gloom.

I stop walking, stop moving, stop breathing. The room goes totally dark. I remember running through pitch-black marsh channels with Eko on the Outer Banks, and I use the sixth sense I developed there to keep from falling.

"Superb balance, Jack. I see that darkness is your friend. I am also fond of it." The colonel's eyes gleam like a cat's in the blackness. "Do you believe in an afterlife? I don't. Once you die, you're mud."

Suddenly light starts to come back on. But not from overhead. From the sides of the pool. It's a strange light, a purplish glow that fluoresces in from the edges.

"But while you're alive, you're almost akin to a god," the colonel whispers. "And how especially sweet to be young and in love. This girl cares for you very deeply, Jack. Aware that you were to blame for her captivity, even in her moments of deepest misery, she would not renounce you. Now you can reward her. Tell me everything you know and I'll let you both go. You can live another sixty years together in bliss. Where is Kidah?"

"Don't you think I would tell you if I knew?" I plead, and fear shakes like a white flag in my voice. "I don't even know him. I've never met him. I don't owe him anything. I don't owe my father anything. He betrayed me and lied to me. I hate them all. But I do love P.J. I beg you to spare us. I'll do anything you say. But I can't tell you something if I don't know it."

The pulsing purple light has now radiated from the edges of the pool to its center. And in that center, directly beneath me, I glimpse a churning mass. It looks like a giant knot, trying very hard to untie itself.

"You might still be holding back from me," the colonel growls. "Your father was capable of such strength. But we all have limits. The most primal human fear, Jack, is not being torn apart or even devoured. It's being invaded by a foreign entity, being eaten from the inside out. The candirú is the only vertebrate that parasitizes humans. We're not its primary food source. It likes to lodge inside the gill flap of fish. It erects a sharp spine to hold itself in place. Then it feeds on the blood in the gills. When it has sucked sufficient blood, it detaches and swims out, and sinks into the river mud to digest its feast. The fish host swims away, not greatly harmed."

As the purple pulse-glow intensifies, I see that the knotted mass is really the shadowy reflection of a thousand tiny fish, swarming together and breaking apart. They're not swimming in the corners of the pool. They're hanging out right beneath me. Somehow, they know where I am.

"In humans, on the other hand," the colonel continues with relish, "the candirú is like a tiny kamikaze with teeth. It's attracted to blood and urine. It swims into an orifice—the urethra, the vagina, or the anus. It erects its spine and sucks blood. But then it can't swim out. It can only go deeper, continuing to feast on blood and tissue till the hemorrhages kill the host."

I can see them very clearly now. A thousand tiny snakelike shadows, coiling and untying beneath me, roiling the surface of the water with their hunger for blood.

The bridge continues to narrow. It can't be more than three inches wide now—the sides of my feet protrude over its edges. I keep my weight centered, and try to keep my concentration equally fixed. But that's nearly impossible as the colonel finishes his vivid warnings.

"And the pain, Jack! Think what it must be like to be eaten from the inside! They're insatiable, indefatigable. Legend says that they can even swim up a urine stream. It's unclear whether this is true, but I can tell you that natives on certain parts of the Orinoco don't ever relieve themselves into the river. Of course, if you and P.J. were to fall into this pool, they wouldn't have to resort to such extreme measures to get at you. You'd be coming right to their dinner table, so to speak."

His words stoke my rising fear, twisting it tighter, so that I tremble and have to move my arms quickly just to stay on the beam. I can picture myself dying in the horrible way he describes. And P.J., too, right next to me.

"You may have noticed that the surface of the water is five feet beneath the floor," the colonel drones on. "That's for safety— I wouldn't want any of the little devils to jump out when I come to visit them. But it also keeps anyone who falls into the pool from climbing out. The walls have been sanded down so that they're smooth, to make sure there are no fingerholds. Once you drop in, all you can do is splash around, hip deep, and wait for them. Or you can try to drown yourself, which is surprisingly difficult. The body's impulse to stay alive is remarkably strong, even with the certain knowledge that one would be far better off dead. Jack, if I can't persuade you to reveal Kidah's hiding place, perhaps someone else can. She's been following this whole discussion. Shall I let her talk to you for a few moments?"

P.J.'s voice is shrill and desperate, but also, even at this horrible moment, tender. "Jack, tell him what he wants! I want to see my parents again. I don't want to die here. Whatever it is, whatever secret you're protecting, it can't be worth this. I beg you, *please . . .*"

"*I don't know anything,*" I shout back.

"*Jack, he's holding me out over the pool!*"

"*I swear I don't.*"

The colonel's command booms over our panicked voices: "*Walk to me or I drop her, Jack.*"

"*I can't. It's too dark.*"

"*Walk!*"

I force myself to take a step. The plastic beam is an inch wide now—silhouetted against the purple pool below, it looks like a string. I'm doing a high-wire act over the most painful death imaginable. "*I'm coming.*"

"*Be careful, Jack!*"

I remember Eko's training. Once I bent sand grain by grain. Once I ran at top speed through a dark marsh, avoiding branches and holes by sensing their presence. I use that extra sense now. Step by step. Seeing the wire in my mind's eye and moving across it in measured steps . . .

"*Where is Kidah? Tell me and this will all be over. Otherwise I drop her!*"

"*Jack! For God's sake tell him everything!*"

"*Kidah came back over the centuries to stop you.*"

"*He can't stop me!*"

"*They believe he can. But they lost track of him.*"

"*Why did they need you?*"

"*They think I can help find him. But I don't have a clue. I don't know if he's in a town or out in the rain forest. I don't know if he's in a cave or on a mountaintop. I swear—I don't even know where to start looking!*"

It's not going to work. I can feel the bridge narrowing from a string to a wire, and then to a hair.

And he's going to drop P.J. in the pool. I'm close enough to the colonel to sense it. P.J. feels it, too. She's too terrified to scream out a warning, but I can hear it in her gasping breaths.

I start to tumble off the strand of plastic at the same moment he drops P.J. Time freezes.

I'm on the Outer Banks, on a beach, at sunset. Eko is teaching me to fly. "Steer with your whole body," she says. "You are a point of light, moving in the darkness."

I am a point of light now, above an abyss. I spread my arms and dive forward, and somehow grab P.J. as she screams and starts to plummet. My momentum carries us back over the edge of the pit to the stone floor.

✸

50

I lie there in darkness, holding P.J. tight. This girl. This girl from Hadley-by-Hudson who I love and have come so far to find. Only her. She clutches me back and whimpers, and I am crying, too.

I know we're still in grave danger. There's nothing I can do. The ordeal of crossing the bridge was too much for me. The panic that I suppressed for so long now seizes control. I'm exhausted. My legs cramp into Gordian knots. My right foot starts to throb. I shake uncontrollably.

I sense the colonel standing above us, watching. There's no way I can get up and fight him. We're at his mercy. But he doesn't push us into the pool. He doesn't strangle us.

I'm vaguely aware of time passing. Other men creep hesitantly into the room, summoned by their commander.

They stay back as he bends close to me, and his voice is soft and musical again. "Well done, Jack. I like survivors. I reward the brave. You told me what you know. It's of little use to me, but I will keep my side of the bargain and let you both go. Here are my terms. Leave the rain forest. Never return. Never help the People of Dann again, or I will find you."

I lie there on the stone floor, clutching P.J. and trying not to shiver. He's clearly waiting for some sort of response. Somehow I manage to look up at him and nod. Then I gasp, "My dog."

"You can take that mindless cur if you want."

"And the boy."

"Fine. I have no use for a tongueless twit."

I know I should stop. I can feel P.J.'s heart beating fearfully. I should quit while I'm ahead, and get her out of here. If he really is willing to let us go, we should make a beeline for the nearest exit and not look back till we're in North America. Still, I can't stop myself from gasping out, "Ernesto . . . and the kids in the cell . . ."

The colonel laughs. "Such nerve! Who are you? Moses? You want to lead your people out of bondage? The truth is, I have no use for them. Weak as they are, and diseased and addle-brained, they'll slow you down. But if you want them, you can have them. It will give me a chance to empty the stinking refuse from my prison. Take your chosen people and head out into the wilderness."

He nods to his henchmen. "Get them out of here."

Strong arms haul us up. P.J. and I won't release each other, so the guards half carry, half drag us to a door behind where the colonel was standing.

As we pass him, he reaches out and puts a restraining hand on my shoulder. It's a soft hand, but it tightens till it feels like he might snap my collarbone. His voice sounds in my ear: "Good-bye, Jack. I've told you the truth and I'm giving you a chance at a happy life, which is more than your own father ever did. Remember one thing—if you ever make contact with Kidah, or try to help the Dannites in any way, I'll find you and make you wish you had fallen into that pool with the candirú."

51

It's an armada of the pathetic. In twos and threes they are let out of their dark cells and stumble down to the river under the watchful eyes of armed guards.

P.J. and I stand near a dozen dugout canoes, holding hands silently, and we watch the sad parade approach. They limp and sway and lean on each other for support—men, boys, and even a few women and little kids. Some of them have tremors, others have been in prison for so long that they look terrified at the prospect of freedom. The colonel's phrase comes to mind—the weak, the diseased, and the addle-brained. He has indeed opened his prison's gates to cast out the wretched refuse of his teeming cells.

All the men and boys from my old cell are there. Mudinho, our young companion from the Andes, now looks to be inseparable from Gisco. He waves at me and smiles, glad that I'm okay and pleased to be out in the sunlight. Then he hops into a canoe and snaps his fingers, and Gisco bounds in after him and settles down by his feet. I watch him pat the dog's snout and give Gisco's ears a good scratch. The old Gisco would have bitten his fingers off, or at least made a bitingly sarcastic comment. But the new Gisco just drools and wags his mop of a tail.

I help P.J. into a canoe. We haven't spoken much since we were let out of the colonel's fish-tank torture chamber. I think she's experiencing post-traumatic shock—if that's possible, since our trauma is not over yet. She watches me at all times, as if afraid that if she so much as blinks too hard I may vanish into the steamy air.

I sit in front of her and grab a paddle. These canoes are not the sleek machine-tooled and outboard-powered craft that the colonel's soldiers used to rescue us from the caimans. The dugout P.J. and I clamber into is thirty feet long, and appears to have been chewed by fire from a single log. Its worn hull has an impressive assortment of nicks and knife slashes, not to mention dried chicken feathers glued on with blood.

My guess is that the colonel's men intercept fishermen and traders on the river and take whatever they want, including the old dugouts themselves. Our canoe must have belonged to a poultry vendor, who butchered his birds right on the bow. The other canoes in our group look equally decrepit. Something tells me we are being sent off into the wilds of the Amazon with the oldest, flimsiest, and leakiest vessels in the colonel's fleet.

I have no idea how I will steer this rudderless log downriver with only a flattened pole to paddle with, but Ernesto comes to my rescue. The self-declared governor general of the free and wild Amazon quietly takes control of the situation. He assigns the weakest of the prisoners to ride with the strongest, and the most experienced native paddlers to help the clueless settlers and city dwellers. P.J. and I fall into that last category, so Ernesto directs the Korubo chief himself to our canoe.

The chief has undergone a transformation. His eyes are alive now, his very skin seems to be waking up. He jumps into our dugout and pushes off strongly from the mud bank, and soon we are in the lead position, gliding swiftly downriver. Eko taught me to paddle a kayak on the Outer Banks, so even with the flattened pole I'm able to generate some power as he steers expertly from the back.

The colonel's compound extends for more than a mile and we pass impressive military fortifications and docks with gunboats. Then the river narrows, and a metal gate runs from bank to bank. At the bottleneck, two soldiers stand outside a concrete guard station. One cradles an enormous rocket launcher in his arms as lovingly as if it were a newborn. I get the feeling he'd like nothing better than to pick off our canoes for target practice.

We slow down as we approach the gate, till we're barely moving. The second soldier raises a cell phone and whispers a few words. Then he disappears into the guard station. A minute later we hear the whirring of electronic controls and the metal gate lifts like a drawbridge.

We paddle under it, and the current stiffens and sweeps us downriver. Soon the metal gate is just a pinprick of gleaming light against the lush background. When it vanishes behind a leafy curve in the bank, and the roof of the guard station sinks out of sight, I hear whooping and clapping and one Indian man breaks into song.

I understand their joy. "We made it," I whisper to P.J., turning to take her hand. "Now we're free."

She looks at me. I still have great trouble believing we're actually here together, in the Amazon. But it's undeniably P.J. in the flesh, barely two feet from me, in a fast-moving canoe, her long auburn hair trailing in the breeze.

The same soft lips I used to kiss when we necked in our favorite lookout over the Hudson, when I had nothing more to worry about than an algebra test, now part slightly. The bright eyes that used to dance when they saw me approaching her hall locker in the morning are clouded with shock and worry, but they focus on me.

P.J. hasn't said much since we escaped from the candirú pit, so I don't expect a reply. But she whispers back, "That place is living death, Jack. And that man . . ." She breaks off for a second, and then finishes bravely, "But I dreamed of you, and that gave me hope."

"I dreamed of you, too," I reply quickly. "Real vivid dreams, like I could see you and hear you and almost touch you. I knew you were in danger and it drove me crazy that I couldn't do anything. P.J., it's my fault that this happened. I'm so very sorry . . ."

I stop talking, explaining, and apologizing. She's gone again—disappeared into some safer place deep inside herself. There will be time for conversation later. Now we need to get away.

I resume paddling and try to concentrate on the dangers in the river ahead. From jaguars to candirú, I know how deadly this place can be, but I still feel oddly optimistic.

P.J. said it well—the colonel's prison was living death. Whatever exotic animal, vegetable, and mineral horrors the Amazon holds seem far less threatening than the human monster we've just left behind.

52

The Korubo chief paddles in a steady rhythm. The other canoes are strung out in a long chain behind us. Some of them have three or four passengers, others as many as ten. The chief's concentration is unceasing—his eyes sweep from bank to bank. He keeps us on a fairly straight course, but every now and then he veers to one side. He never offers an explanation for these changes of direction, but his reasoning often becomes alarmingly evident.

We barely avoid a column of black flies so tiny they're invisible from thirty yards away. I hear them before I see them—they swarm in a funnel cloud, in such a frenzy that they make the air hum. One of them lands on my arm and takes a bite before I flick it away. There must be billions of them in the tornado-shaped cloud that seems to reach from river to sky. As we pass close, the melodic hum sharpens to a shrill, voracious whine.

Later, just as we're about to pass under an enormous tree, the chief steers us into deeper water. The tree has long branches that overhang the river, with dark vines trailing down. As we paddle past, I notice that the thickest of the vines is yellow with black spots. It seems to sense our approach, and moves a few feet away!

P.J. spots it moving, and she puts a hand on my shoulder. "Jack! It's a giant snake!"

"Don't worry, it's just a big, dumb anaconda," I try to reassure her. But "big" doesn't begin to do justice to this colossal serpent. Its tail is wrapped around a high branch, its thirty-foot body dangles down, and its head is submerged. I follow the curve of its yellow neck beneath the surface and spot its trowel-shaped head riding the current. Only its nostrils poke above the water as it waits for something tasty to swim past.

The anaconda's slitted eyes rise slowly above the surface to study us. "It knows we're here!" P.J.'s hand trembles on my back.

"Canoes probably aren't high on the list of favorite anaconda foods," I tell her. "Anyway, I'm bringing you back to Hadley in one piece. I intend to personally walk you up the front steps and deliver you to your father."

I hesitate for a second, remembering my reception in our hometown, and decide not to mention that her parents called the police to arrest me, and that her dad took a swing at me. Instead I glance back at her and say, "They're okay, by the way. Your parents, I mean. I saw them a few weeks ago. They're very worried about you, but they're keeping faith."

P.J. doesn't say anything, but a tear rolls slowly down her

cheek. I wipe it away, and whisper, "Sorry, but I thought you'd want to know that." She nods very slightly, leans over, and kisses me on the neck.

I can tell she's getting stronger with every hour we put between ourselves and the colonel's dungeon. Soon we'll be able to have a real conversation. I look forward to that moment, but I also fear it. Will she believe what's happened? Can she ever find a way to forgive me?

Islands start popping up in the river like green buoys. Some of them are just tangles of swampy grass, others feature towering trees. They split the river in half and then in thirds, till we're completely lost in a shifting wonderland of green islets, bays, and inlets.

I have no idea where we're heading, and I don't really care. When we stop for the night there will be plenty of time to discuss routes and strategy. Right now I'm focused on taking care of P.J., and avoiding biting flies, half-submerged anacondas, and whatever other exotic dangers the dark waters conceal.

✳

53

We stop for the night on an island in the center of the river. It's just exposed grass and mud, with a grove of what look like mangrove trees. A danger light starts flashing in my mind—the island is inhabited! Several canoes lie side by side on the mud beach, just above the waterline. As we draw closer, I see that they're not canoes but giant black caimans, watching our slow approach with hungry, reddish yellow eyes.

I don't really want to hop out of our canoe with the caimans so close, but when the chief jumps into the chest-deep water I reluctantly follow his lead. Soon we're pulling our dugouts up the slippery bank, barely fifty feet from the latter-day dinosaurs.

"Won't they mind us intruding on their turf?" I ask Ernesto as we walk back to help with the other canoes. "How can we get a good night's sleep knowing they may decide to use us for a midnight snack?"

"Don't worry. Caimans are smart," our leader assures me. "They never take risks. They'll hear our voices, see our fire, and leave us alone. But since they're on the island, nothing else will come too close."

Using caimans as our personal security system seems like a dangerous plan, but this is not my world.

The sun touches the treetops, and the Amazon night starts to put its dark arms around us. The river glows a deep shade of purple-black. With every passing minute the animal-and-insect chorus rises in volume and intensity. Night feeders prepare to hunt. Are those frogs, calling to one another? Could that hungry roar be a jaguar? The one we met before screeched.

The fading light lends urgency to our need to make camp. Ernesto and the chief divide us up and assign tasks. P.J. and I are sent with a group of mostly women and kids to the grove of trees. I soon learn one reason we stopped here. The branches are heavy with a star-shaped fruit that has a slightly bitter taste but is quite edible.

We gather dozens of them. I put on a little juggling act for P.J., and one of the four fruits I have circling from hand to hand falls out of the loop and plunks me on the nose. The impact makes me lose my balance and tumble off a low branch onto the grass. I land gracelessly, on my butt. When I look up, several of the kids are laughing.

I glance over at P.J. and she's smiling, too. It's the most natural smile I've seen from her thus far.

When we get back with our fruit, I see that the other work

crews have been busy. There's a roaring fire going. I can't begin to describe how comforting a big fire is with the darkness of the Amazon all around us. Enormous leaves have been interlaced to form a sleeping platform. Someone's even managed to spear a few fish, and they're sizzling away on spits.

I must eat a dozen or so of the fruits, not to mention my share of fish. I see Mudinho chowing down also, and flipping bits of fish to Gisco, who gobbles them up before they hit the ground. At least my old traveling companion still enjoys a good meal.

When we finish eating I realize that night has fallen. Darkness doesn't really "fall" in cities, or even suburbs, but in the Amazon it comes down like the shadow of death itself. There's a depth and density to the rain forest night—the billions of eerie sounds as creatures devour weaker creatures, the swampy smells that ooze off the river, the shifting shadows that joust at the edges of the firelight—beyond anything I've ever experienced.

I try to be brave for P.J.'s sake, but the truth is the sounds make me jumpy, the smells seem to stick to my skin, and the shadows conjure up nightmares. I'll be very glad when the sun comes up.

Guards are posted, and the other members of our group find places to lie down on the sleeping platform. Gisco and Mudinho curl up near the fire, and both of them appear to fall asleep within seconds. They seem to have blind faith that the people sleeping on either side of them will somehow protect them. I hope the old saying about there being safety in numbers is rooted in truth.

"Should we catch some sleep?" I ask P.J. "We have a big day ahead of us. I think there's some space over there . . ."

But she takes my hand and draws me away from the sleeping platform, to the opposite side of the fire. "No," she whispers. "I think it's time for us to talk."

54

On a rock by a fire in the heart of the Amazon I sit down next to my high school sweetheart and prepare to explain to her the details of exactly how I came to destroy her life.

We're facing away from the fire, looking out at the shadowy bank and the wide, star-specked river. Every few seconds a fish breaks the surface to gobble an insect, and the ripples make the reflected Milky Way tremble and reshape itself. We're sitting so close that our shoulders brush. I put my arm around P.J., but she gently undrapes it and enfolds my fingers in her own, holding my hand on her lap, keeping me captive.

She's waiting for my story, and she has every right to hear it. I suck in a big breath, but I can't figure out what to say or where to begin. So I exhale silently.

P.J. has always understood me better than anyone. She comes to my rescue, speaking first, bringing us back to the unlikely place where it all started. "Do you remember the first time we kissed?" she asks softly.

"Of course. In the old gym," I reply, unsure where she's going but very content to follow. "Under the bleachers. On a Tuesday. I'll never forget it."

"After we broke apart we looked into each other's eyes, and then we kissed again," she reminds me softly. "The first kiss was just fun and recklessness and curiosity. But the second one was much more serious. It sealed it. Do you know why I kissed you that second time, Jack?"

It's a simple question, but I can't seem to come up with the right answer. "We'd been friends for so long. Since third grade," I mumble. "You must have known I was crazy about you. I used to dream about you. And we always respected each other so much. You laughed at my jokes. And—"

"Shut up," P.J. commands with a little chuckle, gently squeezing my hand.

"Okay. Sorry."

"It wasn't just that you liked me, Jack. A couple of other boys did, too."

"Dozens," I admit. "I was jealous of all of them."

"You had your share of female admirers," she reminds me. "It also wasn't that we were such good friends. Nor even how cute you looked under the bleachers that day, with those wide shoulders and those bright blue eyes of yours."

"What then?" I demand. "Pheromones? Did I smell nice?"

"You smelled okay," she admits grudgingly. "But you were no flower garden. No, it was something I saw in your eyes after that first kiss." P.J.'s whisper becomes softer. "A kind of genuineness . . . and sincerity. I knew somehow that I could trust you—that you weren't just a bozo jock with raging hormones. I especially knew that you'd always tell me the truth. And you always did." She lets go of my hand and moves a few inches away, so that our shoulders no longer touch. "So tell me the truth now."

"Okay," I whisper back. "But one question first: what if the truth doesn't make any sense?"

"The truth always makes sense," P.J. assures me, sounding more and more like the healthy, grounded, decisive girl I remember from Hadley. "That's why it's the truth."

"You're wrong about that," I tell her. "But judge for yourself. Here goes. The truth, the whole truth, and nothing but the truth." I suck in another big breath, and this time I know exactly where to begin. "It started that day I scored all the points in that stupid football game. Afterward, we went to the Hadley Diner to celebrate. I thought I saw a man's eyes flash. You laughed and said I must be on mind-bending drugs."

"I remember." P.J. nods. "People were taking your picture. I thought you must have seen a flashbulb . . ."

"There were no hallucinogenic drugs or camera flashes involved. A tall man's eyes flashed white to silvery. They marked me, somehow. And, even weirder, when I got home, my dad knew what it meant."

"What did your dad say?" she wants to know, drawn in.

So I tell her. Odd step by step, harrowing adventure by adventure, mind-blowing event by event.

P.J. doesn't listen passively or accept things on faith. She interrupts with probing questions.

"Why didn't you at least call me?" she wants to know when I describe my escape to Manhattan. "Or e-mail me?"

"I was afraid you were being watched. I wasn't sure who was chasing me, but I knew they were powerful. I was scared that if I tried to contact you, I might put you in danger."

"Okay. I see that. But you could have dropped a postcard in a mailbox. Or called a mutual friend and left a message for me. You could have tried something, anything . . ."

"Maybe you're right," I concede. "My dad had just told me he wasn't my real father and my mom wasn't my real mother. Then he sacrificed his life for me to get away. My whole world flipped upside down and backward. It was a hard time to know what to do . . ."

"A very hard time," P.J. agrees, and the pain in her voice is palpable. "The police were convinced I knew something. They interrogated me for days. Meanwhile I was worrying about you so much I couldn't sleep. Couldn't eat. I lost fifteen pounds. My hair started to fall out. I was certain that if you were still alive, you would call. You would reach out to me. You would know what I was going through and you'd find a way. But you didn't . . ."

"Maybe that was because I was running for my life," I blurt out, and for just a second anger rings in my voice. I stop and take a few breaths, and get myself back under control. "I went from a

monster in a Manhattan penthouse to a speeding train to a motorcycle gang. You weren't there, P.J. You don't know what it was
like. So I don't know how you can judge me." I pick up my story
and describe meeting Gisco, and how he tricked me into going to
the Outer Banks, and ditched me in a locked barn.

Then I hesitate a long beat, and I start to tell her about Eko.

55

P.J. lets me get through the whole Outer Banks part of the
story without interrupting. Then she asks softly, "So you were
able to dive to the bottom of the ocean because this Eko girl gave
you a necklace with magic beads?"

"Not magic," I tell her. "Condensed oxygen in solid form."

"Where's the necklace?"

"Right here." I take it off my neck and pass it to her.

"You still wear it?"

"I might need it again. You never know."

"No, you never do." She fingers the beads, and then looks
right at me. "It's nice. She has good taste." P.J.'s eyes probe my
own.

I hold her gaze and don't say anything.

Seconds pass.

"So what happened next?" P.J. finally asks. "You were in an
open boat with that telepathic dog, in a storm."

So I finish my strange tale. I describe surviving the hurricane,
and being picked up by the trawler *Lizabetta*, and how I was taken
to Dargon's island, where I found Firestorm and used it to wreck
the trawler fleet.

"So I guess I did what I was supposed to do," I tell her. "I fulfilled my mission—the reason I was sent back a thousand years. On some level, that means a lot. But when Eko and Gisco disappeared . . . I was suddenly left all alone. I started to realize that I'd saved a future I didn't know, and completely screwed up my life in the present."

"My life, too," P.J. says softly. "I was walking home from a babysitting job when a town police car pulled up. A cop waved me over, and asked me if I'd seen a gray van drive by. I leaned down to answer, and he sprayed something cold on my face. When I woke up I was bound and gagged, and on my way to the Amazon. No goodbyes to Mom and Dad, no idea what was happening. Just . . . taken."

"I'm sorry," I say. "I don't know what I could have done to prevent it, but it's terrible."

"Yes," she agrees. "Look, Jack, I want to believe your story. I accept that you got caught up in something huge and confusing, which neither of us fully understands. I've seen the colonel and how strange and powerful he is. But . . . a lot of what you just told me is pretty incredible. I can't just swallow it all down in one big gulp." Her tone hardens slightly. "Nor can I forget everything's that's happened to me . . . or completely forgive."

"Then where do we go from here?"

She lets my question float on the fetid night air for a few seconds. "Out of the Amazon," she finally suggests.

"Literally or metaphorically?"

"Both. We're lost in a dark jungle. Let's find a safe path out."

"Together?"

She turns her head to look at me. "Do you still love me, Jack?"

I look back into those eyes that I missed so much, for so long. "More than ever," I tell her. "You're right, my story was incredible. But it was true. And when you're swept up in an adventure like that, and you find yourself fighting off Gorms and helping weird time travelers try to save endangered future worlds, you gradually realize that the only thing that really matters is . . ."

"The girl next door?" P.J. suggests softly.

My fingers gently trace the curve of her cheek. "You never lived next door to me."

"Just down the block," she replies, and her lips are so close I can feel the warmth of her whisper.

"That hardly makes us neighbors," I point out. My own voice trembles as I ask her, "Do you know why I kissed you back in the gym that day?"

"Why, Jack?"

"You looked so damn cute, in your tight jeans and red sweater. No bozo jock with raging hormones could have resisted."

She smiles and her eyes sparkle in the firelight. "You really know how to speak to a girl's soul."

"And you smelled good, too," I tell her, as our lips brush. "And you do now."

"Hold me, Jack," she requests. I take her tightly in my arms. "Kiss me." I kiss her, hard and true. "Never let me go again," she whispers.

"I won't," I promise. But even as I hold her tight, I wonder to myself if there's any way I can ever really get even a part of my old life back.

56

For breakfast we eat bitter fruit and discuss strategy. The previous afternoon we put twenty watery miles between the colonel and ourselves. Now we've reached a crossroads: we can wind our way deeper into one of the wildest sections of the Amazon, or we can head out of the forest, toward the nearest decent-size city.

Some of the Indians would prefer to seek sanctuary in the unmapped jungle, but one of the women and two of the kids in our group are running high fevers and need urgent medical care. We all want to stick together, so the decision is made to strike out for civilization.

"It's a small city, but it has a hospital," Ernesto tells P.J. and me as we drag our canoes back to the river.

"What about an airport?" I ask.

"Don't expect jumbo jets, but you can catch a flight to Rio or São Paulo."

And from there to New York, I think, but I don't fill in the blank out loud. Let's take this one step at a time.

"Do you think this small city will have a hotel room with clean sheets and hot breakfasts?" P.J. asks.

"Definitely," Ernesto assures her with a smile. "I can also promise you a long, hot soak in a big bathtub."

"Say no more," P.J. tells him with an answering grin.

Our honest talk the evening before, followed by a sweet sleep with her head on my chest and my arm draped protectively around her, seems to have done wonders for P.J. Her eyes are brighter, her speech is more hopeful, and even her sense of humor is coming back. Give her a pancake breakfast and a soak in a hot tub and she'll be as good as new.

Soon we're out on the river again, leading the procession of canoes. P.J. sits in the front and requests a paddle of her own. She wields it like a club, whacking the water as she tries to speed us on our way.

"If you splash you're doing it wrong," I tell her, recalling Eko's kayaking lessons. "Don't just use your arms. Try to put your legs and back into it."

On her next stroke P.J. slaps the water harder, splashing both the chief and me.

The Korubo chief glares at her, but his warrior's scowl melts into a grin, and he splashes her right back. The next thing I know I'm trapped in the middle of a no-holds-barred water fight between a highly skilled Amazon chieftain and a stubborn American girl. It's hard to say who wins, but I'm the one sitting between them, so I definitely end up the big loser, soaked from head to foot.

People in nearby canoes laugh and shout advice. I spot Mudinho grinning and apparently having the time of his life watching me take an unwanted bath. We're all feeling relaxed and hopeful, eager to leave this nightmare behind.

For an hour we make fast progress down a wide and gently flowing stretch of river. Then the current picks up, and as we come around a bend I hear a grating roar. The chief stops us and points.

The river ahead flows level for a hundred yards, and then descends in precipitous steps. Swirling white eddies funnel around sharp-edged boulders. Logs and debris have become trapped all along the way, beached on shallows or pinned to boulders by the current. There's even a dead tree, stripped of its bark, with long, naked branches reaching out like the useless arms of a stranded swimmer.

Ernesto paddles up, and there's a brief conference. We could try a portage, but it's apparently an arduous and time-consuming thing to drag a dozen canoes through thick rain forest. Ernesto and the chief decide that the rapids don't look too dangerous, and we should risk shooting them.

The chief, P.J., and I have the dubious honor of going first. The chief speaks to us, and Ernesto translates. "He will steer. You two keep low. The higher you sit, the more"—Ernesto searches for the word—"unstable your canoe will be. Keep the nose pointed downriver, and if you see a rock, push off before it smashes you."

All the other canoes form a semicircle and watch as we inch forward.

"Ready?" I ask P.J.

"I always knew you were trouble, Jack Danielson," she replies, tight-lipped. "How did I ever let you get me into this?"

"What's life without a little spice?" I ask, trying to hide my own fear. I signal to the chief that we're ready, and he gives a quick thrust with his paddle. The current grabs us and down we plunge, into the rapids.

The water roars around us like an angry creature with a sore throat and an empty belly. Now it's a snake, now an ogre. It coils and hisses and sprays us with venom. Enormous white fingers reach over the sides of our dugout as if trying to climb in and devour us.

The chief does a masterful job of steering from the back, picking out safe channels where the water funnels through rocks cleanly. We move in jerks and starts and sometimes in spine-jarring drops, when the bottom seems to fall from under us and we plummet a foot or two before smacking back down.

When we're almost free and clear, the current suddenly pins us to a boulder. The water pressure may flip us or snap us in half at any moment. The chief paddles valiantly, but he can't extricate us. I lean way out and push my paddle against the boulder. P.J. joins me. Inch by inch we're able to shove our canoe forward till the current catches the stern and the boat swings away.

We shoot out through the last gate of boulders, and the roaring water subsides into placid river again.

"*We made it!*" P.J. shouts and lets out a whoop of pure triumph. The chief emits an answering triumphant bellow, and I pound my chest and give my best Tarzan imitation.

Each canoe that makes the treacherous descent goes to school on the previous one's mistakes. Gisco and Mudinho come down second to last. I know the boy can't swim, but there's not a trace of fear in his eyes as he helps paddle their dugout through the roaring torrent.

Gisco appears to have no recognition at all of the dangers around him. While it's true that the big dog is as buoyant as a manatee, the old Gisco would have been hugging the floor of the canoe and cutting deals with the Great Dog God. But the sweet-natured simpleminded hound who sits near Mudinho just cocks his big ears and peers around at the roiling rapids as if contemplating a midmorning bath.

57

Lunch is nuts and berries, eaten on a great flat rock that looks like a giant's table. A troop of monkeys finds us hilarious—they hoot and cackle above us, showing off as they swing back and forth on vines.

The truth is I wouldn't mind a nice hot pastrami sandwich. "At least this trip is lowering my cholesterol," I say to P.J. as I crunch a nut between my teeth.

"That was never your problem," she tells me. "By the way, nice paddling back there in the white water, Bozo."

It was her pet name for me. I almost tear up when I hear it. "Nice pushing off rocks," I manage to say back.

"I hate to admit it, but this part of the trip is almost fun."

"I'm sure there's something nasty up ahead that will try to devour us," I tell her.

"Nothing like an optimistic attitude." P.J. pauses, and lowers her voice. "Jack, I'm sorry if I was tough on you last night. I really want to believe your story."

I put my arm around her. "I don't even believe it myself half the time. What's important is that we're back together. Now, how about a kiss, sugar lips?"

"Here? In front of everyone?"

"Why not?" I demand. "Think of it as a public declaration that we're going steady."

"Next you're going to ask me to wear your stinky varsity jacket." She leans toward me. "Just don't go for second base," she whispers, "or you're caiman feed."

She gives me a big, sweet smooch.

When we break apart, I see the Korubo chief watching us and smiling. He walks over, slaps me on the back, congratulating me man to man, and then points to our canoe. Time to get going again.

The sun is high overhead now, an orange-yellow blowtorch firing through the narrow gash the river rends in the tree cover. P.J. rides in the front of our canoe, her long hair blowing back toward me as we gather speed. She's getting the hang of paddling, splashing less and digging in more. She bends and straightens, and I watch the muscles of her back and legs flex and release, enjoying her every graceful movement.

With three strong paddlers, and helped by the swift current, our canoe shoots forward. Even though I know the small city is still far away, we're traveling so fast that part of me expects to see a shack or a motorboat around every bend. But we see no one— no rubber tappers, no fur traders, not even a native fisherman.

The river narrows between rocky banks and the current picks up even more. "At this rate we'll be home before supper," P.J. shouts back to me.

"You gonna invite me in for cookies?"

"If you behave yourself." She turns and flashes me a grin.

And that's when the trouble starts.

First I hear the roar. I recognize the sound immediately. But this roar is of a whole different magnitude from the rapids we traversed earlier.

Then we round a bend and I see the forest floor all around us fall away into a deep rift valley. The river drops with it. Steam boils up and hangs in the air at the spot where the gleaming water starts its several-hundred-foot descent.

The chief steers us closer to a bank, and from this angle we get a little better view of what lies ahead.

It's not Niagara, but it's plenty big and outrageously loud, a liquid rock concert with drums and bass and a light show. There are four separate stretches of white water, spanning a distance of more than a mile. The first two feature spectacular cataracts, with tons of water cascading over rocks, sending up tall geysers of silvery spray.

"No way I'm going down that!" P.J. says.

"We'll have to portage," I agree.

Ernesto has paddled over to us. "Yes. We'll lose a day, maybe more, but there's no alternative," he agrees sadly. "Let's get everyone over to the bank and we'll start cutting trees to use as rollers for the canoes—"

And that's when the guns open up.

※

58

A loud *rat-tat-tat* erupts from the far bank and bullets whistle into the water near us.

"Must be hunters . . . or tribesmen . . . *But those sound like semi-*

automatics!" Ernesto shouts in confusion, his usually calm face panicked. He rips off his white shirt and waves it back and forth, desperately trying to signal that we come in peace.

In a flash, I realize what must be happening. I recall how at the end of my Firestorm quest, Dargon cut off one of my fingers and planted a tracking device in the plaster cast. Like father like son. The colonel let us go, but he must have planted a bug in one of the canoes. In our last conversation, he compared me to Moses. Now, too late, it occurs to me that Ramses reconsidered and sent his army after the Israelites, to wipe them out. "It's the colonel's men," I tell Ernesto. "They followed us here."

"This way! To shore!" Ernesto shouts and directs the canoes toward the near bank. But as if anticipating his command, a submachine gun opens up from beneath the trees on the near bank, less than fifty feet away.

The first blast rips a three-inch hole in the chest of the governor general of the free and wild Amazon.

Our fearless leader is blown clear out of his canoe by the blast. Time slows down. He seems to hang in midair, his arms waving. A long stream of blood unthreads from his chest while his handsome face is contorted in pain and disbelief. Then a second burst of bullets rips his body nearly in half, and he disappears into the river.

There are shrieks from nearby canoes. Everyone sees what is happening, but no one knows what to do.

The chief paddles us quickly away from the gun on the near bank, to the center of the river. The other canoes follow us out, but there's no place to hide.

The ambush has been well planned. We can't get away by paddling back upriver because the guns are on either bank, right at the narrows. If we try to pass between them, the crossfire will blow us to matchsticks. If we stay out here, they'll pick us off one by one. And we can't escape downriver, over the rapids, because it would be like trying to go down Niagara Falls in a barrel.

The canoe right next to us comes under fire. The man standing at its prow manages to dive off. A second later, the four men and one woman remaining on board are shredded alive. Their bodies dance grotesquely as bullets thud into them, and then skulls and chests explode and riddled, eviscerated corpses are blasted over the side.

"*Jack!*" I look over. P.J. is half standing, horrified. "*We're next.*"

She's right. I can almost feel the soldiers on both banks adjusting their aim. But she's also wrong. Because there's no way I'll let that happen. Even the best traps have a way out, and the only possible escape from this one is roaring just in front of us. Every now and then, someone does make it down Niagara Falls in a barrel.

"Down the falls!" I shout to the Korubo chief, pointing with my arm. "*It's the only way!*"

He doesn't speak a word of English, but we exchange one desperate look and he understands.

We turn the canoe and head straight for the cataracts. I see the other canoes follow us toward the hissing and steaming entrance to a watery hell.

✴

59

We paddle for the abyss. It's strange to be racing toward almost certain death, straining for it, as if it also represents the only possible chance at salvation.

Bullets hiss around us. Three more canoes are hit. Pieces of splintered wood flap by like flying fish. Horrific screams ring out so sharply that they pierce even the thunder of the falls. Patches of white water churn scarlet. I see men and women bobbing desperately in the river, their eyes wild with the fear of drowning.

I want to try to rescue them, but there's nothing we can do. The crossfire is too intense, and the current is sweeping us along too quickly. If we did succeed in slowing down, we'd be machine-gunned in seconds.

I have to save P.J. That's all I'm thinking. You got her into this. Do whatever it takes. Get her out.

A bullet rips through the prow of our canoe. Knocks us off line. The chief straightens us. A second bullet smashes in. A third! They've found our range.

I dive forward and cover P.J. with my body. She cringes. I hold her tight. Wait to be shredded. Hope the first bullet is a head shot that kills me. But just before that happens, the bottom drops out of the world.

We tilt so far forward it seems like we will spin end over end. Instead, we plunge. Down, down, down, with the roaring all around us and the spray in our eyes. Blinded. Deafened. Holding P.J. and waiting for it to end.

Surely we're going to hit a boulder and crack apart. Certainly we're going to get sucked up in a whirlpool and drown. Positively we must roll upside down and be flayed alive against the rocky bottom.

But we don't founder or roll or crack apart.

I glance back. The Korubo chief is sitting proudly in his place, somehow keeping us on a relatively safe course. He doesn't look scared at all. In fact, he's smiling. I understand that he's doing what he was born to do, and that he'd much rather die this way than in the colonel's foul prison. His bravery gives me the strength to help.

I let go of P.J., sit back up, and begin to paddle. We're almost through the first section of falls. We barely avoid a giant boulder, and veer away from the dangerous clutches of a dead tree.

Then we reach the next huge cataract, tip over the edge, and down we go! Our canoe is in free fall. I try to keep my wits about me and help the chief pick out a safe landing spot. When we finally splash down in an explosion of spray, my first thought is that we made it!

Then I see that the front of our canoe is empty. We've lost P.J.! The impact knocked her out. I search the churning river and spot her, being swept toward the next set of monster rapids. She reaches up an arm and seems to wave, perhaps saying good-bye.

I dive over the side. The river grabs me in its powerful arms, but I fight back with everything I have. Always been a powerful swimmer. The best in my grade, in my school, in my town. Aced junior and senior lifesaving. Won gold medals at the town races. Once swam across the Hudson and back to win a bet. Now I put every ounce of strength and skill I have into saving P.J.

She's trying desperately to slow herself—to avoid being swept down the next waterfall. Foot by foot I claw my way through the white water, moving ever closer to her. I'll have only one chance to grab her. We're perilously close to the lip of the thundering cataract.

Too late. She's gone over! I've lost her! No, there she is, clinging to a rock at the very edge.

I grab a leg. Yank her back from the abyss. Find a handhold on the sharp rock she was clinging to. The chief sees us, and steers the canoe in our direction. But there's no way he can possibly rescue us. We're too close to the edge of the watery precipice.

P.J.'s freaking out. Thinks she's gonna die. I grab her in a lifeguard hold. Push off the rock. Kick and stroke and fight my way back against the current.

Somehow I make it to the canoe. The chief reaches down. Grabs P.J.'s arms. Tries to paddle and haul her up at the same moment. I try to anchor us against the current and push her up. She calms down enough to help. I push, he pulls, she climbs, and suddenly she's in.

Saved her! Our eyes meet for a fraction of a second. She knows I just saved her life.

BAM! Something slams me on the side of the head. A rock? A floating branch? I fade out, and come back to consciousness whirling in limbo. Fight my way up to the surface.

"*Jack! Jack!*" I see P.J. in the canoe, searching for me, as they tip over the edge of the falls.

I try to wave back, to let her know I'm alive.

And then I go over a different part of the falls. No canoe. Just Jack. Forget about negotiating Niagara Falls in a barrel. Try doing it in just shorts and some sandals.

BAM, another rock sucker punches me. OOWW, something knifes me in the ribs. WWWHHISSHHT, I'm whirled upside down in an eddy. ZZZZTTTT, I bust loose only to be sandpapered by the rocky bottom.

It's like trying to fight twelve big guys who are armed with different weapons. One knifes you, one clubs you, while the next guy loads up with brass knuckles.

Still I refuse to give in. Beaten and bruised and bloody as I am, I kick back to the surface one final time.

See a canoe in the distance. P.J. and the chief are flying over white water, already far in front of me.

She's half standing in the canoe, looking backward.

And then something massive comes between us.

A boulder, clenching like a giant's fist. No time to duck. No way to block it.

I actually hear my skull CRACK open against it, and the darkness rushes in.

✹

60

This is what happens when you die. You sail and sink and whirl back to the woman who gave birth to you.

"Jack? Jack?" a soft voice calls out to me.

Is it my mother, Mira, regretting sending her baby away, reaching across the centuries to try to reclaim me as I die?

Too late, Mom.

Is it P.J., swept away from me by the falls, calling one last time to her lost love?

Too late, my dear. I'm finished.

Skimming over water. Must be one of the rivers of hell. Hope it's Lethe. Let me drink and forget.

There's a dark figure in front of me, poling the skiff forward. Is it Charon, the ferryman who takes dead souls across to Hades? He's supposed to be a winged demon with a double hammer. I can't make out the details, but I see his hunched shadow working us toward the gloomy bank.

We reach the far shore. All movement stops.

Now there will be only the darkness of the damned. But I still feel sunlight.

I'm being held in warm arms. Bathed. Taken care of.

Something cool on my skin. Ointment?

Water is drizzled onto my lips. Not from the river Lethe. It doesn't make me forget. It gives me strength, and helps me to remember.

"Jack, Jack? Can you hear me?" That same familiar voice again, but now I know it's not Mira or P.J.

I open my eyes. We didn't cross the Styx. Haven't arrived in Hades. Hell can't be this green and lush.

The shadowy figure bending over me is not a demon with a double hammer.

Quite the opposite. Soft skin. Red lips.

A caring hand strokes my forehead tenderly. Compassionate eyes peer down at me, filled with worry. Sad and beautiful eyes, deep and glittering with purpose. "Jack. Can you hear me?"

I don't have the strength to speak, so I answer her telepathically: Yes, Eko.

Thank God! You've been out for three days. Twice I thought I'd lost you.

P.J.?

You had a concussion. Busted ribs. By the time I pulled you out, you'd swallowed half the river.

Where's P.J.? Did you save her, too?

Focus on yourself. You've just had a brush with death. Are you hungry? Do you think you can keep down solid food?

It takes a tremendous effort, but I suck in a breath and open my mouth and the words explode out: *"Is she here? Did you save her?"*

"I could only save you."

"No!"

"Yes. It's vital that you live. You are the beacon of hope."

"Let me die." Sinking back into a pit of darkness, craving a drink of oblivion from Lethe, and a one-way ticket to the shadowy shores of Hades.

✸

61

Movement, always forward. Downriver. I can feel the tug of the current. Eko, where are we going?

The only way left to us. Rest.

Never a woman given to long explanations. Silent, sad, mysterious.

Turn us around. We have to search for P.J.

No, Jack. We have to continue on. Trust me.

Even telepathy is draining. I'm still in pain, half floating in darkness.

I don't trust you.

You should. I care for you deeply.

Then take me back to the falls. Help me find P.J.

Impossible. Rest.

Something tart squeezed between my lips. Berries.

The bandages over my ribs being changed.

Leaves are tucked under my head like a soft pillow.

The soothing voice singing to me. Not in English. Sounds like Japanese.

My dreams take me to a place I visited once before.

A diamond-shaped valley surrounded by cliff walls. Four mighty rivers spilling down in a succession of great cascades, hissing into the same boiling cauldron.

A lush island floats in the center of this whirlpool, a jungle Eden. I glimpse towering trees and pink flowers as big as umbrellas. Giant men are on the island, too—I see their shadowy faces. They're unmoving, unblinking.

One gaunt face is much larger than the rest. It could almost be just a wind-chiseled crag. Insects crawl over it, birds circle it, and flowers bloom near it, as if they all find the essence of vitality in its lifeless repose.

Someone is watching me. A keenly intelligent gaze. Human eyes! Vaguely familiar and spooky. Ghoul-like. Egyptian mummy eyes, encased in a sand-dry face.

The face is ancient, but the eyes are childlike.

I hear music! Flutes, rattles. And human voices, chanting hypnotically.

That wise old face leans closer.

"Who are you?" I ask. "What do you want from me?"

The old lips open. One word. "Destiny."

"To hell with destiny," I tell him. "It only brings misery. I want to save P.J. Can you help me?"

The old face smiles sadly.

I open my eyes. Try to sit up.

The pain is excruciating. I sink back down, defeated.

Dawn light is streaking over the river. A morning breeze rustles the leaves.

I'm on a grassy bank, near a canoe. Eko is thirty feet away, sitting on a rock that juts out into the river. She looks like a forest nymph, a dryad or a naiad. Long flowing black hair, lissome body, gleaming bare almond skin. She's meditating, her arms spread wide as if she's embracing the trees, the river, and the lightening sky.

One look at her is all it takes to understand how she kept me alive, fed, and protected while I was unconscious. She lives on such close terms with nature that she seems to be a part of this green expanse of threatening wilderness.

I remember her on the Outer Banks—how she communed with the birds of prey and the dolphins of the deep. I can tell it's the same for her here—she probably knows every edible plant, every medicinal shrub. It wouldn't surprise me if she could converse with caimans, and perhaps the chattering monkeys give her navigational advice.

Nature nymph nonpareil though she may be, I'm aware that her skills serve her own agenda. She's a priestess, a functionary, carrying out the will of the People of Dann. She's bringing me somewhere for her own purposes, or theirs. Definitely not mine.

What I need to do is clear: go back and find P.J.

"Never let me go again," she whispered the night we sat by the firelight.

"I won't," I promised her.

I sit back up. My damaged ribs stab me. I cross my arms over my body, locking in the pain. Hold on to it, I tell myself. Use it to stay conscious.

I start to crawl across the mud. It's slow going, but I make it to the canoe. Drag myself up and over the side. Find a paddle. Silently push off from the grassy bank.

I glance at Eko—she hasn't moved. The rock she's meditating on is a short distance downriver. If the current pulls me past her, she'll spot the canoe.

So, weak as I am, there's only one way to go. Upriver. I can't possibly paddle a canoe against the current in this condition. Somehow I manage it. There's no way I can make it back to the falls and find P.J.—this is a fool's errand. Well, I guess I'm a fool.

I force my arms to move, the muscles of my shoulders to work. Dig, pull, lift. Every stroke is agony.

It seems to take an hour for me to make it around the first bend, but finally I do. Eko slowly vanishes behind the curtain of trees. I hate to leave her in the rain forest without a canoe, but I know she can fend for herself. This is my only chance to save P.J.

I'm the master of my fate again. And that's when I see the silver torpedo bearing down on my canoe!

✸

62

It's not a torpedo, it's a whale. I can see it above the waterline, gasping oxygen. But we're in fresh water and it has scales, so it has to be some kind of humongous air-breathing fish.

I try to paddle around it, but I'm already exhausted and it's coming on much too fast. It dives and I prepare to use the paddle to ward it away when it surfaces again.

A flock of brightly plumed birds is skimming five feet above the river. As they pass near my canoe, the gigantic fish suddenly launches itself out of the water like a flying oil tank and snags one of the birds in its mouth. The rest of the flock veers away, shrieking wildly. As the lunker water-to-air predator falls back into the river, its massive tail clips the bow of my dugout.

My canoe flips wildly, and I'm thrown far and clear. Before I can grab the upside-down dugout, the current catches it and carries it away downstream.

The fin-tailed colossus turns slowly in my direction. It must be twelve feet long and weigh six hundred pounds. I see that it has teeth. It finishes off the rest of the bird in one gulp and looks at me curiously. Does it eat humans? Does it know whether it eats humans or not?

The good news is that it slowly swims off. The bad news is I'm now floundering in the middle of the river, more than forty feet from either bank, too weak to swim.

My nose and mouth sink beneath the surface, and I try to breathe water. I come up sputtering. That's one.

Panic gives me the strength to take a few pathetic strokes. But I'm just flapping my exhausted arms.

I sink down again, and try to hold my breath. My eyes are open and I see the muddy bottom. The stems of water plants. Tiny fish. This will soon be my resting place.

My mouth opens and the river rushes in. I pop up, choking. That's two. The next one will finish me.

Is a voice in the distance shouting my name? I manage one last kick and then I sink down a third and final time.

Blackness edges in on the fringes of my consciousness, like a curtain slowly being drawn across a lighted stage.

I'm just barely aware of a shape diving toward me. Is it the freshwater killer whale, coming back for a bite?

Hands grab me. Strong legs kick us to the surface.

Eko tows me to the bank. She opens my mouth, turns my head to the side, and tries to breathe life into me.

I flash in and out as she pinches my nose closed and gives me mouth-to-mouth. It's no use. I can't breathe the oxygen she's trying to give me.

Suddenly I go into spasm, kicking and gagging.

Eko turns me on my side as water streams out my mouth. Finally it's all gone, and I can gasp in air again.

She looks down at me, hands on her hips. "What did you think you were doing?"

"P.J.," I gasp.

"Even if she survived the falls, how could you ever hope to find her? You could never make it back that far upriver in your condition. You barely made it fifty feet."

I nod and gasp out, "Had to try. Would have gone farther. Hit a whale. Do better next time."

Eko's eyes remain furious, but something else kindles in them. Grudging admiration. "It was a pirarucu," she says softly. "The largest freshwater fish in the world. They breathe air, but they're not whales. They're almost extinct, but you managed to find a pretty good specimen."

I look right back into those angry black eyes. "P.J.," I whisper. "The truth."

Eko nods slowly. "Okay. I believe your girlfriend is still alive. But you can't go back and try to save her. The more you search for her, Jack, the more you will make her death a certainty. In fact, the only way you can possibly help her is to come with me."

63

In Eko's canoe, drifting downriver, listening to explanations I don't want to believe.

"The only reason the Dark Lord let you go is because he was hoping you'd lead him to Kidah," she tells me. "When you turned toward the city, and he saw that you were heading out of the forest, he immediately ordered your death. His men are scouring the rain forest now, searching for you. It was their mistake that you survived the ambush. The colonel is not tolerant of mistakes."

"If they don't find me, he'll kill them?"

"Without a doubt," Eko agrees. "That's why the search for you has become so intense." She has a talent for matter-of-factly breaking bad news. "They're scanning the forest with low-flying drones, and they're paying thousands of natives to fan out in canoes. Of course, they're also searching for the other members of your party who survived the ambush, and they're always on the lookout for Kidah, but the primary focus now is you."

"So if I go back and search for P.J., I'll be sailing right into their hands?"

"And if you should find her, or even come close, you'll just be drawing more danger upon her."

Eko's fingers touch my wrist. She looks into my eyes. "You asked for the truth, Jack—see if you can handle it. The more you seek her out, the more danger you bring to her. Your love for her and your desire to be with her can only bring her pain, suffering, and ultimately death. That is the sad irony of your relationship with Peggy Jane Peters."

"P.J.," I correct her sharply.

"This is not her struggle. If you really love her, let her go. She is not of your world."

I yank my wrist free. "She and I grew up together. You're the one who's not of my world. And I think maybe you didn't save P.J. because you're jealous of her."

Eko looks surprised. "Don't be ridiculous."

"We're speaking the truth," I remind her. "Can't you handle it, Eko?"

"I'm not some lovesick teenager. I'm on a mission to save the earth."

"You're also a woman, and a prophecy said we were going to be married."

Eko shrugs. "What will be, will be. The point is that the colonel will hunt for you till he finds you, and he's also looking for P.J. You can't run away or even hide from him for very long, and neither can your girlfriend."

"She's with a Korubo chief who knows the forest."

"And I'm sure he's done the smart thing and abandoned the canoes," Eko tells me. "It's much easier for the colonel's men to spot people who are out on rivers, where they can be seen from the air. If the chief leads P.J. and the others deep into the forest, and they take refuge with a tribe, they can hide out for a little while."

"Then why didn't we abandon our canoe?" I ask.

Eko hesitates a moment, and when she answers, her voice

rings with a zeal that comes from absolute faith. I remind myself that she is a priestess, and has dedicated her life to a cause. "This canoe is the only possible chance of getting where we need to go," she whispers.

"And where is that?"

"We must find the Mysterious Kidah," she declares.

I recall what Gisco told me about him in the balloon. The greatest genius of the future, who apparently decided to play hide-and-seek just when all the cosmic chips were put out on the table. "What good will that do? If he's really so powerful, and he's cut and run, that's his choice. We'll never flush him out. End of story."

"We can't let the story end that way. We need to find out why he disappeared, and help him, and get him to lead us. He alone can kill the colonel. If he does, he'll save my future world. And at the same time, you and"—she hesitates—"P.J. will no longer have anything to fear. So we have a common cause: find Kidah. Help him defeat the Colonel. It's the last, best chance for all of us."

I mull it over. She may well be right, but I don't want to leave P.J. again and go off on some wild-goose chase, or rather wild-wizard chase. "When the colonel released me, he warned me that if I ever helped the Dannites or searched for Kidah, he'd track me down and make me pay."

"He'll do that anyway," Eko assures me. "He already tried to kill you at the falls."

"I hate to provide him with any more incentives."

"His warnings to you about Kidah should be all the proof you need that this is his only weak point, and therefore the only chance we have."

I sort of know what she means. I remember how desperate the colonel was to learn of Kidah's whereabouts. When he demanded information about the missing sorcerer from me, fear rang in his voice. I felt it then, above the candirú pit, and I know it now: this fiend from the future, who is not shy about wiping out rain forests and changing the destiny of entire worlds, is scared of a little lost wizard.

"Okay," I say finally. "I accept that it's our only chance. I won't try to escape again." I hesitate and then promise, reluctantly, "I'll go with you, and do what I can to help."

Eko gives me a tiny smile and we resume paddling.

After a time, I add, "And by the way, Eko, for what it's worth, thanks for saving my life."

"Twice," she reminds me. "You're welcome."

64

Deeper, ever deeper into the most unmapped, unexplored section of the Amazon.

No drones with DNA scanners fly overhead, and even if they did, they would never spot us here. We are paddling through a flooded forest. The winding labyrinth of watery channels is shielded from the air by an impenetrable curtain of interlaced branches. Sunlight itself can't pierce the leaf cover—what filters down to us is a faint greenish luminescence that imbues every animal, plant, and rock with a cartoonish emerald glow.

No dugout canoes with paid native spies pass near us—we haven't seen any evidence of other humans in days. No footprints. No native huts. No smoke from distant fires.

It feels like we've entered a prehistoric forest, and are not only paddling farther and farther from civilization but also backward in time, to an untouched wilderness in a bygone era before man started to muck the planet up. There are no Cessnas droning low overhead searching for mahogany, or logging trucks rumbling down freshly hacked forest trails. But it wouldn't surprise me to see a pterodactyl plane down from the trees, or a stegosaurus rumble out of the underbrush with its spiked tail swinging.

A few lines of Longfellow's "Evangeline" come to me as I paddle:

> *This is the forest primeval. The murmuring pines and the hemlocks,*
> *Bearded with moss, and in garments green, indistinct in the twilight . . .*

But of course I'm not seeing pines and hemlocks. I'm seeing spiny-trunked pupunhas and towering maparajubas. They are bearded with moss like the pines and hemlocks in Longfellow's poem, but they're also mustached with lichen and sideburned with fungus. Stringy vines hang down from them like unruly hair, and woody lianas dangle like thick, sloppily tied hippie braids.

The trees' green garments are indistinct not only in the twilight, but all day long in this world of low light. They include ferns with enormous fronds that cloak the trees' massive root systems, and all manner of clinging epiphytes that gird the trunks like armor or tart them up like flowery lingerie.

Eko has mastered the habits of every giant tree and gnomish shrub in this forest primeval. She uses her knowledge to nurse me, feed me, and protect me while I slowly recover. It feels strange to have to rely for the basic necessities of life on a woman so soon after another young woman completely depended on me.

There Eko is, in the soft dawn light, spearing a fish for me to eat even though she's a strict vegetarian. And there, at noon, a knife in her mouth, as she scales a palm to cut fruit for our lunch. And at night, lighting a fire to keep us warm and then lying next to me. "Try to sleep, Jack. Those screams are far away."

"But they sound so close, Eko . . . and so human."

"A snake is eating a monkey. The monkey's friends are protesting from the high branches, but there's nothing they can do. Now it's over. They've swung away to mourn him. Close your eyes. We're safe here. I'll sing to you."

I feel guilty being with her after all the promises I made to P.J. by the fireside. But it's obvious I wouldn't last long in this predator-filled hothouse without Eko's knowledge and vigilance.

As I get stronger, and start to be able to paddle without pain, and swim, and even climb trees, she uses her forest savvy to protect me from my own self-destruction.

"Careful, Jack," she warns as I prepare to dive off our canoe headfirst.

"Don't worry, I see that big black rock."

"That's not a rock," she informs me. "It's a giant freshwater electric eel."

"You're kidding. I don't see any eyes."

"They're almost blind. They sense movement by sending out low-level electric fields. When they locate prey, they increase the voltage. They have enough juice to kill caimans."

A few hours later, I find a shallow pond that seems perfect for learning to spearfish. As I stalk a fish with visions of cooking it on a spit, Eko shouts that I should get out of the water.

I reluctantly let my lunch swim away and clamber up the bank. "Now what? Was it poisonous?"

"No," Eko tells me, "it would have made a delicious lunch. And then you would have, too. See those flashes of red?"

I follow the direction of her finger and peer down at a far corner of the pond. "What are they?"

"A school of red-bellied piranhas. The most dangerous members of the piranha family. And it's not known for being a warm and cuddly family."

I spot dozens of them, small and barely moving. It looks like nap time at the piranha kindergarten. "I read that piranhas rarely attack humans," I tell her.

"True for most of the year," Eko agrees. "They've got easier things to eat. But when the forest floods and then starts to dry out, they get trapped in ponds like this. As the food thins, they get hungrier and hungrier. If you'd caught that fish and spilled its blood, they'd have been onto you in a heartbeat. Their teeth are like razors—a school that size can strip a bone clean in seconds."

Eko's lessons pay off. Pretty soon I am spearfishing in the right pools, and diving off the canoe at safe moments. I still feel the urgency of our mission, and I worry constantly about P.J., but I also start to notice a subtle change in the way I think about the rain forest.

It stops being an alien and terrifying place, filled with living land mines. Instead, I begin to savor its unique beauty. And with that change, almost despite myself, I start enjoying my time with Eko.

65

Is she flirting with me, or is our closeness just a byproduct of sharing a dangerous mission through breathtaking terrain? Is it part of Eko's agenda to design moments when we feel intimate, or is the attraction mutual, and am I as much to blame as she is? It's hard to tell, but I can't deny that it's happening.

It happens when I see her emerging from her morning swim, without a shred of clothing or self-consciousness. She smiles at me and I wave back, and try not to stare at her.

It happens at noon when we walk through thick brush and she thinks I might have picked up tiny ticks. She has to check me for them, which involves running her fingers over my scalp, and then sifting them through my body hair.

At night, by the fire, we sleep near each other. We started doing this when I was helpless, and she had to protect me. As I got stronger, we never stopped. Maybe it makes tactical sense for us to be so close—we can guard each other and share information about snake hisses and growls from the underbrush. Or maybe we like exchanging whispers and feeling the warmth from each other's bodies. There's probably truth in both explanations.

Whatever's happening, I struggle valiantly against it, but I can't completely prevent it.

They're such very different women. It made me feel manly to come to P.J.'s rescue, to find her and win her back and start leading her out of the rain forest. And to be fair to her, P.J.'s hardly a shrinking violet.

But Eko is superior to me in surmounting just about every challenge we meet. She's braver than I am, stronger, too, and a far better swimmer. She radiates a mature, athletic sexiness and an unspoken confidence that I will come to my senses and we will end up together.

As we spend long hours in each other's company, the temptations become greater and my defenses start to weaken.

One late afternoon, as we prepare to make camp, Eko suddenly stops moving on a rocky bluff above a freshwater lagoon. She turns her head and stands motionless, all her senses on high alert. I watch her face and try to figure out what dangerous predator's scent she's just picked up. Is a herd of peccaries about to burst from the bush, tusks gleaming as they charge?

Then Eko does something she almost never does—she smiles. It's not a small, guarded smile either. She flashes a big, delighted grin that lights up her usually serious face. "Come," she says, "time for a swim."

"But we have to build a sleeping platform and finish getting the wood for the fire before it gets dark . . ."

Eko grabs the branches I was collecting and tosses them into the water. "We can do that later," she says. "Now I want to introduce you to some friends."

I start to ask what she's talking about, and the next thing I know she's pushed me off the cliff and dived in after me. I surface just as she hits the water. "What the heck was that about, and who are your friends . . . ?"

My question dies on my lips as Eko takes off in flight. She soars two, three, four feet in the air, rising above the dark lagoon. Even Eko can't jump that high, especially from shoulder-deep water. Then I see that she's getting a lift, on the back of a bright pink dolphin!

The dolphin must weigh several hundred pounds, but it swims with grace and rubberlike flexibility. I see that it has a hump on its back instead of a dorsal fin. Its head pivots all the way around to look down at me, and it smiles. Eko grins, too, sharing a joke at my expense.

I feel something moving under me. Another pink dolphin! It gets me in the position it wants, and then rises with me on its back. I feel myself being launched out of the lagoon, and suddenly I'm flying next to Eko! We both laugh out loud at the wonderment of the moment.

We spend half an hour swimming with the two pink dolphins in the purple twilight of the Amazon evening. I can't shake the feeling that we're on a kind of enchanted double date. The dolphins have long beaks, friendly faces, and silky-smooth skin. They're clearly devoted to each other, and they also love Eko, who can communicate with them telepathically.

I can't find their wavelength, but it doesn't take telepathy to figure out that they're every bit as smart as we are, not to mention fun-loving and mischievous.

As the sun starts to sink, one of them tugs my shorts off and swims away with them. I cover up and move into deeper water as my shorts are deposited by dolphin beak on a branch of a distant floating tree. "Eko, did you tell him to do that?"

"They're naked and I'm naked, so it seems only fair."

"Fair to who?"

"Stop asking so many questions!" She laughs and then springs forward and dunks me.

It's hard to win a dunk fight with a martial arts expert, but I feint right, go left, and dunk her right back. In a second we're laughing and wrestling with each other, all knotted up in a jujitsu hold that could lead to strangulation or impregnation if it's pushed much farther.

I didn't plan it, but innocent fun changes into something much more serious. In a heartbeat we're locked together, looking into each other's eyes. Our heads incline. Our lips brush . . .

With a tremendous effort I break away and swim off underwater. Eko doesn't chase me.

I stay away for a few long minutes, retrieve my shorts, and get my body back under control. When I swim back we resume the fun and games with our pink humpbacked friends, and try to pretend that nothing happened.

Soon the last light glimmers across the water and the dolphins swim off. We stand on the bluff and watch them leap to the starlight and wave goodbye with their tails.

Then they're gone, and we're alone together.

Eko and I build a fire and sit awkwardly close.

"That was great," I say truthfully. "I didn't know there were freshwater dolphins."

"There are only five species in the entire world," she replies softly. "The others live in places like the Yangtze and the Ganges, but the pink river dolphins of the Amazon are by far the smartest. Loggers shoot them for food, so there are only a few hundred left." She turns toward me, and her sad eyes have never looked more beautiful. "Soon they'll all be gone."

"That's terrible," I murmur. "They're so gentle."

"And smart," she adds softly. "Their brain capacity is much larger than humans'. It's too bad you couldn't talk to them, Jack—you missed a treat."

"I didn't miss it entirely," I whisper back, and our eyes meet. I was talking about the dolphins, but my remark takes on a second meaning.

Eko leans into me and my arm goes around her.

Suddenly we're looking into each other's eyes, reliving our wrestling match in the lagoon. The memory of how good it felt is right there with us, as hot as the campfire roaring in front of us.

Eko squeezes my hand. "Don't be afraid," she whispers. "If it feels right, trust it." Her face has been warmed by the firelight, and I feel it turn slowly, her cheek sliding over mine.

Our lips find each other, and this time I don't pull away. Her kiss is soft, and when our tongues touch she trembles. How can such a strong woman become so vulnerable so quickly? "I missed you," she whispers. "I was afraid I would never see you again."

"I missed you, too," I tell her truthfully. "I thought you were dead when you disappeared over the ocean. Where did you go? What happened?"

Instead of answering she shivers in my arms and I feel her loneliness and her longing. She whispers my name, and her hands are on my face, my shoulders, sliding down my arms. We're drinking each other in, inhaling each other, devouring each other, and it does feel right, or maybe I'm not even thinking at all, I'm too busy feeling . . .

A log falls over in the fire, and sends up a shower of sparks. It's a tiny thing, but it fractures the mood.

And in that split-second pause, I remember sitting with P.J. in front of just such a fire on just such a dark Amazon night.

The memory strikes me like a punch.

Eko feels the shock of it and releases me. She watches silently as I reel back, stand up, and stagger away out of the bright ring of firelight.

66

The morning after our fireside embrace, Eko withdraws into herself. She becomes silent and, at the same time, extravigilant. I interpret her new mood to mean that we are nearing our journey's end.

I can't be sure because things are awkward between us. We don't discuss the previous evening, but there are accidental slips when our hands brush, and moments when we look into each other's eyes and then glance quickly away. Even steering the canoe is uncomfortable—as our paddles rise and fall in rhythm, I know we're both thinking about what happened by the fire, and where it almost led.

My efforts to pull away and keep my emotional distance prevent me from pressing her too hard for information about our mission. I helped create this barrier between us, so I can't break it down. But something is clearly wrong. Eko's wary eyes sweep the thickly forested banks.

I steal glances at her face and try to figure out why she's suddenly on high alert. Are we close to Kidah? Is there some hidden danger lurking? I completely trust Eko's forest skills, but I'm bothered by a growing sense that she herself doesn't know what she's looking for, and that we're now wandering aimlessly.

Eko has never told me exactly how we'll know when we're getting close to Kidah. Now, as we paddle silently into what feels like the pulsing auricle of the heart of darkness, I'm painfully aware of my own ignorance. I don't know where we're headed, and I have no idea what we're looking for, or what we're supposed to do if and when we find it.

The rain forest can't possibly get any denser or wilder. When a ray of light somehow squeezes down between the leaves to the forest floor, it's such a rare event that you can see it far off, like the stab of an usher's pen-flashlight in a dark theater.

The birds and animals we encounter here are of an improbable variety and an otherworldly strangeness. It's as if Noah's ark docked in this patch of rain forest midway through its ancient cruise, and the most unusual passengers hopped off into these trees and pools two by two, and have remained ever since. I spot harpy eagles and giant anteaters with mouths like vacuum cleaners, spiny rats and tree frogs as bright as Christmas lights.

We pass a tree with distinctive, oblong green leaves, and Eko stops pensively scanning the forest long enough to give it a curious stare.

"What is it?" I ask.

"A cinchona tree," she tells me. "Quinine, which prevents malaria, is distilled from its bark. Loggers have pretty much wiped them all out, but that's a lovely specimen." Its leaves seem to drip down like teardrops in the fading greenish light. "Strange that humans should do such harm to trees that have done us so much good."

Darkness comes on, but we don't pull over. The howls and barks and shrieks from nocturnal predators seem louder and more threatening than any we've heard before.

I find myself longing for the light and heat of a big fire. "Eko, shouldn't we stop and make a camp?"

"Not tonight," she mutters.

"Why not?"

"I don't think we'll need to."

I understand that withdrawing is one of Eko's ways of protecting herself. And I remember from the Outer Banks that when she's on a mission and it gets dangerous, she doesn't like to divulge details. But I can't just sit silently in this canoe as the Amazon closes in around us for the kill.

"Eko, please tell me what's wrong. You seem worried."

She doesn't answer, or even give me a glance.

"Let me help. What are we looking for? I think we passed that same tall tree three hours ago."

"Four."

"So we are going in circles! Do you have a plan? Will you at least tell me what we're searching for?"

Her resistance to answering is almost palpable. She wants to do this alone. But she knows I won't let it drop, so she finally tells me, "It's not a what. It's a who."

"Kidah?"

"Maybe."

"What do you mean maybe? Who else could it be? Did he come back in time with a traveling companion?"

"No. He came alone. But he may have found friends."

A monkey's hoot mocks her answer. "Eko, we've been traveling for more than a week, and we haven't seen anyone. No natives, no canoes, no huts, not even a footprint. I don't think it's very likely your wizard popped out of the air in these parts and found a sympathetic social circle."

"It's different for him," she whispers. And now she's not just worried. She's definitely spooked.

"In what way?"

Eko opens her mouth, but doesn't manage an answer.

"Come on," I plead softly. "Whatever it is, tell me. If you're worried, then I'm scared to death. Look, I'm sorry about last night. I sincerely apologize. I know things are awkward between us now. But you're full of information about pink dolphins and cinchona trees. Can't you give me a hint about what's really going on? Why is it different for Kidah here? How could he possibly find friends when there's nobody around?"

Eko turns from scanning the trees to look at me. Perhaps my apology touched her. "Because he's from here."

"What? I thought he was from the future."

"Yes, but his ancestors were from the Amazon. The legends say he is descended from a long line of shamans."

"So you think Kidah's backcountry relatives might have found him somehow? And they took him in?"

She doesn't answer, she just looks beyond me, to the shadowy outlines of the surrounding forest.

I grab her wrist. "Isn't that a stretch?" I demand. "If there was a tribe here, wouldn't we have seen some evidence of it by now? I don't think there's another human around for a thousand miles."

"The fact that we haven't seen anyone could mean we're close," she says cryptically, and pulls her wrist free.

I hear something truly weird. It's discordant yet rhythmic, tuneless but beautiful and compelling. Is it the trilling of a tone-deaf songbird? The ravings of a mad monkey? Or are human voices chanting in a way I've never heard before? "Eko, please stop talking in riddles."

"According to legend, Kidah's ancestral tribe had no contact with any outsiders. Even the other indigenous tribes weren't sure they really existed. They were nicknamed the People of the Forest because they lived in perfect harmony with the plants and animals."

I glance around at the shadowy trunks of giant trees pressing in on us from the narrow banks. "If the People of the Forest are really here, why haven't we seen any signs of them?"

"If the legends are true and they live in such a pure and natural way," she answers softly, "their ability to move through the rain forest with total stealth would be of a far higher order than mine."

I begin to understand why Eko is getting nervous. It must be scary for the queen of the jungle to come up against people whose skills and knowledge surpass her own.

"Okay," I say, "I get it. They can stay hidden if they want. But you sense that they're close? Your instincts tell you that we're moving into their neighborhood?"

Eko's head moves in an almost imperceptible nod.

"So what do we do? We can't track them, right? They leave no footprints, and need no marked trails. They might not even sleep in huts or build fires. How will we possibly find them?"

"We won't," Eko whispers. "They'll find us."

There's a quiver at the end of her whisper. She half stands in the canoe, raises her arms out to her sides, and stares fixedly at some shadowy ferns along the bank.

The ferns move. Fan out. Men!

They're four feet tall. Athletically built, totally naked, and covered with streaks of war paint. They hold long spears.

No, wait, not spears. Shafts but no spearheads. They raise them to their lips.

Blowguns, pointed right at us!

✳

67

Don't move, Eko cautions me telepathically.

I'm not moving, I'm not even breathing, I assure her, looking back at the muscular warriors on the bank. They have long dark hair and bright black eyes and distended earlobes that hang down several inches and appear to be pierced and decorated with small, sharpened bones.

Good, because their arrows have been rubbed with the venom of golden poison dart frogs—the most lethal toxin known to man. If one of them pricks you, it's over.

I consider diving into the river and trying to escape by swimming underwater. As if anticipating my thoughts, two more warriors emerge from the trees on the far bank, also aiming blowguns at us. I spot several more tribesmen perched motionless on high branches. If I tried to dive over the side, I'd have half a dozen poison darts sticking out of me before I hit the water.

Tell them we come in friendship, I suggest to Eko. Maybe I could give them my bead necklace as a peace offering. Or they might like my sandals.

They have no use for your sandals, Jack. Except maybe eating them.

As long as they don't eat me.

It's not out of the question.

I ask myself what Gisco would do at this moment. He would probably be begging the Great Dog God to spare his life, while promising all sorts of self-degradations and deprivations in return. Sadly, I don't think the Great Dog God has much pull when it comes to pygmy warriors with frog-poisoned blow darts. We'll have to find a way out of this by ourselves. Eko, can you talk to them?

I'm trying.

You can joke with dolphins. I've seen you get inside the heads of birds in flight. How can you not be able to say a friendly hello to these fellow human beings?

I have to find them first. Telepathically.

One warrior barks out a few syllables. Perhaps he's asking a polite question, like: "Hi, would you like to join our tribe for a spot of tea?" But it sounds more like a gruff command with a murderous intent: "Kill them quickly and let's see how they taste with citrus sauce."

Eko, they're going to shoot! I can see it in their eyes.

I believe you're right.

For God's sake, find a way to talk to them!

I can't. I'll have to draw them a picture.

What? How?

Eko slowly raises her right arm above her head. She extends her index finger.

The warriors on both banks pause for a second before launching darts at us to see what she has in mind. I'm a little curious, too. Whatever you're up to, Eko, it better be good. They have their fingers on the triggers . . . or rather their lips on the blowguns . . .

Sometimes I forget that Eko has an alternate career as High Priestess of Dann. I'm not sure exactly what this entails, but she usually has a couple of spectacular tricks up her sleeve, or in this case her index finger, that can come in very handy.

She half closes her eyes and concentrates very hard. I see orange-brown energy radiating from her eyes, flowing up her arm to her right hand. She begins to draw in the air, or maybe on the air. It's like a plane doing skywriting, except that Eko is not using smoke. I'm not sure what she is using, but her finger moves slowly and artistically, somewhere between a magician's wand and a sketch artist's charcoal. As her hand sweeps back and forth, a dark image slowly takes shape.

The warriors gasp and back away a few steps. Surprise shows in their proud, fierce faces. I guess they've never seen anyone write on air before.

Neither have I for that matter.

Still holding their blowguns at the ready, they whisper among themselves. Several of them point excitedly at the mysterious black image hanging in the air just above me.

I watch their faces to try to read my fate, and I see something unexpected in their eyes. Not just surprise at Eko's skywriting, or fear of unknown intruders with magical powers. I also see glimmers of recognition. She's drawing something they know!

I turn my head and stare up at it. It's hard for me to see Eko's sketch clearly, since I'm standing almost directly beneath it. I surreptitiously slide over a few inches, and from this new angle I can see that it's a face.

To my surprise, I also recognize it.

It's a face I've seen several times on this journey in my dreams—an old man's mummylike features, with playful, childlike eyes. Even this crude drawing conveys the impression of someone with great life force, who exists outside of time and place. An Einstein. A Gandhi.

Or, I surmise, as the warriors make a collective decision and lower their blowguns, it just might be the sphinxlike face of the Mysterious Kidah.

68

The forest trail we tromp along in single file is not blazed. Plants haven't been cut back from it or even noticeably thinned. If I were on my own I could never find it, and if I strayed off it by a few feet I would forever lose its winding thread. But as I march on through the thick brush, with warriors in front of and behind me, I'm aware that this crude, twisting footpath is the only passageway through an otherwise impenetrable forest.

Eko is walking less than ten feet ahead of me, but the vegetation all around us is so dense that I lose sight of her each time the path twists. The warrior behind me touches me on the shoulder several times, nudging me back on course. Once I hear a hiss and look down to see that he's just saved me from stepping on a coiled viper.

A scarlet macaw hurls outraged parrot curses down at us, as if rebuking us for making so much noise outside its neighborhood bodega. A lizard leaps from the ground and snares a blue butterfly in flight. The reptile eats the lovely insect head first, and its jaws seem to dismantle the still-flapping blue wings in a brutal demonstration of reverse origami. Behind us, a rain forest jackhammer opens up—perhaps a giant woodpecker is taking on a hardwood.

Eko, we should try to mark this trail so we can find our way back to our canoe. It could be our only way out of here.

Not anymore, she responds. *Don't you hear that thumping sound?*

I thought it might be a woodpecker.

The two warriors they left behind are using rocks to smash up our canoe.

Why are they doing that?

It makes perfect tactical sense. Just in case we do escape, they're making sure we can never paddle out of the forest and reveal the location of their tribe.

Great, then how are we going to get out of here?

We're not.

Where are they taking us?

I don't know.

I take it you're not having much luck reaching them telepathically?

Actually I'm getting closer. I can sense some of their thoughts.

Are you picking up anything useful?

You're annoying them by making so much noise.

What are you talking about? I'm not saying a word.

Try to walk more quietly.

Now that Eko has called my attention to it, I become aware of the sounds of my own walking—my knees swishing leaves, my sandals snapping up and down, my labored breathing as we press on in the heat. Eko and the tribesmen move silently. Ten of us are following this trail, but from a short distance away it probably sounds as if only one city slicker is blundering along.

I try to walk quietly. No sense in giving our hosts a headache. I want their minds tranquil so that Eko can reach them. I sort of understand what she means about how she's zeroing in on the warriors telepathically.

Mind reading is not a simple or direct means of communication, like speaking out loud or writing a letter. It has limitations, and gradations of clarity, and the hardest part of all is finding the right wavelength to make contact with someone for the first time.

Eko, of course, is a far better and more experienced telepath than I am. Given time, I have no doubt she'll find the right frequency to exchange cogitations with these tribesmen. I just hope she makes friendly contact before they put us in a giant pot and light a fire under us.

The warriors slow. One of them tilts his head back, puts his hands to his lips, and makes a high-pitched birdlike trill that echoes away through the trees.

A few seconds later we hear an answering trill.

Is he doing a Tarzan routine and exchanging pleasantries with the forest creatures, or is he letting his tribe's lookouts know that we've arrived?

We walk forward, and I have the creepy sensation that we're being watched. I scan the underbrush, but I can't see anyone. No eyes scrutinize us, no spears or blow darts aim at us, and no feet softly pad after our own. Still, I sense their presence. Eko, I think someone's out there.

Yes, I feel it, too.

Can you see them?

Of course not. We'll only be able to see them when they choose to reveal themselves.

Are they going to kill us?

If they wanted to, they would have done so back at the river.

Why? Wouldn't it make more sense to have us march back on our own, and then slaughter us? It would save them the trouble of lugging our bodies through the forest.

They're used to carrying dead animals home from their hunts. If they wanted to kill us, they would have done it without bringing us home and exposing their children to whatever unknown dangers we represent.

I hope you're right. So what should we do?

Nothing. Just be your normal friendly self. Whatever happens, don't run away or act violent.

I try to obey Eko's instructions and put aside all thoughts of fight or flight. But the feeling that we're being watched intensifies. Did someone shake that vine, or was it pushed by the wind? Is that a monkey screeching overhead? It sounds vaguely human, and I see one of the warriors smile and nod his head slightly.

We burst through a layer of brush and suddenly the welcoming committee is waiting for us. There must be twenty of them. Women. Kids. Toddlers. They're almost all completely naked. Some of them hold clubs and spears.

They react at the sight of us. I realize for the first time how strange we must look. Eko is a foot taller than the tallest of them, and I have six inches on her. Then there's my blond hair and blue eyes. If what Eko said about them is true, they've never seen any outsiders before. We must look like Martians.

The women and children surround me. Some are smiling. Others look scared. They begin to touch me experimentally. They're laughing and whispering. Someone gives me a hard pinch. Ouch. Eko, what should I do?

Go with it. They're just curious.

I see that she's also surrounded.

They hang on my arms and crawl between my legs. Before I know it they've toppled me, and I sink helplessly beneath the mass of a dozen men, women, and children, all pinching me and sniffing my hair and tugging at my ears.

One grinning little brat even bites my leg. I don't think it's cannibalism, just curiosity—he wants to know how I taste.

69

I try to get to a kneeling position, but there's too much weight on me. It feels like half the tribe is sitting on my back.

Curious hands sweep over me. They tug my hair and my beard. They slip off my sandals. Slide off my shorts. Eko!

No harm done. They're not big on clothing.

I manage to look up from my prone position and spot a kid running off with my shorts on his head like a safari hat. Another kid grabs them and soon it's a big game of capture the shorts.

Meanwhile, an old woman has gotten hold of one of my sandals. She sniffs it and then discards it disgustedly into the underbrush, as if tossing away a ham sandwich that has gone stale.

Suddenly they all let me go and start to back off. I'm not sure what's spooked them, but I'm glad to get back to my feet.

Eko is also standing. We're both completely naked.

I feel a little exposed, I tell her.

Get used to it.

There are women and kids. It's not . . . natural.

It's totally natural. Try to look on the bright side. At least they didn't eat you.

One of them took a bite. What's happening now? Why did they just back off?

The shaman is coming.

An old man saunters up, wearing something strange on his head. It looks like a cross between a bad toupee and an extremely lifelike Halloween mask. As he gets closer, I see that it's a jaguar skin, complete with the enormous cat's head, which stares at me with lifeless eyes.

I feel myself shiver. Eko, what exactly is a shaman?

The spiritual authority of the tribe. They'll do whatever he says, so try to stay on his good side.

I look back at him and smile.

The old guy makes no effort to be friendly back. He has a leathery face, cracked and wrinkled, like a catcher's mitt that has been left out in the sun all season. His hair is white, and when he opens his mouth I see only three teeth. But wizened and worn down though he may be, his eyes are penetrating and they scrutinize me with care.

They remind me of the Mysterious Kidah's eyes. Come to think of it, this old shaman bears more than a passing resemblance to the sphinxlike figure who croaked out the word "destiny" to me in my out-of-body vision.

This shaman now literally holds Eko's and my destinies in his gnarled old fingers, and he doesn't look favorably disposed. He scowls at us and asks a few questions of the warriors who brought us back.

The warriors reply, pointing to Eko's index finger, and no doubt describing how she drew a picture on the air.

The old medicine man grumbles. He's not happy, or maybe the spirits he communes with are not pleased. At any rate, he looks like he's ready to sign our death warrants. His face hardens as he looks us up and down one last time, and I notice that the women and kids have pulled back, and the warriors have stepped closer and are holding weapons.

Eko, we should run for it.

Don't move.

The warrior standing nearest to me flicks his eyes from my neck to my heart to my groin. He's measuring me for a strike and trying to choose between death spots.

Eko, this shaman doesn't like us one bit. If he gives a thumbs-down, they're going to slice and dice us. Let's at least make a fight of it.

No, stay still and remain silent. Keep smiling.

I smile at the warrior, who seems to have settled on my throat as the best target. He looks back impassively, his fingers tightening on his spiked war club.

Then an odd thing happens. The fierce old shaman looks shocked for a second, and then he steps forward, peers up into Eko's face, and breaks into a wide grin.

Next the stone-faced warriors break into smiles, and finally the women and kids start to catch whatever happy germs are going around. They giggle and flash grins at Eko.

I take it you figured out a way to get through to them? I ask Eko.

She's smiling back at them. *Yes. They have such lovely, uncluttered minds.*

They were about to slaughter us.

It was nothing personal or cruel. They love but they don't hate. Death is a natural part of life for them. It's all around them, in the rain forest every day.

The kids run back up to us, smiling and laughing. They take our hands and lead us forward. All of a sudden we're the flavor of the day again.

I find it a little hard to adjust to these mood swings. One minute we're about to be eviscerated by blunt weapons, the next we're treated like honored guests.

Where are they taking us now? I ask Eko.

To see Kidah, she replies, with an uncharacteristic mix of dread and awe. *Or at least what's left of him.*

✶

hear running water. The kids pull me around some palm trees, and I see a river spilling down rocks in a small and beautiful waterfall. A dozen huts are built around a clearing near the pool at the bottom of the falls. They look like miniature versions of the longhouses that the American Indians used to build. They have a framework of posts and poles, covered with sheets of bark and palm leaves.

One of the huts is smaller than the rest, with an animal skin for a door. The children lead me to it and then run off. Eko, what is this place?

The spirit home, she says. *Part medicine lodge, part holy of holies. Whatever is inside, be respectful.*

The old shaman walks up and lifts the skin, and Eko and I bend and enter.

The medicine lodge is dark and smells faintly of incense. As my eyes adjust to the gloom I'm disappointed to note that there are no statues or paintings or masks, just what looks like a fire pit in the middle, with a small hole in the thatch above it for smoke to escape.

Where are the spirits? I ask Eko. Don't they have totem poles or giant golden idols?

She doesn't bother to respond. She's turned away from me, to the darkest wall of the hut. I turn in that direction and hear something, and then I glimpse movement.

Live animals are kept tethered in the far corner of the hut— birds, rodents, snakes, and even giant insects. Maybe they use them for sacrifices.

I step closer, and see that the creatures are all free. They're not caged or tied up. The birds could fly away. The snakes could slither off. The large butterflies could flitter up through the opening in the thatch.

They don't. They want to stay here.

And then I see why.

They're keeping a corpse company. Perched motionless on his still limbs. Fluttering above his bloodless face. As I watch, a gorgeous golden butterfly lands softly on his shock of white hair. Seconds later, a brightly plumed songbird flies in through the opening in the thatched roof. It sings a few melodic notes as it circles the lodge and finally lands at the dead man's feet.

The shaman lights a torch from a glowing ember in the fire pit and walks over. In the flickering light I see the face of the corpse clearly. It's a small face, desiccated and mummylike. He looks like he could have been lying here for a thousand years. Eko, it's Kidah, right?

She looks too shocked to respond telepathically. She just gives a tiny nod, and sinks to one knee beside him.

I glance back, and see that the chief and the other elders of the tribe are watching carefully.

I guess we got here too late, Eko, I say.

She's kneeling before Kidah, all her attention focused on him. In the torchlight, I see that even though he has the face of a mummy, and his limbs are as stiff and wooden as the lodge poles, his chest is moving shallowly up and down. He's still alive!

Eko touches his face. She spreads her hands wide and assumes the tense, meditative pose of a priestess in a deep trance. A strange keening sound breaks from her lips and repeats itself, over and over again. It's not a word, nor a tune from a song. It's an ululation. An urgent appeal from some mysterious place deep inside her.

I'm positive that the shaman has never heard anything like this supplication from a thousand years in the future, but he seems to understand Eko's behavior in a way that I don't. He gives an answering chant in his own language, and the chant is taken up by the warriors standing around.

I recognize the singsong chant I heard in my dream.

Eko's arms are spread wide over the wizard. I can feel her reaching out to him on a deep telepathic level.

Suddenly the warriors gasp and their chanting falters as a nimbus of lambent silvery energy kindles around Eko. It lights her beautiful face and sparks outward from her extended fingers, till it flows from her to Kidah. The birds, insects, and animals shrink away from this mysterious flame.

Bathed from head to foot in the silvery radiance, the sleeping wizard reacts. He stirs slightly and his eyelids flutter. I half expect him to sit up in bed, like Sleeping Beauty awakening in the fairy tale. But Kidah doesn't wake, or even yawn or roll over. His eyelids close again, and his body becomes rigid once more.

Eko snaps out of her trance and topples toward the floor. I catch her and see that she's conscious, just utterly exhausted by whatever she just tried to do. "Are you okay?" I whisper.

I failed. I couldn't wake him. You have to try.

Me? What can I do? Reviving slumbering wizards wasn't in the curriculum in Hadley High School.

She looks up at me. *You are the beacon of hope, and you are also your father's son. Please, you must try.*

Okay, but . . . try to do what?

What you were born to do, she tells me. *Save the forest. Save the future. It's all up to you.*

I step past her, to the foot of the platform. Look down at the old man lying flat on his back. I think I'd have better luck trying to rouse King Tutankhamen. "Okay, old fellow," I whisper. "Hocus-pocus, wake up and focus. We've got to save P.J. and stop that spidery colonel from destroying the earth, so rise and shine."

There's no response. It's like trying to wake up a slab of marble. I reach down and touch his sandpaper-dry forehead, and try contacting him telepathically. Yo, Kidah. Time to get vertical. Snap out of it!

Still nothing. Faintly, behind me, I hear the tribal chants rising and falling.

I turn back to Eko and the shaman and shrug. "Sorry."

They're staring up at me. Way up. I realize that I've levitated off the floor! I'm floating above Kidah.

A pulsing blue light glimmers from my father's watch and flickers over the walls of the hut.

I look down at Kidah, and with the help of that magical blue light I'm suddenly very close to him, touching him, probing the inside of his mind. I sense how extraordinary that mind is, or was. Because it's not there. Just a yawning and empty abyss.

The dark emptiness of it starts to swallow me. I pull back, crash hard to the floor, and black out.

71

I wake to the heat of a roaring fire. I register that I'm outside, that it's late afternoon in the rain forest, and that something is crawling through my scalp.

I open my eyes and see Eko's beautiful face looking down at me worriedly. She has my head on her lap and she's stroking my hair. She looks relieved that I'm awake.

"What happened?" I ask her.

"You tried your best," she says softly. "You literally knocked yourself out."

"You did, too," I tell her. "He almost opened his eyes. I really thought you were going to wake him."

"I touched him," Eko agrees. "But I couldn't find his essence."

"I know what you mean," I whisper. "I felt like I was about to establish contact. And then I tumbled into some kind of chasm. Do you think he's brain-dead?"

Eko shakes her head. "No, he's still there, somewhere. The Dark Army has awful techniques of twisting people's minds. Kidah would normally be able to fight off such an assault, but when he traveled back through time he exposed himself, and they must have taken advantage of his vulnerability."

I remember poor Gisco, and what the colonel did to the thought processes of my dear canine traveling companion. "Is there any way we can untwist it?" I ask.

"I'm not sure," Eko admits. "We did everything we could. And the shaman has tried everything he knows."

I sit up with an effort, and feel dizzy for a few seconds. Then it passes and I'm able to look around at the wooden huts and the two dozen or so men, women, and kids who are watching us silently.

"How did they find Kidah in the first place?" I ask her, looking back at them. "And why did they take him in?"

Eko has apparently communicated enough telepathically with the shaman to know the answers. "They found him stumbling aimlessly through the forest," she tells me. "Birds and animals were circling him, giving him a magical nature escort. The tribesmen had never seen anything like it. They recognized Kidah as a special person, a great spirit. He collapsed, and they brought him back to their holiest place. He's been lying there ever since, and the birds and animals and insects still come to him . . ."

Several women walk over carrying large baskets. They smile down at us, and Eko looks back at them, nods, and stands.

"What's up?" I ask.

"There's going to be a ceremonial banquet tonight in our honor," she informs me.

"Great, I'm starving. What's on the menu?"

"I don't know exactly," Eko admits. "I can't get a read on it. It's their local delicacy. Something they farm. Maybe manioc or cassava. They're going to harvest it now, and want to know if we'd like to come along."

"Count me in," I tell her, and get shakily to my feet. "Do you know how long it's been since I had a good meal, let alone a banquet? Let's go!"

A dozen of us tromp off through the woods to harvest the feast. I'm famished, but as we make our way through increasingly dank underbrush I grow wary. What fruit or vegetables could they possibly grow in this fetid forest?

We draw near some fallen palm logs, and I start to smell a musky, rotten stench. "What do you think it is, Eko? Mushrooms? Truffles?"

"I'm not sure. But I wouldn't get your hopes up."

We reach the logs. I see that the hearts of the toppled palms have already been removed and, I presume, eaten long ago. But the fibrous pith has been left in the trunks to rot. The women pry it out with sticks.

It gives off a heavy, rancid odor. Eko, our lunch is starting to seem less appealing.

She doesn't look happy either. Eko's a vegetarian, but she's also very practical. *Whatever it is, we'll eat it and we'll like it. We're their guests now, but they can turn on us in a second,* she reminds me telepathically.

They lay the rotten pith down and crack it open with rocks. Inside, white creatures the size of golf balls are rolling around. At first I think they're mice.

A little girl scoops one up in her hands and shows it to me with a smile. It's a humongous grub. I smile back at her as I choke down nausea.

A large bushel basket's worth of grubs is gathered up and lugged back to the huts with great anticipation. I'm wondering how I'm going to be able to force myself to eat the loathsome larvae. But they're not served up right away.

Before the banquet, there's a performance. The warriors who found us, wearing war paint and brandishing weapons, act out a dramatic version of the event. They sing and dance and mime how they spied our canoe, how they aimed their blowguns and we surrendered, and then the great miracle of Eko drawing her picture in the air.

The women and kids listen, enthralled. I watch the spellbound children and realize that since they don't have any TV or movies, this is their entertainment and education rolled into one.

Finally it's time for dinner. I'm famished, but I'm also dreading this particular meal. But Eko was right—we're their guests and if this is their delicacy, we have to find a way to eat it.

First the heads are bitten off the still-squirming grubs, and their guts are yanked out. Then they are wrapped in leaves and roasted. With great fanfare the first two grubs of the day are pulled from the fire and handed to Eko and me.

I unwrap the leafy package and hesitate. It's sizzling but it still looks alive and very . . . grubby.

I glance at Eko. I've seen her face bull sharks and Dark Army assassins without blanching, but as she holds the leafy grub taco she looks like she could throw up for a week. Hey, I've finally found the Ninja Babe's weak spot!

Bon appétit, Eko, I shout out to her telepathically, and force myself to take a bite. At first I gag, but the truth is, it's not utterly awful. It tastes like low-grade Canadian bacon. I smile and take another bite, and our hosts whoop and whistle.

Then I turn dramatically to Eko, drawing the attention of the whole tribe to their female guest. Your turn, I remind her telepathically as they all watch expectantly. Remember to join the clean plate club, Eko.

Her panicked eyes flick to me and then refocus on the greasy white grub like it's a grenade that may detonate at any second.

Her hands shake as she raises it to her mouth. Somehow she manages to produce a feeble smile for the onlookers as she opens her mouth and takes a tentative bite.

I see her barely suppress vomiting with sheer willpower and instead force the muscles of her throat to swallow it down.

"She likes it," I tell the tribe members, who don't understand my English, but figure out my enthusiastic licking of lips and rubbing of belly and miming that they should send a second helping in Eko's direction.

Children cheer and jump up and down and then selflessly scoop more grubs out of the fire and unwrap them for Eko, who soon has a daunting stack in front of her.

We can't risk offending them, I remind her. Better finish them all.

I'll get you for this, Beacon of Hope, Eko replies. *Don't think that I won't.*

72

The early bird gets the worm and I suppose the early tribesman must get the grub, because the People of the Forest go to sleep shortly after darkness falls.

They sleep in hammocks made from hemp, strung up inside the huts. *I told them we were married,* Eko informs me as we follow them into the dark hut. *Otherwise, they're very curious about both of us and things might get uncomfortable. They're not at all inhibited about sex.*

Posing as a married couple is probably a good idea, I agree.

But when Eko and I crawl into the hammock together, things

become uncomfortable precisely because they are so comfortable. I try to keep a discreet distance from her, but soon tumble out onto the floor. Laughter erupts from hammocks on all sides. Helpful tribe members mime that we have to sleep in each other's arms for stability.

I crawl back into the hammock, and Eko and I hold each other. "Good night, husband," she whispers.

"Sweet dreams, wife," I whisper back, trying unsuccessfully to ignore the heat and closeness of her body, not to mention the feel of her breasts against my chest.

"You don't seem like you're that tired," Eko teases. "In fact, your body feels extremely awake."

"I'm doing the best I can," I mutter back. "Good night, Eko. Sleep tight. I don't think the bedbugs are going to bite because our hosts have probably eaten them already."

I shut my eyes and try to sleep, but it's a sham and we both know it. A sound soon makes things even worse.

A couple is making love. We can hear their gasps, and see their hammock lurch in the moonlight that filters in from outside.

No one else seems to pay them any attention. All around us men, women, and children are starting to nod off, except for the amorous pair, who are panting loudly.

They're doing well. It's hard to make love in a hammock, Eko tells me, as if she's had lots of experience.

I'll take your word for it.

You don't have to.

Meaning?

We could let nature take its course. She kisses me. *I'm not the kind of high priestess who kisses and tells.*

If I was ever tempted, I reply, kissing her back on the forehead and then gritting my teeth and turning away. We better save our strength, Eko. How long do you think the savages will let us visit with them before they eat us?

She registers shock telepathically. *You really think they're savages?*

Oh, come on, I respond. They eat grubs, they wear bones in their ears and dance around the campfire waving clubs, they go around butt-naked all day, and they make love in public.

As if to punctuate my thought, the couple in the hammock finish up loudly, and then sink into silence.

I don't mean to be judgmental, I add, but you have to admit they're not civilized or technologically advanced.

I've seen the end result of civilization, Eko fires back angrily. *Before I came back on this mission I smelled it and heard it and even tasted it. I saw what the advanced technologies of the self-described smartest species to ever walk the earth did to this green and beautiful planet. And if I were you, I wouldn't be so quick to label these tribesmen, who treat the trees and animals around them with such respect, as savages.*

Eko trembles and I hold her tighter. Okay, what did you see? I ask. You haven't told me anything about what happened after you blinked out over the Atlantic. Gisco said he was called back. Is that what happened to you?

Yes, she admits reluctantly. She's always hated talking about herself or revealing details of a mission.

But I need to know what's going on. We seem to have reached a dead end, not only to her mission but also to my hopes of saving those I love. P.J. is in hiding and maybe dead. Gisco has had his mind twisted. The Mysterious Kidah is a washout. We're going to have to improvise our own way out of this mess, and to do that I need to understand what's going on.

How did the future get so messed up? I demand. How could cutting down trees in this rain forest lead to such a global hell? And, by the way, if we can't revive Kidah, what's plan B? Is there some way we can fight the colonel ourselves? Surely, with the whole future at stake, the Danns had a clever backup plan?

Eko's heart is racing. She presses her body close to me and I can feel her desperation. *There was no backup plan, Jack. No one can do this but Kidah. He's our only hope, the only chance we have. We've got to find a way to wake him up.*

73

We stay with the People of the Forest for three days. They don't use calendars, but I'm acutely aware of the passage of time. By now the colonel and his highly motivated search parties have probably found P.J. I'm tormented by the idea that he's taking out his fury at not being able to locate me on the girl I love.

Eko spends a lot of time in the medicine lodge, trying to revive Kidah. She meditates near him and sings sacred songs to him, she mixes potions and drizzles them onto his lips, and she burns concoctions of flowers and herbs in the fire pit. Kidah slumbers on, unaware of all the fuss.

I make my own journeys to the medicine hut. I tell him about P.J. and why he needs to wake up and help. I try to dial him up telepathically. When no one's looking I even try to slap the old wizard awake.

Nothing works. He lies motionless, barely breathing.

As the days pass, we become rain forest celebrities. More and more tribesmen keep arriving on foot and in flimsy bark canoes to get a look at us. Eko explains that they're from different nomadic clans, and that our hosts are enjoying showing us off to all their cousins.

I get to know the People of the Forest better, and I slowly become convinced that Eko was right, and that I should be careful in labeling them savages.

They're all healthy and mentally alert. I've never seen a parent punish a child, or a child rebel against a mother or father. Even the little kids come and go through the dark trees as they please—they are the masters of their world, romping through a vast playground. They learn from their parents to use everything and to waste nothing, and they treat the forest with great respect.

I recall my old classmates in Hadley who grew up in air-conditioned houses, addicted to television, computers, and cell phones. Many of them barely noticed the world around them. They had no sense that they were at all linked to their environment, let alone responsible for it.

As I watch the tribe's pure and simple life, I keep wondering if technological progress must necessarily lead humanity to ruin. When Eve bit the apple, did it all have to turn out so badly? Or did we just jump ahead too quickly, and make a few wrong turns?

Weighty questions, no time for answers. Every day that we lose increases the chance that P.J. and Gisco will be caught and killed, and that the colonel will extend his power and destruction to the point where it's irreversible.

After three days, I reach my breaking point. Eko has just spent hours in the medicine lodge, trying to rouse Kidah. When she leaves, I enter.

She must have been burning something in the pit—the place smells foul. I sit down next to the slumbering wizard, and a bird perches on my shoulder. I put my ear to Kidah's bony chest. I can feel his faint breaths.

Suddenly I know for a certainty that we're never going to be able to wake him. We could stay here for a month, and Eko could try every possible incantation and potion, and none of it would work.

P.J. will die. Gisco will be skinned for a rug in the colonel's library. The trees will all be burned down. The future will go up in the smoke of the present. We have to try something else.

I go in search of Eko, to confront her with this bitter reality, but I can't find her. A six-year-old boy I've made friends with watches me search and guesses who I'm looking for. He points downriver, to a hidden spot near the pool beneath the waterfall.

I follow his finger, leave the village behind, and soon spot Eko sitting by herself on a log above the still water. She's not meditating. I think she may be crying.

74

I walk over and sit down next to Eko.

She turns her face away, and blinks back tears.

"He's never going to wake up, is he?" I ask softly.

She shakes her head. "It's over. We've lost. The Dark Lord has won. The future will be as he wills it."

"And what does he want?" I ask. "You might as well tell me. What did you see when they called you back?"

She hesitates and gazes out at the water spilling down the rocks, and then at the still pool at our feet. "One minute we were flying over the Atlantic, and you were holding me tightly," she whispers. "Then, in the snap of a finger, I was catapulted through space-time. I thought maybe I had died and was on my way to an afterlife. But instead of heaven or hell, I ended up on an operating table with masked figures hovering over me."

"The Dannites brought you back to try to save you?" I guess.

Eko nods. "I was barely conscious. I remember thinking that if I survived their medical procedures I was going to wake up in paradise because you and I had used Firestorm to turn the future into a new Eden."

"But when you woke up, you weren't in Eden?"

Eko is silent, but her beautiful black eyes brim with regret.

She looked this way on the Outer Banks, on the rooftop of our beach house, when she first explained to me why she had come back a thousand years. She wanted to turn the future in a better direction, but she was tormented by memories of the ravaged, dying planet she had left behind.

Now she's looking down at the smooth surface of the black-bottom pool. I sense that as she sits here watching a water bug crawl across the mirrored branches, in her mind she's flashing forward through the centuries to the world she found herself in when the Dannites saved her life.

I take her hand. "Tell me what you saw."

When Eko finally speaks, it's in a haunted whisper. "Ground so parched that every step was fire-walking. Hot oceans boiling up endless typhoons with winds strong enough to knock down mountains. Air that could not be breathed, and unfiltered sunlight that could kill."

"How did it get that way?" I press. "How could cutting down trees in the Amazon do that to the future earth?"

Her fingers close around my hand. She speaks very softly: "If we were flying through space right now, looking down at the earth together, we would see that it has two thin and vulnerable layers, the oceans and the atmosphere. Both are crucial for life. When we destroyed Dargon's trawler fleet, we saved the oceans. So the colonel has come back to the Turning Point to attack and destroy the other layer—the atmosphere."

I recall photos of the earth from space—the shimmering blue oceans and the puffy white clouds. It makes sense—his son targeted one, and now he's come back to destroy the other. "How does cutting down trees in the Amazon destroy the atmosphere?"

"Along with the destruction of the oceans by bottom trawling, the greatest damage to the earth at the Turning Point was to the atmosphere," Eko replies. "Great quantities of greenhouse gases, and especially carbon dioxide, were released."

"Sure, I studied global warming in school," I agree. "But even now people are trying to find ways to reduce gas emissions and repair the damage."

"And nature has its own defenses, its own cleaning system," Eko tells me. "The trees of the rain forest cleanse the air of carbon dioxide and produce oxygen. If you burn the rain forest, the trees can never do their cleaning job again. At the same time, you convert millions of them into vast clouds of carbon dioxide."

"It's a double whammy," I suggest softly.

"Yes. At a certain point, the earth just gives up."

"You make the earth sound like a person."

She nods. "It is, in a way. And that's what Kidah was going to do. He couldn't fight the colonel on his own, either. He was going to try to find the spirit of the rain forest, and harness its force, just the way you partnered with Firestorm. But only you could locate Firestorm, and only Kidah knew where the spirit of the forest dwells. And we can't wake him. So it's over."

I look down at the placid pool and see that the water bug has made it safely to a floating leaf, and is now sailing along on his own green yacht.

"No, it's not over," I tell Eko softly. "I know also. I saw it in a dream."

75

We set out with Kidah in a convoy of fragile canoes. The People of the Forest don't burn and chisel dugouts from trees for long voyages. They patch together flimsy canoes of bark that last only a few days. I hope that will be long enough.

The members of our expeditionary force are an eclectic

bunch—Eko, Jack Danielson, the shaman, two strong young warriors, and the oldest surviving member of the People of the Forest tribe. She's a bent old woman who looks to be at least a hundred, although she's probably just in her seventies. She has no teeth, she's missing three fingers, and she's blind in one eye. But she's the key to the whole puzzle.

I had Eko use telepathy to tell the shaman about my out-of-body journey to a wondrous diamond-shaped valley. I described it for him carefully—the imposing cliff walls, the four rivers with cataracts, and the giant men with shadowy faces who guard a lush and mysterious island.

The shaman immediately nodded and gave the place a name. It is part of their lore, their oral history, passed down from generation to generation. He said he had never been there himself, but he knew someone who had.

A mighty shaman years and years ago had found the fabled spot, and had taken his daughter along. The daughter still lived, and might be able to show us the way.

Now we are in three small canoes, following a winding river through forest so thick that even the tribesmen seem spooked. Eko and I are in one small canoe, with the Mysterious Kidah laid out between us on a bed that may become his bier if we don't find the valley soon. I can tell that the wizard is losing his tenuous grasp on life. He is sinking deeper into himself, and his breathing is now so shallow that I can barely see his chest move.

We're not traveling through flat rain forest anymore but moving into hill country. As the river narrows, the trees on either side link branches to weave a green-brown ceiling that completely obscures the sky. The tribesmen begin chanting—it's creepy to be on a tiny and fragile craft, sailing along into ever-darkening gloom.

The Mysterious Kidah never moves or makes a sound, but he's very much a part of this trip because of the effect he has on the wildlife around us. We're accompanied by an ever-changing escort of forest well-wishers. Dusky-headed parakeets swoop over us and bawl their favorite karaoke ballads. Squirrel monkeys turn trapeze tricks for our benefit. A bearlike tamandua genuflects from the bank.

Suddenly we burst from darkness to daylight. The ceiling of branches retracts as leafy banks give way to rocky embankments. The river flows faster, pressed between cliff faces. We hear a roaring up ahead, and I'm now an experienced enough canoer to know what that sound means.

The shaman steers quickly to a rocky bank, and we follow. Soon all three canoes have been dragged out of the water and stowed safely in the brush. The two young warriors pick up Kidah on an improvised litter, and our party creeps toward the thunderous sound.

As we move forward, I notice that the shaman seems to be growing younger and more vibrant. His wrinkled face smoothes out and his stride becomes springier. At the start of our journey, the hunched old woman hobbled along on a walking stick. Now she carries the stick in her right hand and uses it to swat away thorns. The two young warriors at first struggled to carry Kidah over the rough terrain, but with each step their burden seems to lighten, and they bound along like twin mountain goats.

I feel the power of the place myself. It's restorative, regenerative. All the aches and pains from my many wounds begin to melt away. I feel wide awake and energized, like I just woke up from the best sleep of my life to a beautiful spring morning filled with promise.

We draw close to the edge of the abyss. The shaman stops first and stands stock-still, gazing down in rapture. One by one we join him on a great stone that protrudes like a natural balcony out over the precipice.

Over the lip of the enchanted chasm into which we are now peering, four mighty rivers burst into space. They tumble down the rock-ribbed mountainsides from all points of the compass in roaring cataracts. The boulders that line those torrents seem to dance in the sun as their sharp edges skewer the current, shooting up fountains of froth.

The four great waterfalls hiss and bubble down the cliff faces into a diamond-shaped valley where they form a witches' cauldron of a whirlpool. In the center of that swirling lake floats an emerald island so lush that it gleams in the sun like a jewel in a watery crown. One by one, picking our way down the mountainside on the single narrow trail, we head for that shimmering sapphire.

How can an old shaman possibly pick his way over razor-edged rocks or an aged crone, even with Eko's and my help, negotiate her way over yawning crevices? But halfway down she flings her walking stick aside and climbs down with nimble, sprightly steps. The two warriors carrying the slumbering Kidah bring up the rear, easily surmounting the roughest crags despite the added weight of the wizard.

And then we're slipping and sliding down the lower slopes, to the rocky banks of the swirling lake. We stand there together, marveling at the scenery and wondering what to do next. It's like looking down into a giant Jacuzzi that doesn't have an "off" switch. Every few moments geysers of spray hurl up from one or another of the cataracts and splash us from head to foot, while a warm and fragrant mist perpetually hangs over the entire valley.

Looking across at the island, we see trees that look like green skyscrapers, and pink and violet flowers as big and bright as beach umbrellas. Several dark, giant faces frown at us through breaks in the foliage.

"How are we ever going to get across?" I ask Eko. "If we try to swim we'll drown. There are no bridges."

Eko nods, her eyes running over the rocky banks. "And there are no trees on this shore to build a boat. Let me ask the shaman."

The shaman in turn asks the old woman, who smiles and chatters back at him in their singsong language. She now has the energy and demeanor of a middle-aged woman, and occasionally I see the mannerisms of a teenager or the carefree facial expressions of a young girl. She returns to the memories of her girlhood and informs the shaman that she knows a way across.

76

We pick our way around the perimeter of the lake to a sheltered spot between two massive boulders. Deep in the shadowy recesses of the cavern we glimpse something.

"What is it?" I ask Eko.

"She says her father built a raft, and had warriors drag it down the trail. He blessed it with special spells, and left it here after they returned from the island."

Eko and I climb down to see the craft. It's in remarkable condition considering that it was built decades ago. Perhaps it was protected from the elements by the rock overhang, or perhaps the magic spells worked. Time in this valley doesn't seem to have the corrosive, ravaging effects it has everywhere else.

The two warriors help us drag the raft out of dry shadow into misty sunshine. It's made from logs that were lashed together with hemp ropes. There are a few crosspieces for passengers to stand on, and a palm tree mast. In the sheltered cavern we find the moldy but still-serviceable animal-skin sail.

"That raft must be more than fifty years old," I warn Eko. "It may crack apart in the current. If we overturn, the whirlpool will suck us right down."

Eko also looks concerned as she studies the wooden craft. "If it worked fifty years ago, it should work now."

"What if her memories are playing tricks on her?"

Eko considers for a moment, and we both study the wrinkled face of the old woman. She's climbed onto the raft and is looking across at the beckoning island, smiling toothlessly at the trees on the far shore.

"Sometimes you just have to trust people," Eko tells me, and steps onto the raft. The shaman follows her, as do the two warriors bearing the Mysterious Kidah.

I hesitate a second more. "I hope you know what you're doing," I tell Eko, and climb aboard.

The old animal-skin sail is raised and we push off. For a horrible moment we're caught by the swirling current. There's a sucking sound around us as we begin to circle the island at ever-greater speed, and I can feel the hemp ropes straining and the old logs beginning to weaken and crack.

Eko, we're circling the drain and we're about to be flushed down! I cry out telepathically.

Suddenly the old sail billows as if it's caught a wind. I don't feel even a faint breeze at my back, but whatever force is driving us is strong enough to push us out of the grip of the whirlpool. We sail straight across as if pulled by an invisible tugboat.

When our raft bumps gently against the green bank of the island, I immediately hop off, glad to be on solid ground again. But the bank is not solid—it's a soft bed of moss and grass that extends right down to the water. My toes sink in an inch, as if I've just jumped onto a luxurious carpet.

We pull the raft onto the green bank and set off to explore the jungle Eden. The surrounding cliff walls are barren, which makes the explosion of life on this island even more striking. The smell hits me first—it's a sugary but not cloying odor of fruits, leaves, and flowers that reminds me of a candy store.

Flowers are everywhere, underfoot, high above us, and on hanging vines. Eko names a few of them for me—rainbow orchids and golden Amazon roses and scarlet forest flames that are so bright I can barely stand to look at them.

The old woman begins to walk toward the center of the island, and we follow her. She seems to know just where she's headed, and her eyes shine brightly like those of a little girl leading the way to her secret playhouse. The foliage is lush but not impenetrable—unlike in the rain forest, sunlight shines down here, filtering through the trees and reflecting off the walls of the chasm.

There must be more birds here than on whole continents. They're perched side by side on branches like church choirs or warbling solo from mossy mounds like happy drunks in an alley. They seem to have no fear at all of humans, and as we walk, parakeets and hummingbirds land on our shoulders and twitter encouragingly in our ears.

"What is this place?" I ask Eko in an awed whisper.

"I don't know," she admits. "The People of the Forest don't have a name for it. In their legends, the spirits of the rain forest have lived here since time began."

Perhaps those spirits once had physical presences, and were worshipped by ancient forest dwellers. That might explain the dozens of imposing statues that look down on us as we press forward.

They remind me of the stone statues on Easter Island—humanlike faces on pedestals that resemble torsos. Each face is distinct, as if the ancient artists were striving to capture personalizing qualities like strength, courage, and compassion. The smallest of the monoliths are ten feet high; the largest must be thirty feet and weigh fifteen tons. I can't fathom the work it must have taken to carve and transport them. It seems impossible for humans to have done it without modern technology, but then I recall the pyramids of Egypt, built thousands of years ago.

The shaman, the old woman, and the warriors pause each

time we come to a statue. The warriors seem bewildered and frightened and bow slightly as if in obeisance. The medicine man scrutinizes the carved faces and sings softly to them, perhaps reciting prayers. And the old woman simply smiles up at them like they're long-lost friends.

Near the center of the island is a stand of giant trees, with trunks so thick that two-lane roads could be cut through them. I look up their straight, spiked trunks to the top where majestic crowns of branches explode into color with green leaves and creamy pink flowers.

"Are they redwoods?" I ask Eko.

"Kapok trees," she tells me. "Thousands of years old and sacred. The Mayans called them the trees of life, and believed that their roots reached down to the underworld, and their branches supported the heavens."

In the center of the stand of kapok trees sits a statue that is much larger than all the rest. It could almost be a rain-washed hill or a wind-chiseled crag. I look up and study the gaunt, shadowy visage. The hollow eyes and angular nose and mouth somehow manage to convey an impression of both strength and kindness, and also a sort of tolerant melancholy, as if this great forest spirit is resigned to the foolishness around him.

The monolith is as lifeless as the black stone it was carved from yet also vibrant as the vortex of all life on this enchanted island. Butterflies swarm it, parrots and toucans perch on it, and thousands of flowers bloom around it, attracting pollinating insects that sing and chirp and whistle.

A human cry of pain shatters the bucolic moment. I look down and see the Mysterious Kidah moving about, writhing as if trying to shake off invisible ropes. His lips curl back, and he screams again in wordless agony.

The warriors carrying Kidah start to lose their grip as he thrashes about, and they look terrified by his wrenching shrieks.

They lay him down on a bed of moss and wildflowers at the foot of the great stone figure and back away.

Then the birds and the bugs leave us. One minute we're being serenaded by hundreds of songbirds and the next there's an eerie silence. The butterflies and beetles, dragonflies and centipedes also flutter off or slither away as if they sense something that they want no part of.

"What is it, Eko? What's coming?"

She doesn't look back at me. She's looking up into the sunny afternoon sky. And so, I notice, is the old shaman, who has begun a strange, herky-jerky dance.

77

The sky blackens, the wind picks up, and the temperature starts to drop precipitously.

There's a flash of lightning, a cymbal crash of thunder, and an icy driving rain begins that would feel more appropriate in northern Maine than in this spiritual cradle of the Amazon.

I watch lightning flash across the face of the stone statue while hundreds of birds take frightened flight, cawing and shrieking as they try to escape the downpour by flying up and over the walls of the chasm to the surrounding rain forest, which may provide more shelter.

"Is it the end of the world?" I ask Eko, only half kidding.

"It's a friagem," she tells me.

"A what?"

"A freak storm that sometimes hits the rain forest. Polar air from the Antarctic finds its way north, claws a path over the Andes, and collides with the steamy air over the Amazon basin. Anything can happen in a friagem!"

As if to make her point, the howling cold wind uproots a tree near us.

The shaman, the warriors, and the old woman retreat to the shelter of the kapok trees. These giants have withstood thousands of years of Amazon climate, and the shaman is betting that they will withstand this friagem.

Eko starts to follow them. I glance down at Kidah on his mossy bed beneath the idol. He's getting lashed by cold wind and blasted by rain. It's hard to tell whether he'll drown or freeze first. "Eko, we can't leave him."

"He's where he needs to be," she tells me. "Come." She takes my arm and draws me away.

We sit out the cold squall inside the partly hollow trunk of a giant kapok tree. I stick my head out when the wind is howling its hardest and the rain is coming down in icy sheets, and see a bolt of lightning flash down and strike a direct hit on the giant idol.

The massive stone face glows red, as if drinking energy and heat from the blast. Its lifeless features seem to move and twitch as the red glow animates its deeply set eyes and flows over its angular nose to the base of the torso, where it covers Kidah like a fiery blanket.

As quickly as it came, the freak storm passes. The sky lightens, and rays of sunshine filter down. Birds circle down from the heights, and a cheerful rainbow appears in a sky that had just been as dark as death.

We leave the shelter of the kapok tree and walk back toward the stone idol. A thin coating of frost from the cold snap clings to the ferns and the wildflowers.

Kidah is no longer writhing and moaning. He is lying still, and from a short distance away I am positive that he's dead. "He froze to death in that storm," I tell Eko.

"No," she says, "he's breathing. He's just asleep."

We gather around the slumbering wizard, and for a few seconds the six of us just watch him. There's a faint smile on his dry old lips, and he looks very much at peace. "We didn't come here to watch him snore," I finally tell Eko. "He's your friend. Wake him up."

"He's not my friend," she says nervously. "I've never met him before. He's . . . reclusive and legendary, the most famous man of my time. You are the beacon of hope. You should wake him up."

I start to reach down and then hesitate. "He looks like he's enjoying this sleep. What if he doesn't take kindly to being woken up, and turns me into a frog? No, I think you should do it, Eko."

"Don't be silly," she says. "He won't turn you into a frog. He's not that kind of wizard. His magic is the gentle sorcery of wisdom and truth."

"Maybe so, but I still don't want to wake him up," I tell her. "This is your mission and your wizard. Now stop being such a chicken and start behaving like a Priestess of Dann."

The shaman suddenly pushes forward and bends to Kidah. He gives the wizard a good hard shake, as if from one old medicine man to another.

Kidah's eyes snap open. For a moment he has no pupils or irises. Just empty holes. And inside those holes we see clouds swirling.

The shaman pulls back with a frightened gasp. He leads the warriors and the old woman several steps away, and they peer out from behind the stone idol.

Kidah blinks twice, and his eyes become the eyes of an old man, bleary and unfocused. He looks up at us, still unknowing and unspeaking.

We all stand there waiting silently to hear the first words of the greatest mind of the future.

I can almost hear my heart thumping. What deep truth will this living oracle impart to us as he wakes from the dead? Will he explain the purpose of life or the secret of death? Will he unravel the mystery of my own destiny and explain why I was sent back in time to live a childhood that was a lie, or predict how my future will unfold?

Kidah's eyes slowly focus. They may be the eyes of an old man, but they're exceptionally bright. They almost seem to glow. It's clear that he knows where he is now. His mouth opens. His tongue creeps out and wets his lips. Finally he says, in a hoarse whisper, "Wow, who turned out the lights?"

I glance at Eko, and ask her telepathically: That's it? Who turned out the lights? Are you sure he's the mastermind of the future? Because, frankly, I expected a little more. Based on what I'm seeing, the Dark Lord will eat him for breakfast.

Eko steps by me and bows her head to Kidah. "Great Soul of Dann," she says in a reverent voice, "something happened to your mind when you made the passage back through the tunnel of years."

"You're not kidding," Kidah says. "Talk about headaches. Who are you?"

"Eko," she says, "Priestess of Dann." She bows her head again. "It's a true honor, O Great Soul, knower of the past, revealer of what lies ahead—"

"Please," he says, holding up a hand. "No mumbo jumbo before lunch. Just call me uncle." He studies her for a second more. "You're a nice girl," he says, "but you should try to smile more."

I think to myself that that's actually pretty good advice for Eko.

The old wizard's eyes swing in my direction. "And who are you?"

"Jack Danielson," I say, holding out my hand.

"No you're not," he says, studying me carefully. And then he bursts into delighted laughter, jumps to his feet, and gives me a hug.

78

I have had a few unexpected hugs in my life, but never one quite this odd. The time-traveling Tiresias squeezes me tightly and chortles in my ear, "My boy, you're the spitting image of your father. But where did you get that Jack nonsense? Your name is Jair, which means 'he shines'—and I can see that it suits you."

His words rake up all my insecurities. I pull away forcefully and look back at him. "No, my name is Jack Danielson. I'm glad you're okay, and we do need your help, but I *don't* need you to tell me who I am."

Again, the chortling laugh. "Yes, yes, your father's son indeed. Stubborn. Bullheaded. One could never tell him anything. I once beat him in chess and he tried to break the board over my head." He glances from me to Eko. "So, you two are an item?"

I recall that he was the one who prophesied that we would one day be married, and that our descendants would be as numerous as the stars in the sky. "No, sir," I say. "We're just friends."

"Just friends?" he roars. "Are you blind?" Then he glances at Eko and sees her blush. "Never mind," he says, "there's time for all that later. Who ate your toe?"

At least the mastermind of the future is pretty good at changing the subject. "The colonel," I answer.

"What colonel?"

"Colonel Aranha."

"Colonel Piranha?" he repeats. "Speak up. I'm a little hard of hearing."

"The Dark Lord. I don't know what his name is, but I'm sure you know who I mean. He's part man, part spider."

The effect on the wizard is immediate. The laughter is gone. The merry twinkle vanishes from his eyes and is replaced by iron determination. "So he's here? Have you seen him? But of course you have. No, you don't have to explain anything. I can get it all from her."

Eko freezes. Her head jerks up and her eyes roll into her head. I can tell he's doing some kind of telepathic suction job, downloading all he needs to know. Then Eko's head snaps back down, and she's as good as new.

"Sheesh," the wizard says, "what a mess! There's no time to lose. Where's that guy who woke me up? You can never find a good shaman when you need one."

He calls something out to the old shaman, who is still hiding behind the stone statue. Apparently they like the same jokes, because the shaman goes from being terrified to laughing uproariously in about three seconds flat.

Next Kidah speaks to the old woman. She grins and answers back almost flirtatiously, and he purses his lips and then nods his understanding. "She's staying," he informs Eko and me. "She says she wants to die here. I told the old gal it looks to me like she still has a lot of dancing left in her, but I understand her choice."

Finally he says a few words to the warriors, who immediately turn and start leading him through the trees toward the raft.

"Come," he tells us, and for a guy who's just awakened from a deep coma, he's covering ground pretty fast. "Hurry. Every minute is precious."

"Where exactly are we going?" I ask, struggling to keep up.

"To raise an army," Kidah says as if it's the simplest thing in the world. "We must smite the forces of darkness. The spirit of the forest will lead us into battle. And, oh yeah, I also need some lunch."

79

The Mysterious Kidah turns out to be an amiable traveling companion. As we paddle back to the village, he cracks jokes with the monkeys that swing overhead and croons songs to the birds that serenade our boat.

He doesn't wave a wand and conjure ham sandwiches for lunch or pull an outboard motor out of a hat. But I notice that the current of the river slows. It flowed quickly toward the chasm on the first leg of our journey, but as we head home the current diminishes till the river is perfectly still, allowing us to paddle easily upstream.

I ask Kidah about my father. "He's a good friend of mine," the wizard says. "And I've known your mother since she was a little girl. What do you want to know?"

Confronted with this potential treasure trove of information about my parents, only one question comes to mind. "I'm their only son, right?"

"Yes. Their only child. They both love you deeply."

I hear my voice sharpen and swell a little louder. "Then how could they send me away?"

"There was no choice," Kidah says simply.

"There must have been a choice," I protest. "There are always alternatives. You just have to find them."

"Who told you that nonsense?" Kidah asks.

"A mother and a father don't give up their child," I respond, and anger rings in my voice. "That's a given." Eko listens from the bow of the canoe, but she doesn't interrupt. "They don't pop him in a time machine and send him back to be raised by strangers and live a lie."

"It was your destiny and you have to find a way to accept it," Kidah tells me gently.

"Then my destiny sucks."

"Of course it sucks," he agrees. "Destiny almost always sucks. You can let the weight crush you, or you can accept it. But whatever you do, quit whining about your parents. No boy ever got a better pair."

He sets his paddle down and a big grin spreads across his face. "And now I may finally get that hot meal." We come around a bend and I see all the kids and adults of the village waiting on the bank. A roar goes up from them at the sight of us, and Kidah waves and shouts back.

Kidah doesn't do any wizardly tricks to win their trust or put them in awe. He just hops out of the canoe and greets the tribe members one by one, hugging them and mussing the hair of the kids and pointing to his belly as if to ask when the welcoming feast will start.

I can tell that Eko is dreading another banquet of grubs *en papillote*, and I'm not exactly looking forward to it either. Luckily, the tribe goes all out for Kidah, and grubs are just one of the menu options available. There is also roast peccary and wild fowl and a dozen varieties of fresh fruit, none of which I've ever seen before.

Kidah has a remarkable appetite for such a small man, and his table manners are not exactly polished. "I feel like I haven't had a decent meal in a thousand years!" he laughs, tearing into a huge peccary haunch and wiping the grease off his cheek with the back of his hand. Then, to the delight of the kids, he lets loose a prodigious belch.

After the feast the shaman and the warriors recount the expedition to revive Kidah in songs and dances. I can't understand the words, but I can follow the narrative as our expedition descends into the chasm, sails on the flimsy raft, and survives the friagem. The shaman does a wicked impersonation of Kidah slowly waking up from his sleep and looking around with bleary, stupefied eyes.

When the shaman finishes, to much laughter, the kids all point to Kidah. The wizard walks to the center of the clearing, enjoying his moment in the spotlight. First he sings. It's a slow tune, beautiful and very sad, and I sense it's a song about loss. I'm not sure whether it's a dirge for a dying world or a ballad about a lost young love, but by the time he finishes, several of the old men and women have tears running down their cheeks.

Then Kidah dances out a story that involves different rain forest animals. He does an obnoxious howler monkey, and a peeved peccary, charging around the circle of kids with his index fingers out as tusks. The kids scream and dart out of the way.

Kidah's dance ends with a battle between an eagle and a tarantula. His tarantula is fearsome, and reminds me quite a bit of Colonel Aranha, but his eagle is noble and overpowering. It bites the head off the thrashing tarantula to end the dance, and I find myself hoping that this kids' show is also a divination of things to come.

Kidah closes his act with magic tricks. None of them are what you might expect from the great sorcerer of the next millennium. He does some sleight of hand that the kids love. Finally he asks a boy to come forward.

This boy was bitten on the calf by a poisonous snake years ago. With the help of the shaman's nature cures the child survived, but his leg never recovered. I've watched him at play, gamely running after the other kids, dragging his useless limb. Now Kidah waves him over, and the boy hesitantly hobbles out to the center of the clearing.

Kidah does a sleight-of-hand trick to relax him, pulling a grub out of his ear. Then he makes the boy lie flat on the ground and waves his hand. The boy slowly levitates as the onlookers gasp. Kidah reaches out and touches the boy's right leg with his hand. There's a flash of blinding light, as if someone's snapped a picture.

The boy falls to the ground. His parents rush to him, but he waves them away. He gets to his feet, and looks down as if sensing something odd. He takes a few small, experimental steps. A cry of pure joy breaks from his lips. He begins running in a circle, still emitting the happy scream. Then he starts hopping on his right leg, like a drunken rabbit, and all his playmates hop along with him, shrieking with shared ebullience.

The kids hop away in a deliriously happy kangaroo conga line, and the elders thank Kidah with words and many embraces. I watch the boy's mother walk up, trembling with the emotion of what she's just witnessed, and thank the old wizard with just her eyes. Kidah bows back to her and then mimes that it's time for sleep.

They lead him to a hammock, and one by one the tribesmen go to sleep around him. I tell Eko that I'm not tired and she should turn in. She heads for the hut, and I walk down to the river and sit on a large stone.

There's a full moon out, and through the crack of trees above the river I can see its rough surface clearly. I wonder if P.J. is staring up at the same pale craters from some rain forest hiding spot, and if we'll find her as we march on the colonel and his minions.

It seems incredible that this little old man thinks he has a chance to bring down the mighty Colonel Aranha and his well-armed and deeply entrenched forces. A few hours ago I wouldn't have given the wrinkled wizard a snowball's chance in the Amazon. But when that boy started walking and then running, I felt something bounding up inside me as well.

Perhaps it was hope that this could all somehow turn out okay.

High above me the moon seems to wink, as if advising me to keep faith.

"Easy for you to say," I mutter back out loud. And then I realize that I'm not alone.

The Mysterious Kidah has stolen out of the hut and has joined me at the water's edge.

80

Were you talking to yourself?" Kidah asks me.

"No, I was speaking to the moon."

"I see," he says, looking baffled. "Well, I don't want to intrude on that conversation. But if you and the moon are finished, I'd love a little company."

I shrug and slide over, and he sits down on the rock next to me. For a while we're both quiet, watching the bright chain of moonlight on the black river.

"Can't sleep?" I finally ask him.

"I had enough sleep over the past couple of months," he says.

"I guess so. You were really out."

"The strange thing was that I was conscious the whole time, but I couldn't speak or move. They tied my mind in a pretty good knot."

"Yeah." I nod. "They did the same thing to Gisco."

The wizard reacts. "You know Gisco?"

"He came back with Eko. I've spent a lot of time with him. How do you know him?"

"I knew his grandfather," Kidah answers with a chuckle. "What a rascal! We once meditated together, and while I was in a deep trance he ate my lunch and took off."

I have to grin at this.

"Is Gisco like his grandpa?" Kidah asks.

"Worse," I say. And then I fall silent again, thinking about what the colonel did to Gisco, and wondering if the poor pooch will ever get his mind unknotted.

Kidah is silent also. The night wind picks up and shuffles the leaves like playing cards. A bat flaps out of the night shadows and lands on the wizard's wrist. He strokes the bat's head the way one would pet a kitten, and then flicks his hand upward and the night creature takes wing. "What about you, Jack?" Kidah asks, and I take note that he's using my preferred name. "Why can't you sleep?"

"Just . . . thinking."

"Warriors need to sleep before a battle," he advises me.

"I'm hardly a warrior. Is a battle really coming?"

"Definitely," he says.

"But the colonel has a whole army regiment at his disposal. I've seen them. Thousands of soldiers. Heavy artillery. Helicopters. Gunships."

"I have no doubt that he's prepared to vigorously defend himself," Kidah replies, with obvious respect for his foe.

"Yes, he is," I tell him. "Where are we going to get our army?"

He nods toward the hut of sleeping tribesmen. "I thought some of those warriors might join us."

I shrug. "A dozen small men with blowguns."

"Men are men. And others will join us. We should go to sleep now." But the wizard doesn't stand up. He's watching me carefully. "Unless you want to talk a bit. It's a nice night. Perhaps you want to ask me something?"

"No, that's okay, sir."

He unexpectedly reaches out and puts a leathery arm over my shoulder. "Try calling me uncle. You know, Jack, I was a very close friend of your father. And whatever my limitations, I'm sure I give better answers than the moon."

I mull it over for a few seconds. "Okay, Uncle."

"That's better."

"What's my mom like? You said you've known her since she was a little girl."

Kidah nods, closes his eyes, and rocks back and forth. "Yes, I've known Mira since she was a young orphan. She entered the priesthood, and the Caretakers became her cause, her education, and her family, just as they did for your friend Eko. I remember first seeing her as a girl of seven or eight, dressed in the white robes of a novitiate. Even then she stood out. Not just for her beauty. She was such a serious child. And she had the most angelic voice."

"I think I've heard her sing," I tell him in a whisper. "It was in the Andes, when we were trapped. She saved us. Sometimes, in moments of great danger, I get the feeling that she and my dad are looking out for me."

"A thousand years is a formidable barrier, but love often finds a way," Kidah says. "I'll be honest with you, Jair, I mean Jack. Mira never recovered from having to part with you. Perhaps you can understand how an orphan, denied her own family when she was a child, would find it especially hard to give up her baby."

I remember the excruciating sadness of the song I heard high up in the Andes, and nod slowly. "Where is she now? What's happened to my mom?"

"When your father was captured by the Dark Army, she took over the resistance. She's fought very bravely, but it hasn't gone well."

"So I've heard."

"You're her last best hope."

"No," I say, "I did my job and found you. Now you're the man with the plan."

"We'll do it together," Kidah says. "But we'd better get some shut-eye first." He stands. "Coming?"

I hesitate and then take his hand. "Okay, Uncle."

81

We leave at dawn, and a dozen warriors of the tribe go with us. They're aware that by venturing beyond their borders they will be revealing their existence and inviting trouble. Kidah has explained to them that the entire rain forest is threatened, and told them why he's risking his life now to try to stop the damage.

We hike through the forest to the river where Eko and I first encountered the tribesmen. There we find the remains of our dugout, destroyed by rocks and set on fire for good measure. The warriors expertly begin assembling small bark canoes, and soon have six of them ready to go.

The shaman decides not to go with us—he explains that he must stay behind and care for his people. He says an emotional farewell to Kidah, and the two men embrace. Watching the great wizard of the future and the medicine man of the People of the Forest standing next to each other, you would find it easy to mistake them for brothers.

When we push off and head downriver, the old shaman stands alone on the bank and follows us with his eyes till the leafy canopy descends between us and hides him from view.

We're soon in the vast flooded forest. It took Eko and me days to paddle through it, but we're following a different route out. Kidah rides in the lead canoe, picking his way carefully. He seems to navigate by instinct, and is never at a loss over which branch of the maze to take. "How does he know where he's going?" I ask Eko.

She shrugs. "The same way he healed that boy's leg. Magic."

"I don't believe in magic," I tell her. "I believe in medicine and global positioning devices."

"At a certain point," Eko responds, "sorcery and science become one. Kidah was our top scientist. He used mathematics and physics to design powerful weapons, like Archimedes three thousand years earlier. Then he left the People of Dann to live alone on a mountaintop, cultivating the secrets of mind over matter that I started to teach you on the Outer Banks. You learned to bend lines of sand, but he can make boulders fly through the air. Over time, his scientific studies and his psychic gifts merged, and he became"—she pauses—"what he is today."

"And what is that?" I ask, studying the little man in the canoe in front of us as he paddles tirelessly forward.

"Unique," she says.

"Let's just hope he's up to the task," I mutter, remembering the candirú pool. "I have a feeling that losing a battle to Colonel Aranha is no fun at all."

We're cheered along on our journey by an ever-changing menagerie of birds, beasts, and fish. They dip low overhead, watch us from fern-curtained banks, and swim lazy circles around our canoes. It's fun to be the center of rain forest attention, although sometimes it's also a bit perilous. A manatee, slow-moving as a garbage scow, gets so close that he nearly overturns our canoe.

Kidah's new route soon pays dividends. We leave the flooded forest in the early afternoon, and enter a fast-flowing river system. An hour later, the warriors who are accompanying us start to look nervous. I watch how they urgently whisper back and forth from one canoe to the other, sometimes using words and other times relying on anxious-sounding birdcalls.

"They must be freaking out at being so far from home," I speculate to Eko.

"No, that's not what's spooking them," she says. "We've moved into an inhabited area. They've picked up the scents and sounds of another tribe."

Kidah soon slows his canoe till it's barely moving and drifts toward a bank. The rest of us follow his example.

The leaves part as we get close, and we see several dozen men in war paint standing with weapons raised.

The old wizard motions that we should all stay still. Then he dives over the side and swims to shore. He walks up the bank dripping wet, smiling and shaking water out of his white hair. They surround him, and he explains the situation to them in their own language. I don't know how he got this gift of tongues, but it works miracles in gaining the trust of skeptical warriors with spears.

This tribe has heard rumors for generations of the People of the Forest. We are welcomed with great respect, and soon seated in their ceremonial clearing enjoying a big feast. Eko and I get a lot of attention for our height and exotic looks, but Kidah remains the star of the show.

According to Eko, he can perform miracles with his magical mind, but he doesn't choose to impress them that way. Instead, he picks a far more mundane way of helping them.

They are having a problem with architecture. Their medicine lodge, twice the size of the biggest hut of the People of the Forest, is built on muddy ground and has nearly buckled. Kidah surveys the site and finds three poles that have rotted through and need to be replaced.

In a few hours the work is finished and the home of their spirits is as good as new. The repair job wasn't difficult, but apparently it made just the right impression. Six of their warriors agree to come along with us in two dugout canoes.

This scenario, with minor variations, unfolds again and again as we make our slow way toward a showdown with Colonel Aranha. Each time we encounter a suspicious tribe, Kidah finds a simple way to win their trust. He cures a sick elder or he removes an infestation of giant rats. The grateful tribe listens to his explanation of our mission, and decides to contribute manpower.

From a dozen men our ranks soon swell to more than a hundred. I notice that while the tribesmen are fascinated by each other, they travel with their own clans. I wonder how long this quickly assembled ragtag army can hang together, and how well we'll fight when the time comes.

It gradually dawns on me that Kidah is not merely recruiting warriors. Majestic birds of prey fly spirals over our convoy—I see eagles and hawks and condors with wingspans like jumbo jets. Jaguars follow our progress on treetop highways. On the opposite bank a squadron of simians swing along in a chattering group that literally makes a monkey out of military discipline.

We soon start to encounter tribes who wear more clothing, and who have guns and even motorboats. We are now too numerous to all descend on a village, so Kidah, Eko, and I take a small delegation of tribesmen with us for the initial parley. On one such trip, when we swim to shore, we are confronted with a dozen rifles poking out of the underbrush, aimed at our chests.

Kidah looks a little dismayed and raises his arms. He shouts at them in their own language, and someone shouts back angrily from the foliage.

"What is it?" I ask. "Don't they want to join us?"

Kidah shrugs. "No, they're a very tough and solitary tribe. They say they don't need friends. They're especially eager to get rid of some friends of yours who are eating them out of house and home."

I look back at him in shock. "What?"

Just then a familiar telepathic voice says: *Well, if it isn't the beacon of hope! I hope you've brought some food with you, because the rain forest cuisine, while providing ample sustenance in the nut and fruit areas, is not exactly what the Italians would call* la gastronomia maxima.

Gisco! I shout, and run right for the rifle barrels. Eko tries to hold me back, but I pull free and charge ahead all by myself.

I burst through the branches and see a dozen tough-looking tribesmen expertly aiming guns at me, their fingers on the triggers.

But I barely give them a glance. I dive at the rotund dog and wrap him in a bear hug, or at least a fat-dog hug. I think I even kiss him on his hairy jowls, and I believe Gisco licks my cheek twice. Then I see Mudinho sprinting toward us and he jumps on Gisco's back and grabs hold of my neck. Soon we're rolling on the ground in a joyful three-way embrace that even a highly suspicious squadron of Amazon warriors can't help grinning at.

82

How did you recover? I demand from Gisco when we finally break the hug. The last time I saw you, the colonel had turned your mind into mashed potatoes.

This paragon of boyhood nursed me back to health, Gisco replies, indicating Mudinho with an enthusiastic flick of the snout. *He took care of me with the love and compassion that only a devoted lad can shower on a sick dog, and after a while the fog began to lift. I'm so glad I convinced you to bring him along with us.*

That's not exactly what happened . . . I start to object.

Hideous to think of a fine young fellow like this left to the mercies of criminals and brutes in the Andes. Of course we had to save him! And he's repaid the favor with interest. He fed me, he looked after me, he somehow got us away when the colonel's men tracked us down and attacked us from helicopter gunships . . .

Gisco stops in mid-thought when he sees the horrified look on my face.

I force myself to ask him: Was P.J. with you when you were attacked?

The dog nods. *She was in a canoe behind us.*

What happened to her?

It was chaos, Jack, so it's hard to say for sure. I wasn't in my proper mind yet, but even if I had been, there was nothing to be done. They shot her canoe apart.

I feel mounting dread, and can barely bring myself to whisper telepathically, Gisco, is she dead?

I don't know, he admits. *The chief was with her. They shot him in the back. He made it to shore and lived long enough to lead us to this tribe and convince them to take us in. None of us saw what happened to P.J. Sorry, old fellow. They may have captured her . . .*

Or they may have blown her away! For a second I'm flooded with rage. How could you leave her like that?

Dear boy, I hate to point out that you left her under rather similar circumstances.

I was washed away down a waterfall!

And we were trying to survive a helicopter attack.

I look back at him and see great sympathy in his big dog eyes. Okay. You're right. I can't blame you.

Your feelings are quite understandable. But there's only one person to blame and we're headed in his direction. She's a survivor, Jack. Maybe we'll find her there.

Maybe we will, I agree, and walk off. I stand alone for several minutes, watching the river flow by. Gisco, Mudinho, and Eko throw glances at me but don't disturb me.

I can't stop picturing P.J. being gunned down from above.

She's a strong swimmer and I'm sure she would have made it to shore if given the chance. But they killed the chief, who was in her canoe, and was good at surviving, too. I force myself to confront a bitter reality: now, when I'm finally in a position to fight the colonel, P.J.'s probably lying at the bottom of a muddy Amazon river.

A gentle hand taps me on the shoulder. I turn, expecting Eko or Mudinho, but it's Kidah. He reaches out and touches my cheek, and for a second it's like a small door has opened and I'm inside his mind.

I see images of a brutal future world: children trying to breathe impossibly thin air, old people roasting alive in unfiltered solar glare, and a lethal sandstorm.

And then I'm looking back into Kidah's face, and the wizard's eyes are no longer twinkling and childlike. For a second they're overflowing with anger and determination to avenge innocent lives brutally cut short. "He's a monster," he whispers. "He brings agony and loss with him. Now you understand the pain of my world. Shall we go?"

I give him a slight nod. "Let's find this guy."

Members of our group glance at my face as we walk up, and they must see something frightening there, because no one dares to say another word to me.

83

They must know we're coming. We're in a flotilla of two hundred canoes, fully exposed as we move up the winding river, ever closer to the colonel and his troops.

What those soldiers fail to realize is that not only are we being led by a wizard, but we've also got several hundred native warriors who have more combined rain forest savvy than has ever been assembled on one muddy river before. These Indian fighters could sniff out a three-toed Amazon rat at a distance of five miles. So it's not surprising that dozens of them suddenly prick up their ears and pull their canoes over to the bank at just about the same moment. They inform the city slicker from Hadley-by-Hudson that a mile upriver, the colonel has set a trap.

Kidah responds with a stratagem of his own. His plan is simple. Our canoes will continue forward on the river, as if oblivious to any danger ahead. At the same time, a small group of picked warriors will crawl through the brush and try to surprise the colonel's men. As soon as I hear the plan I volunteer to join the sneak attack.

Eko and Gisco try to talk me out of it. "You weren't raised in the forest," Eko reminds me. "If you step on a stick or spook a bird, your fellow warriors may die."

She's got a point, old fellow, Gisco adds. *There are times to fight and there are times to stay in the canoe.*

But Kidah taps me on the shoulder, signifying that I'm now part of the advance brigade.

Minutes later I'm crawling through thick brush with a dozen of the toughest young warriors in the Amazon. I've got a knife in my teeth, freeing my hands to push thorny branches out of the way. I use all the skills Eko taught me on the Outer Banks, and everything I've learned from watching the People of the Forest.

Even so, I make more noise than the forest ninjas on either side of me. They slither between trees and over ferns as silently as serpents, and when I make a tiny noise they all freeze and throw me cautionary glances.

We are moving parallel to the river. Every so often through a gap in the foliage I can see green water and the canoes that are trailing a few hundred feet behind us. I spot Eko in one of the lead canoes, looking very anxious.

Gisco and Mudinho are a little way back, and the devious dog is a much better actor than the High Priestess. I'm sure he's also worried about me, but he's slouched down in the canoe with a nonchalant, tired expression as his droopy ears flick flies off his face. He looks like a bored tourist.

A hand touches my shoulder. It's the warrior leading our attack. He brings us all to a halt and points. There's a clearing up ahead, and thickets of what look like the nastiest thorn bushes in the world.

Then I see something move inside one of them, and realize that they're not briars but rather camouflaged fortifications. This is the ambush the colonel has set. He's hidden big guns facing the river, manned by soldiers ready to kill everyone in our flotilla. Our leader waves his hand and our platoon creeps forward.

I can taste the metal knife in my mouth. I'm thinking of P.J. and what she must have felt when the first bullet struck her from above. As we near the gun emplacements I remind myself that one of these soldiers could have been in the helicopters that attacked P.J.

There's no way to keep behind cover when you have to cross a clearing, so for the last twenty yards we break out of the brush and run.

Sprinting through low grass. Expecting to hear someone shout out an alarm at every step. Shots will ring out. I'll feel the sting of bullets in my neck or my chest, and stumble down to my final resting place.

But there's no alarm. The low grass softens our footsteps, and no one hears us coming.

I've always been a fast runner. The same legs that once carried me more than three hundred yards in a high school football game now drive me first across the clearing. I spot a leafy door built into the wall of a hut, and I push in as quickly and silently as I can.

Two soldiers are inside. One is sleeping. The other stands next to a machine gun, sipping from a cup as he peers out a narrow slit of window at the river.

I think he's just sighted the canoes. He turns to wake his sleeping comrade, and sees me. He opens his mouth and at the same time hurls the cup out of his right hand as he raises his arm to ward off my knife thrust.

I step inside his guard and stab him in the throat. I feel the blade sink an inch deep into soft tissue. I must have sliced the carotid artery, because blood spurts. The soldier gapes at me in surprise, and his hands go up to his neck, as if he wants to take the knife out and cap the bleeding.

Our eyes meet. He's as young as I am. He reaches a bloody hand toward me. Then he reels two steps sideways and collapses on the floor, making low gurgling sounds.

His comrade jumps up, but an Indian warrior has followed me into the hut and makes short work of him.

I stagger outside, sink to my knees, and vomit. My whole body begins shaking, and I suddenly feel weak.

I've killed before, but it was never like this. Dargon was an archfiend. The bat creatures were trying to rip out my jugular. But this was a fellow human being, just about my age, and his warm blood is all over me.

As I kneel in the grass, dizzy and weak, I remind myself that the guy I just killed was fighting for the colonel. He was aiming machine guns at people I love.

But even so, I can't seem to stand up.

Luckily, the Indian warriors quickly finish what I started. Within seconds, and without a shot being fired, the colonel's men are all blowgunned, knifed, or garroted.

Two of the warriors come over to check on me. When they

see that I'm okay, they gently help me to my feet. They seem to understand what I'm going through. Perhaps they had similar reactions after their own first kills.

The other warriors are standing together, facing out toward the river and the oncoming canoes. They're waving to the canoes, signaling that it's now safe to come on. And Kidah is waving back from the second canoe.

I spot Eko paddling quickly, scanning the bank for me.

Mudinho spots me and raises a paddle in salute, and Gisco waves a proud paw.

And that's when the guns open up at us, and the colonel's real ambush begins.

84

They're on the opposite bank, spaced well apart, and expertly hidden. Our own Indian warriors could not have concealed themselves any better. In fact, it wouldn't surprise me if many of the men now attacking us turned out to be Indians from other parts of the Amazon. I'm sure for a fistful of money the colonel could buy himself some native manpower.

I see in a flash that there was a reason that the gun emplacements in the clearing were only crudely concealed. The colonel meant for us to see them and concentrate on them. They were a decoy to distract us from the true hidden threat. And now that trap closes around us with deadly precision.

Semiautomatic weapons, howitzers, and rocket launchers rake the river with a lethal hail of lead and metal. Canoes split apart and burst into flame. Proud warriors scream and leap into the river. I spot Eko diving off her canoe, and Gisco dog-paddling for the closest bank, with Mudinho clinging to his back.

But there's no place to go. The colonel's men waited to attack till the canoes entered a stretch of river with nearly impenetrable thorn bushes on either bank.

I get the idea of turning one of the machine guns in the gun emplacement on the colonel's men, so I duck back into a hut. I run to the large gun, which is pointed out at the river, and see that it has no bullets. As always, the colonel is one big step ahead of me.

The narrow window of the hut gives me a perfect vantage point to view the unfolding ambush. The canoes are now empty on the river. Many of them have been shattered or even splintered by bullets. Hundreds of Indians are swimming or wading to shore. They're screaming as bullets shred them alive. Our rain forest crusade to stop the colonel has utterly failed. In minutes, our war-painted army will be decimated.

Then I realize that the hail of bullets is lessening. And the bullets and rockets that are being fired are wildly missing their targets. Screams still ring out, but they're coming from the thickets along the shore where the colonel's men lie concealed.

I see one of the soldiers burst from beneath a bush, ripping off his camouflage outfit, screaming as if he's on fire. A heartbeat later, a second soldier bolts from hiding, his gun still in his hands. He screams and fires wildly into the ferns at his feet, and then turns his gun on himself and blows his own head off his shoulders.

I peer across the river at the thick foliage on the opposite bank, trying to guess what he was firing at. Are monkeys swinging down from the trees and attacking, or jaguars bounding out of the bush?

I scan the foliage carefully, but I can't spot any large rain forest predators on the attack. But I do notice that the colonel's men aren't alone in giving up their leafy hiding places and fleeing toward the river. The ground itself seems to be moving, driving all manner of wildlife before it.

Insects are fleeing. Rodents are evacuating, rats and mice and capybaras as big as goats are leaping into the river like lemmings. Ground birds take wing and rise in riotous throngs. Traumatized monkeys climb skyward, seeking the security of the very highest branches.

.A slow tide of red-brown mud is oozing out of the jungle, squeezing and shifting, and slowly covering everything in its path. Except that mud doesn't change course willfully. Mud can't flow uphill, or use tactical skill to find hidden soldiers and then chase them down.

Ants! Millions of them. Marching in columns in their own highly disciplined army. Eating leaves. Scattering rodents. Putting to flight birds and beetles. And surrounding and devouring the colonel's soldiers.

I see one man directly across the river jump from his concealed lair in a tree, shrieking pitifully. He manages to rip off all his clothes, and runs for the river stark naked, swatting at his body. But he is cut off by a moving carpet of ants. They crawl up his legs and swarm over his genitals. They reach his face and cover his eyes. Blinded, he trips and falls, and instantly disappears beneath the swarm, as if drowning in a low tide.

His shrieks continue for a few moments, and then stop.

The whole rain forest is silent again. The colonel's men who lay in ambush now lie dead on the bank. The ants pull back, receding like an outgoing tide. I can't bear to even look at some of their victims, almost completely stripped of flesh.

Kidah waves from a rock on the bank, and a hundred or so canoes come into view. I realize that most of our flotilla stayed back, out of reach of the enemy guns. Kidah anticipated that the gun emplacements were a ruse, and that the real attack would come from the opposite bank.

Did he play along, using a calculated risk to set an even cleverer and more deadly trap? Check and mate.

The hundred or so surviving canoes don't continue upriver. They pull over to the bank near Kidah, and the Indians get out.

The warriors I'm with join them, and I follow along. I guess we were too exposed on the river, so Kidah has decided to press on overland. We start hiking through the thick brush, forging our own trail through the green wilderness. It's late afternoon, and we're soon deep in the dark rain forest, safely beneath the seamless canopy. The colonel may know we're coming, but he'll never be able to track us, even with air surveillance.

85

Darkness falls, but we don't break off our march. Kidah leads the way through the forest, carrying a torch. It's just a tree branch that was soaked in some potion he concocted, and then set alight. As it flames, it casts a wide circle of silvery radiance, and it never seems to burn down. He holds the torch high over his head, and we stream after him through the darkness, the way the Israelites must have stayed close to Moses after he used his staff to part the Red Sea.

The rain forest has always been threatening to me at night, but as I follow behind that old wizard, with three hundred Indian warriors marching by my side, the beasts that scream and growl no longer feel like my enemies. I've joined cause with them, and even the darkness that shrouds us so completely seems somehow to be trying to protect us.

Now and then helicopters drone overhead, searching the rivers in vain for us. I'm certain we will soon burst out of the sheltering trees and find ourselves right in the colonel's fortified backyard. The final round of this fight is coming very soon.

I keep flashing back to the young soldier I stabbed. I recall the shock in his eyes, his desperate attempts to repair the damage my blade inflicted, and then how quickly he toppled and bled out. He had such a wild look in his eyes. Was it fear, or did he flash to his mother, or a girlfriend, or to some cherished future plans that would now never be realized?

Was he planning to marry? Did he think about the children he would never have? Did he call on his God to save him?

You were heroic to volunteer for that sneak attack, Gisco tells me, sensing my somber mood. *Did something happen back there, old fellow?*

Yes, I tell him. But I don't want to talk about it.

We'll respect your silence, Eko promises from my other side, and for a few steps I feel the reassuring touch of her hand on my shoulder.

The trees whisper in the night wind and I find myself remembering the woman who raised me. I picture her kneeling, weeding her garden, and glancing up with a smile to watch me sink baskets in the hoop over our driveway. I recall Dad throwing footballs to me in Hadley Park, and reading me *Treasure Island* with all the different pirate voices. How strange to think that they were both living out a lie, and that they're gone now. I wonder if I'll be seeing them soon, and how they'll explain themselves.

P.J. may be there, too, if the helicopter gunship got her. Did she think of me with her final breath? Did she curse me for getting her into this mess, and then leaving after I promised that I would never desert her again? If there is an afterlife, and I die in battle, I've got questions to ask, and lots of explaining to do.

Suddenly I become conscious of a flame over my head. Kidah is walking next to me, and our procession has reshaped itself behind him so that we're now leading the parade. Eko, Gisco, and Mudinho drop back to give us space.

"You were far away," he observes quietly. "What were you thinking about?"

"I was wondering if there is an afterlife."

He nods. "A natural thing for a young man to ponder before a battle."

I look at that wrinkled old face in the flickering torchlight. "Well, is there?"

"How should I know?"

"You're the great wizard of the future."

He grins and then shrugs. "Do you know what the Buddha answered when his disciples asked him what would happen after they died? He said, 'Why do you ask me about death when you don't yet begin to understand life?' "

"I don't understand life either," I mutter miserably. "It's pointless. Everyone you love dies. Everything you believe turns out to be a lie. Every vow you make, destiny forces you to break. I stabbed a kid to death back there, and he could have been my brother." I shiver. "And then you die and the worms eat you. What a swell deal."

Kidah looks back at me and bursts into low laughter. "Wow," he says. "And I thought I had problems." He slowly lowers his arm and suddenly the flaming torch is right in front of me. "Would you hold this for a second, Jack? My arm is starting to cramp up."

I don't believe that his arm is cramping, but I reach out and take the torch.

It's just a tree branch, but when I touch it I feel its power. For a moment I'm not only leading an army through the rain forest, but I'm also plugged into something bright and vibrant and very beautiful.

I can feel the men around me, the jaguars prowling through the trees, the snakes slithering between fern stalks, the raptors circling high above us, and untold billions of insects creeping and crawling through grass and over leaves. We're not just leading an army—we're at the convergence of a great web of life, and tears run down my cheeks as I take it all in at once.

I understand that by letting me carry the torch, Kidah is answering my question. He's showing me that we're risking our lives for a cause greater than ourselves.

"Thanks," Kidah says, holding out his hand for the torch. "I needed the break." As he takes the burning brand back, he smiles and says, "Anyway, I think you're already carrying a torch for someone else." His voice drops. "I don't know much more about the afterlife than you do, but I think you just might run into her again."

"You do?" I ask eagerly.

The wizard looks back at me and for a moment his eyes vanish. All I see are twin holes with clouds. It's as creepy as it was the first time I saw him do this, when he woke up under the stone idol.

I hear people around us gasp, and I pull back in fear. Then he's Kidah again, smiling at me. "Seek and you shall find," he whispers, giving my arm a squeeze. "And try not to look so glum. It's bad for morale."

I manage a small smile. "Okay. Point taken."

"That's better," he says. "Now I'd better go rally the troops." He starts to go and then turns back and adds, "Oh, as for the worms eating your corpse, I wouldn't worry about it. In the rain forest, it's the ants and the beetles that will get you."

✸

86

One minute we're walking through trees beneath the protection of the canopy, and the next we emerge into a field of stumps and weeds and dust. Searchlights sweep the darkness and find us.

Alarms blare. I glimpse the colonel's tall fence far ahead of us, and hear the shouts of guards on watchtowers.

Kidah darts forward, across the open field, and for a little old man he puts on a pretty impressive burst of speed. We follow him, and a determined shout goes up from three hundred throats, in dozens of different tribal languages.

I lend my voice to the swelling roar. *"Chaaaarrrrrge!"*

As I run, I register that it is suddenly getting much colder. A freezing night wind blasts us harder and harder. The first bullets from the guard towers whistle down through that wind and tattoo the ground around our running feet.

A grassy field separates the forest from the fence that guards the colonel's base. We need only a few minutes to cross the half mile of open ground, but each second when you're exposed before enemy guns is a lifetime.

We don't cross this no-man's-land alone. A mysterious legion of dark forms breaks from the trees and runs alongside us. I'm passed by a jaguar that covers fifteen feet with each enormous bound. A dozen peccaries stampede by, their tusks glinting in the spotlights.

Two machine guns open up at us. Their earsplitting RAT-TAT-TAT sounds like the ominous thunder that precedes a summer squall. Then the rain of lead hits us.

I've heard the phrase "war is hell," but I've never really un-

derstood it before. Now I'm in the middle of that hell, with pain
and death sweeping the field all around me.

A young Indian warrior running near me cries out and then
collapses to the ground, holding his stomach. I break stride for a
moment and glance down at him. Bullets have sliced his belly
open like a melon, and his guts are spilling out onto the dust. As I
start running again, I nearly trip on the thrashing, screeching
body of a monkey that has had both its legs shot off.

There's no safety here, no way to minimize the danger, no
magic charm against this murderous, maiming barrage. The only
two options open to us are to continue forward, into what seems
like certain death, or to turn back toward the safety of the forest.

No one turns back.

Kidah holds his torch above his head as he runs. It makes him
an easier target, but the sight of the flame gives us the courage to
keep following. Now I understand why armies through the centuries always carried standards into battle. As long as the stan-
dard bearer lives, his bravery and momentum carry his army
forward.

The freezing wind shifts so that it's behind us, pushing us on
toward the fence.

A laser weapon sizzles down at us and in seconds sets the
grass on fire. I see an eagle streak through the white-hot beam and
turn into a flying cinder.

Two helicopters appear as if from the dark side of the moon,
and their guns join the deadly barrage.

There's no possible escape. We're being blasted from all directions at once, lit up with lasers and shredded with machine guns.
Even if we tried to make it back to the trees, we wouldn't get
halfway there. Our army will be obliterated in seconds.

I know I'm going to die, but I still keep running forward, following the torch, shouting, *"Chaaaarrrrrge!"*

The helicopters swoop low to strafe us, pinpointing us with

their own powerful searchlights. One of the lights finds me, and the helicopter flies right toward me.

I stop running and watch the copter come on, mesmerized by the bright light and the chance to watch my own doom unfold. The copters are now so close that their pilots and gunners are visible, taking final, deadly aim.

In the glare of the searchlights, I see a funnel-shaped black cloud rise quickly from the ground. It envelops and swallows both helicopters. I've seen such a funnel cloud once before, when P.J. and I were paddling with the Korubo chief.

Gnats. Tiny mites. Billions upon billions of them.

The copters' guns fire wildly from inside the inky cloud, as if trying to shoot holes in an unknown foe. Then the guns fall silent as the two aircraft lose their bearings.

I try to imagine what's going on inside them—pilots suddenly unable to see out blackened windows, frantically trying to pull out of their dives, relying on navigational controls. The tiniest mites breach the interior of the cockpits, flying in through air exhaust systems and cannon muzzles. They crawl down throats and fly onto the pupils of eyes. More and more microscopic bugs pour in, till the cabins are awash with them.

BLAM, one of the copters crashes into the stumpy ground and explodes.

WHHIIRFF, the other one zigzags down and is swallowed up by the trees at the edge of the forest.

As I watch the helicopters fall from the sky, I remember the army ants that broke up the colonel's ambush on the river. It's ironic that the rain forest's smallest and most despised creatures are now coming to the aid of its largest ones, and turning the tide of the battle.

I start sprinting again. We're close to the fence now. I can see a machine gun and a laser weapon clearly, mounted atop platforms on the guard towers. I spot the colonel himself taking control of the laser weapon and aiming it at Kidah and his torch.

The personal battle between these two titans from the future has now been joined, and it promises to be a brief one. The white-hot beam flashes across the dark field, searing a savage path toward the wizard.

87

Kidah flings his torch high into the air, like a cheerleader tossing a baton. When the burning branch reaches the apex of its arc, the flame turns blue and then goes out. At the same second, the searchlights crisscrossing the clearing all pulse and then blink off, as if the colonel's electric generators were shorted out by the extinguishing of the wizard's torch.

For a heartbeat, the vast field is plunged into pitch darkness. I stop running and begin to pick my way forward.

Then an apocalyptic peal of thunder rips the sky open, and a blazing bolt of energy flashes down like a serpent's forked tongue. A laser from the sky streaks toward the man-made laser atop the guard tower.

A shadow dives off the platform a split second before the lightning strikes. I'm pretty sure it was the colonel, making a desperate escape. Then the bolt from the stormy black sky flashes into the guard tower, and nothing is left standing save a few scorched and twisted metal bars.

I reach the fence in the first wave of attackers, and start climbing. It was probably electrified, but the blue pulse of Kidah's torch took care of that. Even so, it's not easy to climb a three-story fence in rainy darkness.

Amazon warriors hit the wire and start climbing beneath me. Dozens of Indians wrestle their way up the mesh, trying to get secure hand- and footholds in the gusting downpour. They're used to scaling palm trees, and pass me on the way up, but coils of razor wire at the top stop them. Monkeys outstrip the warriors, but also stop when they hit the concentric rings of tiny blades.

We hang near the top, unable to climb over and too weak to clamber back down. Our combined weight makes the fence sag, but the posts still hold.

Then the whirlwind comes. It's the mother of all friagems, a frigid blast that made it over the Andes and now howls like a monster as it gusts at our backs. The colonel wanted to destroy the earth with global warming, which hits the poles most severely. They're getting some of their own back now. For a moment we're pinned to the fence by the force of this Antarctic gale. It pushes my chest flat against the wire so that I can barely breathe.

These powerful winds would normally whistle harmlessly through the mesh fence. But the hundreds of us clinging near the top give the storm something substantial to blow against. Our backs become like the cloth of a sail, and as the friagem pushes against us, the metal barrier buckles and grinds and begins to give way.

The mesh dips inward, bowing submissively before the force of the blast. Then the posts start to snap, and soon large sections of the fence begin curling to the ground. We ride them all the way down, pick our way gingerly over the razor wire, and race off toward the colonel's compound.

A wave of threatening shapes surges from the darkness to stop us. They're soldiers and prison guards, armed with guns, clubs, and knives.

A guard with the long hair of Samson and the build of a rugby professional swings a club at me. I sense the blow coming, and just duck under it. I wrap him up in a two-legged wrestling takedown, and lift him off his feet. He's still trying to club me as he falls, but my head is tucked tight to his chest and he has no target. I slam him down and his skull thunks against a rock. The impact knocks him cold. I grab his club and run forward.

The outline of the colonel's compound looms in the darkness. I recognize the prison where I was confined. Something tells me that if P.J. is alive, that's where I'll find her. I feel a surge of adrenaline, and leap forward with a savage shout.

The struggle grows fiercer as the colonel's men become more desperate. This is hand-to-hand fighting, the way it must have been for a Spartan phalanx or a Roman legion. I'm stabbed in the hip, and a second later a soldier grabs me from behind and tries to gouge out my right eye.

He's got me in a headlock that I can't break, while his thumb grinds into my eye socket. Then his grip relaxes and he falls to the ground. Eko has run a spear straight through him. Thanks, Ninja Girl, I owe you one.

Twenty feet away, a prison guard grabs Mudinho and raises a club to brain him. Gisco darts over so fast he's a blur, and sinks his canines deep into the guard's calf. The guard screams and tries to kick the snarling hound away. Mudinho jumps on the guard's back and soon the three of them are rolling around on the ground.

Fifty yards to the prison. Half a football field. The rain freezes into hail that comes pelting down at us like iron Ping-Pong balls.

I press forward, leading the final charge. Blood runs down my nose and cheeks, into my mouth. I feel its heat and taste its salty tang and it stirs me to a new level of savagery. This is pure blood rage. Punches and kicks don't faze me. I will not be denied.

Lightning strobes the battlefield and I see images that I will never forget. A soldier is gutted by a peccary's tusks. The wild pig lifts him off his feet and runs around in circles, while the impaled man's arms and legs flail in the air. A guard hacks at a jaguar with an ax. The big cat dodges, and then leaps forward and catches the man's head in its jaws. The ax clatters to the ground as the guard pushes with his hands against the jaguar's neck, trying to extricate himself. The cat bites down, there's a crunching sound, and the soldier goes limp.

I hurdle two dead bodies and reach the prison's front door. It's chained and locked. I punch it and kick it and beat on it with the club, but it doesn't give an inch.

Then I step back and do the most difficult thing there is to do on a battlefield—I force myself back under control. Eko taught me how to use mind over matter on the Outer Banks, but to do so now I have to shut out all this mayhem. And that takes a colossal act of will.

I close my eyes and visualize bursting through darkness into light. When the image in my mind is real enough, I jump off my right foot and kick with my left. The sole of my foot explodes into the door, and the chains snap like Christmas ribbons.

I'm inside.

88

I sprint through the labyrinth of dark and narrow corridors. The electricity is out, so I rely on the sixth sense of navigating in darkness that Eko taught me.

No one challenges me or tries to stop me; the guards must all have gone out to fight. It feels strange to run down these long black hallways alone, listening to my own echoing footsteps.

I turn a corner, and starlight filters in through a high window. The silence is fractured by two dozen frantic voices pleading for help.

Prisoners! Women and kids. They reach out through the bars

of their cell with desperate hands, and beg in a dozen different languages for food and water.

I sprint three or four steps past their cell and then stop and slowly turn back. I was once a prisoner in this very dungeon. I had the same empty stomach and the same desperate eyes. Even in my haste to find P.J., I can't ignore their suffering.

The massive door to their cell is locked and bolted, and the ancient steel bars are more than two inches thick and deeply rooted into the stone floor.

As I stand there examining the lock from the outside, the women and kids wave even more desperately, their voices rising in panic. I figure they're probably misinterpreting my hesitation as a lack of interest.

One thin little girl of eight or nine catches my eye. She's not moving or shouting, just squinting up at me with terrified eyes.

I figure I must look pretty scary with battle scars all over my body and blood running down my face. I reach up and wipe away some blood with the back of my hand, and give her a tiny smile.

Her eyes grow still wider in horror. It dawns on me that she's not scared of me, but for me.

I duck quickly to one side, and a club as big as a baseball bat smashes into the metal where my head was a second ago. The blow would have killed me.

I dive away as a hulking guard takes another vicious swing and just misses. I bounce off a side wall, somersault high over his head, jump on his back, and slap on a choke hold from behind.

The big man bucks like a bull and snaps like a gator, but there's no escape. He runs backward into a wall, trying to knock me off, but I take the hit and increase the pressure. He soon sinks to his knees, gasping.

His face starts to turn red and he goes into final contortions. As he twists wildly, I get a look at the side of his face. I know this man!

He was the biggest of the trio of guards who led me to the candirú chamber. His struggles lessen, and I can tell he's at the edge of blacking out from lack of oxygen.

I let him slip to the floor, and stand over him so that he can see my face. The side of my bare foot presses into his windpipe. I let him breathe just enough to keep him conscious. "Look at me," I shout at him. I point to my face. "*Look at me!* Do you remember who I am?"

He can't understand my English, but he looks up, and I see a glint of recognition in his eyes.

"Where is she?" I ask him, miming long hair and a girl's figure. "*La señorita?* P.J. The girl I love. *Mi amor.* Is she down in the candirú room?" I point downward. "Or up in the private dungeon wing?" I point upstairs. "Tell me where she is or you die."

I increase the pressure on his throat and he gags and raises a shaking finger to point upward.

I'm not sure what to do with him. If I let him live, he'll probably sound the alert and then find a weapon and come after me again. But I can't just kill him in cold blood.

I reach down and grab hold of his uniform and drag him to his feet. He's almost too dizzy to stand, gasping in breaths of air and trying to shake out the cobwebs. I judo-throw him ten feet so that he crashes into the bars and sinks back to the floor.

Twenty arms reach for him. The guard screams as vengeful women grab clumps of his hair, starving children's fingers latch onto his ears, and the gnarled hands of tough old women secure his legs. He writhes, but there are too many of them and he can't break free. Other hands reach through the bars for the big key ring on his belt.

I take off down the hallway, confident that the prisoners will free themselves and mete out justice to their jailer.

I'm running through darkness again, but this time I know where to go. I reach a flight of stairs and take them four at a time.

Even a jaguar would be impressed by these bounds. At the top, a long corridor unfolds like a black ribbon. I fly down it at full sprint.

Smoke is in the air—someone must have set the prison on fire. Voices echo from far off, triumphant yells and agonized screams. The women and kids must be using the key ring to free other prisoners, and when the swelling mob encounters jailers it sounds like they exact swift revenge.

There are no more flights to climb and no more hallways to traverse. I'm at the top now, the penthouse of the penitentiary. The corridor terminates fifty feet ahead.

At the very end is a blue circular door. It looks like the entry hatch to a rocket.

I reach for it, and recall with a shiver the similarly shaped black door to the candirú chamber.

89

The blue hatch is open and I push into the chamber.

It's large and windowed, and in daylight must offer views of the compound and the surrounding forest stretching away to the horizon. Now it's dark and gloomy.

I glance out the bank of windows nearest me, and glimpse the battle raging below.

I turn back to the shadowy chamber. In the center of the room, a figure stands motionless, towering from floor to ceiling. Is it a statue? A giant guarding his tenebrous lair? I step forward cautiously and realize that whatever it is, it's not standing, but rather suspended from the ceiling.

Something moves above me, and the room starts to grow cold. I feel the whoosh of wind and the damp of rain. A segment of the roof is retracting! Starlight filters down, and I reexamine the large figure. It's not a statue, nor a giant standing guard. It's P.J., hanging from the ceiling!

She's dangling upside down from chains, so that her long hair brushes the floor. She moans very faintly. She's alive!

I run to her. And then I hear an ungodly sound.

It's a rustle above the roar of the wind. A whisper that is at once delicate and deafening because it portends the approach of something dreadful.

Lightning flashes and I see them fly down at us through the opening in the ceiling. Red eyes, muscular and lithe ratlike bodies, gleaming teeth. Bats!

I remember reading that there are nearly a thousand different kinds of bats in the Amazon, including the only true vampire bats in the world. They sleep by day and hunt by night, and their preferred food is mammals.

I can't fight them, can't swat them away. There are too many of them—there must be twenty thousand! I wrap P.J. in my arms and hold her tight.

The stench of them is noxious! Their bodies are wet and cold! They cover my face, crawl through my hair, nip at me with razor-sharp teeth to draw blood, and then lap it up with tiny tongues.

There's nothing I can do. I hear myself screaming, and P.J. is screaming, too.

I force my mind to work. Loathsome as these bloodsuckers are, they are also nature's creatures. I remember the way it felt to hold Kidah's torch, and how, for a few moments, I was one with all the animals of the rain forest, big and small, cuddly and repulsive.

I clutch P.J. tightly and try to shut out the pain and horror of the bat attack, and to recapture that feeling of being an integral part of the rain forest quilt of life.

When I held the torch I felt the jaguars prowling through darkness, the monkeys swinging in the trees, and the ants and beetles in the grass and ferns. We were all linked together, all joined with a common cause.

Now I open my mind up to the bats. I feel their hunger for blood, their joy at being part of the feeding swarm, the sonar that allows them to zero in on us. Instead of being repelled by them, I reach out to them and try to touch their essence.

The rain forest is their home. They have as much to lose if it vanishes as anyone. We are all part of the same web of life, and if it is frayed and destroyed no cave will be deep enough to shelter these bats, and no midnight will be dark enough to shield them from destruction.

For a moment I feel myself fractured into a thousand pieces, wheeling and darting around the dark chamber on thousands of tiny wings.

And then I'm Jack again, and the black cloud dissipates, like smoke blown away by a strong wind. Off they go, through the roof aperture, and P.J. whimpers in my arms.

"It's okay. They're gone," I tell her. "And I'm taking you home."

She cries out again, with words. "Jack, he's here!"

A man enters the room through the blue hatch door, and pauses to shut and lock it. Then he turns to face us.

I recognize the colonel, even though he's significantly altered. The shock of white hair is the same, and the muscular build, and he watches me with the same black eyes. But this is no librarian on steroids. This is unmistakably the Dark Lord!

"You did well with the bats," he says, and his voice is mocking. "So the old charlatan taught you some tricks, and now you're the sorcerer's apprentice? If I were you I would make myself disappear." His voice hardens. "I warned you not to find Kidah. I spared your life. I ordered you to leave the forest forever."

"And then you sent your men to ambush us," I remind him, stepping protectively in front of P.J.

He doesn't appear to even hear me. "But you didn't listen," he continues, advancing toward me. He no longer walks like a man. He scuttles, and his arms and shoulders twitch as his legs move. "You found Kidah and revived him. For that you and your lady friend will pay in blood." He's more spider than man now, and he looks hungry.

I should be terrified, but I'm not. My knees should be knocking and my voice should be quaking, but anger comes to my rescue.

"That's right, I defied you," I answer him, curling my fingers into fists and settling into a fighting pose. "Listen to those screams outside. Your army is being destroyed as we speak. Your buildings are on fire. Your power in the Amazon is smashed. As for P.J., the only way for you to ever hurt her again is to get through me now. So why don't you stop mouthing off and take your best shot."

If a tarantula can smile, that's what he does. His eyes ignite like twin black suns. "Gladly," he whispers. And he charges.

✳

90

The last time we fought, I threw the best kick of my life at him, and he grabbed my foot in midair. His speed and strength were superhuman.

I want him to believe I'm angry enough to make the same mistake again. My defiant words and insults were intended to make him think I'm so blinded by my own fury that I can't think straight. I lower my head and charge at him as if I've gone completely berserk.

But I know what I'm doing. The only way to beat this guy is to use his own power against him.

We come together hard, and his charge knocks me backward. Instead of resisting, I give way. As I fall back, my hands grab his arms and pull him down with me, so that I incorporate the force and momentum of his charge in my spin. My knees come under his chest, and at the right second I kick him up and away. Spider man goes flying fifteen feet and cracks into a large window.

The back of his head smashes hard into the thick glass pane, shattering it. The impact would stun almost anyone. The Dark Lord falls to the floor, but he pops right back up. A shard from the broken pane must have cut him. He's bleeding, and he doesn't look pleased.

He comes at me again, and I have no more tricks up my sleeve, so I try to knock his head off with a straight right. It's a good punch, but he ducks it and grabs me.

It's my turn to fly through the air, and instead of a window he tosses me into a stone wall. I hit it and feel my spine crack, and then I black out for a moment. P.J.'s screams bring me back. *"Jack, he's coming! Jaaaaackkkk!"*

Sure enough, he's advancing at me through the gloom, ready to finish me off. I climb back to my feet, but something is broken on my right side and I can't stand up straight. I move hunched over, holding my side.

His mouth opens. His teeth have disappeared. Long fangs glint. He's going to rip out my jugular and enjoy every bloody throb. There's no way I can stop him.

I back up to the window. Feel the cold air. This is the pane his head struck and shattered!

I get an idea and glance down. Shards of broken glass glint on the floor. He springs at me, and I bend, scoop up a glass shard in my hands, and stab upward.

I aim for his throat, but he turns his head and I only succeed in slicing him open from ear to jaw.

The Dark Lord staggers back with a bellow of pain and rage. "I will make you wish that whore of Dann never gave birth to you," he growls, and comes in for the kill.

I've never seen anyone move so fast. He's a blur, coming right at me, and there's no time to get out of the way. I try a kick, but he blocks it with such force that he breaks my right leg.

I collapse, screaming in pain, and crawl away from him across the floor.

The Dark Lord laughs. "Where are you going, young one? You do remind me of your father sometimes. He screamed and tried to crawl away, also. But I had my fun with him, and we're just getting started here."

P.J. sees my agony and screams, and he turns and smiles at her. "You're next, my dear. Wait your turn."

He steps toward me again, and this time I'm absolutely helpless. I roll away as far as I can, till I hit the wall. And then I just lie there and wait for him.

He stands above me, enjoying my fear for a long second. "So," he says, "this is the Prince of Dann, the light of the world, the beacon of hope?" Then he reaches down. But before his fingers close on me, all the lights in the chamber suddenly blink back on.

As if guessing what's about to happen the Dark Lord whirls around, just in time to see the blue hatch door explode inward.

✳

91

Kidah steps into the room.

"So you've come," the Dark Lord whispers, and there's fear and fury in his voice.

"Yes, I've come to stop you," Kidah answers calmly. "This world has enough problems of its own without a monster like you."

The Dark Lord has no answer for that except an all-out attack. He forgets about me and runs right at the wizard. It's like a tarantula charging a tiny white mouse.

But the mouse doesn't give an inch. Kidah stands his ground, and raises a hand. A white light shoots out of his palm and zaps into the Dark Lord. It seems to cling to him, to play about him, to grow brighter and brighter.

The Dark Lord shrieks in pain and begins rolling around on the floor, as if trying to extinguish the flames. But whatever is consuming him cannot easily be put out. The more he rolls around screaming, the brighter the light seems to burn.

Eko runs into the chamber, just in time to see the Dark Lord go into his death throes. His screams reach a pinnacle of agony, and then he curls up and shrivels into himself. But he doesn't die. He transforms.

Where a man writhed on the ground, a black spider the size of a basketball stands defiantly. It shakes out its bristly legs, and peers at us with its eight chilling eyes.

Kidah shoots another white light at the spider, but it dodges to one side.

"Don't let it get away!" Eko shouts, and throws a silver knife at it. Her knife severs one of the spider's eight legs and it hisses wildly, and then runs to the windows.

It crawls up the pane that was shattered during our fight, and squeezes out the crack. It scuttles down the other side of the glass and drops off into the night.

"It's wounded. We must hunt it down and kill it now!" Kidah declares. He hurries to the window and touches the glass with both palms. He doesn't push it hard, but the thick pane explodes outward. The wizard turns to me, raises one arm in farewell, and then turns back and jumps out of sight into the darkness.

Eko is left alone with us. I can tell she's in a hurry to join the chase, but she runs over to me. "Jack, are you okay?"

"I've been better," I tell her. "Help P.J."

Eko takes a few precious seconds to free P.J. from her chains and get her upright again.

My high school girlfriend and the Ninja Babe are finally face-to-face.

"Thank you," P.J. whispers.

"You're welcome. I'm Eko."

"I know who you are," P.J. tells her. "And I know what you want."

Eko looks back at her, and then glances toward the broken window. "I feel for you," Eko whispers. "You can have him back for now, but in the end he is destined to be mine."

She runs to the window in four long steps, puts her arms out in front of her, and dives into blackness.

92

Two sleek outboard canoes hum down a river toward the lights of the small city ahead.

P.J. is nestled in my arms. She hasn't slept since we left the colonel's compound, which was thoroughly destroyed in the battle. I haven't slept much either—it hurts when I lie down, it hurts when I roll over, and it even aches each time I breathe.

I guess we both have some healing to do.

We haven't discussed the battle or speculated about whether Kidah tracked down and destroyed the Dark Lord.

We just hold each other tightly and let the canoe carry us swiftly down the wide, pitch-black channel.

It's a beautiful and hypermodern craft, from the colonel's own private collection. The powerful outboard motor eats up the long miles. I can steer it and hold P.J. at the same time. She feels very good in my arms.

In the canoe behind us, Gisco and Mudinho ride together. As the lights of the city glimmer closer, Mudinho slows their canoe and Gisco raises a paw in unexpected farewell.

I wave back, and ask him telepathically: Aren't you coming with us?

I may catch up with you eventually, Gisco answers. *But this loyal lad saved my life, and a dog always repays a debt. In a little village by a mountain lake there's a mother living in grief because her eight-year-old son was stolen by drug bandits. I'm going to help bring him home.*

I understand, I tell him. I hope you find her. It's a noble thing to try. Godspeed.

Yes, a truly selfless errand of mercy, Gisco agrees. *But I do hear she's*

the best cook in her village. Mudinho says she can do things with roast
pork that are miraculous, and her chicken with pumpkin seeds is beyond
compare. So off I go on my mission of self-sacrifice. Au revoir.

They veer off one way, and we go the other. Mudinho steers
their canoe with his right hand and waves with his left. Gisco
watches me with sad eyes and then stands on his hind legs and
blows a kiss at P.J.

"That's some dog," P.J. observes softly.

"One of a kind," I agree. "And some boy, too. I think they're
going to do okay together."

We watch till their canoe grows tiny in the distance.

The sky is lightening to the east. A new dawn is breaking over
the treetops. I press my cheek to P.J.'s and confess, "It's strange,
considering what we've been through, but I've gotten to like this
glorious rain forest."

"I'm ready for home," she whispers back. Then I feel her
shiver. "What about us, Jack? How are we going to do together?
Do you think we can ever really go home, or get back what we
had?" Doubt and fear sharpen her whisper. "That monster survived. And the wizard. And Eko, too. It's not over. It may never
be over."

I hold her closer, and plant the softest of kisses on her neck.
"It's over for me."

P.J. nods and kisses me back. "Okay," she whispers. "That's
what I want, too." She's quiet for a few seconds, mulling it over.
"But what if they don't let you go? From what you've told me,
you're caught between two worlds. And even if this is the one you
grew up in and are comfortable with, you're really one of them.
Your parents are alive in the future. And your enemies, too. You
were born into their struggle. You're of their time."

I look back into her worried face and words fail me. I glance
down and end up staring at my father's watch. The blue hands
glint on the white background.

I take the watch off my wrist and fling it far out over the dark river. It gleams when it hits the water, and then it quickly sinks out of sight.

"What did you do that for?" P.J. asks. "Didn't that come from your father?"

"Yup. But I'm no longer operating on his time." I hold her even tighter. "Look, I hope we helped save this incredible rain forest, and protect the atmosphere. I think we might have done some good to planet Earth, and improved the chances for future generations. But as far as I'm concerned, it's finished now. My connection to them and their time is sinking to the bottom of this river. Right now all I want is to live my life, my own insignificant Jack Danielson life, with you."

She looks back at me, and I see all the suffering and trauma she's been through. She's a different person from the happy-go-lucky girl I fell in love with back in Hadley. "Do you think that's at all realistic, Jack?"

"Sure," I say.

She looks incredulous but cautiously hopeful. "Okay. Where do we start?"

"I'm going to start with a hamburger," I tell her. "For you, I recommend a long soak in a hot tub."

P.J. looks back at me for several long seconds, and I think she's going to cry. A tear slides down her cheek, but then the corners of her mouth tilt upward into a brave smile. "Bozo," she whispers, "you got yourself a deal."

I take her hand, and we motor on down the river. As we come to a wide bend, I glance back.

The spot where I dropped my father's watch is now illuminated by an eerie blue glow. It seems to spread out, lighting the palms on either bank. As we speed away from it, it reaches out across our rippling wake and touches me.

For a long moment I feel my father's presence—he's right there in the boat with us! I sense that he knows what I've accomplished in the Amazon and he's pleased and very proud. He grasps how I feel about P.J., and he's bemused. But he also knows what I just told her, and he wants to correct me. I can almost hear his whisper from a thousand years away: "You're my son, Jack. You belong to us. You cannot change your destiny."

I turn the throttle up and we speed around the bend. P.J. nestles into my shoulder and I give her hand a squeeze as the shimmering blue glow fades away into the watery wilderness behind us.

GOFISH

DAVID KLASS

What did you want to be when you grew up?
For a long time, I wanted to be a base-ball player. I was a pitcher, and then, as I got older, a first baseman. Later on, I considered being a doctor and volunteered in a hospital during college. But telling stories seemed to be what I was best at.

When did you realize you wanted to be a writer?
I started writing short stories in my early teens, and midway through college, I began to consider it as a career.

What's your first childhood memory?
When I was four, my parents took us to India for a year. My father was an anthropologist who was doing a study of a small village there. My earliest memories are of India: the smell of the spices, the festivals, going to a missionary school, hearing about President Kennedy's assassination over the radio, and being bitten by a rabid dog. I still remember a little Bengali.

What's your most embarrassing childhood memory?
When I was in second grade, I stuck a paper clip in a wall socket and nearly electrocuted myself.

As a young person, who did you look up to most?
I was blessed with wonderful parents. My father was a wise, gentle, funny man who loved us dearly and read to us every night. My mother is a novelist who is probably responsible for the fact that her three children all grew up to be writers.

What was your worst subject in school?
I didn't like algebra, and I struggled with physics. It's strange, because these days, I find theoretical physics to be fascinating. I still don't like algebra.

What was your first job?
My first full-time job was selling a book called *Basic Wiring* over the telephone. I couldn't believe anyone would actually buy it, but every day, I managed to sell a dozen or so copies. I truly hated calling complete strangers during their dinner hour and trying to sell them a book that I would have never read myself.

How did you celebrate publishing your first book?
I sold my first novel, *The Atami Dragons*, to Scribner when I was twenty-three years old. I was living in a small town in Japan, and I celebrated by going out that night with some friends for a Japanese feast.

Where you do write your books?
I used to write at home, or in coffee shops or libraries, but now that I have two small kids, I rent an office in midtown Manhattan.

Where do you find inspiration for your writing?
I wait for a story to grab me. Sometimes, I hear the voice of the main character and try to let him tell his story through me. That's what happened when I started to write *You Don't Know Me* and *Firestorm*. Other times, I become interested in an issue and slowly flesh out a story around it. An example of this is *California Blue*.

Which of your characters is most like you?
I don't think that any of my characters are really like me. John in *You Don't Know Me* was drawn from some of my memories of myself in junior high school. Jack in *Firestorm* also has a bit of me in him—I loved sports and poetry, and even as a kid, I thought that the global environment was fragile and under assault.

When you finish a book, who reads it first?
My father used to read my books first—he read at a great speed and caught all spelling and grammatical errors. I miss him terribly.

Are you a morning person or a night owl?
I'm a morning person. I get up in darkness, and do some of my best writing while the rest of my family is sleeping.

What's your idea of the best meal ever?
A three-hour dinner in the Italian countryside with good friends and a nice bottle of wine or two.

Which do you like better: cats or dogs?
I like dogs—the bigger the better. I married a woman with a cat, and now we're stuck with two of them. One doesn't get everything one wants in life.

What do you value most in your friends?

I like friends who are smart and funny, genuine and loyal, interesting and a little quirky, but at the same time, rock solid when it comes to the most foundational qualities.

Where do you go for peace and quiet?

I write alone in an office, so finding peace and quiet is not a problem. When I need noise and to be around other people during the day, I go to a gym and play pickup basketball. I enjoy coming home in the evening to two kids who want to sword fight and play hide-and-seek.

What makes you laugh out loud?

Both my son, Gabriel, and my daughter, Madeleine, are very funny. I laugh out loud when they make fun of me, which they do quite often.

What's your favorite song?

I don't think I have a favorite song, but I sing the kids "Puff the Magic Dragon" every night at bedtime. I confess that after a few years, it has stopped being one of my favorites. I'm ready for a new one.

Who is your favorite fictional character?

I loved John le Carre's character Jerry Westerby. And when I was younger, I liked Edmond Dantes from *The Count of Monte Cristo*.

What are you most afraid of?

I'm most afraid of not being able to protect my kids in what I see as an increasingly dangerous world. We live in Manhattan, and September 11th is a very powerful memory.

What time of the year do you like best?
I love autumn. I lived in Los Angeles for ten years and I missed the change of seasons. It didn't rain for two years after I moved there. Then I decided to throw a barbecue party. As soon as I lit the grill, a downpour started. I knew I'd better move back east.

What is your favorite TV show?
I enjoyed *The Sopranos* and was sorry to see it finish. I watch a lot of sports and news shows, but don't really have a favorite dramatic show. When I was growing up, I loved *Star Trek* and *Kung Fu*.

If you were stranded on a desert island, who would you want for company?
If I was stranded on a desert island, it would be the perfect time for a family vacation.

If you could travel in time, where you would go?
I would like to accompany Hannibal on his march over the Alps. I would also love to go back to Athens just before the Peloponnesian War.

What's the best advice you have ever received about writing?
I remember an essay by Rudyard Kipling where he talks about following his Daemon—an inner voice that was infallible in telling a story well. I am the least mystical person around, but I do believe that somehow, in some way, a writer must try to be led by his characters rather than force them to do his will.

What do you want readers to remember about your books?

I don't have set goals that I want readers to remember from my books. I hope they enjoy them, and in the case of *Firestorm* and the Caretaker Trilogy, I hope they get a heightened sense of how fragile this planet is, and how we're at a crucial turning point.

What would you do if you ever stopped writing?

I think I would shift from one writing form to another. I also write screenplays, and I would love to try writing plays for the stage. I directed a bit of theater years ago, and it would be a dream to write and direct my own play.

What do you like best about yourself?

I guess what I like best about myself is the time and energy I devote to my kids. They are a true blessing.

What is your worst habit?

My worst habit is probably wasting so much time watching sports events on TV that I really don't care about. A football game can gobble up three or four hours.

What do you consider to be your greatest accomplishment?

As a writer, I'm proud of several of my books: *You Don't Know Me*, *California Blue*, *Wrestling with Honor*, and *Firestorm*. Probably the hardest thing I've ever done is go to Hollywood without connections and become a successful screenwriter. It took seven years of struggle and near-starvation. But my greatest accomplishment is building a family.

What do you wish you could do better?

There are many things I wish I could do better. Here are a few, in no particular order: Sing, draw, dribble a soccer ball, write crisper dialogue, speak better Italian and Japanese, understand string theory, shoot jump shots from three-point range, and devote more of my time to good causes.

What would your readers be most surprised to learn about you?
Many of my YA book readers are surprised to learn that I have a double career, and that I spend most of my time writing action movies for Hollywood. It's a big jump from a novel like *You Don't Know Me* to a movie like *Walking Tall* or *Kiss the Girls*.

*K*eep reading for an excerpt from Book 3 of
The Caretaker Trilogy: **Timelock**,
available now in hardcover from Farrar, Straus and Giroux.

EXCERPT

Manhattan. Seven-thirty in the evening. Indian summer. No way it should be this warm in late September, but I'm sweating in my T-shirt as I run through the gloaming and feel the cold prickle on the back of my neck. Someone is watching me. Now. Here. Close by.

Had enough sentence fragments yet? My English teacher said they were a weakness of mine. But that was more than a year ago, when I was a senior at Hadley High School, leading a relatively normal life.

I'm not in Hadley anymore, and I can never go back. Too much has happened to me since then. Firestorm adventure to save the oceans, over. Whirlwind trip to the Amazon, completed. I'm a year older. I hope a bit wiser. But I still like sentence fragments. They generate pace. If you want speed, stick around, my friend. If you enjoy weird, don't budge from that chair.

I feel that prickle again. Glance around quickly. Gangly guy in spandex checking his fancy stopwatch for lap time. Cute chick with red hair bopping along the wrong way, listening to her music, making all the other runners veer around her. Family of four jogging in pairs, mother-son, father-daughter. Everyone looks a bit strange.

This is Manhattan, after all. Hundreds of people in the park on a warm autumn evening doing their funky big-city things and surreptitiously checking each other out.

That's why I'm here. I came to the Big Apple because it seemed like a good place to lose myself and start over. Shed a skin. Jump into the bubbling stew. Melting pot supreme.

Got a job working construction. See a lot of P.J. who's a freshman at Barnard College. There are days when I work fifteen hours and no one gives me a second look, and I almost believe that it's possible for me to live a relatively normal life.

And then there are the moments like this when I know I'm kidding myself.

I do a three-sixty, looking for telltale signs. No tall cyborgs. No bat creatures. No one dodges my gaze.

Could be a false alarm. Maybe I'm paranoid. Except that deep down I know it's real. Can't spitball who's watching me, but I'm positive they're out there.

I have only two choices, neither of them particularly appealing. I can wait for them to make their move. Or I can try to run away.

I pick up the pace as darkness settles over the reservoir. Outside the park, the lights of Central Park West and Fifth Avenue blink on. An urban constellation frames an oasis of dark, rippling water. I've seen the world a bit. Swum deep under the oceans to a virgin sea mount. Found the hidden valley of the Amazon. A beautiful evening in Manhattan is still a pretty spectacular thing.

I'm running fast now. Passing people. Arms pumping. No one can keep up with me. But they don't have to.

Whoever's watching me may be stationary, following my laps from a bench. Or maybe they're ensconced high up in an apartment overlooking the park, like the Gorm who lured me to her penthouse lair, watching me through a window with nightscopes. Or it could be a kid, or a mechanical bird, or even a shape-shifting squirrel.

I first felt the prickle one week ago, at P.J.'s dinner party. I admit I was nervous anyway.

Nice of her to invite me, but I didn't fit in. P.J.'s new friends. The college set. A dozen Columbia and Barnard freshmen. Giggling about a charming anthropology professor with endless eccentric anecdotes and complaining about an arduous chem lab. Comparing reading lists and writing assignments. Trying out new words, new hairstyles, and post–high school personas on each other.

One goofy guy not in college. Didn't even finish high school. Nice to meet you, Jack. What do you do? Oh, really, you work construction? How do you know P.J.? High school friend? Well, nice talking to you.

We're eating in the garden of a Greek restaurant downtown. I'm trying to pretend that I don't mind being completely ignored. Go ahead and converse. Posture. Pontificate. I'll just concentrate on this plate of kabobs.

I listen politely as I unskewer lamb chunks with my hands, calloused from heavy work. The physics phenom sitting next to me keeps stealing glances at my missing pinky. Want to know how I lost that one, Einstein? A fiend named Dargon cut it off on a trawler, while his thugs held me down. But don't mind me. Go on making fun of your linear algebra teaching assistant's stutter. I'm riveted.

P.J. isn't fooled. She's watching me. I give her a nonchalant grin and she smiles back. Okay, prep school lacrosse star. Tell her about your family's spread in the Hamptons. She'll listen and nod, but I'm the one who will be walking her home tonight. I'm the one who will be riding up in the elevator with her, to her dorm room. I'm the one who will follow her into the common room, past her three roommates, to her tiny bedroom filled with books.

And guess what? You may have the hip clothes and the

preppy cool and the million-dollar summer house, but I'm the one who will put my arms around her and kiss her on her soft warm lips, and tell her I love her.

Except that she definitely seems interested in that place in Bridgehampton. And the lacrosse player is smart enough not to go after her too aggressively, but rather he makes it a group thing. Somehow a party starts to get planned there, a big bash with costumes and a live band. And I don't think I'm on the guest list.

I excuse myself and head to the bathroom. Twenty other tables in the garden. Glasses clinking. Silverware clanking. And that's when I feel it.

On the back of my neck. The tactile equivalent of someone raking his fingernails across a blackboard. It makes me squirm and wheel around.

All I see are couples sipping wine and spooning lemon chicken soup by candlelight. There are a few large groups digging into platters of stuffed grape leaves and devouring baby lamb chops as they banter back and forth.

I burst inside and check out the bar, the waiters, and the kitchen staff. They're all busy with plates and trays and glasses. "The bathroom's down there, sir," a waiter explains, misinterpreting my distress.

Seconds later I'm in the bathroom splashing cold water on my face and trying to calm down. Because this is the nightmare I live with. That they'll find me again. Hunt me down. Rip off the bandage and open the scar.

And now it's happened.

I knew it instantly, at that dinner party, standing in the courtyard of the Greek restaurant. Sure, I tried to convince myself that it had just been a chill breeze on the back of my neck. But as I looked at myself in the bathroom mirror, I knew they had found me and it was starting all over again.

I knew it with even more certainty two days later at the construction site, hard hat on and tool belt in place, stepping out on a high girder. Couldn't afford to shiver up there, but I felt the cold prickle again. All of Manhattan below. Dozens of office buildings. Anyone could be watching me.

So now, in Central Park, it isn't a complete surprise. But this is strike three. No use pretending anymore. I go into full sprint for the last hundred yards, and as I fly along, arms pumping, I force myself to face the bitter truth. Have to act quickly. Take time off my job. Go out of town for a while. Maybe get myself a weapon. And most difficult of all, I must tell P.J.

She's so happy at Barnard, living a normal life again. She never told her parents what happened after she disappeared from Hadley. She feigned amnesia. They brought her to psychologists and specialists, and finally they just gave up and were glad she came back to them.

Now she's starting to enjoy life again. Making new friends. Taking classes. Excelling in art. Touring galleries. Going home on weekends to see her folks.

At the same time, I've noticed she's stopped talking to me about our Amazon experiences. If I bring it up, she'll nod and mumble a few words. But she herself never mentions it. She's put the whole thing behind her. Wiped the slate clean.

She won't enjoy hearing that it's not over. That it may never be over. But I have no choice. Because the Dark Army kidnapped her once. They may try again. She's a player in this now. If they've found me, they probably also know that she's here, so she has to be on her guard.

I finish my ten miles and leave the park, breathing hard. Normally, I would enjoy this feeling after a good run, my blood pumping, my wet shirt sticking to my chest and back as the evening wind blows. But the prospect of telling P.J. fills me with dread. I can imagine the look in her eyes when she hears it. Don't, Jack. Please stop now.

But there's no choice. No delay possible. I have to tell her. Tonight. At nine o'clock, when she comes home from the library. If I don't warn her and something happens, I'll never forgive myself.

So instead of heading to my own tiny room, I jog to Broadway and head uptown toward Barnard.

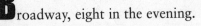

Broadway, eight in the evening.

Not the bohemian Broadway of Soho or the Village, or the touristy, glitzy Broadway of Times Square and the Theater District. This is the authentic Broadway for me, where New York starts to feel ethnic again.

I hear hip-hop. Smell pizza. Signs start popping up in Spanish. There's a curry joint. A Korean grocery. The White Lotus Karate Academy with a class going on inside. I peer through the window. Manhattanites of all different sizes and races learning to kick and punch. I bet Eko could show them a few tricks.

I haven't heard from the Ninja Babe since she jumped out a window in the Amazon in pursuit of a spider who was really the Dark Lord. Gisco hasn't dropped me a postcard either. I wonder if he returned Mudinho to his village.

Just thinking about such things as I walk up Broadway makes me realize how wacky my life is. All around me is a pulsing city crammed with an endless variety of people returning home from school and work. They've come here from the ends of the earth, and have wildly different lives and sets of problems to worry about, but at least they're all playing in the same ballpark of reality.

None of them are plagued by memories of dark masterminds from a thousand years hence who shape-shift into tarantulas and scuttle off into the rain forest. None of them miss wizards or telepathic dogs or beautiful ninja babes, who have probably all returned to their now-pristine future world.

I walk faster, attempting to leave the memories and the doubts behind. But the most upsetting question of all continues to tug at me: Isn't that mysterious far future world really my world, since I was born into it, and both my parents still live there?

No, I tell myself. Don't walk down that path. It leads straight to madness. I've crawled out of the rabbit hole. It's time to draw a line. I am Jack Danielson now, construction worker. Public library user. Young man about town. On the way to see my ladylove.

But deep down I know it's not over. That's why they were watching me at the restaurant, at the construction site, and tonight at the reservoir. And that's why I need to warn P.J., even if she freaks.

I'm more than halfway to Barnard. Starting to freak a bit myself. Because I know that whatever words I use to tell her, however gently I break the news, I'm going to scare the daylights out of her. Worse than that. I'm going to widen the gulf between us. She'll once again associate me with a nightmare she's trying hard to forget.

Eventually, in her effort to construct a normal life, she'll reach for something safe and traditional. End up with the lacrosse player. Can I really blame her?

I pound my fist into my hand so hard it makes a smacking sound. People glance over at me. Yes, damn it, I can blame her. We love each other. Love is supposed to conquer all. Even the weird stuff. But what can I do?

Four blocks from P.J.'s dorm, I get the idea. It pops into my head out of the dark sky. Don't show up with bad news *and* empty-handed, dummy. Bring her something to sweeten the mood a bit. What do all girls love? Flowers.

Now I'm not a candy and flowers kind of a guy. My presents to P.J. usually run more along the lines of a new book that I've enjoyed, or a CD she can listen to while I give her a back rub.

Come to think of it, I don't even think P.J. likes candy. But she does like flowers.

And here's a nice corner flower store—the Gotham Garden. Surprisingly, it's still open and ready for business. There's a display of orchids outside. A sign in the window promises: "Bouquets made to order. Let our flowers touch the heart of your special one."

Yes, please touch her. Just what I need.

I push the door open and head inside.

Flower displays floor to ceiling. Roses. Tulips. Lilies. Irises. Dozens of vibrant blooms that I can't identify, but then I'm no flower expert.

Two young shop workers are performing menial tasks. A bored girl with a pierced nose sorts ferns. A big guy in a Giants cap sweeps up fallen leaves.

"Excuse me," I say, "but I need some help."

"Stanley!" the fern sorter calls. Then she tilts back her head, opens her mouth wide, and bellows: "STANLEY. CUSTOMER."

A pudgy middle-aged man hurries out of the flower-cooler room, wiping his hands on a towel. His bald head gleams under the lights and his eyeglasses are crooked. He looks me over quickly, taking in my shorts and sweaty T-shirt, perhaps wondering if I've got any money. "Evening," he says, "how can I help you."

I take out the thin wallet I carry when I run, to put his mind at rest. "I'd like to buy a dozen red roses."

"You've come to the right place. We have some real beauties," he assures me and then hesitates. "But are you sure you wouldn't want something a little more interesting? I could make you up a nice mixed bouquet?"

"Thanks, but I can't go too far wrong with red roses," I point out. "And I'm in a bit of a hurry."

"You got it," he says, sounding a little disappointed. Then he smiles. "Roses are red, violets are blue, she'll love them, so she'll love you."

The guy sweeping up snorts derisively, and the girl sorting ferns turns to me and says, "Forgive him. He's a nice man, but he can't help himself."

"Nothing wrong with a little poetry to break up the tedium of life," the florist replies with a defensive smile. And then, conspiratorially: "Tell you what, son. Meredith is gonna get your roses. Let me show you some truly special flowers that just came in, so that maybe next time I can talk you into a mixed bouquet."

I glance at my watch. "I really don't have . . ."

He's already opened the door of the cooler room and is ushering me inside. "It'll take two minutes, while she's clipping and wrapping your roses. You won't lose any time. Humor me. A flower of beauty is a joy forever."

I don't have it in me to be rude to a man who paraphrases John Keats and makes up his own bad doggerel. So I nod and walk in through the held-open door. It clicks shut behind us and we're alone in the cooler.

Big white pots on racks. Each pot is filled with a different type of flower. There's a long wooden table in the center, which I guess is used for assembling bouquets. It's not icy cold, like a meat locker. But it is chilly.

"I'm sweaty from running," I tell him. "This probably isn't such a good idea . . ."

But he's pulled a magnificent purple flower out of a pot and is holding it for my inspection. "Take a look at this baby. Just came in. It's called a Moon Shadow."

"Beautiful," I murmur. "Now I'd better go . . ."

"Take a whiff. You can almost taste the color."

I hesitate and inhale the Moon Shadow's aroma. Never smelled anything quite like it. It does smell like the very essence of purple.

The cloying, syrupy stench seems to flow up my nose and mouth and take up residence deep in my lungs.

I feel an urge to sit down. "I think I better be heading out," I say, and step toward the door.

"Absolutely," the little man agrees, but he's standing in my way. "Meredith, are his roses ready?"

I see that the girl who was sorting ferns has slipped into the cooler. She walks to the pots and starts spritzing them with a sprayer-gun. "Al is just wrapping them up now. One more minute."

I feel a little light-headed. The florist smiles sympathetically. "Sit down for a second, why don't you?" he says. "Al, bring over that chair."

The big guy with the Giants cap has also come into the cooler. He hurries over with what looks like an office chair, on wheels. "Here, buddy, take a load off."

What are they all doing in the cooler with me?

Who's minding the store?

Where did this leather office chair come from?

I register these questions, but most of all I know I have to get out of here fast. I force my legs to move. One step. Two. The shop workers don't try to stop me.

They just wait. I've almost made it to the door. I seem to be moving in slow motion. Feet are heavy. Muscles don't respond.

But my brain still works. No wonder the idea to buy P.J. flowers popped into my head right before I passed this store. It was planted. Some sort of telepathic suggestion. I fell into a trap.

I reach for the handle. But the door now seems heavy. I manage to pull it open an inch. "Help me," I mumble.

"Beacon of Hope, you're the one who needs to help us," the bald florist says.

✳